Relive the stories that started it all!

STAR WARS®

THE EMPIRE STRIKES BACK®

RETURN OF THE JEDI®

Also available as

THE STAR WARS® TRILOGY

And journey across the galaxy
with Han Solo and Chewbacca in

STAR WARS®: THE HAN SOLO ADVENTURES

A GUIDE TO THE

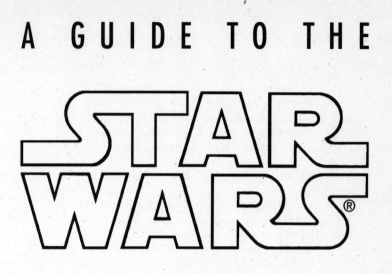

STAR WARS®

UNIVERSE

SECOND EDITION, REVISED AND EXPANDED

BILL SLAVICSEK

A DEL REY® BOOK

BALLANTINE BOOKS · NEW YORK

TM, ® and copyright © 1994 by Lucasfilm Ltd.

LIBRARY OF CONGRESS CATALOGING-IN-PUBLICATION DATA
Slavicsek, Bill.
A guide to the Star wars universe / Bill Slavicsek. — 2nd ed.,
rev. and expanded.
p. cm.
"A Del Rey book."
ISBN 0-345-38625-6
1. Star wars films—Encyclopedias. I. Title.
PN1995.9.S695S63 1994
791.43'75—dc20   93-46930
CIP

Text design by Holly Johnson

Cover design by Andy Baris

Cover art by Ralph McQuarrie

Manufactured in the United States of America

First Edition: March 1994

10 9 8

For everyone who remembers the first time they saw *Star Wars*—the place, the moment, the feelings of awe and wonder. May the Force never lose its magic . . .

Thanks to M'iko (Jade), Dale (Caine), Les (Fahjay), and Steven (K'tarrk), who wanted to play Star Wars when I most needed to get back into the proper frame of mind.

Special thanks to George Lucas for creating this far-away galaxy, to all the other authors whose collected works contributed to this guide, to West End Games for expanding the wealth of detail known about this long-ago time, and to Lucy Autrey Wilson and Sue Rostoni at Lucasfilm for letting me gather all this stuff into one place.

ACKNOWLEDGMENTS

We would like to express thanks to those who assisted in the preparation of this book:

June Brigman
Ellen Key Harris
Allan Kausch
Sue Rostoni
West End Games

A long time ago in a galaxy far, far away ...

A FEW NOTES ABOUT WHAT FOLLOWS

The entries in this book are presented in alphabetical order. They give a brief explanation of each person, place, and thing, but they are far from complete. There are many rich details that simply could not fit into the space allotted to each entry. Interested readers are encouraged to track down the original sources for a complete view of whichever particular entries capture their attention. A complete bibliography is included for that purpose.

Each entry starts with one of the following symbols: ☸ or ☻. ☸ indicates that the information that follows is drawn from an original Lucasfilm source—the films, the radio dramas, or the original novelizations. ☻ indicates that the information is drawn from an officially licensed source that may or may not agree with George Lucas's vision of the Star Wars galaxy.

All entries are also listed by category in the beginning of the book. Should a reader not know or remember a specific name or term, it may be found by glancing over the listing for the appropriate category.

The categories are as follows:

Alien Creatures, Species, Families
Battles, Wars, Historical Events

Characters and Characters' Names
Devices and Things
Droid Names and Types
Food, Medicines, Chemicals
Geology, Plant Life
Places, Worlds, Customs, Institutions
Terminology, Slang, Colloquialisms, and Other
    Abstractions
Vehicles and Vessels
Weaponry

Because it is often difficult to differentiate first and last names of aliens and people from the many non-Terran cultures, multiword entries have been alphabetized by their first word. For example, "Han Solo" will be found under "H," and "Admiral Ozzel" will be found under "A." This system is used for both the category lists and the main portion of the *Guide*.

ENTRY CODES AND SOURCES

BFE —*Ewoks: The Battle for Endor*, MGM/UA, 1986. ☻

BGS —Battle for the Golden Sun, Douglas Kaufman, West End Games, Honesdale, Pennsylvania, 1988. ☻

BI —Black Ice, Paul Murphy and Bill Slavicsek, West End Games, Honesdale, Pennsylvania, 1990. ☻

CCC —Crisis on Cloud City, Christopher Kubasik, West End Games, Honesdale, Pennsylvania, 1989. ☻

CP —Star Wars Campaign Pack, Paul Murphy, West End Games, Honesdale, Pennsylvania, 1988. ☻

DE —*Star Wars: Dark Empire* issues 1–6, Tom Veitch and Cam Kennedy, Dark Horse Comics, Milwaukee, Oregon, 1991–1992. ☻

DESB —*Star Wars: Dark Empire Sourcebook*, Michael Allen Horne, West End Games, Honesdale, Pennsylvania, 1993. ☻

DFR —*Dark Force Rising*, Timothy Zahn, Bantam Spectra Books, New York, 1992. ☻

DFRSB —*Dark Force Rising Sourcebook*, Bill Slavicsek, West End Games, Honesdale, Pennsylvania, 1992. ☻

DOE —Domain of Evil, Jim Bambra, West End Games, Honesdale, Pennsylvania, 1991. ☻

DSTC —*Death Star Technical Companion*, Bill Slavicsek, West End Games, Honesdale, Pennsylvania, 1991. ☻

DTV —*Droids* animated television shows, Episodes 1–13, 1985. ☻

DU —Death in the Undercity, Michael Nystul, West End Games, Honesdale, Pennsylvania, 1990. ☻

EA —*The Ewok Adventure*, MGM/UA, 1984. ☻

ESB —*Star Wars V: The Empire Strikes Back* film, 20th Century Fox, 1980; *Star Wars: The Empire Strikes Back* novelization, Donald F. Glut, Del Rey Books, New York, 1980. ☻

ESBR —*Star Wars: The Empire Strikes Back*, National Public Radio dramatizations, Episodes 1–10, 1980. ☻

ETV —*Ewoks* animated television show, Episodes 1–26, 1986. ☻

FG —*Cracken's Rebel Field Guide*, Christopher Kubasik, West End Games, Honesdale, Pennsylvania, 1991. ☻

GA —Graveyard of Alderaan, Bill Slavicsek, West End Games, Honesdale, Pennsylvania, 1991. ☻

GDV —*The Glove of Darth Vader*, Paul Davids and Hollace Davids, Bantam Skylark Books, New York, 1992. ☻

GG1 —*Galaxy Guide 1: A New Hope*, Grant Boucher, West End Games, Honesdale, Pennsylvania, 1989. ☻

GG2 —*Galaxy Guide 2: Yavin and Bespin*, Jonatha Caspian, Christopher Kubasik, Bill Slavicsek and C.J. Tramontana, West End Games, Honesdale, Pennsylvania, 1989. ☻

GG3 —*Galaxy Guide 3: The Empire Strikes Back*, Michael Stern, West End Games, Honesdale, Pennsylvania, 1989. ☻

GG4 —*Galaxy Guide 4: Alien Races*, Troy Denning, West End Games, Honesdale, Pennsylvania, 1989. ☻

GG5 —*Galaxy Guide 5: Return of the Jedi*, Michael Stern, West End Games, Honesdale, Pennsylvania, 1990. ☻

GG6 —*Galaxy Guide 6: Tramp Freighters*, Mark Rein-Hagen and Stewart Wieck, West End Games, Honesdale, Pennsylvania, 1990. ☻

GQ —Game Chambers of Questal, Robert Kern, West End Games, Honesdale, Pennsylvania, 1990. ☻

GW —Star Wars comic strip, Archie Goodwin and Al Williamson, Russ Cochran Publisher, West Plains, Missouri, 1991. ☻

HE —*Heir to the Empire*, Timothy Zahn, Bantam Spectra Books, New York, 1991. ☻

HESB —*Heir to the Empire Sourcebook*, Bill Slavicsek, West End Games, Honesdale, Pennsylvania, 1992. ☻

HLL —*Han Solo and the Lost Legacy*, Brian Daley, Del Rey Books, New York, 1980. ☻

HSE —*Han Solo at Stars' End*, Brian Daley, Del Rey Books, New York, 1979. ☻

HSR —*Han Solo's Revenge*, Brian Daley, Del Rey Books, New York, 1979. ☻

IC —The Isus Coordinates, Christopher Kubasik, West End Games, Honesdale, Pennsylvania, 1990. ☻

ISB —*Imperial Sourcebook*, Greg Gorden, West End Games, Honesdale, Pennsylvania, 1989. ☻

LC —*The Last Command*, Timothy Zahn, Bantam Spectra Books, New York, 1993. ☻

LCF —*Lando Calrissian and the Flamewind of Oseon*, L. Neil Smith, Del Rey Books, New York, 1983. ☻

LCJ —*The Lost City of the Jedi*, Paul Davids and Hollace Davids, Bantam Skylark Books, New York, 1992. ☻

LCM —*Lando Calrissian and the Mindharp of Sharu*, L. Neil Smith, Del Rey Books, New York, 1983. ☻

LCS —*Lando Calrissian and the Starcave of ThonBoka*, L. Neil Smith, Del Rey Books, New York, 1983. ☻

ML —Mission to Lianna, Joanne E. Wyrick, West End Games, Honesdale, Pennsylvania, 1992. ☻

MMY —*Mission from Mount Yoda*, Paul Davids and Hollace Davids, Bantam Skylark Books, New York, 1993. ☻

OS —Otherspace, Bill Slavicsek, West End Games, Honesdale, Pennsylvania, 1989. ☻

OS2 —Otherspace II: Invasion, Douglas Kaufman, West End Games, Honesdale, Pennsylvania, 1989. ●

PC —The Politics of Contraband, Gary Haynes, Paul Arden Lidberg, Brian J. Murphy, William Olmesdahl, and Eric S. Trautmann, West End Games, Honesdale, Pennsylvania, 1992. ●

PDS —*Prophets of the Dark Side*, Paul Davids and Hollace Davids, Bantam Skylark Books, New York, 1993. ●

PG1 —*Planets of the Galaxy, Volume One*, Grant Boucher, Julie Boucher and Bill Smith, West End Games, Honesdale, Pennsylvania, 1991. ●

PG2 —*Planets of the Galaxy, Volume Two*, John Terra, West End Games, Honesdale, Pennsylvania, 1992. ●

PM —Planet of the Mist, Nigel Findley, West End Games, Honesdale, Pennsylvania, 1992. ●

QE —*Queen of the Empire*, Paul Davids and Hollace Davids, Bantam Skylark Books, New York, 1993. ●

RJ —*Star Wars VI: Return of the Jedi* film, 20th Century Fox, 1983; *Star Wars: Return of the Jedi* novelization, James Kahn, Del Rey Books, New York, 1983. ☻

RM —Riders of the Maelstrom, Ray Winninger, West End Games, Honesdale, Pennsylvania, 1989. ●

RSB —*The Rebel Alliance Sourcebook*, Paul Murphy, West End Games, Honesdale, Pennsylvania, 1990. ●

SF —Starfall, Rob Jenkins and Michael Stern, West End Games, Honesdale, Pennsylvania, 1989. ●

SFS —Strike Force: Shantipole, Ken Rolston and Steve Gilbert, West End Games, Honesdale, Pennsylvania, 1988. ●

SH —Scavenger Hunt, Brad Freeman, West End Games, Honesdale, Pennsylvania, 1989. ●

SME —*Splinter of the Mind's Eye*, Alan Dean Foster, Del Rey Books, New York, 1978. ●

SW —*Star Wars IV: A New Hope* film, 20th Century Fox, 1977; Star Wars novelization, George Lucas, Del Rey Books, New York, 1976. ☻

SWR —*Star Wars*, National Public Radio dramatizations, Episodes 1–13, 1977. ☢

SWRPG —*Star Wars: The Roleplaying Game*, Greg Costikyan, West End Games, New York, 1987. ☢

SWRPG2 —Star Wars: The Roleplaying Game, Second Edition, Bill Smith, West End Games, Honesdale, Pennsylvania, 1992. ☢

SWSB —*Star Wars Sourcebook*, Bill Slavicsek and Curtis Smith, West End Games, New York, 1987. ☢

SWWS —*Star Wars: The Wookiee Storybook*, Random House, New York, 1979. ☢

TA —The Abduction, Chuck Truett, West End Games, Honesdale, Pennsylvania, 1992. ☢

TGH —The Great Heep, animated television show, 1986. ☢

TM —Tatooine Manhunt, Bill Slavicsek and Daniel Greenberg, West End Games, New York, 1988. ☢

WC —*Wanted by Cracken*, Louis J. Prosperi, West End Games, Honesdale, Pennsylvania, 1993. ☢

ZHR —*Zorba the Hutt's Revenge*, Paul Davids and Hollace Davids, Bantam Skylark Books, New York, 1992. ☢

ADDITIONAL BIBLIOGRAPHY

A Guide to the Star Wars Universe, Raymond L. Velasco, Del Rey Books, New York, 1984.

Art of the Empire Strikes Back, Ballantine Books, New York, 1980.

Art of Return of the Jedi, Ballantine Books, New York, 1983.

Art of Star Wars, Ballantine Books, New York, 1979.

"Soldiers of the Empire," Anthony Fredrickson, *The World of Star Wars: A Compendium of Fact and Fantasy from Star Wars and the Empire Strikes Back*, Paradise Press, Inc., Ridgefield, Connecticut, 1981.

"Star Wars Android Assembly Manual" (for R2-D2 and C-3PO model kits), MPC Corporation, 1977.

Star Wars: Return of the Jedi Official Collectors Edition, Paradise Press, Inc., Newtown, Connecticut, 1983.

Star Wars: Return of the Jedi Portfolio, Ralph McQuarrie, Ballantine Books, New York, 1983.

Star Wars: Return of the Jedi Sketchbook, Joe Johnston and Nilo Rodis-Jamero, Ballantine Books, New York, 1983.

Star Wars Rules Companion, Greg Gorden, West End Games, Honesdale, Pennsylvania, 1989.

Star Wars: The Empire Strikes Back Notebook, Ballantine Books, New York, 1980.

Star Wars: The Empire Strikes Back Official Collectors Edition, Paradise Press, Inc., Ridgefield, Connecticut, 1980.

"Star Wars: The Full Story," *Screen Superstar*, Paradise Press, Inc., Ridgefield, Connecticut, 1977.

Star Wars TV Special, 1977.

The Star Wars Album: Official Collectors Edition, Ballantine Books, New York, 1977.

The Star Wars Portfolio, Ralph McQuarrie, Ballantine Books, New York, 1977.

The Star Wars Sketchbook, Joe Johnston, Ballantine Books, New York, 1977.

STARFIGHTER SUBLIGHT SPEED
COMPARISON CHART

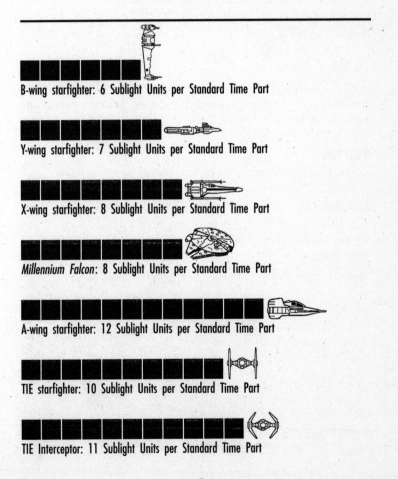

B-wing starfighter: 6 Sublight Units per Standard Time Part

Y-wing starfighter: 7 Sublight Units per Standard Time Part

X-wing starfighter: 8 Sublight Units per Standard Time Part

Millennium Falcon: 8 Sublight Units per Standard Time Part

A-wing starfighter: 12 Sublight Units per Standard Time Part

TIE starfighter: 10 Sublight Units per Standard Time Part

TIE Interceptor: 11 Sublight Units per Standard Time Part

TIME LINE OF IMPORTANT EVENTS
IN THE STAR WARS GALAXY

25,000 + BSW4
The Old Republic, the first galaxy-wide government is formed; Jedi Knights appear; period of galactic peace and expansion begins.

896 BSW4
Yoda, the Jedi Master, born.

200 BSW4
Chewbacca the Wookiee born on Kashyyyk.

112 BSW4
C-3PO activated.

60 BSW4
Obi-Wan Kenobi, Jedi Knight, born.

BSW4=Before the events of *Star Wars IV: A New Hope*; **ASW4**=After the events of *Star Wars IV: A New Hope*.

55 BSW4
Anakin Skywalker born.

48 BSW4
Mon Mothma, Senator and Alliance leader, born on Chandrila.

35 BSW4
Clone Wars end.

29 BSW4
Han Solo born in Corellian star system.

Fall of the Republic
A dark period of corruption and social injustice sweeps through the Republic, paving the way for Senator Palpatine's rise to power.

18 BSW4
Luke Skywalker and Leia Organa born and placed in hiding; Anakin Skywalker becomes Darth Vader; Jedi Knights hunted and killed; Palpatine becomes Emperor; Empire formed; first stirrings of rebellion begin.

Star Wars IV
The events of *Star Wars IV: A New Hope* occur; first Death Star destroyed at the Battle of Yavin.

3 ASW4
The events of *Star Wars V: The Empire Strikes Back* occur; Battle of Hoth takes place.

4 ASW4
The events of *Star Wars VI: Return of the Jedi* occur; Galactic Civil War ends with the Battle of Endor; the New Republic is formed; Imperial remnants fight on.

9 ASW4

The events of the novels *Heir to the Empire, Dark Force Rising*, and *The Last Command* occur; Leia and Han's son and daughter, Jacen and Jaina, born.

10 ASW4

The events of the *Dark Empire* comic series, #1–6, occur; Leia and Han's son Anakin born.

ALIEN CREATURES, SPECIES, FAMILIES

Abyssin
Altorian
Amanaman
Ammuud clans
Anomid
Aqualish
Arachnor
Arcona
Baga
ball creature of Duroon
bantha
Barabel
battle dogs
Biituian
Bilar
Bimm
Bith
blase tree goat
blope
bonegnawer
bordok
Bothan
Brubb

Bubo
Calamarian
Canu
Cavrilhu Pirates
Chadra-Fan
Charon
Chubb
Chubbits
Columi
Corellian
Coway
Defel
Devaronian
dewback
dianoga
digworm
dinko
divto
Drang
Duinuogwuin
Dulok
durkii
Duros

Elomin
Ewok
firefolk
Fuzzum
Gamorrean
Givin
Golden Sun
Gotal
gravel-maggots
Greenies
gundark
Gupin
Hammerhead
hanadak
Herglic
howlrunner
Ho'Din
humming peeper
Hutt
Ingey
Ithorian (Hammerhead)
Ixll
Jawa
Jenet
Jindas
Kamarian
kete
Kitonak
kleex
Kowakian monkey-lizard
Krayt dragon
kroyie
Kubaz
Lake Spirit of Mimban
lantern bird
Lorrdian

makants
Malorm Family
mantigrue
Marauders
Massassi
Mimbanite
mogo
Mon Calamari
morrt
mudmen
Myneyrsh
mynock
nashtah
neks
nerf
night beast
nightcrawler
Nikto
Noghri
Obroan
Ortolan
Oswaft
owriss
Phlog
Pho Ph'eahian
preducor
Psadan
pterosaur
Pui-ui
Quarren (Squid Head)
rakazzak beast
Ranats
rancor
Rishii
Rodian
Rukh

Ruurian
rycrit
sand sloth
Sand People (Tusken
    Raiders)
Sarlacc
Sauropteroid
Sedrian
Sentinel
Shistavanen
Sic-six
Skandits
Sljee
Sluiss
space slug
Squib
Squid Head
Strum
sungwas
Swimmer
Swimming People
Talz
tauntaun
Theelin
Tin-Tin Dwarf
Togorian

Trianii
trompa
Tulgah
Tusken Raider
Twi'lek
Ugnaught
Ugor
urchin
Verpine
vornskr
wampa ice creature
wandrella
webweaver
Weequay
Whaladon
Whiphid
Wistie
womp rat
Wookiee
Yak Face
Yaka
yayax
ysalamiri
Yuzzem
yuzzum
Zeebo

BATTLES, WARS, HISTORICAL EVENTS

Battle of Endor, The
Battle of Calamari, The
Battle of Hoth, The
Battle of Taanab, The
Battle of Yavin, The

Clone Wars
Galactic Civil War, The
Kanz Disorders
Taanab
Third Battle of Vontor, The

CHARACTERS AND CHARACTERS' NAMES

Adar Tallon
Admiral Ackbar
Admiral Drayson
Admiral Griff
Admiral Motti
Admiral Ozzel
Admiral Screed
Afyon
Anakin Skywalker
Anakin Solo
Anky Fremp
Arhul Hextrophon
Asha
Askha Boda
Atuarre
Auren Yomm
Aves
Badure
Bail Organa
Baji
Bane Nothos
Barada
Batcheela

Beedo
Ben (Obi-Wan) Kenobi
Beru Lars
Ber'asco
Bib Fortuna
Big Bunji
Biggs Darklighter
Bin Essada
Bithabus the Mystifier
Boba Fett
Bodo Baas
Bondo
Borsk Fey'lya
Bossk
Bot
Boushh
Bozzie
Brasck
Briil Twins
Calrissian
Camie
Captain Afyon
Captain Antilles

Captain Brandei
Captain Colton
Captain Dorja
Captain Dunwell
Captain Needa
Captain Neva
Captain Pellaeon
Captain Piett
Captain Syub Snunb
Captain Virgilio
Captain-Supervisor
   Grammel
Cass
Catarine Towani
Charal
Chewbacca (Chewie)
Chief Chirpa
Chief Muskov
Chin
Chirpa
Chituhr
Chubb Scutt
Chukha-Trok
Cindel Towani
Cobak
Coby
Colton
Commander Bane Nothos
Commander Klev
Commander Narra
Commander Orlok
Commander Silver Fyre
Commander Willard
Commodore Zuggs
Controller Jhoff
Covell

Cycy Loctob
C'baoth
Dack
Darth Vader (Lord Vader,
   Dark Lord of the Sith)
Deak
Deej
Defeen
Demma Moll
Dengar
Deppo
Derlin
Dobah
Doc
Dodonna
Dorja
Dr. Arakkus
Dravis
Drayson
Droopy McCool
Dunhausen
Dunwell
Dustangle
Dustini
Dutch
Dyyz Nataz
D'rag
Egome Fass
Elarles
Emperor, The (Palpatine)
Engret
Ephant Mon
Erpham Warrick
Exozone
Fadoop
Fandar

Fidge
Figrin D'an
Fiolla of Lorrd
Fixer
Freedom's Sons
Fugo
Gaff
Gallandro
Gank Killers
Gargan
Garindan
Garm Bel Iblis
Gee Long
General Covell
General Dodonna
General Madine
General Rieekan
General Tagge
General Veers
Ghent
Gillespee
Gorax
Gorm the Dissolver
Gornash
Gorneesh
Governor Bin Essada
Governor Tarkin
Grammel
Grand Admiral Thrawn
Grand Moff Dunhausen
Grand Moff Hissa
Grand Moff Muzzer
Grand Moff Tarkin
Grand Moff Thistleborn
Greedo
Gribbet

Griff
Grigmin
Gwig
Halla
Han Solo
Hasti Troujow
Heater
Hermi Odle
Hideaz Quill-Face
High Prophet Jedgar
Hija
Hin
Hirken
Hissa
Hissal
Hobbie
Hoom
Hoona
Hoover
H'kig
Ido
Inspector Keek
Irenez
Ishi Tib
Izrina
Jabba the Hutt
Jacen Solo
Jaina Solo
Jak Sazz
Janson
Jedgar
Jeremitt Towani
Jerjerrod
Jessa
Jhoff
Jodo Kast

Jord Dusat
Jorus C'baoth
Joruus C'baoth
Jyn Oban
J'uoch
Kabe
Kadann
Kaink
Kane Griggs
Karrde
Kasarax
Kea Moll
Kee
Keeheen
Ken
Kendalina
Kez-Iban
Khabarakh
King Gorneesh
Klaatu
Klev
Koong
Kraaken
Kybo Ren
Labria
Lando Calrissian
Lanni Troujow
Latara
Leeni
Leia Organa
Leviathor
Lieutenant Hija
Lieutenant Page
Lieutenant Tschel
Lisstik
Lo Khan

Lobot
Logray
Lord Tion
Lord of the Sith
Luke Skywalker
Lumat
Luuke Skywalker
Luwingo
Lwyll
Mace Towani
Madine
Magg
Major Derlin
Mako Spince
Malani
Mal'ary'ush
Mandalore Warriors
Mara Jade
Marso
Master Thon
Max Rebo
Max Rebo Band
Mazzic
Meerian Hammerhead
Megadeath
Moff Jerjerrod
Moff Tarkin
Momaw Nadon
Mon Julpa
Mon Mothma
Mooth
Mor Glayyd
Morag
Motti
Muftak
Mungo Baobob

Murgoob, The Great
Muskov
Muzzer
Mystra
Nahkee
NaQuoit Bandits
Narra
Needa
Neema
Neva
Nien Nunb
Niles Ferrier
Nilz Yomm
Nippett
Noa
Obi-Wan Kenobi
Odumin
Oola
Organa
Orlok
Owen Lars
Ozzel
Page
Pakka
Palpatine
Paploo
Par'tah
Pellaeon
Piett
Piggy
Ploovo Two-For-One
Ponda Baba
Pops
Porkins
Pote Snitkin
Priests of Ninn

Princess Leia Organa
Prophet Gornash
Prophets of the Dark Side
Puggles Trodd
Queen Rana
Ra-Lee
Ralrra
Raskar
Ree-Yees
Rekkon
Rieekan
Roa
Rokur Gepta
Romort Raort
Roofoo (Doctor Evazan,
    Doctor Cornelius)
R'all
Sabador
Salacious Crumb
Salla Zend
Salporin
Sate Pestage
Screed
Seggor Tels
Sena Leikvold Midanyl
Senator Palpatine
Serpent Masters
Shada
Shazeen
Shrag Brothers
Shug Ninx
Silver Fyre
Sise Fromm
Skorr
Skynx
Slick

Snaggletooth
Snunb
Solo
Sonniod
Spray of Tynna
Spurch Goa
Squeak
Supreme Commander
   Skywalker
Supreme Prophet
Sy Snootles
Syub Snunb
S'ybll
Tagge
Talon Karrde
Tanith Shire
Targeter
Tarkin
Tarrik
Tarrin
Tav Breil'lya
Teebo
Teek
Terak
Thall Joben
Thistleborn
Thrawn
Tibor
Tig Fromm
Tion
Toda
Tonnika sisters
Torm
Torve
Tregga
Triclops

Trioculus
Tschel
Tyrann
Ulic Qel-Droma
Umak Leth
Umwak
Uul-Rha-Shan
Vader
Varn
Veers
Vima-Da-Boda
Vinda
Virgilio
Vonzel
Voren Na'al
Vrad Dodonna
Wadda
Wedge Antilles
Wicket W. Warrick
Wiley
Willard
Windy
Winter
Wormie
Xim the Despot
Yoda
Zardra
Zatec-Cha
Zebulon Dak
Zev
Zev Veers
Zlarb
Zorba the Hutt
Zuckuss
Zuggs
Zut

DEVICES AND THINGS

acceleration compensator
alluvial damper
antigrav
antigrav drive
armored defense platform
astrogation computer
beamdrill
breath mask
caller
carbon-freezing chamber
cargo lifter
central lifter
cloaking device
com-scan
comlink
comm unit
computer probe
condenser unit
crystal oscillator
data card
data pad
decoder
deflection tower

deflector shield
directional landing beacon
drop shaft
ejection seat
electrobinoculars
electrorangefinder
electrotelescope
emergency stud
energy cell
escape pod
freeze-floating control
fusioncutter
glow rod
gravity well projector
gyro-balance circuitry
holocomm
Holocron
holocube
holoprojector
homing beacon
horizontal booster
hurlothrumbic generator
hydrospanner

hyperdrive
hyperdrive motivator
hyperspace compass
hyperspace transponder
interrogator
interruptor template
ion engine
irradiator
Jedi Holocron
landing claw
lantern of sacred light
Leth universal energy cage
lift tube
light table
lightspeed engine
locomotor
macrobinoculars
macrofuser
main drive
mole miner
motivator
nav computer
orbit dock
paralight system
particle shielding
pelvic servomotor
photoreceptor
plastoid
power converter
power coupling
power prybar
power terminal
pressor
prosthetic replacements

reactivate switch
recording rod
remote
repulsor
repulsorlift engine
restraining bolt
S-foil
scan grid
sensor
servo-grip
servodriver
shield
shield generator
slave circuit
Spaarti cloning cylinder
sublight drive
synth-flesh
target remote
targeting computer
telesponder
terrain following sensor
thermal coil
Thrella Well
tracomp
tractor beam
transfer register
transparisteel
vaporator
vibroscalpel
vocabulator
warming unit
weapon detector
zenomach

DROIDS, NAMES AND TYPES

agrirobot
assassin droid
astromech droid
Atedeate
BG-J38
binary load lifter
Bix
BL-17
Blue Max
Bollux
C-Ratt
C-3PO (See-Threepio)
CB-99
Chip
Choco
detainment droid
DJ-88 (Dee-Jay)
EV-9D9 (Eve-Ninedenine)
freight droid
Frija
FX-7
gladiator droid

Great Heep, the
HC-100
human replica droid
Hunter-Killer probot
IG-88 (Phlutdroid)
interrogator droid
KT-10
KT-18
Mark II Reactor Drone
Mark X Executioner
medical droid
Ninedenine
Phlutdroid
power droid
probe droid
probot
Proto One
R2-D2 (Artoo-Detoo)
R2 unit
R5 unit
R5-D4
R7 unit

See-Threepio
sentient tank
talkdroid
Too-Onebee (2-1B)

treadwell robot
Vuffi Raa
war droid
ZZ-4Z (Zee Zee)

FOOD, MEDICINES, CHEMICALS

avabush spice
bacta
carbonite
dipill
elba beer
flameout
lumni-spice

L'lahsh
Norvanian grog
phobium
R'alla mineral water
spice
Tibanna gas

GEOLOGY, PLANT LIFE

Adegan crystals
asaari tree
blumfruit
chak-root
ch'hala tree
fungus of the Rokna tree
gimer stick
ilum crystals
Kaiburr Crystal
kholm-grass

light dust
lommite
quickclay
ryll
Soul Trees
Spirit Tree
tentacle bush
Tree of Light
t'ill
wroshyr trees

PLACES, WORLDS, CUSTOMS, INSTITUTIONS

Abregado
Abregado-rae
Academy, The
Adega
Akrit'tar
Alderaan
Ammuud
Anchorhead
Annoo
Anoat
Aquaris
Arbo Maze
Aridus
Athega
Badlands
Barhu
Beggar's Canyon
Berchest
Bespin
Bestine
Biitu
Bilbringi
Bimmisaari

Blue Nebula, the
Bnach
Bodgen
Bonadan
Bonadan Spaceport
    Southeast II
Boonta
Borderland Regions
Bpfassh
Brigia
Byss
Byss Bistro
Calius saj Leeloo
Carkoon, Great Pit of
Cell 2187
Chad
Chandrila
Churba
Cinnagar
Circarpous IV
Circarpous XIV
Circarpous V
Circarpous Major

Cloak of the Sith
Cloud City
Colonies, the
Commenor
Core Worlds, The
Corellia
Corporate Sector, the
Corulag
Coruscant
Cron Drift
Cyax
Cyborrea
Da Soocha
Dagobah
Daluuj
Dantooine
Deep Core Security Zone
Deep Galactic Core
Dellalt
Deneba
Derra IV
Detention Block AA-23
Docking Bay 45
Docking Bay 94
Domed City of Aquarius
droid harem
dukha
Dune Sea, The
Duro
Duroon
Echo Station Three-Eight
Elom
Emperor's Citadel, The
Emperor's Throne Room
Empress Teta
Endor (Sanctuary Moon)

escape pod station
Etti IV
Expansion Region
fifth moon of Da Soocha
Fire Rings of Fornax
floating cities of Calamari
Fondor
Fortress of Tawntoom
Free-Flight Dance Dome,
    the
fuel ore processing plant
Galactic Core
Gamorr
Gargon
Great Pit of Carkoon
Gyndine
Hologram Fun World
Honoghr
Hoth
Hurcha
Hyllyard City
Ilic
Imperial City
Imperial Freight Complex
Imperial garrison
Ingo
Inner Rim Territories
Ithor
Jomark
Jovan Station
Jundland Wastes
Junkfort Station
Kabal
Kalla
Kamar
Kashyyyk

Kessel
Khuiumin
Kir
Kirdo
Laakteen Depot
Lafra
Landing Zone, The
Lesser Plooriod Cluster
Lianna
Lost City of the Jedi
Lur
Manarai Mountains
Massassi
meditation chamber
Mid Rim
Mimban
Minos Cluster
Moltok
Mon Calamari
Mos Eisley
Mount Yoda
Mount Tantiss
Myrkr
Mytus VII
Nal Hutta
Nar Shaddaa
New Alderaan
New Cov
Nkllon
Nomad City
Norval II
Nunurra
Obroa-skai
Orbiting Shipyard Alpha
Ord Mantell
Ord Pardron

Orron III
Ossus
Ottega
Outer Rim Territories
Outpost Beta
Pantolomin
Paradise
Peregrine's Nest
Pinnacle Base
Platform 327
Rakrir
Ralltiir
Rampa
Rethin Sea
Rishi
Roche Asteroid Field
Roon
Roonadan
Rudrig
Ruuria
Rwookrrorro
Ryloth
Saheelindeel
Sanctuary Moon (Endor)
Simoom
Sluis Van
Space Station Kwenn
Space Station Scardia
Spacers' Garage
Stars' End
Stenness
Sullust
Tammuz-an
Tatoo I, Tatoo II
Tatooine
Tawntoom

TERMINOLOGY, SLANG, COLLOQUIALISMS, AND OTHER ABSTRACTIONS

abo
affect mind
Analysis Bureau
anticoncussion field
approach vector
armament rating
artificial gravity
Assassin's Guild
Basic
Big L
Blue Five
Blue Four
Blue Leader
Blue Six
Blue Squad
Blue Squadron
Blue Three
Blue Two
Blue Wing
Bocce
bounce
Bureau of Operations
burnout

chromasheath
chrono
Colonial Games
combat sense
command control voice
COMPNOR
control mind
Corellian Bloodstripe
Corporate Sector
   Authority, the
Council of Elders
credit standard
crystalline vertex
cyberostasis
Cyborg Operations
dark side, the
Dark Force
Dark Jedi
Dark Side Adepts
Dark Side Compendium
Declaration of a New
   Republic
Delta Source

Doonium
dormo-shock
DRAPAC
driit
droid
dura-armor
durasheet
durasteel
Echo Base
Emperor's Hand
Emperor's Inner Circle
Empire, the
energy gate
Espo
feathers of light
Festival of Hoods
Final Jump, The
Force, The
Force lightning
Force sensitive
Force storm
forward tech station
fusion furnace
Galactic Constitution
gameboard
Gamor Run, the
Gold Five
Gold Leader
Gold Two
Gold Wing
Goldenrod
gravel storm
Gray Leader
Gray Wing
Green Leader
Green Squadron

Green Wing
haul jets
hibernation sickness
High Council of Alderaan,
    The
High Court of Alderaan
hologram
holograph
holographic recording mode
holomonster
HoloNet
House Glayyd
House Reesbon
human-droid relations
    specialist
hyperspace
hyperspace commo
hyperspace wormhole
ILKO
illuminescences
Ilthmar Gambit
Imperial Charter
Imperial gunner
Imperial Hyperspace
    Security Net
Imperial Intelligence
Imperial Royal Guard
Imperial Sovereign
    Protectors
Imperial stormtroopers
Imperialization
Inner Council
insignia of the New
    Republic
Internal Organization
    Bureau

Jedi Code, the
Jedi Knights
Jedi Master
jizz-wailer
John D
jubilee wheel
Katana fleet
Katarn Commandos
Kessel Run
Krath, the
Light Festival
Light Spirit
maitrakh
Maker, the
Malkite Poisoner
manumitting
medical cocoon
medpac
memory flush
moisture farm
Mookiee
nergon 14
New Order, the
New Republic, the
Night Spirit
normal space
Old Republic, the
Omega Signal
otherspace
Outbound Flight Project
outlaw tech
Page's Commandos
phototropic shielding
Point 5
program trap
Project Decoy

protocol droid
Provisional Council
ray shielding
realspace
Rebel Alliance, the
Rebellion, the
Rebels
Red Five
Red Leader
Red Two
Red Wing
Renegade Flight
Renegade Leader
Renegades
retinal print
reversion
Rogue Flight
Rogue Four
Rogue Guard
Rogue Leader
Rogue Squadron
Rogue Three
Royal Two
sabacc
sandwhirl
Scavs
scout trooper
sector
Senate, Imperial
shelter container
shimmersilk
shock-ball
short-term memory
  enhancement
Sith, the
Skyhook

smuggling guilds
snowtrooper
Sovereign Protectors
spacer
spacing
ST 321
Standard Time Part
stang
Starhunter Intergalactic
    Menagerie
starshipwright
stim-shot
stormtrooper
Survivors
tech dome
telekinetic kill

Tetan Elite
thermal cape
thermosuit
Tiree
Triannii Ranger
Ubese
Ubiqtorate
Vector
voice manipulation
Voice Override: Epsilon
    Actual
Wookiee honor family
Wookiee life debt
xenoarchaeology
Zyggurats

VEHICLES AND VESSELS

A-9 Vigilance Interceptor
A-wing starfighter
Accuser
Adjucator
airspeeder
All Terrain Armored
    Transport (AT-AT)
All Terrain Personal
    Transport (AT-PT)
All Terrian Scout Transport
    (AT-ST)
Allegiance
amphibion
Antares Six
aqua-skimmer
assault frigate
assault shuttle
AT-AT
AT-PT
AT-ST
autohopper
Avenger
B-wing starfighter

Black Ice
Blockade Runner
bulk freighter
Calamari minisub
capital ship
Carrack-class light cruiser
Chariot LAV
Chimaera
cloud car
compact assault vehicle
consular ship
container ship
Coral Vanda
Corellian Corvette
Corellian gunship
Death's Head
Deep Core haulers
Defiance
Devastator
Dreadnaught
drone barge
drop ship
dungeon ship

E-wing starfighter
Eclipse
Emancipator
escort carrier
escort frigate
Executor
flitter
floater
floating fortress
gravsled
Guardian patrol ship
hang glider
Headquarter's Frigate, the
herd ship
Home One
hoverscout
Hutt caravel
Hutt floater
Hyperspace Marauder
I-7 attack ship
    (Howlrunner)
Imperial customs vessel
Imperial Star Destroyer
Imperial walker
Incom Skyhopper T-16
Incom T-65
Interdictor-class cruiser
IRD
Judicator
juggernaut
Kuari Princess
Lady of Mindor
Lady Luck
Lambda-class shuttle
Lancer-class frigate
landspeeder

Liberator
Liberty
lighter
maintenance hauler
medical frigate
Millennium Falcon
mobile command base
Mon Calamari star cruiser
passenger liner
Peregrine
Permondiri Explorer
pinnace
pocket cruiser
Quamar Messenger
Queen of Ranroon
Rand Ecliptic
Rebel Star
Relentless
robot starfighters
sail barge
sand skimmer
sandcrawler
Scardia Voyager
Scimitar assault bomber
scout walker
Shannador's Revenge
shieldship
Silver Speeder
skiff
skimmer
Skipray blastboat
skyhopper
Slave I
Slave II
snowspeeder
snubfighter

space barge
speeder
speeder bike
speeder transport
star cruiser
Star Destroyer
Star Galleon
Star Runner
Starlight Intruder
stock light freighter
Strike-class medium cruiser
Subjugator
Sunfighter Franchise, The
Super Star Destroyer
swamp crawler
swoop
system patrol craft
T-47
T-16
Tantive IV

TIE crawler
TIE fighter
transport ship
treaded neutron torches
   (TNTs)
Tydirium
U-33
V-wing airspeeder
Victory-class Star Destroyer
walker
wave walker
Whaladon hunting ship
Wild Karrde
X-222
X-wing starfighter
XP-38
Y-wing starfighter
Z-95 Headhunter
Zorba's Express

WEAPONRY

battle wagon
beam tube
blaster
bowcaster
concussion missle
dart shooter
Death Star, the
disruptor
electro-jabber
energy battery
flechette missile
flechette cannister
force pike
forward gun pod
gaderffii
ion cannon
laser cannon
lightsaber
missile tube

orbital gun platform
palmgun
power gem
proton torpedo
proton grenade
quarrel
seeker
Silencer-7
sleeper bomb
Stokhli spray stick
tank droid
thermal detonator
torpedo sphere
turbolaser
vibro-cutter
vibro-ax
vibro-shiv
vibroblade
World Devastator

A GUIDE TO THE

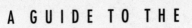

UNIVERSE

A

A-9 Vigilance Interceptor

🌑 The newest Imperial starfighter, the A-9 Vigilance Interceptor first saw action against New Republic forces during the events that led to the return of the Emperor. [DE]

A-wing starfighter

🔵 The A-wing, a lightweight, wedge-shaped military starfighter, made its first appearance late in the galactic civil

A-wing starfighter

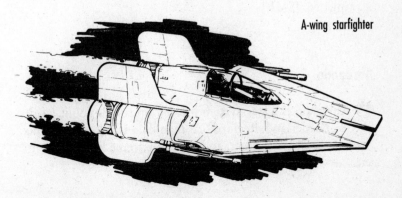

war on the side of the Rebel Alliance. Designed for high speed and maneuverability, the A-wing carries two wing-mounted, pivoting blaster cannons, a sophisticated targeting computer and sensor array, and light combat shields. Built for ship-to-ship combat and to serve as escort craft for larger starships, it was the Alliance's answer to the Empire's newer TIE fighter models. Two extra-large real-space power plants and low total mass make this the fastest combat starfighter in either arsenal, beating out even the TIE interceptor for pure speed in normal space. [RJ]

⊕ The A-wing was developed secretly during the early days of the Rebellion. It has excellent sensor and communications countermeasures, including a power-jamming package to blind targets before it strikes. Since this starfighter was first introduced, its mission profile has undergone some significant modifications. It has been determined through trial and error that the high-speed craft is better suited to hit-and-fade operations than to escort duty. [SWSB, DFR]

abo

⊕ Abo is an Imperial slang word for the native inhabitants of a planet. [SME]

Abregado

⊕ Abregado is a star system located on the Republic's side of the Borderland Regions. A manufacturing center links the worlds of the system, and it is of extreme importance to the New Republic. [HE, HESB]

Abregado-rae

⟐ Abregado-rae is a spaceport world within the Abregado star system. During the time of the Empire, the spaceport was considered on par with the worst places in the Rim Territories. Now, since the birth of the New Republic, civilization has come to the world. A bright, painfully clean cityscape rises over the landing pits, but the wild air of all spaceports (created by the mix of cultures and species) hangs over the place. The world is ruled by a repressive bureaucracy that is still struggling to bring outlying clans into line. [HE, HESB]

Abyssin

⟐ Abyssins are two-meter-tall humanoid bipeds with long limbs, well-muscled bodies, and single, slit-pupiled eyes. They are natives of the planet Byss, an arid but sporadically fertile planet located in the binary star system of Byss and Abyss. [GG4]

Academy, The

⟐ Youths across the galaxy once dreamed of attending the Academy in hopes of finding a life of service and adventure. An elite educational institution, the Academy produces highly trained personnel to fill posts in the Exploration, Military, and Merchant Services. Under the rule of the Emperor, the Academy has slowly turned into the training ground for Imperial officers. The Academy has a reputation for a competitive selection process and a rigorous curriculum. [SW, SWR]

⊕ While everyone talks of "the Academy," more than one single facility makes up this galaxy-wide institution. Under the jurisdiction of the Empire, the Academy trains people for service in all branches of the Imperial Military. If there is one location and facility that people think of when they think of the Academy, it is Raithal Academy in the Core region. [ISB]

acceleration compensator

⊕ The acceleration compensator provides artificial gravity and neutralizes the effects of high-speed maneuvering for crew and cargo aboard space vessels. The *Millennium Falcon*, for example, is equipped with such a device. [HSE]

Accuser

⊕ The Imperial Star Destroyer *Accuser* was one of two captured by the Alliance during the Battle of Endor. Lando Calrissian and Wedge Antilles commanded the renamed *Emancipator* during the Battle of Calamari. [DE, DESB]

Ackbar

See Admiral Ackbar.

Adar Tallon

⊕ Adar Tallon was a brilliant naval commander and military strategist who served in the Old Republic. Many of the space-combat tactics he developed are still in use by both the Empire and the Alliance. When the Old Republic gave way to the Empire, Tallon faked his own death and settled on Tatooine to hide. A group of Rebel agents found Tallon and convinced him to join the Alliance, adding another important leader to the cause of galactic freedom. [TM]

Adega

⊕ The Adega star system, located in the Outer Rim Territories, was the site of an important Jedi stronghold in ancient times. [DE]

Adegan crystals

⊕ Adegan crystals were the types most commonly used in the construction of ancient lightsabers. These naturally occurring crystals spontaneously emit powerful bursts of light and energy when resonant frequencies are run through them. Also known as Ilum crystals. [DE]

Adjucator

⊕ One of two Imperial Star Destroyers captured by the Alliance during the Battle of Endor, the *Adjucator* was renamed the *Liberator* and placed under the command of Luke Skywalker. After Coruscant was recaptured by the Empire, *Liberator* crashed into Imperial City as the result of damage sustained during combat. Luke's skillful deployment of the Star Destroyer's shields and repulsorlifts prevented the death of the crew. [DE, DESB]

Admiral Ackbar

Admiral Ackbar

Admiral Ackbar is a respected member of the Mon Calamari species who serves as one of Mon Mothma's two senior Rebel Alliance advisers. He was one of the military tacticians who developed the plans for the Alliance surprise attack on the second Death Star battle station. He prefers to lead important assaults personally, and was in command aboard his personal flagship during the Battle of Endor. His prime military specialty is in the area of Imperial defense procedures. [RJ]

Ackbar made a study of Imperial tactics and defenses while serving as slave to Grand Moff Tarkin. Rebel agents released him from servitude during a failed attempt to assassinate the Grand Moff. He used his newfound freedom to return to his homeworld, where he convinced his normally peaceful people to join the Rebels, bringing a much-needed fleet of capital ships into the Alliance arsenal. [SWSB]

Shortly after the Battle of Yavin, Ackbar proposed a plan for dealing with Imperial escort frigates. He argued that a specially designed starfighter was the Alliance's best hope—at least until more funds became available or the number of Rebel capital ships dramatically increased. With the aid of the Verpine, a renowned race of shipbuilders, Ackbar developed the B-wing starfighter. [SFS]

Since the rise of the New Republic, Ackbar has been named Commander-in-Chief of Republic military operations. He serves on the Provisional Council and the ruling Inner Council of the New Republic, helping to forge the new galactic government. With the help of Luke Skywalker and his companions, a recent Imperial plot was foiled and Ackbar was proven innocent of charges of treason. [HE, DFR, LC]

Admiral Drayson

🌑 Admiral Drayson is a high-ranking officer in the New Republic military. Unlike most other officers of his stature, Drayson did not begin his career as either an Old Republic or Imperial officer. He was in charge of the Chandrila system defense forces, serving as Admiral of the Chandrila Defense Fleet for many years. During this time, he came to know Senator Mon Mothma, Chandrila's representative to the Old Republic (and later Imperial) Senate. She was impressed with his efforts, which caused a dramatic decrease in pirate and smuggling activity in Chandrila space. Years later, Mon Mothma asked Drayson to command her headquarters ship in the Alliance. When the New Republic was formed, he was given the rank of admiral and put in charge of the fleet attached to the Provisional Council and the capital system of Coruscant. [DFR, DFRSB]

Admiral Griff

⬡ Admiral Griff was the fleet admiral who supervised the construction of Darth Vader's *Super*-class Star Destroyer *Executor*. Admiral Griff was also in charge of the Imperial Blockade of Yavin Four after the destruction of the first Death Star. He and his ship were destroyed when, in an attempt to intercept the fleeing Rebel fleet, Griff miscalculated a hyperspace jump and dropped out of hyperspace onto the *Executor*. [GW]

Admiral Motti

⬡ Admiral Motti was the senior Imperial commander in charge of operations on the original Death Star battle station. He died when the station was destroyed. [SW]

Admiral Ozzel

⬡ The Imperial officer named Admiral Ozzel was in command of Lord Darth Vader's task force during the events leading up to the Battle of Hoth. The Imperial Death Squadron, as the task force was dubbed, consisted of Vader's flagship *Executor* and five Imperial Star Destroyers. Ozzel's contempt for the Rebels and his unwillingness to see the Alliance as a credible threat led to his downfall. When he brought the task force out of hyperspace within Hoth's sensor range, Vader eliminated the admiral for prematurely alerting the Rebels and for "being as clumsy as he is stupid." [ESB]

Admiral Screed

☺ Admiral Screed was the Emperor's right-hand man during the early days of the Empire. He was a no-nonsense military man, easily recognizable due to the electronic patch he wore over one eye. The droids R2-D2 and C-3PO had various encounters with Screed during this period of time. [DTV]

affect mind

☺ Through the use of the Force control, sense, and alter technique called *affect mind*, a Jedi Knight can alter another person's perceptions. Affect mind creates illusions or blocks real sensory inputs, altering a person's memories so that the person remembers things differently or fails to remember a particular occurrence. [SWRPG, SWRPG2, DFRSB]

Afyon

See Captain Afyon.

agrirobot

☺ An agrirobot is a primitive droid programmed to tend the land and harvest foodstuffs. These machines come in a variety of forms, each designated to fulfill a primary function. Models include harvesters, sowers, sprayers, and packagers. [HSE]

airspeeder

🌀 Any type of airship designed to operate within a planet's atmosphere is called an airspeeder. The term is usually applied to repulsorlift vehicles that fly high above the ground. [HLL, SWSB]

Akrit'tar

🌀 Akrit'tar is one of the galaxy's many penal colony worlds. [HSR]

Alderaan

🌀 The adopted homeworld of Leia Organa, Alderaan was once a shining star in the Old Republic. It spawned such heroes as Bail Organa, Leia's adopted father, who fought beside Obi-Wan Kenobi during the Clone Wars. The horrors of the Clone Wars convinced Alderaan to take a new stance once peace was restored. The planetary government instituted a philosophy of pacifism and banned all weapons from the planet. Due to the tyrannical acts and unchallenged injustices of the Emperor's New Order, many young people, including Senator Leia Organa, began to question Alderaan's pacifistic policies. As the New Order became more open in its tyranny, Alderaan became more supportive of the growing Rebellion. Some even believe that the Alliance was born on this world. Before Alderaan could officially join the Alliance and rebuild its military might, the Empire destroyed the entire planet as a demonstration of the original Death Star's destructive capabilities. [SW, SWR]

✦ When Alderaan dismantled its massive war machine, its government decided to hide the weapons where no one would be able to find them. At the same time, the weapons would be readily available should the planet ever need to protect itself or its beliefs. The weapons were stored aboard a massive armory ship named *Another Chance*, which was then programmed to continually jump through hyperspace until the Council of Elders called it home. Sightings of a ghost ship in the asteroid ruins of Alderaan's orbit (called the Graveyard) have been attributed to this legendary vessel. [GA]

Allegiance

✦ The Super Star Destroyer *Allegiance* was the Imperial command ship at the Battle of Calamari. [DE]

All Terrain Armored Transport (AT-AT)

✦ The four-legged combat vehicle called an All Terrain Armored Transport (AT-AT), or "walker," serves as both a troop transport and an assault craft. It provides high-powered support to Imperial ground forces. An individual walker stands over fifteen meters tall, has blaster-impervious armor plating, and resembles a mechanical beast as it strides across the battlefield. The movable "head" contains the crew deck, with a pilot's station, gunner's station, and commanding officer/combat coordination station. A walker's armament consists of heavy blaster cannons mounted on each side of the head and under the "chin." [ESB]

✦ When the Empire began to design its military war machine, it sought weapons to match the terror inspired by

13

All Terrain Armored Transport/AT-AT and All Terrain Armored Scout Transport/AT-ST

Star Destroyers and unending hordes of stormtroopers. The AT-AT, an unstoppable juggernaut of fear and fury, fit in well with the Imperial doctrine of rule by terror. A walker carries troops and light vehicles into combat areas, marching fearlessly through most defenses. The massive AT-AT kneels to unload its troops, lowering assault ramps from the rear portion of its armored body. [SWSB]

All Terrain Personal Transport (AT-PT)

The All Terrain Personal Transport, or AT-PT, is the an-cestor of the modern Imperial walker. This experimental weapon was developed by the Old Republic as a personal weapons platform for ground soldiers. Like a scaled-down version of the scout walker, it was supposed to turn a com-mon soldier into a walking fortress. The majority of AT-PTs were installed aboard the legendary *Katana* fleet, and when that fleet was lost the project was abandoned. A soldier fills a crowded control pod nestled between two multijointed legs. In the armored pod, slightly raised above the battle-field, the soldier controls a twin blaster cannon, a concus-

14

sion grenade launcher, and a primitive combat sensor package. [DFR, DFRSB]

All Terrain Scout Transport (AT-ST)

☺ Modeled after the larger AT-AT, the All Terrain Scout Transport (AT-ST) serves as a reconnaissance or defense vehicle. Lightweight and built for speed, the "chicken" or "scout walker" runs on two metal legs. The two-man crew sits in a small, armored command pod. With its maneuverability and quickness, a scout walker provides covering fire for ground troops or defends the flanks and undersides of the AT-ATs. The seven-meter-tall AT-ST has chin- and side-mounted blaster cannons, a concussion grenade launcher, and feet claws for cutting through fixed defenses. [ESB, RJ]

alluvial damper

☺ A subsystem of a starship's hyperdrive unit, an alluvial damper blocks the emission of ion particles by moving a servo-controlled plate, thus regulating the amount of thrust. [ESB]

Altorian

☺ There are two species of intelligent Altorians living on the planet Altor 14. The Avogwi, or Altorian Birds, are two-meter-tall predatory birds with three opposable fingers on the apex of their wings. The Nuiwit, or Altorian Lizards, are bipedal reptiles about 1.5 meters tall. While the Avogwi are primitive and lawless, the Nuiwit possess a highly structured and harmonious society. [GG4]

Amanaman

The long-armed alien with big hands who carried a three-headed staff and spent time in Jabba the Hutt's court was a member of the Amanaman race, more commonly known as Head Hunters. [RJ]

Ammuud

The planet Ammuud is governed by a feudal coalition of seven clans, under a contract from the Corporate Sector Authority. Its rigid code of honor is known throughout Authority space. [HSR]

Ammuud clans

Ammuud clans are feudal families that govern the planet Ammuud. A Corporate Sector Authority retainer demands that each clan provide forces for its port security. Two of the more prominent clans are House Reesbon and House Glayyd. [HSR]

amphibion

Amphibions are the amphibious assault vessels that were used by New Republic Sea Commandos in the Battle of Calamari. [DE]

Anakin Skywalker

The father of Luke Skywalker and Leia Organa, Anakin

Skywalker was a hero of the Clone Wars. He demonstrated an unusually high level of flying and fighting talent due to his innate ability to tap the Force. Later, as a student of the Jedi Knight Obi-Wan Kenobi, Anakin honed his use of the Force to near perfection. Unfortunately, the young Knight was lured to the dark side by the Emperor and transformed into the evil Darth Vader. [RJ]

Anakin Solo

⊕ Anakin Solo is the son of Han Solo and Leia Organa Solo. Like his mother, siblings, and Uncle Luke, Anakin is strong in the Force. He was born approximately six years after the Battle of Endor, during the events surrounding the rebirth of the Emperor. [DE]

Analysis Bureau

⊕ A division of Imperial Intelligence, the Analysis Bureau takes the data gathered by other divisions and examines it for patterns and other relevant information. It also looks for trends in social data, and watches for hidden messages in the carrier-wave codes of comm broadcasts. Its decryption experts can break most coded communications in very short periods of time. [ISB]

Anchorhead

⊕ Anchorhead, a slow-paced, quiet, moisture-farming community, is located on the desert flats of the planet Tatooine. Luke Skywalker grew up on a farm outside Anchorhead, spending much of his free time in the sleepy town. [SW]

Anky Fremp

⚉ Anky Fremp is one of the nonhuman denizens of the streets of Nar Shaddaa. [DE]

Annihilator

⚉ When the droid Bollux participated in Han Solo's ploy to deceive Viceprex Hirken, he pretended to be the gladiator droid Annihilator, a member of Madam Atuarre's Roving Performers. In this guise, Bollux hoped to help Solo and their companions infiltrate the Authority penal colony known as "Stars' End." [HSE]

Annoo

⚉ Annoo is an agricultural planet. Demma Moll and her daughter had a farm complex there during the early days of the Empire, at which time the gangster Sise Fromm maintained a stronghold on the planet as well. [DTV]

Annoo-dat

⚉ The Annoo-dat are a species of reptilian humanoids from the planet Annoo. They have heavy-lidded eyes, flat noses, and spotted faces. [DTV]

Anoat

⚉ The Anoat star system is adjacent to the Hoth system.

It was in this largely deserted star system that Han Solo managed to lose the Imperial Star Destroyers that chased his *Millennium Falcon* from the Rebel base on Hoth. [ESB]

Anomid

⊛ Anomids are a humanoid species native to the Yablari system. These beings are born without vocal cords, and wear elaborate vocalizer masks to produce synthesized sounds so that they can communicate with other species. The technologically advanced Anomids dress in long hooded robes and like to travel the galaxy as tourists whenever they can. [RM]

Antares Six

⊛ *Antares Six* was one of the two New Republic escort frigates that accompanied the *Millennium Falcon* to Coruscant to rescue the crew of the *Liberator*. [DE]

anticoncussion field

⊛ An anticoncussion field is a magnetic shield used to protect buildings, fortifications, space stations, and space outposts from damage by solid objects. This type of field works best in preventing small objects from colliding with otherwise unprotected structures. Anticoncussion fields cannot protect against combat-rated projectiles or energy weapons, as they are much weaker than particle and ray shielding. [HSE]

antigrav

⊛ Any machine or device that counters the normal effects of gravity. The most common antigrav is the repulsorlift engine. [SW]

antigrav drive

⊛ A starship or speeder propulsion system that works by countering the normal effects of gravity. An antigrav drive only works when a large gravity mass is nearby, such as within the gravity well of a planet. The most common antigrav drive is the repulsorlift engine. [SW]

Antilles

See Captain Antilles.

approach vector

⊛ An approach vector is generated by a ship's nav computer. The computer-generated trajectory places a ship on an intercept course with another ship or other target for purposes of attack or rendezvous. [ESBR]

aqua-skimmer

⊛ An aqua-skimmer is a vehicle used on Aquaris for underwater travel. [GW]

Aqualish

⊛ Aqualish is the species name of the walrus-faced humanoids from the planet Ando, a world covered by water, swamp islands, and rocky outcroppings. One of the aliens who picked a fight with Luke Skywalker at the Mos Eisley Cantina was an Aqualish. [GG1, GG4, GDV]

Aquaris

⊛ The water-covered world called Aquaris is allied with the Rebellion and home to Silver Fyre. [GW]

Arachnor

⊛ An Arachnor is a giant, spiderlike creature that spins very sticky webs. It is native to the planet Arzid. [PDS]

Arbo Maze

⊛ The Arbo Maze on the forest moon of Endor is a thicket of trees so dense and convoluted that most beings and creatures that wander into it become hopelessly lost—including Ewoks. [ETV]

Arcona

⊛ The scaleless reptiloids called Arcona are limbed snakes with flat, anvil-shaped heads and clear, marblelike eyes. They come from the hot world of Cona, in the Teke Ro system. An Arcona makes a brief appearance during the cantina scene in *Star Wars IV: A New Hope*. [GG4]

Area illumination bank

⊕ An area illumination bank, or illumigrid, is made up of a battery of lights. The flood of light such a bank gives off can illuminate a very large area, such as a spaceport or public arena. [HLL]

Arhul Hextrophon

⊕ Arhul Hextrophon is the executive secretary and master historian for the Alliance High Command. [SWSB, GG1]

Aridus

⊕ Luke Skywalker went looking for Ben Kenobi on the distant, harsh, desert world called Aridus. As it turned out, an imposter was posing as Kenobi as part of Vader's plan to capture Luke. [GW]

armament rating

⊕ All space vessels have armament ratings. These classifications specify the level of defensive and offensive weaponry a particular ship packs. A ship's armament rating is contained within its ID profile. The classifications are O (no weaponry), 1 (light defensive weapons only), 2 (light defensive and offensive capabilities), 3 (medium defensive and offensive), and 4 (heavy defensive and offensive weaponry).

Specific classifications are determined by the number and type of weapons, the maximum range, the associated fire control computers, and the maximum output of the ship's power plants. Armament ratings are also called weapons ratings. [HSR, SWR]

armored defense platform

Many star systems protect themselves from outside threats with strategically placed armored defense platforms. These battle stations have little maneuverability, so where they are placed on the perimeter of a system or deep-space docking facility is usually very important. Heavily armed, these stations come equipped with multiple turbolaser batteries, proton torpedo launch ports, and tractor beam projectors. While these battle stations cannot stand alone against a full-scale fleet offensive, they are perfect for dealing with pirate raids and smuggler ships trying to flee a system. [HE, HESB]

artificial gravity

Artificial gravity is a force produced by technological machines to control the weight or weightlessness of beings and items in a specific environment (such as a space station or vessel). These machines, called grav generators, adapt low- or high-gravity environments to the needs of specific biological types working or living within the area. [HSE]

Artoo-Detoo

See R2-D2.

asaari tree

⚇ The asaari trees of the planet Bimmisaari can move their leafy branches of their own accord, though their roots are firmly anchored in the ground. [HE, HESB]

Asha

⚇ Asha is a red-furred Ewok huntress who was raised by a family of creatures called Korrina after being separated from her mother and her younger sister Kneesaa. [ETV]

Askha Boda

⚇ The ancient Jedi Askha Boda was captured and murdered by the Emperor during the Jedi extermination that marked the start of the New Order. Askha possessed the Jedi Holocron at the time of his capture. [DE]

assassin droid

⚇ Assassin droids are intelligent killing machines. These automated weapons systems are programmed to hunt down specific targets and destroy them. Assassin droids have been illegal for several decades, but many of these deadly droids are covertly serving the Empire and criminal organizations. Some are even free-roaming automatons who have broken their own programming or are still following orders given them in the distant past. These droids were originally designed to locate and eliminate escaped criminals or other outlaws for the Old Republic and were soon employed in the corrupt competitions of the decaying Senate. Ironically, it was the Emperor himself who banned the use of assassin droids with the rise of his New Order, because the droids were being used against his own forces. [SWSB]

Assassin's Guild

🏵 The Assassin's Guild is a secret society of professional mercenaries who perform contract terminations. Contracts can be so specialized as to require specialized mercs, so the Guild has different sub-guilds, including the feared bounty-hunter division. The best members form their own sub-guild, called the Elite Circle. Members are voted into the Circle by their peers. The Circle services the most prominent clients, whose operations are so big as to require special attention. Most members of the Assassin's Guild are wanted criminals, so the Guild operates in secret. Even its headquarters is hidden, and few members even know its location. They must contact the Guild via comlink or through some other covert means. [HLL]

assault frigate

🏵 When the Alliance needed capital ships to fill the ranks of its growing fleet, it designed the assault frigate. Using the framework of the Old Republic Dreadnaught, Alliance engineers modified the vessel to create a combat starship. By stripping away huge portions of the superstructure in order to lower fuel consumption and increase engine capacity, and by adding two dorsal solar fins, the techs made the vessel faster and more maneuverable. To meet the demands of limited crew complements, being-operated work stations were retooled to allow for droid- and computer-controlled stations. Once all of the modifications were completed, the barest hint of the original structure remained. Assault frigates have no docking bays. However, twenty umbilical docking tubes are scattered about the hull to accommodate transports, light freighters, and starfighters. After the Battle of Endor, the New Republic continues to use these vessels. Assault frigates patrolling the Borderland Regions are the New Republic's first line of defense against Imperial aggression. A few have been taken off combat duty to serve as cargo transports until full-scale galactic trade can be resumed. [RSB, HESB]

assault shuttle

The Imperial assault shuttle is a heavily armored, thirty-meter-long spacecraft equipped with tractor beam generators and projectors, full sensor suites, power harpoon guns, concussion missile launchers, and automatic blaster cannons. Its five-person crew is trained to engage enemy ships and serve as field support for the zero-g stormtroopers they ferry about. Assault shuttles are designed to serve as launch platforms for zero-g troopers, and they can easily carry forty of the armored space warriors within their main holds. Assault shuttles are among the best shielded vehicles in the Imperial fleet. They can operate in space and in planetary atmospheres, and their limited nav computers can handle up to three hyperspace jumps before needing base-assisted reprogramming. [ISB]

astrogation computer

See nav computer.

astromech droid

✹ Astromech droids specialize in starship maintenance and repair. Some models also assist with piloting and navigation. Luke Skywalker's droid, R2-D2, is an astromech droid. [SW]

✹ Astromech droids interface with starship computers to monitor and diagnose flight performance. They initiate repairs when necessary and augment navigational, astrogational, and piloting capacity. The popular R2 unit, designed by Industrial Automaton, has an extensive sensor package and a variety of tools that assist its jack-of-all-trades programming. [SWSB]

AT-AT

See All Terrain Armored Transport.

AT-PT

See All Terrain Personal Transport.

AT-ST

See All Terrain Scout Transport.

Atedeate

✹ The thin-faced droid Atedeate, or 8D8, worked in Jabba the Hutt's robot operation center as a subordinate to Ninedenine. [RJ]

Athega

The Athega star system has no life-bearing worlds, but its lifeless rocks are great sources of raw materials and resources. However, the intense heat given off by the system's sun has always hindered potential entrepreneurs, for even shielded starships can not long stand the pounding rays of heat and radiation. With the creation of a new kind of spacecraft called a shieldship, Lando Calrissian was able to set up a mining operation on the planet Nkllon, located in the Athega system. [HE, HESB]

Atuarre

Atuarre was the female Triannii trying to locate political prisoners held by the Corporate Sector Authority. Prior to her personal mission and meeting with Han Solo, Atuarre worked as an apprentice agronomist on the planet Orron III. [HSE]

aura blossom

Aura blossoms are beautiful, indigo-blue flowers that glow brightly. They grow on the forest moon of Endor. [ETV]

Auren Yomm

During the early days of the Empire, when R2-D2 and C-3PO were involved in various adventures, they met the then-fifteen-year-old girl named Auren Yomm. She lived in the Umboo colony of Róon, where she demonstrated the skills and talents of an excellent athlete. She often led her competitive team, which included the sleek droid Bix, to victory in the Colonial Games. Her parents were Nilz and Bola Yomm. [DTV]

Authority Cash Voucher

🌀 Authority Cash Vouchers can be obtained and redeemed at any Corporate Sector Authority Currency Exchange Center. Authority worlds do not accept Imperial or Republic credits, so Cash Vouchers are needed to pay for goods and services when traveling within the Corporate Sector. When entering Corporate Sector space, travelers must surrender and exchange other moneys for Cash Vouchers or risk legal ramifications. [HSE]

autohopper

🌀 Autohoppers are self-propelled, unmanned vehicles that follow a preprogrammed course. Routing is controlled by a central instruction processor, or CIP. CIPs can be programmed to remember time and locations of specific job assignments. Certain variables can also be punched into the CIP, including geography and weather fluctuations. [HLL]

avabush spice

🌀 The spice called avabush has the property of causing sleepiness. It also acts as a truth serum, and is used as such by interrogators who know of it. Imperials frequently serve the spice in liquid refreshments or baked into sweets. [ZHR, PDS]

Avenger

The Imperial Star Destroyer *Avenger* was part of the task force assigned to locate Rebel forces after the Battle of Yavin. *Avenger* was temporarily incapacitated during the Battle of Hoth. [ESB]

Aves

One of Talon Karrde's ranking associates, Aves has served with the smuggler chief since the earliest days of his operation. His role is to stay close to Karrde, serving as an adviser and comm officer. In this capacity, he coordinates the activities of field operatives as a sort of ship dispatcher for the smugglers. [HE, DFR, LC, HESB]

B

B-wing starfighter

The uniquely shaped B-wing fighter adds four power plants and a command pod to a primary airfoil to create one of the most heavily armed starfighters in the Alliance arsenal. Two movable secondary airfoils form a cross midway between the command pod and the primary airfoil wingtip. These alter their position during flight: they ex-

B-wing starfighter

tend fully to bring the starfighter's maximum concentration of firepower to bear and tuck into the primary airfoil when in cruise mode. The command pod employs a radical design, using an automatic gyroscopically stabilized suspension system to keep the pod in a fixed position. The airfoil rotates around the stabilized pod, creating a flexible firing platform while the pilot experiences none of the effects of rapid spins, twists, or turns. The primary and two secondary wingtips sport ion cannons, while the command pod features a mounted laser cannon. Other weapons include two internally mounted proton torpedo launchers and two small blaster cannons. These starfighters played a key role in the Alliance victory at the Battle of Endor. [RJ]

⚙ In response to the growing success of Imperial escort warships, Admiral Ackbar conceived and headed the Shantipole Project. With the aid of the Verpine colonies of Slayn and Korpil, Ackbar designed the B-wing. The ship combines speed with armor and armament, thus creating a formidable starfighter to aid the Rebel Alliance. Designed as a pure starfighter, the B-wing originally had no hyperdrive capability. Hyperdrives were added to the design prior to the Battle of Endor. [SWSB, SFS]

bacta

☾ The chemical compound bacta is a wonder of modern science. With it, all but the most serious wounds can be treated and healed like new. Bacta must be applied in a solution of clear synthetic fluid which mimics the body's own vital liquids. A patient is fully immersed in this fluid within specially designed rejuvenation tanks (also called bacta tanks). The gelatinous, translucent red bacta is added to the clear fluid where it interacts to form a bacterial medium.

This bacterial medium seeks out traumatized flesh, then promotes regeneration and tissue growth to rapidly heal wounds without scarring.

After Luke Skywalker suffered injuries battling a wampa ice creature on Hoth, he was treated within a bacta rejuvenation tank. [ESB]

Badlands

The Badlands of the planet Kamar is a flat, desolate area near the arid equator. Inhabitants of this region are commonly called Badlanders. Han Solo and Chewbacca spent some time in this region after the Corporate Sector Authority became overly interested in their location. [HSR]

Badure

Badure was one of Han Solo's military mentors. Badure, who also went by the nickname Trooper, taught Solo almost everything he knows about flying. After leaving the military, Badure crossed paths with Solo a number of times. He even saved Solo and the Wookiee Chewbacca after an aborted spice run to Kessel. Many years before, Han Solo had saved Badure when a training mission turned bad. Just prior to Solo's connection with the Rebel Alliance, Badure enlisted Han and Chewbacca in his quest to locate the lost treasure of the cargo vessel *Queen of Ranroon*. [HLL]

Baga

Baga is a small baby bordok and the pet of the Ewok named Wicket. [ETV]

Bail Organa

Bail Organa was the foster father of Princess Leia Organa. He fought in the Clone Wars, battling at the side of Obi-Wan Kenobi and other heroes of the period. As a native of the planet Alderaan, he served as Viceroy and First Chairman of the Alderaan system up until the time of his death, when the planet was destroyed by the original Death Star battle station. [SW, SWR, RJ]

Baji

The Ho'Din named Baji is a healer and medicine man who once lived on Yavin Four. Wise and peaceful, Baji speaks in rhyme. On Yavin, he spent much of his time gathering the roots and plants necessary to make his medicines. He also collected rare plants that he feared were nearing extinction. These he transported to his home planet of Moltok for further study by his botanist colleagues. The Empire captured him and forced him to cure the blindness that afflicted Trioculus. Afterward, he was kept as an Imperial staff physician until he was rescued by the Rebel Alliance. He now lives on Dagobah, tending medicinal plants he grows in an Alliance greenhouse. [LCJ, QE]

ball creature of Duroon

The ball creature of Duroon is a docile herbivore. Nocturnal in nature, it gets its name from its spherical shape and natural locomotion. It propels itself like a ball, bouncing from place to place. [HSE]

Bane Nothos

See Commander Bane Nothos.

bantha

(🔴) Banthas are large quadrupeds with long, thick fur and bright, inquisitive eyes. Long spiral horns grow in pairs from the heads of male banthas. On the planet Tatooine, banthas are used as beasts of burden by the moisture farmers and as pack animals by the Sand People. [SW]

(🔵) These large herbivores are extremely adaptable, able to live on a variety of worlds and in a wide range of climates. They can survive for weeks without food or water. Males grow as large as three meters at the shoulders, while female banthas are slightly smaller. The domesticated bantha can be found throughout the galaxy, and wild bantha herds thunder across many worlds. Because of its widespread presence, the bantha's world of origin has been lost in the distant past. Almost every planet where the creatures exist claims to be the home world of the bantha.

Banthas are used for many things, depending on which part of the galaxy they are found in. Herders raise the huge beasts for food and clothing. Some of the finest restaurants serve bantha steaks, and bantha-skin boots and cloaks are popular among the upper classes.

These magnificent creatures have even inspired a religion. Priests of the Dim-U religion are devoted to the mystery of the bantha. These priests and their followers believe that a great message of universal importance has been hidden in the simple bantha, and that once the mystery is solved, an incredible age of peace and bounty will begin. [SWSB, TM]

Barabel

🔵 Barabels are bipedal reptiloids who stand from 1.75 to 2.5 meters tall. Horny black scales cover their bodies, and long, sharp teeth fill their mouths. They inhabit the dark, humid world of Barab I. Though spice smugglers and other criminals often use the world as a refuge, it rarely receives open galactic traffic. Therefore, the Barabel species is not widely known and few of the reptiloids have found their way off-planet. The underground spaceport of Alater-ka is crude by Core standards, but sporting hunters fill the tourist lodges to hunt the terrible beasts that inhabit the world. Some Barabels have taken jobs as porters and guides, and a few have even left the world with bounty hunter commissions, but the majority of the species remains untamed and uncivilized. They have a deep respect for Jedi Knights, and a few have tried to emulate the Jedi tradition despite little aptitude in the Force. This respect goes back to the time of the Barabel War, when the primitive hunters split into two factions over access to choice hunting grounds. Passing Jedi Knights intervened and negotiated a peaceful solution, keeping the Barabels from killing themselves needlessly. [GG4, DFR, DFRSB]

Barada

🔵 Barada was one of Jabba the Hutt's guards on the planet Tatooine. He died when Luke Skywalker and his companions freed Han Solo from Jabba's clutches in the Tatooine wilderness. [RJ]

🔵 Barada, a native of the planet Klatooine, was sold into indentured servitude as punishment for a crime he committed in his youth. The crime lord Jabba the Hutt won Barada's contract and put him to work in the repulsorpool. He quickly took charge, becoming responsible for the procurement, modification, crew, and care of all of Jabba's repulsorlift vehicles. He took his job to heart, serving as captain of the skiffs when they went into battle or when Jabba wanted to travel. [GG5]

Barhu

Barhu, a boiling-hot ball of lifeless rock, is a planet in the Churba star system. [DFR, DFRSB]

Basic

The common language of the galaxy, based upon the language of the human civilizations of the Core Worlds, is called Basic. It became the standard trade and diplomatic language during the time of the Old Republic, and has remained in use to the current day. [SWRPG, SWSB, SWRPG2, HESB]

Batcheela

The old female Ewok named Batcheela is the mother of Teebo and Malani. [ETV]

battle dogs

See neks.

Battle of Calamari, the

The water world of Calamari was the first planet attacked by the reborn Emperor's World Devastators in the conflict now known as the Battle of Calamari. The homeworld of the Mon Calamari suffered great damage, but the new Imperial war machines were eventually stopped thanks to the actions of Luke Skywalker. [DE]

Battle of Endor, the

The Battle of Endor has been called the most decisive engagement of the Galactic Civil War. The Alliance to Restore Freedom to the Galaxy and the Galactic Empire clashed near the forest moon of Endor in a battle that saw the deaths of both Emperor Palpatine and Darth Vader.

The Empire had selected the forest moon as the construction site for its second Death Star battle station. Bothan spies intercepted information that named the secret construction site and provided its location. In addition, those same spies learned that the Emperor himself was heading to Endor in order to supervise the final stages of construction. The Alliance decided that this would be its best opportunity not only to strike a blow at the Imperial war machine, but to get at the Emperor outside his impenetrable Imperial City fortress.

As Admiral Ackbar gathered the Rebel Alliance fleet around the planet Sullust, a special strike team was sent ahead to sabotage the shield generator protecting the unfinished Death Star. The strike team, led by Han Solo and including Luke Skywalker, Leia Organa, Chewbacca, the droids R2-D2 and C-3PO, and a squad of Rebel commandos, used a stolen Imperial shuttle to get through the Empire's forces and down to Endor's forest moon. The timing had to be perfect. The strike team had to disable or destroy the shield generator by the time the Rebel fleet emerged from hyperspace so that the surprise attack could begin.

Unfortunately, the information that many Bothans died to deliver to Alliance High Command was a deception planned by the Emperor himself. The unfinished Death Star was not as helpless as it appeared, for its superlaser was fully operational. As for the strike team, a full legion of stormtroopers and other Imperial soldiers were waiting to defend the shield generator and capture the Rebel commandos. While the strike team battled the Empire on Endor's moon, the Rebel fleet arrived to find the protective shield still in place. The battle, it seemed, was over before it had begun.

The Emperor's plan called for the Imperial fleet to remain in reserve on the far side of the moon while swarms of TIE fighters engaged the outnumbered Rebel ships. Alliance starfighters met their Imperial counterparts in dramatic dogfights as the Emperor looked on. The onslaught of TIEs was but the first stage of the Emperor's trap. The second stage involved turning the Death Star's prime weapon upon the Alliance's capital ships—vaporizing each one in its path with a single shot.

Lando Calrissian, leading the Alliance starfighters from the command seat of the *Millennium Falcon*, convinced Ackbar on a new course of action. By engaging the poised but as yet docile Star Destroyers in ship-to-ship combat, the Rebel ships would be using the Empire's own vessels as protection from the Death Star's weapon. Of course, the Star Destroyers were also more powerful than the Rebel ships, but not by the magnitude of the Death Star. The Alliance had bought itself some time, but it still needed the strike team to succeed if it was going to have a chance at winning the day.

On the forest moon, the native Ewoks became the key to victory. The primitive natives had been dismissed as inconsequential by the Imperial troops, but this mistake was to be the Empire's undoing. The same Ewoks who had befriended the strike team helped free them, allowing Han and his companions to carry out the sabotage mission. When the shield generators were destroyed, the protective shield surrounding the Death Star disappeared.

As soon as the opening presented itself, Lando Calrissian and his starfighters moved to attack. The *Falcon* and Wedge Antilles' X-wing flew into the unfinished Death Star's superstructure and fired proton torpedoes at the battle station's power regulator. Simultaneously, Lando Calrissian fired concussion missiles at the main reactor. The resulting explosions destroyed the Death Star, and the Imperial fleet immediately lost the central, powerful evil that had been its cohesive force. Without the Emperor, the dark side became diffuse, nondirected, and the Imperial forces were plunged into confusion, desperation, and damp fear. What remained of the Imperial fleet scattered and this phase of the Galactic Civil War came to an end. [RJ]

Battle of Hoth, the

🟦 The Battle of Hoth was one of the worst defeats the Rebel Alliance suffered during the Galactic Civil War. After winning a major victory at the Battle of Yavin, the Alliance spent the next three years running from the Imperial fleet. It evacuated and relocated its command base many times during this period in an effort to avoid a confrontation with the Imperial armada assembled to locate and destroy it. Finally the Alliance thought it had found the perfect location for its secret base. The Hoth system was off the beaten galactic path, and its sixth planet's inhospitable climate of ice and snow seemed a perfect place to hide the Rebels. The base was just nearing completion when one of the many Imperial probe droids searching the galaxy happened to discover the Rebel presence.

A mistake made by Admiral Ozzel gave the Rebels time to evacuate Hoth, though they still suffered grave losses. Ozzel brought the Imperial fleet out of hyperspace too close to the Hoth system, alerting the Rebels to its arrival. The Rebels were able to activate the shields protecting the base, making a bombardment from space impossible. As the Rebels prepared to escape, the Imperial Star Destroyers moved into position around the planet and Imperial ground forces dropped to the surface beyond the range of the planetary shields. Once on the ground, a squadron of AT-AT walkers and several legions of modified stormtroopers advanced on the Rebel base.

Alliance High Command knew it had to turn to desperate measures if it was going to successfully complete the evacuation. While the most important staff and material was loaded into transports and blasted off the planet, the ill-prepared Rebel soldiers moved to engage the Imperials with conventional warfare. Heavy casualties were the order of the day as the Rebellion lost many brave soldiers and much valuable equipment. But the Rebels' holding action delayed the Imperials long enough to get the command personnel away, and the planet-based ion cannon temporarily disabled any Star Destroyers that moved into the escape path of the Rebel transports.

When the battle ended, the Imperials had won a major tactical victory—their first in over three years. The Rebels were routed and their ships barely escaped the Imperial blockade intact. This was the culmination of a dark time for the Alliance, and it directly influenced the Rebels to try an all-or-nothing attack at Endor one year later. [ESB]

Battle of Taanab, the

Before Lando Calrissian joined the Rebellion against the Empire or served as baron-administer of Cloud City, he participated in the small but significant Battle of Taanab. It was at Taanab that Lando demonstrated not only his ability to lead, but his knack for devising winning tactics in the face of overwhelming odds—and this reputation was what prompted the Alliance to place him in command of its starfighters during the Battle of Endor.

The details of the Battle of Taanab are now part of spacer legend. Pirates from the planet Norulac seasonally raided the agrarian world of Taanab for spoils. Lando Calrissian was on Taanab refueling his ship when a Norulackian raid took place. Lando decided to aid the Taanabians because the pirates had damaged his ship and because they were taking advantage of defenseless farmers, but mostly because someone bet him he couldn't beat the Norulackians. With superior tactics, amazing flying, the help of the farmers, and a lot of luck, Lando managed to destroy the attacking space pirates and foil the raid. [RJ]

Battle of Yavin, the

The Battle of Yavin was the first major engagement of the Galactic Civil War—and the first major tactical victory for the Rebel Alliance. The battle occurred in the shadow of Yavin, near its fourth moon. This was not a planned engagement. Instead, it was the result of the actions of Rebel spies, the capture of Princess Leia Organa, and her eventual escape from the original Death Star battle station.

Rebel spies stole the plans for the Empire's newest weapon of mass destruction, barely escaping with their lives. They were chased across the galaxy, finally transferring the stolen data to the consular ship carrying Princess Leia Organa of Alderaan. The Princess had a two-fold mission: she was to receive the stolen data for transport back to Alderaan, where it could then be used by the Rebellion to discover the Death Star's vulnerabilities. On the way, she was to seek out the reclusive Jedi Knight Obi-Wan Kenobi in his hiding place on Tatooine and convince him to aid the growing Rebellion in its fight against Imperial injustice. But before she could complete either of these missions, the Empire intercepted her ship as it entered orbit around Tatooine.

The Imperials, under the command of Lord Darth Vader, quickly overwhelmed the small contingent of soldiers aboard the consular ship and began an intensive search for the stolen plans. With time running out, the Princess placed the technical readouts into the memory banks of the astromech droid R2-D2. She gave it specific orders to get off the ship and present itself to Obi-Wan Kenobi. The brave droid eluded capture and, along with its counterpart C-3PO, used an escape pod to reach the planet's surface. Through a series of adventures that brought the droids into the possession of Luke Skywalker and saw the dramatic rescue of Princess Leia in Han Solo's *Millennium Falcon*, the secret plans finally reached the Alliance base on Yavin's fourth moon.

Rebel technicians and tacticians quickly studied the technical readouts of the Death Star and devised a risky plan for combating the dreaded battle station. The plan utilized the limited number of starfighters the alliance could muster at that point in time, for there were few capital ships in the Rebel arsenal. There was no time to rehearse the daring plan, for the Death Star had followed the *Falcon* to the Yavin star system. The Alliance quickly assembled every spaceworthy vessel at hand and launched the attack. The Rebel forces had a limited amount of time, for once the Death Star orbited clear of Yavin, the moon holding the secret base would be in line for the full power of the battle station's primary weapon—a weapon that had turned Alderaan into molten shards only days before.

The stakes for the Alliance were high. There seemed to be only two possible outcomes: survival or total destruction. For the Empire, the moment held the promise of a swift end to the upstart Rebellion, as its most important cells were trapped on the jungle moon. The success of the Rebel plan depended on the ability of a single starfighter to navigate the trenches carved in the Death Star's surface while avoiding laser-tower fire and TIE fighters. Then the pilot had to target a small thermal exhaust vent and score a direct hit with a proton torpedo; anything less would not cause the chain reaction needed to explode the power core. After suffering massive losses and demonstrating high levels of skill and bravery, the Rebels seemed to be out of time. One chance remained, and it rested in the hands of the farm boy from Tatooine who was strong in the Force—Luke Skywalker.

Using the power of the Force, and aided by the timely intervention of Han Solo and the *Millennium Falcon*, Luke fired the shot heard 'round the galaxy. The Death Star, along with its crew of many of the most talented officers in the Empire, was destroyed in spectacular fashion. The Alliance quickly grew thanks to this impressive victory, and Luke Skywalker and his companions became known as the heroes of Yavin. [SW]

battle wagon

🌀 The massive Ewok war machine called the battle wagon was originally designed by Erpham Warrick and later restored by his great-grandson Wicket. The wagon sits atop four huge wheels and features a large battering ram topped with a bantha skull. [ETV]

beam tube

🏛️ A beam tube is an antiquated hand-held weapon powered by a backpack generator. [HLL]

beamdrill

🏛️ A beamdrill is a heavy tool used for mining. It employs a high-intensity pulse to disintegrate rock. [HLL]

Beedo

✪ The Rodian named Beedo is a relative of the deceased bounty hunter Greedo. He took his kin's place in Jabba the Hutt's organization until Skywalker, Solo, and Organa took it down prior to the Battle of Endor. It is not known if Beedo survived. [RJ]

Beggar's Canyon

✪ The valley on Tatooine called Beggar's Canyon served as the training ground for Luke Skywalker's aerial skills. Luke and his childhood friends raced skyhoppers and engaged in mock dogfights within its twisting confines. One of Luke's favorite pastimes was to fly his T-16 skyhopper at full throttle while hunting womp rats. [SW, SWR]

Bel Iblis

See Garm Bel Iblis.

Ben (Obi-Wan) Kenobi

Ben (Obi-Wan) Kenobi

Ben Kenobi was the hermit and recluse who lived by the Western Dune Sea on the planet Tatooine. He was considered a crazy old man by the locals, but in reality he was nothing of the sort. For Ben Kenobi once went by the name of Obi-Wan, and he served the Old Republic as a Jedi Knight. Kenobi studied under the Jedi Master Yoda, learning the ways of the Force. When the Clone Wars erupted, Kenobi became a general, fighting alongside Bail Organa of Alderaan and the young pilot Anakin Skywalker. Obi-Wan and Anakin became good friends, sharing many adventures as they battled to protect the galaxy. In fact, Kenobi recognized Anakin's natural Force talents and decided to train him to be a Jedi. But Kenobi wasn't experienced as a teacher, and Anakin was lured to the dark side. Kenobi's pride had terrible consequences for the galaxy.

Much to Kenobi's horror, his friend and pupil was so

corrupted by the dark side of the Force that he became essentially a new person—the Dark Lord Darth Vader. When Kenobi saw what had become of Anakin, he tried to dissuade him and draw him back from the dark side.

According to the *Return of the Jedi* novel, discussion turned to battle, and the two fought fiercely. It ended when the man who had been Anakin Skywalker fell into a pit of molten lava. After that, Kenobi helped hide Anakin's children to protect them from the Emperor and Vader.

In the years that followed, as Vader and the Emperor systematically hunted down and destroyed the Jedi Knights, Kenobi remained in hiding. He remained near Anakin's son, young Luke Skywalker, watching over him and waiting for the moment when he would step in and reveal the young man's destiny to him. The event that triggered the beginning of this revelation was inspired by Anakin's other child, Leia Organa. Leia's foster father told her to seek out Kenobi if she ever was in dire need, and that was what she was doing when the Empire captured her over Tatooine. Kenobi became Luke's mentor and protector, starting his training in the ways of the Force.

On the Death Star, while Luke and Han Solo worked to rescue Princess Leia, Kenobi faced Darth Vader for a final time. He sacrificed his life to help Luke and to advance the cause of the Rebellion, but his sacrifice was not the end. He became one with the Force, a being of light who was much more than the crude matter of flesh and bone. He continued to guide Luke even in death, giving him support in desperate times, leading him to further training with Yoda, and helping him prepare for his final confrontation with Vader. [SW, ESB, RJ]

Ber'asco

Ber'asco is the leader of the alien species called the Charon and commander of the biologically engineered space-craft *Desolate*. Hailing from the dimension known as otherspace, he leads the Charon death cult and anticipates the long-awaited enlightenment that will come with the extermination of all life. [OS]

Berchest

🏛 The planet Berchest remains on the Imperial side of the Borderland Regions even beyond the time of Grand Admiral Thrawn's campaign against the New Republic. The world is best known for its major city, Calius saj Leeloo, the City of Glowing Crystal of Berchest. This city has been a spectacular wonder since the earliest days of the Old Republic. The entire city is nothing more or less than a single gigantic crystal. The saline spray of the dark red-orange waters of the Leefari Sea created the crystal over the eons, while Berchestian artisans have painstakingly sculpted it and nurtured its slow growth, crafting buildings, walkways, and roads directly from the massive crystal. This planet and its crystal city were once a major galactic tourist attraction, but the Clone Wars and the rise of the Empire caused such business to slack off. Using the routes established during its heyday, Berchest then promoted itself as a center of trade and has achieved modest success as an Imperial trading center. Thrawn used Berchest as a troop transfer point for his newly cloned ship crews as he prepared to launch a massive assault on the New Republic. [LC]

Beru Lars

🏛 Beru Lars, along with her husband, Owen, raised Luke Skywalker on Tatooine. She was his foster mother, though Luke called her "Aunt Beru." Imperial stormtroopers killed

Beru and her husband after tracking the droids R2-D2 and C-3PO to the Lars' moisture farm during their search for the stolen Death Star technical plans. [SW]

Bespin

🏵 Bespin, a gaseous planet in the star system of the same name, was the location of the Cloud City mining colony. [ESB]

🏵 Other planets in the Bespin system are Miser, a small, metal-rich world orbiting close to the sun, and Orin, a hostile world with a violent environment. The gas giant's many moons include the satellites called "the twins," H'gaard and Drudonna. The system is also home to a massive asteroid field known as Velser's Ring, which many theorize was once another gas giant. The asteroids are actually chunks of frozen gases and liquids, not metal or stone. [GG2]

Since the Empire established a presence on Bespin, a giant Imperial floating factory barge has been put in place. The barge's factories collect raw materials from the Rethin Sea to produce more war machines. [ZHR]

Bestine

🏵 Bestine was a planet allied with the Alliance which housed a secret Rebel base. It is also the name of a small farming community on the planet Tatooine. [SW, RJ]

BG-J38

🏵 The thin, mantis-headed droid called BG-J38 was in much demand in Jabba the Hutt's court. The droid was an expert hologame player, often serving as an opponent for Jabba or one of his associates. [RJ]

Bib Fortuna

🌀 Bib Fortuna served as Jabba the Hutt's chief lieutenant and majordomo, handling all of the day-to-day operations of Jabba's desert palace. His two skull appendages, called head tails and which are common to his species, exhibit prehensile, sensual, and cognitive functions. [RJ]

🌀 Fortuna was a Twi'lek, from the planet Ryloth. He left his world to seek opportunities in the larger galaxy, eventually joining up with Jabba the Hutt and advancing to the top of the crime lord's court. [SWSB, GG5]

Bib Fortuna

Big Bunji

⊙ Big Bunji, a former associate of Han Solo, got on the smuggler's bad side when he failed to repay a debt in a timely fashion. To demonstrate his displeasure, Solo strafed Bunji's pressure dome with blaster fire. Bunji barely escaped with his life. [HSE]

Big L

⊙ Big L is a spacer slang term for the light barrier. To "cross the Big L" is to jump to lightspeed. [HSE]

Biggs Darklighter

⊙ Biggs Darklighter was a childhood friend of Luke Skywalker. The two grew up together on Tatooine, dreaming of adventures beyond the endless dunes. Biggs finally found a way off Tatooine when he was accepted into the Academy. Upon graduation, Biggs received a post as first mate on the merchant ship *Rand Ecliptic*. However, his ambitions went beyond such mundane service. Biggs had fallen in with Rebel sympathizers while at the Academy, and had made plans to defect to the Alliance at the first opportunity. Biggs was reunited with Luke Skywalker during the Battle of Yavin, where both piloted Rebel X-wings against the Empire's Death Star. Biggs lost his life during this battle. [SW]

Biitu

⊙ The beautiful and peaceful planet Biitu was covered

with lush farmland and inhabited by contented farmers until disaster struck. During the earliest days of the Empire, a droid called the Great Heep installed a fuel-ore processing plant equipped with a moisture-eater which turned the planet into a barren wasteland. [TGH]

Biituian

⚙ The people of the planet Biitu are called the Biituians. These green-skinned, bald-headed humanoids lived mainly as farmers until the coming of the Great Heep and his environment-destroying ore-processing plant. [TGH]

Bilar

⚙ The meter-tall species called Bilars resemble hairless teddy bears with long arms, short legs, two dark eyes, and thin lips formed into perpetual grins. They come from the tropical world of Mima II in the Lar star system. Due to the effects of the Bilar group minds, or claqas, a single member of this species has no more intelligence than a rodent. But when Bilars come together to form a group mind, their intelligence doubles with every new member. Seven-member claqas have genius-level intelligence, and ten-member claqas are not unheard of. These claqas have group personalities that can be unnerving and unpredictable. [GG4]

Bilbringi

⚙ The Bilbringi star system, famous for the Bilbringi Shipyards, was the site of the New Republic's last battle with the Imperial forces under the command of Grand Admiral Thrawn. During the conflict, the New Republic was aided by an armada of smuggling ships led by Aves, Mazzic, and Gillespee. [LC]

Bimm

🌑 The diminutive inhabitants of the planet Bimmisaari are called Bimms. Standing about 1.1 meters tall, the half-furred Bimms wear tooled yellow clothing. They are a friendly people, with singing voices and a love of stories—especially heroic ones. One of their current favorites is the tale of the Battle of Endor, and they are particularly fascinated with the heroic acts of Luke Skywalker. The Bimms are peaceful; weapons are not permitted in their cities. They love to shop, and Bimms do not consider a day complete unless they have engaged in a bout of haggling or discovered a bargain at one of the markets scattered among their planet's forests of asaari trees. They see haggling as a serious art form and abhor stealing. Shoplifting is a capital offense in the eyes of the Bimms. [HE, HESB]

Bimmisaari

🌑 The temperate world of Bimmisaari is covered by swaying trees called asaari trees that move though no wind blows. The world's intelligent inhabitants are called Bimms, who were once nominal members of the Old Republic. The New Republic opened negotiations with this planet five years after the Battle of Endor. Because of its distance from the Core Worlds, Bimmisaari escaped most of the horrors inflicted by the Empire during its galaxy-wide reign. The planet boasts a number of impressive marketplaces, including the one located next to the Tower of Law. During a diplomatic mission to this world, Princess Leia and her party were ambushed by the Noghri. [HE, HESB]

Bin Essada

🌑 Bin Essada was the Imperial military governor presiding over the Circarpous Major star system. This portly man wore his black hair in a curly fashion, with a spiral orange pattern on top. His eyes had pink pupils, hinting at a not-quite-human origin. [SME]

binary load lifter

🌀 Binary load lifters are primitive labor droids designed to move heavy objects. With powerful mechanical claws and either a wheeled or repulsorlift propulsion system, load lifters can be found in spaceports, warehouses, and anywhere else objects must be moved from place to place. [SW]

Bith

🌑 The Bith are bipedal craniopeds—highly evolved humanoids with enlarged craniums. They have large, lidless black eyes, receding noses, and baggy epidermal folds beneath their jawlines. They hail from the world of Clak'dor VII in the Colu system of Mayagil Sector. The cantina band in *Star Wars IV: A New Hope* is made up of Bith aliens. [GG4]

Bithabus the Mystifier

🌀 Bithabus the Mystifier, a member of the Bith species, is a stage magician whose performances are famous throughout the galaxy. He can be seen regularly at Hologram Fun World's Asteroid Theater. [QE]

Bix

⊕ The sleek droid named Bix was Auren Yomm's teammate in the Colonial Games that took place during the early days of the Empire. [DTV]

BL-17

⊕ The droid BL-17 looks very much like See-Threepio. He was owned by the bounty hunter Boba Fett during the early days of the Empire, though it is not known if Fett still has possession of him. BL-17 has the same olive-drab and yellow coloration as Fett's armor and carries a rectangular blaster. [DTV]

Black Ice

⊕ The cargo train *Black Ice* consists of two engine pods set on each end of connected force spheres. Each force sphere is a ball 600 meters in diameter filled with cargo. Command capsules the size of freighters nestle on top of the huge pods' massive fuel cells and engines. [BI]

blase tree goat

⊕ The goatlike blase tree goats live in the great trees of Endor's forest moon. They are lethargic creatures who hang from the tree limbs. [ETV]

blaster

⚓ Blasters are weapons that fire coherent packets of intense light energy, also called bolts. Most blasters have variable levels of intensity, from stun to killing bolts. When a blaster discharges an energy bolt, a smell similar to ozone fills the air. [SW, ESB, RJ]

⚙ Blasters come in a variety of different models: small, easily concealable holdout blasters, sporting blasters, standard blaster pistols, heavy blaster pistols, blaster rifles, and various field and ship-mounted blaster artillery. [SWRPG, SWRPG2]

Blockade Runner

⚓ The Corellian pirates who make use of Corellian corvettes have nicknamed these capital ships Blockade Runners because of their speed and primary use by smugglers and others attempting to circumvent galactic authorities. [SW, SWSB]

blope

⚙ Blopes are hippolike swamp creatures that dwell in the marshy areas of Endor's forest moon. [ETV]

Blue Five

⚓ According to the *Star Wars* novel, Blue Five was the comm-unit designation for Luke Skywalker's X-wing during the Battle of Yavin. In the movie, his designation was Red Five. [SW]

Blue Four

✪ According to the *Star Wars* novel, Blue Four was the comm-unit designation for Rebel pilot Porkin's X-wing during the Battle of Yavin. In the movie, his designation was Red Six. He died during the conflict. [SW]

Blue Leader

✪ According to the *Star Wars* novel, Blue Leader was the veteran Rebel pilot in charge of Blue Squadron during the Battle of Yavin. Blue Leader's real name was Dave, though most of the younger pilots simply called him by his comm-unit designation. As a boy, Blue Leader had met Anakin Skywalker and found his piloting skills very impressive. Unfortunately, Blue Leader and his wingmen, Blue Ten and Blue Twelve, were killed at Yavin. In the movie, his designation was Red Leader. [SW]

At the Battle of Endor, Blue Leader was the Rebel officer commanding one of four Alliance battle wings taking part in the assault against the second Death Star. This Blue Leader died when his fighter was caught in the explosion that destroyed an Imperial communications ship. [RJ]

Blue Max

✪ Blue Max was a miniature droid whose primary function was to process and interpret data. The droid's name came from its deep blue, cubical body. The small droid was equipped with a speech synthesizer, folded appendages, and a monocular photoreceptor that glowed red. Built by a band of roaming outlaw techs, Max was specially designed to fit inside the hollow chest of the labor droid named Bollux. Together, the two droids traveled with Han Solo and Chewbacca for a time prior to Solo's involvement with the Rebellion. [HSR, HSE, HLL]

Blue Nebula, The

The Blue Nebula is an extremely seedy tavern and dining establishment in the Manda spaceport. [DTV]

Blue Six

According to the *Star Wars* novel, Blue Six was the comm-unit designation for Rebel pilot John D's X-wing during the battle of Yavin. In the movie, his designation was Red Four. [SW]

Blue Squad

During the battle of Endor, Blue Squad was one of many A-wing starfighter squadrons in the Alliance's Blue Wing attack element. [RJ]

Blue Squadron

Blue Squadron was one of the New Republic X-wing battle groups to participate in the Battle of Calamari. [DE]

Blue Three

✦ According to the *Star Wars* novel, Blue Three was the comm-unit designation for Rebel pilot Biggs Darklighter's X-wing during the Battle of Yavin. In the movie, his designation was Red Three. He died during the conflict. [SW]

Blue Two

✦ According to the *Star Wars* novel, Blue Two was the comm-unit designation for Rebel pilot Wedge Antilles' X-wing during the Battle of Yavin. In the movie, his designation was Red Two. [SW]

Blue Wing

✦ Blue Wing was the comm-unit designation for Blue Leader's second-in-command at the Battle of Endor. Blue Wing was responsible for coordinating several of the Blue Wing battle groups.

Blue Wing was also one of the main Alliance attack elements participating in the Battle of Endor. [RJ]

blumfruit

✦ The blumfruit is a large, red, egg-shaped berry that grows on Endor's forest moon. Ewoks are especially fond of this food. [ETV]

Bnach

🌐 The scorched, cracked world of Bnach houses an Imperial prison camp. Those imprisoned here labor in rock quarries. [PDS]

Boba Fett

Boba Fett

🌑 Boba Fett is an infamous bounty hunter whose exploits are known throughout the galaxy. He wears Mandalore battle armor—the same used by a group of evil warriors who were defeated by the Jedi Knights during the Clone Wars— but his connection to the Mandalore warriors remains a mystery.

Fett's armor is full of nasty surprises. It is a weapon-covered spacesuit whose armaments include wrist lasers, a jet pack, rocket darts, a grappling lanyard, and a miniature flame projector. The bounty hunter has worked for whoever could pay his exorbitant rates, including Jabba the Hutt and the Empire. In fact, Fett accepted the same commission from both Jabba and Lord Darth Vader, agreeing to hunt down and capture Han Solo after the smuggler escaped from the Hoth system.

Boba Fett succeeded in tracking Solo to Bespin's Cloud City, where Vader had the smuggler encased in carbonite. Then Fett had the frozen Solo placed aboard his ship, *Slave I*, for transport to Jabba's headquarters on Tatooine. During the resulting rescue carried out by Luke Skywalker, Fett was lost in the Great Pit of Carkoon and presumed to be a victim of the dreaded Sarlacc. [ESB, RJ]

✪ Boba Fett escaped from the Great Pit of Carkoon sometime during the intervening six years to show up on Nar Shadda, once again on Han Solo's trail. He claimed that the Sarlacc found him to be "somewhat indigestible." His current contract is to the Hutts, who want him to capture Solo and Princess Leia alive for what they did to Jabba. The Hutts wish to watch when the pair die. [DE]

Bocce

✪ Bocce is one of the languages currently in use on Tatooine. [SW]

Bodgen

✪ The bog moon of Bodgen is a swampy satellite orbiting an unnamed planet. During the early days of the Empire, when R2-D2 and C-3PO were engaged in a variety of adventures, the two droids visited the bog moon. At the time, the pirate captain Kybo Ren was holding Princess Gerin of Tammuz-an on a freighter hidden on the moon. [DTV]

Bodo Baas

● Bodo Baas is the Gatekeeper of the Jedi Holocron, a device that contains the stored teachings of ancient Jedi Masters. The nonhuman Jedi Bodo Baas lived thousands of years ago. His image appears to those who both possess the Holocron and are strong in the Force, to guide them in the use of this legendary source of wisdom and knowledge. [DE]

Bollux

● Bollux was a modified labor droid who traveled with Han Solo and Chewbacca prior to their involvement with the Rebellion. Bollux was altered to carry a miniature droid named Blue Max inside his chest cavity. The labor droid was exceedingly old, and his length of service dated back to his first activation at the great Fondor shipyards. As his model was replaced by newer droids, Bollux took on different jobs in order to avoid deactivation. Over the years, Bollux worked as a construction gang assistant surveyor, a roustabout, and a maintenance assistant until he fell in with a band of outlaw techs. Bollux was a stocky, dent-covered droid, with long arms and hands that hung nearly to his knees. A flat brown primer was all that remained of his once-bright finish. Two unblinking red photoreceptors stared from Bollux's head, and his outdated speech synthesizer gave him a low, slow voice. The droid's current whereabouts are unknown. [HSE, HSR, HLL]

Bonadan

🌀 Bonadan is one of the Corporate Sector Authority's most important factory worlds. The highly industrialized and densely populated planet houses many different intelligent species from all over the galaxy, and interspecies rivalries are common. To keep some semblance of peace and order, weapons are outlawed on the planet. Bonadan authorities use a vast and advanced network of weapon detectors to enforce the ban.

From space, Bonadan is a yellow sphere covered with rust-red strips. The planet looks barren and parched, for whatever plant life that was not deliberately destroyed has died due to careless mining operations, abundant pollutants, and simple neglect. [HSR]

Bonadan Spaceport Southeast II

🌀 Bonadan Spaceport Southeast II is the largest of Bonadan's ten spaceports. [HSR]

Bondo

🌀 Bondo is a jovial, portly being who serves as chieftain of the nomadic Jinda tribe. [ETV]

bonegnawer

🌀 One of the many hazards populating Tatooine's wastes is the dreaded bonegnawer. A bonegnawer is a carnivorous flying creature that lives in the desert wastelands. Its tooth-filled jaws are reputed to be strong enough to crush rock. [SW]

Boonta

🌑 The planet Boonta is famous for its speeder races. The speeder tracks are oval tunnels about sixteen kilometers long. Large viewing screens and a comfortable enclosed viewing area are set aside for spectators. The planet also has a gigantic scrap yard that serves as a graveyard for damaged spaceships. [DTV]

Borderland Regions

🌑 Not an official area of the galaxy listed on astrogation charts, the Borderland Regions nevertheless exists. This militarized zone lies between New Republic and Imperial space, claimed by both sides but controlled by neither. The systems within this area take great pains to stay absolutely neutral until a clear winner emerges from the continuing fray. The day-to-day battles of the continuing Galactic Civil War occur in this large volume of space. [HE, HESB]

bordok

🌑 A bordok is a medium-sized, ponylike animal that Ewoks employ as beasts of burden. [ETV]

Borsk Fey'lya

🌑 The Bothan Borsk Fey'lya leads a significant portion of the Bothan people. He also serves on the New Republic's

Borsk Fey'lya

Provisional and Inner Councils. He brought his Bothan faction into the Alliance after the Battle of Yavin, cutting deals with everyone to achieve a position of power in the galactic union to come. He never got along with Ackbar, who saw him as nothing more than a political opportunist. If not for the fact that the Bothan spies who discovered the location of the second Death Star were from Borsk's faction, he may have disappeared into history. Instead, he has become one of Mon Mothma's most-trusted advisers and a political opponent of Ackbar. Like others of his race, it is natural for him to press advantages and seek opportunities in every opening that presents itself. This nature almost pushed the New Republic to the brink of civil war around the time of the return of the Empire's Grand Admiral Thrawn.

Fey'lya grew up on the Bothan colony world of Kothlis. He is a master diplomat who sometimes appears to be a greedy, self-serving politician, but he is only a typical

Bothan. He has the Bothan lust for power, which he hopes to gain through typical Bothan games of politics. He has continued to keep his hand in a variety of galactic business activities, and often provided funds to Garm Bel Iblis's private war against the Empire in the hopes of gaining an ally once Garm agreed to join the New Republic. Like most Bothans, Fey'lya sees everything in terms of political and persuasive influence. He has no interest in military power, only in making more and more people interested in what he has to say. He also believes that everyone is playing the same game that he is: basing decisions on prestige and not the best course of action. [HE, DFR, LC]

Bossk

ⓦ The reptilian Bossk was one of the bounty hunters contracted by Darth Vader to find the *Millennium Falcon* and her crew after the Battle of Hoth. [ESB]

Bot

ⓦ Bot was the cloaked and mute henchman of Captain-Supervisor Grammel on the planet Circarpous V. His true race and origins are unknown. [SME]

Bothan

ⓦ A species allied to the Rebellion, Bothans have an extensive spy network. Bothan spies were instrumental in locating the site of the second Death Star and discovering that that Emperor was scheduled to supervise the battle station's final stages of construction. Due to their efforts, the Alliance decided to launch the assault that came to be known as the Battle of Endor—the battle that ended this phase of the Galactic Civil War. [RJ]

⦿ Bothans hail from the planet Bothawui, though they inhabit a number of colony worlds. [HE, DFR, LC, DFRSB]

bounce

⦿ Bounce is a casino game that uses guns along with a moving target suspended within an enclosed space. The only hits that score are those that are reflected, or "bounced." Direct hits do not count toward victory. [HSR]

Boushh

⦿ Boushh was the name Leia Organa used when she disguised herself as an Ubese bounty hunter to gain access to Jabba the Hutt's palace. To add authority to her disguise, she presented a captured Chewbacca for Jabba's reward. The ruse was part of an elaborate and well-orchestrated plot to rescue Han Solo from the Huttese crime lord. [RJ]

bowcaster

⦿ A bowcaster, or crossbow laser, is a hand-crafted Wookiee crossbow that fires energy quarrels. Chewbacca the Wookiee uses one of these weapons. [RJ]

Bozzie

⦿ The old Ewok widow named Bozzie is Paploo's pushy, overbearing mother and Kneesaa's aunt. [ETV]

Bpfassh

🌑 Bpfassh system, a member of the New Republic, was one of the targets of a three-system attack launched by Imperial forces as a diversion before the true target, Sluis Van, was hit. The attack was designed to frighten and injure, not destroy completely. The plan was to force Bpfassh and its neighboring systems to call to Sluis Van for aid, which they did. The resulting buildup of rescue ships provided the Empire with ships to steal to bolster the war-reduced Imperial fleet.

The main body in the system is a twin planet orbited by numerous moons. The inhabitants of the twin worlds, called the Bpfasshi, do not like Jedi. In the days of the Clone Wars, a group of Bpfasshi Dark Jedi spread terror throughout the Sluis sector before being stopped by an unknown person (or persons) on Dagobah. [HE, HESB]

Brandei

See Captain Brandei.

Brasck

🌑 Brasck is one of the major smuggling chiefs operating in the Borderland Regions between New Republic and Imperial space. He is a Brubb from the planet Baros, a bipedal reptiloid who once worked as a mercenary for Jabba the Hutt. When Jabba died, Brasck grabbed as many followers as he could and set up his own smuggling operation. He deals in anything, including kidnapping and slaves. His headquarters is the starship *Green Palace*, which he keeps in constant motion in order to avoid the fate that befell his former master. Fearful of ambush and assassination, he always wears body armor and keeps several weapons hidden on his person. [HE, HESB, DFR]

breath mask

🌀 A breath mask is a part of a portable system that supplies life-sustaining gases to a user. The mask portion fits over the nose and mouth, and is connected to a miniature life-support pack that is worn on the belt or carried on the back. Breath masks can also be used by persons who have sustained throat injuries or contracted certain respiratory diseases. Darth Vader had such a device built into his armor. [ESB, RJ]

Brigia

🌀 Brigia is a poor, backward planet in the Tion Hegemony. The University of Rudrig has been providing guidance and aid to Brigia's development and modernization initiative. [HLL]

Briil Twins

🌀 The Briil Twins were former associates of Han Solo who were killed while battling an Imperial cruiser on patrol near the Tion Hegemony. [HSR]

Brubb

🌀 The strong Brubb species are bipedal reptiloids who stand about 1.6 meters tall. They have pitted, knobby hides of dusty yellow, ridged eyes, and flat noses. Males usually have a single tuft of coarse black hair jutting from the tops of their heads. Social beings, they come from the planet Baros and treat visitors to their world as honored guests. [GG4]

Bubo

The creature called Bubo is a pet of a Jawa tribe on Tatooine. The creature has froglike eyes and long, protruding lower teeth. It is unknown if Bubo is its species name or simply an identifying tag given it by the Jawas. [RJ]

bulk freighter

Bulk freighters haul the vast majority of cargo throughout the galaxy. While there are plenty of different models, all bulk freighters are basically boxes with hyperdrive engines. These vessels are small to mid-sized, which allows their owners to keep fuel costs down and gives them access to almost all space docks and ports. Most of these craft have little or no armament, depending on the protection of well-traveled space lanes and the ships that patrol them. While some large companies have their own fleets of freighters, most bulk freighters are independently owned. [SWSB]

Bureau of Operations

A division of Imperial Intelligence, the Bureau of Operations handles all covert operations beyond the scope of resources of the other divisions. It participates in surveillance and infiltration operations, counterintelligence, and assassination missions. [ISB]

burnout

✦ The term "burnout" is spacer jargon for the loss of energy in a ship's power plants. [ESBR]

Byss

✦ The planet Byss is the primary planet in the binary star system of Byss and Abyss. The species named Abyssin hails from this arid yet sporadically fertile world. [GG4]

Hidden deep within the galactic core, another planet with the name Byss has been utterly twisted by the dark side of the Force. On Byss, the Emperor has been establishing the model for the galaxy-wide society he envisioned—a society where everyone and everything is ruled and controlled by the dark side without any need for physical weapons. After the Emperor's ancient body was destroyed by Darth Vader during the events of the Battle of Endor, his spirit was transported to Byss to be installed in a new clone body. Once he was ready, the reborn Emperor reunited his forces over the planet in preparation for a last devastating attack against the New Republic and all others who would deny his rule of the galaxy. [DE]

Byss Bistro

✦ The Byss Bistro is a cantina located within the Imperial Freight Complex on the planet Byss. Freighter crews can find food, drink, and entertainment in this establishment while they wait for their ships to be unloaded. [DE]

C

C-3PO (See-Threepio)

🌀 C-3PO is a protocol droid with specialized programming in droid/human relations and language translation and interpretation. He is bipedal, with a gold-colored body. Among Threepio's standard equipment are visual, auditory,

C-3PO

olfactory, and sensory receptors, a broadband antenna for receiving droid transmissions, and a speech vocabulator. He is fluent in over six million galactic languages. Design specifications for this model droid call for limited creativity circuits to keep embellishment to a minimum. Over the long period since C-3PO's last memory wipe (if he ever even had one), he has apparently developed a talent for telling stories, as evidenced by his dramatic re-creation of the events of the galactic civil war for the Ewoks of Endor's forest moon.

C-3PO claimed that he and his counterpart, R2-D2, were the property of Captain Antilles when they first met Luke Skywalker, though the protocol droid readily accepted Luke as his new master. He even claimed not to have ever heard of Princess Leia, though this seems unlikely. Since meeting up with Luke, C-3PO has shared many adventures with the Heroes of Yavin. He tends to stay close to Princess Leia when Luke is away. [SW, ESB, RJ]

C-Ratt

🌐 C-Ratt is one of Nar Shaddaa's nonhuman residents. [DE]

Calamarian

See Mon Calamari.

Calamari minisub

🌐 A Calamari minisub is a small underwater transport used on the planet Mon Calamari. [GDV]

Calius saj Leeloo

See Berchest.

caller

🔴 Callers are small, hand-held transmitters that summon droids by sending signals to their restraining bolts. These devices also turn restraining bolts on and off, which is why they are also referred to as restraining bolt activators. [SW, SWR]

Calrissian

See Lando Calrissian.

Camie

🔴 Camie was a young woman close to Luke Skywalker's age who lived in Tatooine's Anchorhead community. She frequented the Tosche power station and was the girlfriend of the youth named Fixer. [SW, SWR]

Canu

🔵 The primitive inhabitants of Circarpous V worship a deity called Canu. [SME]

capital ship

Capital ships are any class of huge combat starships designed for deep-space warfare. These vessels normally require large crews to operate, are mounted with huge numbers of weapons batteries and shield projectors, and often carry smaller ships such as shuttles and starfighters in their great hangar bays. Imperial Star Destroyers and Mon Calamari Star Cruisers are common examples of capital-class ships. [SWSB, SWRPG2]

Captain Afyon

Captain Afyon of the New Republic rides the helm of the escort frigate *Larkhess*. He has grown bitter over the years, for he feels that the real work of the new government is done by men like him, while the credit goes to hot-shot starfighter pilots. For more than a year now, his beautiful war ship has been relegated to cargo transport duty, and this bothers him as well. The transport problems facing the New Republic make his current mission profile important, but that does not make it any less frustrating. [HE, HESB]

Captain Antilles

Captain Antilles commanded the Alderaanian consular ship *Tantive IV*. C-3PO claimed that he and R2-D2 belonged to the captain until the ship was captured by the Empire. In the novel version of *Star Wars*, this character was called Captain Colton. [SW, SWR]

Captain Brandei

⊙ Captain Brandei commanded the Imperial Star Destroyer *Judicator*, one of the vessels in Grand Admiral Thrawn's personal armada. He was one of the few senior officers to survive the Battle of Endor, and has been in the command seat of his Star Destroyer ever since. Though he was born on the Outer Rim colony of Mantooine, Brandei grew to loathe the Rebellion and the aliens it treats as equals. He is confident and daring, but never reckless. He believes it is more important to live to fight another day than to die spectacularly for a lost cause. The Empire might lose individual battles to the Rebels, but Brandei believes it will win the war. [DFR, DFRSB]

Captain Colton

See Captain Antilles.

Captain Dorja

⊙ Captain Dorja commands the Imperial Star Destroyer *Relentless*. He has been in charge of that ship since before the Battle of Endor, and his vessel has the distinction of not suffering a single casualty during that conflict. His cautious command style and unwillingness to engage an enemy in direct combat could be the reason, though he believes his holding tactics were the prudent course of action. He comes from a rich family with a long tradition in the Old Republic and Imperial fleets. He was appalled when a junior officer named Pellaeon announced that he was taking charge of the fleet when the battle turned bad, though he agreed with his order to retreat.

Dorja tried unsuccessfully to wrest control from Pellaeon in the five years that followed, though he came very close on a few occasions. Dorja does not like Grand Admiral Thrawn, for the man is obviously not human, not to mention that the *Relentless* was not included in Thrawn's personal armada (which Dorja feels was a calculated insult). He dreams and plots of a way to take control of the Empire so that he can reinstate the true, undiluted glory of the New Order. [DFR, DFRSB]

Captain Dunwell

Captain Dunwell was the crazed human commander of the Whaladon hunting submarine that operated below the waves of Mon Calamari. With his blue uniform, gaudy medals, and neatly trimmed white beard, Captain Dunwell is almost dashing. His obsession destroys this illusion, however. His main goal, which he has pursued for many years, is to capture Leviathor, leader of the Whaladon. [GDV]

Captain Needa

This Imperial officer was in command of the Imperial-class Star Destroyer *Avenger*, which was part of Lord Darth Vader's task force during the events leading up to the Battle of Hoth. It was his ship that took the point during the subsequent search for the *Millennium Falcon*. When Han Solo's vessel escaped, Captain Needa's personal apology to Vader was met with acceptance and a quick death through the powers of the Force's dark side. [ESB]

Captain Neva

⊕ Captain Neva is the Sullustan commander of the New Republic escort frigate *Rebel Star.* [DE]

Captain Pellaeon

⊕ Captain Pellaeon has served in the Imperial fleet (and the Old Republic before it) for nearly fifty years. He is always loyal, always professional. At the Battle of Endor, after his commander was killed, Pellaeon took control of the Star Destroyer *Chimaera* and saved it from certain destruction. The scenes of that fateful battle still haunt him—so many grand ships destroyed, so many promising and established officers killed. Pellaeon took control of the remnants of the fleet that day, bitterly ordering the ships to retreat instead of remaining to fall to the victorious Rebellion. He has done his best to fight back in the five years since, but he is only a simple captain, not a powerful leader like the Emperor or Vader or Grand Admiral Thrawn. It was Pellaeon who received Thrawn's call, announcing that a Grand Admiral had returned. He offered his ship to serve as Thrawn's flagship, and has remained at the Grand Admiral's side throughout the campaign to destroy the New Republic once and for all. [HE, DFR, LC, HESB, DFRSB]

Captain Piett

⊕ Captain Piett served as first officer on Darth Vader's flagship *Executor.* He assisted Admiral Ozzel in overseeing the crew, as well as helping to direct the entire fleet assigned to the flagship. He was promoted to Admiral and given command of the flagship and the fleet after Admiral Ozzel made a fatal mistake during the assault on the Rebel base on Hoth. Piett remained in command of *Executor* through the Battle of Endor, where the Super Star Destroyer was lost in combat with the Rebel fleet. [ESB, RJ]

Captain-Supervisor Grammel

⊛ The square-jawed Captain-Supervisor Grammel commanded the Imperial military garrison on Circarpous V. This mustached, black-and-white-haired administrator was ruthless, routinely torturing prisoners whether he needed information or not. [SME]

Captain Syub Snunb

⊛ Captain Syub Snunb, from the planet Sullust, commands the New Republic escort frigate *Antares Six*. [DE]

Captain Virgilio

⊛ Captain Sarin Virgilio commands the New Republic Escort Frigate *Quenfis*, one of the ships in Admiral Drayson's Home Guard Fleet assigned to protect Coruscant. He has long been a supporter of the Bothans, for he was among the crew of the Alliance ship that helped the Bothan spies return with the plans for the second Death Star battle station. At the time, Virgilio was a young third officer on a Corellian Gunship. The ship picked up a distress call whose code identified its senders as members of a large team of Bothan intelligence agents operating in the outer regions. Of that team, only six survived—but they carried with them the plans and secret location of the second Death Star as well as the Emperor's private schedule, which told when he would be visiting the site. [DFR, DFRSB]

carbon-freezing chamber

(✹) In Bespin's Cloud City, Tibanna gas is stored in carbonite to preserve it during transportation to far-off trade centers. This preservation process is called freezing, and is accomplished in a carbon-freezing chamber. Gas is pumped into the chamber, where it is mixed with molten carbonite. The mix is then flash-frozen to cool the carbonite into a solid. The gas remains trapped within the carbonite block until released at a processing center or market. One of the chambers on Bespin was modified for use on a human so that Darth Vader could safely capture and transport Luke Skywalker back to the Emperor. Before Vader would allow it to be used on Skywalker, it was successfully tested on Han Solo. [ESB]

carbonite

(✹) Carbonite is a strong metal alloy. One of its uses is as a preservative for materials such as Tibanna gas. [ESB]

cargo lifter

(✹) Cargo lifters are large utility airships operated by a single pilot. Usually found in spaceports, these craft are used to load and unload cargo containers and to make short-distance hauls from loading zones to storage facilities in other parts of the port. Older cargo lifter models employ mechanical claws to handle cargo, while newer models make use of tractor-beam and repulsor technology. [HSR]

Carkoon, Great Pit of

See Great Pit of Carkoon.

Carrack-class light cruiser

⊕ One of the smallest capital ships classified as a star cruiser is the *Carrack*-class light cruiser. Approximately 350 meters in length with an optimum crew of one thousand ninety-two, the Carrack has a high proportion of weaponry compared to its size rating. Most are outfitted with ten heavy turbolasers and twenty ion cannons, and there is room for up to five tractor-beam projectors if desired. This vessel's primary mission profile is to serve as the Imperial answer to the Corellian Corvette. The Carrack has no internal hangar bay. Instead, it carries up to four TIE fighters on an external rack. As this small number of starfighters offers little offensive support, the TIEs are used for recon and patrol missions. To compensate for the lack of starfighter support, Carracks have powerful sublight engines for extra speed in realspace, making them among the fastest capital ships in the Imperial fleet. Though Carracks were not originally designed for front-line combat duty, in the period after the Battle of Endor the Empire has been forced to place more and more of these vessels into harm's way. [ISB, HESB]

Cass

☾ Cass was the Imperial officer and adjutant to Grand Moff Tarkin aboard the original Death Star battle station. [SW]

Catarine Towani

🌀 Catarine Towani is the mother of Mace and Cindel. She and her family were marooned on Endor's moon for a time, where they were befriended by the Ewok tribe to which Wicket belongs. [EA, BFE]

Cavrilhu Pirates

🌀 The Cavrilhu Pirates are a gang of marauders who plunder and pillage merchant ships along the various space lanes of the galaxy. Led by Captain Zothip, who commands the gang from his gunship *Void Cutter*, the pirates are the scourge of the Amorris star system. His first mate is a female Togorian named Keta.

Niles Ferrier stole three patrol ships from the pirates to sell to Grand Admiral Thrawn shortly after the failed Imperial action at Sluis Van. Now Zothip wants to inflict painful punishments upon the starship thief, and he has ordered his scouts to watch for Ferrier and his known associates. [DFR, DFRSB]

CB-99

🌀 CB-99 is an old, battered, barrel-shaped droid that once belonged to Jabba the Hutt. After the crime lord died, the droid emerged from its secret hiding place in Jabba's desert palace to present Jabba's hologram will to his beneficiaries. [ZHR]

C'baoth

See Jorus C'baoth and Joruus C'baoth.

Cell 2187

Cell 2187 was the small cell where Princess Leia Organa was held captive during her imprisonment aboard the original Death Star battle station. The cell was located in Detention Block AA-23. [SW]

central ladderwell

On the stock freighter *Millennium Falcon*, the central ladderwell is a tubular passageway running vertically from the top gunwell to the belly gunwell. It connects the cargo-hold deck to the quad laser batteries. Gravity shifts within the tube to always keep occupants oriented correctly. [HSR]

central lifter

On the stock freighter *Millennium Falcon*, the central lifter is a hydraulic piston that raises and lowers the ship's boarding ramp. [ESB]

Chad

The planet Chad is a beautiful, civilized world in a star system of the same name. The Chadra-Fan species comes from the bayous of this planet. [GG4, QE]

Chadra-Fan

The small, quick-witted inhabitants of Chad, the Chadra-Fan, resemble humanoid rodents, with large ears, dark eyes, and flat, circular noses with four nostrils. The fur-covered, rodentlike Chadra-Fan have seven senses. In addition to the five shared by most intelligent species, they are also blessed with infrared sight and an advanced chemoreceptive smell. These small, one-meter-tall beings love to have fun. They tend to be flighty and have short attention spans, though they enjoy tinkering with technological items. A Chadra-Fan can be spotted in the cantina scene of *Star Wars IV: A New Hope*, requesting a drink from the bar. [GG4, QE]

chak-root

⚙ Chak-root is a flavorful red plant that grows in the marshlands of the planet Erysthes. High taxes on the plant have given rise to a profitable venture for smugglers. They avoid the normal channels of distribution and offer chak-root at reduced prices on the Invisible Market. [HSR, HLL]

Chandrila

⚙ Chandrila is the homeworld of Mon Mothma, leader of the Alliance to Restore the Republic. [SWSB]

Charal

⚙ The evil witch Charal has the power to change form at will, thanks to a magical ring she wears. She is the cohort of Terak, king of the marauders. Charal is of indeterminate age. An imposing figure, she has raven-black hair, angular features, and a slender shape, and she wears a cloak of black feathers. She rides a wild, black stallion that also has the ability to change form. [BFE]

Chariot LAV

⊙ The Chariot Light Assault Vehicle (LAV) is a modified military landspeeder used almost exclusively by Imperial forces. Chariots serve as command vehicles for officers during routine planet occupations and other assignments where heavy combat is not expected. These vehicles are more heavily armored than a normal landspeeder, but they are also slower and carry less weaponry than combat landspeeders. These command speeders feature battle-assistance computers that provide hologramic schematics and constant situational updates to the officers on board. With dedicated sensor and communications arrays, they can coordinate the activities of more than a dozen combat units. Combat speeders carry three crew members: the unit's commander, a driver, and a bodyguard/gunner. [ISB, HESB]

Charon

⊙ The Charon come from a dimension termed "otherspace" that seems to exist beyond the confines of the known galaxy. The Charon appear as humanoid arachnids, capable of spinning webs. They are divided into at least two distinct classes: bioscientists and warriors. The bioscientists are the more intelligent of the two, working to keep the biologically based Charon technology and constructs in operating condition. The warriors are more single-minded and aggressive. The Charon come from a homeworld on the verge of being swallowed by a black hole. This condition has led to the development of a death cult whose members believe that the Void is the only constant in the universe. Everything will eventually return to it. Only life seeks to triumph over the Void, so the Charon death cult believes that it is its responsibility to help life along on its unavoidable journey to the Void. When the Charon developed a star drive, instead of saving the species from the dying planet the death cult set out in biologically engineered vessels to spread its dark doctrine of swift death to all life through the galaxy.

As those who have visited the dimension of otherspace can attest, the dead, lifeless galaxy seems to be a testament to the Charon's death worship. [OS, OS2, GG4]

Chewbacca (Chewie)

Chewbacca is a two-meter-tall Wookiee who serves as first mate and copilot on the *Millennium Falcon*. Over two hundred years old, Chewbacca has spent his last few decades at the side of Han Solo. Like all Wookiees, Chewbacca is

Chewbacca

covered in shaggy fur and communicates in a series of grunts, growls, and terrifying roars. He is extremely strong, even for a Wookiee. His deep friendship with Han Solo (who fondly calls him "Chewie") has only intensified over the years. Either would gladly die for the other.

Chewbacca comes from the Wookiee homeworld of Kashyyyk. His weapon of choice is either his massive fists or his bowcaster; both can cause a considerable amount of damage. Besides being a top-notch pilot, Chewbacca is also a mechanic with no small amount of talent. He constantly works to repair and upgrade the *Falcon*, and he has been known to put severely damaged droids back together.

The mighty Chewbacca is used to having a price on his head. He has been marked as a runaway slave and known smuggler by the Empire, chased by bounty hunters working for crime lords, and wanted by the Emperor because of his involvement with the Rebellion. Though brave and powerful, Chewbacca sometimes succumbs to fear. He is especially frightened by things he cannot shoot or rip apart. He likes to win, has a well-developed sense of humor and a huge appetite, behaves very protectively toward his friends, and is equally at ease aboard an advanced space vessel or in the giant trees of his home planet.

Chewbacca acts as the conscience of his friend and partner, Han Solo. He often convinces Solo on a course of action, giving voice to the honor and sense of justice that sometimes hide in Solo's heart. It was the mighty Wookiee who made Solo realize that he had to stand beside his friends at the Battle of Yavin, and it was the Wookiee who was charged with protecting Princess Leia after Han was captured and encased in carbonite.

Through his adventures with the Rebellion, the legend of the mighty Chewbacca has grown. His prowess was especially effective during the Battle of Endor, where he helped rally the Ewoks into a fighting force to be reckoned with.

His actions helped turn the tide of the battle and allowed the Rebel strike team to disable the shield generator protecting the second Death Star. [SW, ESB, RJ, SWTVS, SWWS]

⊙ Chewbacca has been many things over his long life—including slave, smuggler, and Rebel hero. Little is known of his life before he hooked up with Han Solo. At an early age, he exhibited a natural talent toward mechanics, piloting, and all things of a technical nature. He knows Wookiee hand-to-hand combat techniques, and is proficient with the Wookiee bowcaster. He left his world at an early age to see the galaxy, and was happy learning new skills and visiting strange and wondrous places. Then the Empire was established, and the bad times began. Since he was away from his homeworld, Chewbacca was unaware that Kashyyyk had been turned into a slave-labor planet by the Empire. Wookiees were declared a slave species, and it was illegal for free Wookiees to travel the space lanes. Slavers captured Chewbacca, and he spent time performing heavy labor. It was only through the intervention of a young Imperial officer named Han Solo that Chewbacca found freedom. Solo destroyed his military career to free the Wookiee, and Chewbacca immediately decided he owed the Corellian a life debt. He followed Solo around for a long time before the Corellian decided to accept his Wookiee shadow. Their association soon developed into a deep friendship which continues to this day. [HLL, HSE, HSR, SWSB]

ch'hala tree

⊙ Ch'hala trees are greenish-purple trees with slender trunks and leafy tops. The tree has a unique property: when a noise occurs nearby, the tree responds with a burst of red that ripples across the trunk in time to the sound. The Grand Corridor in the Imperial Palace on Coruscant is lined with these beautiful, colorful trees. Unfortunately, the Emperor set them up as a complex spying system called Delta Source. Delta Source, which was responsible for providing Grand Admiral Thrawn with detailed intelligence about New Republic activities, was not a traitor or group of traitors as the Provisional Council thought. By using the natural properties of the ch'hala trees which cause pressure, including sound waves, on the tree trunks to set off small chemical changes in the inner layers of bark, the Emperor developed living circuits for his intelligence-gathering system. Implanted tubes in the trunks continuously sample the chemicals and shunt the information into a module in the taproot. The module takes the chemical data and converts it back into speech, then sends it on to another module for sorting, encrypting, and transmission. Delta Source was nothing more or less than a series of organic microphones. It seems the system has been in place since the earliest days of the Empire, giving the Emperor an edge in all Senate proceedings. [HE, DFR, LC]

Chief Chirpa

Chief Chirpa is a strong-willed Ewok and head of his tribe's Council of Elders. After some confusion and a little hostility, Chirpa decided to befriend the Rebel strike force sent to the moon of Endor to clear the way for the Alliance fleet. He even agreed to send his tribe into battle against the Imperial forces, and his warriors proved to be courageous in the face of a superior fighting force. The gray-furred Chief Chirpa carries a reptilian staff of office and wears the teeth, horns, and bones of animals he has bested in the hunt. [RJ]

Chief Muskov

🌑 Chief Muskov is in charge of the Cloud Police, which protect Bespin's Cloud City. [MMY]

Chimaera

🌑 The Imperial Star Destroyer *Chimaera*, a veteran ship that was involved in the Battle of Endor, became one of the most important ships in the remnants of the Imperial fleet due to the actions of its commander, Captain Pellaeon. When Grand Admiral Thrawn returned from the Unknown Regions, he selected *Chimaera* to serve as his flagship, leaving Pellaeon at its helm. [HE, DFR, LC]

Chin

🌑 Chin, one of Talon Karrde's chief associates, is a middle-aged man from the planet Myrkr. Chin's knowledge of the planet's indigenous life has served Karrde well. Chin's primary responsibility is to care for and train Karrde's pet vornskrs. He had domesticated the creatures and trained them to serve as guards. His understanding of the mysterious ysalamiri led him to develop a method for safety removing them from their tree-branch homes. His other duties include maintaining the security of Karrde's base of operations and overseeing the smooth running of base facilities. [HE, DFR, LC, HESB]

Chip

🌑 The droid called Chip (short for Microchip) is the personal property of the Jedi Prince named Ken. The size and shape of a twelve-year-old boy, Chip kept young Ken company during his stay in the Lost City of the Jedi. He now travels with him as Ken explores the larger galaxy. [LCJ, ZHR, MMY, PDS]

Chirpa

See Chief Chirpa.

Chituhr

Chituhr is the mean-looking animal trainer of the Jinda tribe of Ewoks. [ETV]

Choco

The small, battered, and uncoordinated R2 unit called Choco befriended R2-D2 during the droid's encounters with the Great Heep and his droid harem, years before the start of the Galactic Civil War. [TGH]

chromasheath

An iridescent material that is similar to leather, chromasheath is used for the same purposes. [HSE]

chrono

A chrono measures time. There are personal models which can be carried, as well as models that are built into the controls of starships and other vehicles. [HLL, SWSB]

Chubb

⚫ Chubb was a small, burrowing reptile, and the pet and constant companion of the young boy named Fidge. [TGH]

Chubb Scutt

⚫ Chubb Scutt is one of Nar Shaddaa's nonhuman residents. [DE]

Chubbits

⚫ Chubbits are small reptilian desert dwellers on the planet Aridus. [GW]

Chukha-Trok

⚫ Chukha-Trok is a brave Ewok woodsman known for his skills and forest lore. [ETV]

Churba

⚫ The star system Churba contains eight planets. The first, Barhu, is a boiling-hot ball of lifeless rock. The eighth, Hurcha, is so far from the sun that it is much too cold to support life. The other six worlds, however, all serve some civilized purpose. Churba, the fourth world in the system and the one that gave it its name, is a high-tech planet inhabited by humans and assorted nonhuman species. It is a cosmopolitan metropolis, although not as grand as Corellia or Coruscant. New Cov, the third world orbiting the sun, has no indigenous intelligent species, but its vast jungles teeming with all kinds of natural resources have made it an ideal corporate colony. [DFR, DFRSB]

Cindel Towani

The beautiful, blond, four-year-old girl named Cindel Towani was shipwrecked on Endor's moon with her parents and older brother. She is an innocent, trusting girl with a sweet disposition. She and her family became friends with the Ewok tribe Wicket belongs to. [EA, BFE]

Cinnagar

Cinnagar is the largest city of the seven worlds of the Empress Teta star system. [DE]

Circarpous Major

The Circarpous Major star system is made up of fourteen planets. While many of the system's inhabitants were sympathetic to the cause of the Alliance, they were afraid to become involved and risk the wrath of the Empire. To swing support over to the Rebellion and convince the system to join the Alliance, Princess Leia traveled to Circarpous Major on a diplomatic mission. [SME]

Circarpous IV

The fourth planet in the Circarpous Major star system was to be the site of Princess Leia's diplomatic meeting with Circarpousian resistance groups. Her mission, undertaken shortly after the Battle of Yavin, was to persuade the groups to join the Alliance. She was accompanied on this important mission by Luke Skywalker, and her prime directive was to convince the Circarpousians that the Alliance could withstand the might of the Empire. [SME]

Circarpous V

The fifth planet in the Circarpous Major star system is called Mimban by the locals. It was the site of a secret Imperial mining operation around the time of the Battle of Yavin and immediately thereafter. [SME]

Circarpous XIV

The fourteenth and outermost planet in the Circarpous Major star system was the location of a hidden Rebel base during the initial stages of the Galactic Civil War. [SME]

cloaking device

A cloaking device is a defensive antidetection system still in the experimental stages. During the period depicted in the original *Star Wars* movie trilogy, these devices were too cost- and power-prohibitive to install on anything larger than a starfighter. Even then, the defensive properties rendered the pilot of a cloaked craft blind, making it impossible to conduct any kind of serious mission.

The theory behind cloaking is that a device can be used to disrupt all electromagnetic waves emanating or reflecting from the ship it is installed in. This renders the ship electronically invisible to all sensors. [ESB]

⟐ The Emperor made cloaking technology a priority effort during the building of the second Death Star. The project yielded a working prototype that absorbed sensor radiation, thus disguising the device and anything under its cloak as empty space. Before it could be mass-produced, the Emperor was killed and the Empire shattered. Years later, Grand Admiral Thrawn discovered the prototype in one of the Emperor's hidden storehouses and employed it in his bid to destroy the New Republic. [HE, HESB, DFR, LC]

Cloak of the Sith

⟐ The region of space called the Cloak of the Sith is a huge dark cloud of dangerous meteors, asteroids, and planetoids. To reach the Roon system, ships must chart a course through the Cloak of the Sith. [DTV]

Clone Keepers

⟐ The Clone Keepers are the scientists and attendants responsible for the Emperor's clone vats on the planet Byss. [DE]

Clone Wars

⟐ The Clone Wars was a terrible conflict that erupted during the time of the Old Republic (some thirty-five years prior to the start of *Star Wars IV: A New Hope*). The conflict produced such heroes as Bail Organa, Anakin Skywalker, and Obi-Wan Kenobi, who served as a general. Few details about the period have been revealed, but we know that the Jedi Knights and their allies battled to defend the Old Republic against its enemies. [SW, ESB, RJ]

cloud car

🔰 Cloud cars are any atmospheric flying vehicles that employ both repulsorlifts and ion engines. Typical models consist of twin pods for pilots and passengers. The ion power plant is mounted to the connecting boom. Cloud cars fill a variety of roles. On Cloud City, for example, cloud cars serve as patrol craft and traffic control vehicles. [ESB]

⚙️ The major manufacturer of cloud cars is Bespin Motors. They make a full line of pleasure craft, personal planetary transports, air taxis, and patrol vehicles. Until recently, the only types of cloud cars they did not turn out were models capable of entering into major combat situations. [SWSB]

Cloud City

🔰 The mining outpost and trading station called Cloud City floats high within the atmosphere of the gas-giant planet Bespin. It is a small city of landing platforms, delicate spires, jutting towers, and airy plazas—all held aloft atop a long repulsorlift unipod. Cloud City's major industry is the mining and exporting of Tibanna gas, but it also serves as a merchant outpost and recreational center. While off the main space lanes, those who know about Cloud City arrive to enjoy its many casinos, restaurants, and shopping plazas. In addition to the many spacers who frequent its ports, Cloud City boasts a diverse citizenry of humans, droids, and assorted alien species. [ESB]

⚙️ Cloud City was founded by Lord Ecclessis Figg of Corellia. He started it as a floating work base and slowly developed it into the city it became. [GG2, CCC]

Cobak

⚙ The bounty hunter Cobak is a member of the Bith species. He was hired by Zorba the Hutt to capture Princess Leia. To accomplish this mission, Cobak impersonated Bithabus the Mystifier to lure the Princess into his trap. [QE]

Coby

⚙ Prince Coby, the son of Lord Toda of Tammuz-an, met the droids R2-D2 and C-3PO in the Empire's early days. He was nine years old at the time, and he used spoiled, aggressive behavior to hide his insecurity. [DTV]

Colonial Games

⚙ The Colonial Games are a series of athletic competitions that pit champions from the various colonies of the Roon star system against each other for fun and glory. The main event is the drainsweeper, a kind of no-holds-barred relay race. [DTV]

Colonies, the

⚙ One of the first areas of the galaxy outside the Galactic Core to be settled was the region called the Colonies. This area is now heavily populated and industrialized, with societies as firmly established as those of the Core Worlds, though it lacks the rich history or grand traditions of the ancient centers of civilization. During the Galactic Civil

War, this area was ruthlessly controlled by the Empire. Once the New Republic was formed, much of the area decided to support the new regime. [SWRPG2]

Colton

See Captain Antilles.

Columi

⊙ The Columi are craniopods who grow to be about 1.75 meters tall. Their huge, hairless heads make up fully a third of their size, with throbbing veins and huge black eyes. The rest of their bodies are puny, with thin arms and legs that do not function. This species comes from the planet Columus, where they have devoted themselves to the pursuits of mental activities. All physical work is performed by droids and other machines, which the Columi communicate with via brain-wave transmissions. They are a peaceful, non-aggressive species, who often hire themselves out as advisers and soothsayers. [GG4]

combat sense

⊙ Through the use of this Force sense technique, Jedi Knights can focus the bulk of their attention on the battle at hand. Everything else becomes muted as the Jedi's senses concentrate on the battle currently underway. All opponents become bright images in an otherwise dull landscape, aiding the Jedi in attack and defense. [DFR, DFRSB]

comlink

🔃 A comlink is a personal communications transceiver. It comes in a wide variety of hand-held and headset-mounted models, and contains a transmitter, a receiver, and a power source. The most widely used model is a small palm-sized cylinder, though military units carry large backpack versions with boosted ranges. Comlinks are also built into stormtrooper helmets and provide ship-wide communications aboard large space vessels. [SW, ESB, RJ]

command control voice

🔃 Droids can be programmed to receive command control instructions via a special voice pattern, or command control voice. This voice usually belongs to the droid's master or primary supervisor. [SWR]

Commander Bane Nothos

🔅 The Imperial district commander Bane Nothos was in charge of the operation to locate and destroy Admiral Ackbar's Shantipole Project. He failed, and the Alliance was able to finish work on the new B-wing starfighter. This led to Nothos's demotion, and he was placed in charge of an Outer Rim Territories patrol fleet. He was subsequently captured by the Alliance, placed aboard a Rebel ship for transport to a hidden outpost, and lost in the mysterious dimension called otherspace when a problem developed with the ship's hyperdrive. [SFS, OS]

Commander Klev

⚙ Commander Klev was in charge of *Silencer-7*, one of the Imperial World Devastators at the Battle of Calamari. Klev died when Luke Skywalker tampered with the Master Control Signal and caused *Silencer-7* to crash into the Calamari Ocean. [DE]

Commander Narra

✦ After the death of Red Leader at the Battle of Yavin, Commander Narra was put in charge of the X-wing fighter group to which Luke Skywalker belonged. The pilots of the squadron called Narra "The Boss." Prior to the events at Hoth, Commander Narra lost his life in an Imperial ambush near Derra IV. The Rebel convoy that Narra and his squadron were escorting was attacked by several TIE fighter squadrons. In the wake of this tragedy, Luke Skywalker was promoted to the rank of commander and placed in charge of the fighter group. Under Luke's command, the fighter group became the legendary Rogue Squadron. [ESBR]

Commander Orlok

⚙ Commander Orlok was the Imperial commander in charge of the Imperial Training Center on Daluuj. [GW]

Commander Silver Fyre

⚙ A former smuggler colleague of Han Solo and leader of one of the biggest gangs of mercenaries in the galaxy, Fyre commands the Aquarius Freeholders. He joined the Alliance at the Conference of Uncommitted Worlds held on Kabal. [GW]

Commander Willard

(Rebel symbol) Commander Willard was one of the Alliance officers serving under General Dodonna at the Rebel base on Yavin Four. [SW]

Commenor

(Rebel symbol) The planet Commenor serves as a trading outpost and spaceport for ships traveling the trade routes near the Corellian star system. [SW]

Commodore Zuggs

(Empire symbol) Commodore Zuggs is a bald, beady-eyed Imperial officer who is assigned to Trioculus, serving as the pilot for his Strike Cruiser. [LCJ]

comm unit

(Rebel symbol) A ship-board communications device, a comm unit provides a ship with the ability to transmit and receive communications signals to and from outside sources, including comlinks. [SWSB]

compact assault vehicle

🔘 The compact assault vehicle, or CAV, transforms a single Imperial trooper into a formidable assault force—at least in theory. So far, the CAV has yet to distinguish itself as a weapon of war. These small, single-occupant vehicles are typically equipped with one medium blaster cannon. Tracked wheels provide locomotion, and these small craft can attain fairly impressive speeds. They are suspectible to sensor jamming, however, which could be why they have yet to catch on with Imperial troopers. [ISB]

COMPNOR

🔘 COMPNOR, the Commission for the Preservation of the New Order, was formed in Imperial City as one of Emperor Palpatine's first official actions. It started as a social gathering of idealistic young beings who saw the New Order as a way to turn back the chaos of the dying days of the Old Republic. This populist movement was quickly molded into a powerful political tool of the New Order. Through its subtle manipulations, COMPNOR teaches the galaxy the everyday ethics of the New Order and works to turn the structure of the Old Republic into a relic of the past. [ISB]

computer probe

🔘 A computer probe is a device that provides access to a computer network. Probes come in a variety of sizes and shapes, though the most common are the appendages droids use to tap into computers or portable console units. [HSE]

com-scan

(⊕) Com-scans are specialized sensor sweeps designed to detect the energy that results from the transmission and reception of communication signals. [ESB]

concussion missile

(⊕) Concussion missiles make up part of the armament carried by starfighters. These sublight-speed projectiles cause shock waves on impact. The concussive blasts can penetrate and destroy even heavily armored targets, though they work best when directed against stationary targets. The *Millennium Falcon* carries these weapons as a regular part of its offensive capability. Concussion missiles were used to destroy the second Death Star during the Battle of Endor. [RJ]

condenser unit

(⊕) A condenser unit (also called a thermal coil or warming unit) is a neutronic circuit that radiates high levels of heat through the use of small amounts of energy. These units are frequently found in standard survival kits since they can be used to cook food and provide heat. [SW]

consular ship

(⊕) A consular ship is any vessel officially registered to a member of the Imperial Senate. When consular ships are on diplomatic missions, they are immune to the normal mire of spaceport and deep-space inspection. Since the Senate was disbanded, such courtesies are no longer extended. [SW, SWR]

container ship

🌐 Container ships, or super transports, are among the largest commercial vessels plying the space lanes. Big, slow, and expensive, they are still the most efficient way to transport huge amounts of cargo from system to system. Ease and speed of cargo handling make these vessels so efficient. They haul standardized cargo containers, either rectangular or cylindrical in shape, which are sealed and loaded by automated barges. Some containers are even designed to carry passengers. A single super transport may carry hundreds of various-sized containers for drop-off along its winding route through space. Too large to land on a planet or approach a space dock, container ships must rely on stock light freighters and other small craft to collect and transfer their cargo to orbital ports within a system. [SWSB]

Controller Jhoff

🔴 Controller Jhoff served aboard the Super Star Destroyer *Executor.* His specialty was space traffic control. During the construction of the second Death Star, Jhoff was responsible for clearing, directing, and tracking space traffic into and within the restricted space surrounding Endor's moon. [RJ]

control mind

🌐 Through the use of the control, sense, and alter technique called *control mind*, a Force user can take direct control of other people. They become automatons who must obey the Force user's will. This technique is considered a corruption of the Force, a product of the dark side. The Dark Jedi Joruus C'baoth was a master of this technique. [HE, DFR, LC, DFRSB]

Coral Vanda

🌑 The subocean cruise ship *Coral Vanda* explores the ocean depths of the vacation world of Pantolomin. It makes three-and seven-day excursions through the huge network of coral reefs off the coast of the Tralla continent. It has a very impressive casino, complete with eight ornate gambling halls. Full-wall transparisteel hulls separate each hall from the ocean, giving tourists breathtaking views of sea life and the fabulous reefs. [DFR, DFRSB]

Core Worlds, the

See Galactic Core.

Corellia

🌑 The Corellia star system and its inhabited planets were among the first members of the Old Republic. The system is best known for its fast ships, skilled traders, and the pirates that regularly raid the local space lanes. [SWRPG2]

Corellian

☉ Corellians are a race of humans from the Corellia star system. Han Solo is a Corellian. [SW]

Corellian Bloodstripes

⚙ Corellian Bloodstripes are the red piping that adorns the trousers of some Corellians. Within the Corellian military, these red stripes are worn by individuals who have distinguished themselves through brave and heroic acts. Han Solo wears the Bloodstripes on his trousers. This is his only nod toward his time of military service. [HLL]

Corellian Corvette

⚙ An old, multipurpose capital ship model, the Corellian Corvette still sees service throughout the galaxy. This mid-sized vessel is 150 meters long and can function as a troop carrier, light escort vessel, cargo transport, or passenger liner. Its modular interior can easily be refigured to handle any requirements. Like most Corellian-built ships, the Corvette has a fast sublight drive and a quick hyperjump calculator for fast exits into hyperspace. Because this vessel type sees a lot of duty among the Corellian pirates, authorities have nicknamed it the Blockade Runner. Princess Leia's consular ship *Tantive IV* was a Corellian Corvette. [SWSB]

Corellian gunship

⚙ The dedicated combat capital ship called the Corellian gunship is designed to be fast and deadly. It is 120 meters long, typically mounted with eight double turbolaser cannons, six quad laser cannons, and four concussion missile launch tubes. Engines fill more than half of its interior, while weaponry, computers, and shield generators take up most of the rest of the ship. With a small command crew, tech staff, and lots of gunners, the gunship works very well as an anti-starfighter platform. The Alliance (and later the New Republic) make extensive use of these vessels, and some can even be found in private defense fleets and independent armies. [RSB, DFRSB]

Corporate Sector, the

The Corporate Sector is a portion of the known galaxy set aside for the exclusive use of the Corporate Sector Authority. The Sector consists of tens of thousands of star systems which apparently have no native sentient life-forms. Many of the resources mined from the planets of the Corporate Sector went into the construction of the Imperial war machine. [HLL, HSE, HSR]

Corporate Sector Authority, the

The Corporate Sector Authority is a vast private corporation that was granted a charter by the Empire to control a portion of the galaxy—the Corporate Sector. According to the terms of the charter, the Authority has the right to exploit the resources of the region to the fullest extent. It rules the region in much the same way the Empire ruled the rest of the galaxy, as its charter empowers it to act as owner, employer, landlord, government, police, and military to all persons, places, and things within the Corporate Sector. [HLL, HSE, HSR]

Corulag

Corulag is a planet in the Imperial Core World systems. Lieutenant Page, among others, was born here. [HESB]

Coruscant

⚹ Coruscant is considered the jewel of the Core Worlds. It has been the seat of galactic government from the start, and though the methods of governing have changed more than once, Coruscant has remained constant. The Old Republic built the Senate Hall on this beautiful world. When the Emperor took power, he added to the Presidential Palace to create Imperial Palace, a structure that looms over Senate Hall to this day.

When the New Republic was formed, its members decided to use Coruscant the same way the previous governments had. Imperial City, with its majestic spires and dazzling lights, rests at the base of the snow-covered Manarai Mountains. Once it was called Galactic City, but since the Emperor changed the name it has remained Imperial City.

It is said that Coruscant sets the tone of the entire galaxy. Styles and fads start on this capital world and slowly spread. The level of culture is unsurpassed anywhere else in the Core or beyond, and all of the "standard" measurements used throughout the galaxy are based upon the norms of this planet. Except for a few isolated melees, Coruscant and its area of the Core remained unscathed by the Galactic Civil War. Throughout the collapse of the Old Republic, the time of the Empire, and the rise of the New Republic, the people of Coruscant knew war and hardship only by the news they received. Most saw the shift of governments as the changing of the seasons. Who cares who sits on the seats of power? Coruscant is eternal. Those who were particularly loyal to the Empire fled or were expelled once the New Republic took charge.

Between the end of Grand Admiral Thrawn's threat and the return of the reborn Emperor, the Empire made a successful attack on Coruscant. The New Republic leadership was forced to flee from the capital planet, which was left in ruins by the Imperial onslaught. Now neither side uses it as a ruling platform. Instead, the planet and the system have become a battleground for the continuing struggle between Republic and Empire. [HE, DFR, LC, DE, HESB, DFRSB]

Council of Elders

✪ The Council of Elders is the ruling body among the Ewoks of Endor's moon. The Council is led by Chief Chirpa. [RJ]

Covell

See General Covell.

Coway

✪ The Coway are a troglodyte race of humanoids who inhabit Circarpous V. They are bipedal and covered by a fine gray down. These tribal beings live in caves and wells which were built by the now-extinct Thrella. Coways are fond of charms, but have an intense dislike of surface dwellers. A triumvirate guides the affairs of the tribes. [SME]

credit standard

✪ The credit standard, or credit, is the basic monetary unit used throughout the Empire. The unit is based upon the Old Republic credit and remains in use during the time of the New Republic, though both the New Republic and the Imperial remnants produce their own currency. Most credits are stored and exchanged via computer transaction, but there is credit currency which can be carried and physically exchanged. [SME, SWRPG, HESB]

Cron Drift

⊛ The Cron Drift is a charted sector of the known galaxy. It is the remnant of a trinary system supernova that exploded in the distant past. [HLL, HSE]

crystalline vertex

⊛ Crystalline vertex is the currency used throughout the Corporate Sector to supplement Authority Cash Vouchers. Vertex is made from a crystal mineral found on the planet Kir, deep within the heart of the Corporate Sector. On this planet, Authority mining outposts refine the crystals into a standard size and color. When individuals enter the Corporate Sector, they must turn over all other forms of currency in exchange for vertex crystals or Cash Vouchers. These exchanges occur at Currency Exchange Centers on planets or within the spaceport/perimeter defense stations that guard Authority space. [HSE]

crystal oscillator

⊛ The mysterious object called the crystal oscillator was stolen from the Towanis's shipwrecked star cruiser by Terak's marauders because Terak believed that it was the source of "the power." [BFE]

Cyax

🌀 The Cyax star system is an uncharted, unexplored system far from the galactic trade routes. Though most of the galactic community know nothing about Cyax, the Hutts consider the system to be sacred territory. For over four thousand years they have held it as a place of legend. Many of the worlds in the system bear Huttese names. [DE]

cyberostasis

🌀 The condition called cyberostasis affects droids that have received a traumatic, external shock, have experienced an internal systems defect, or have induced the state as a function of a protective reflex system. In this state, all cybernetic functions within a droid are impaired or halted, usually resulting in shutdown. [HSE]

Cyborg Operations

🌀 Cyborg Operations, one of the departments in Jabba the Hutt's court, was controlled by the droid EV-9D9. Located deep within the dungeons of Jabba's palace, Cyborg Operations was concerned with breaking the programming and personalities of droids through torture and other means before assigning them to tasks and duties in Jabba's organization. [RJ]

Cyborrea

🌀 Cyborrea is the star system where nek battle dogs are bred and trained. [DE]

Cycy Loctob

⚛ Cycy Loctob, one of Nar Shaddaa's alien denizens, makes a living by selling contraband to any and all interested parties. [DE]

D

Dack

(symbol) Young Dack was a Rebel gunner assigned to the Alliance forces on the ice planet Hoth. Among his duties was to serve as gunner on Luke Skywalker's snowspeeder. Dack died defending the Rebel base from Imperial AT-ATs when Skywalker's snowspeeder took a hit from a walker's weapon fire. [ESB]

Dagobah

(symbol) The swamp planet Dagobah resides in an explored but sparsely populated star system of the same name. The planet, shrouded in mist and covered by clinging vegetation, was the home and hiding place of Yoda, the Jedi Master. [ESB]

(symbol) As the principal planet in a star system of the same name, Dagobah is not much to speak of. It has no spaceports and none of the conveniences of modern technology. Its neighbors throughout the Sluis sector consider it to be a haunted place due to its connection to the Dark Jedi of

Bpfassh. The evil rampage of the Dark Jedi came to an end on the swamp planet after the group terrorized the systems of the Sluis sector during the Clone Wars. [HE]

Daluuj

☺ An Imperial Training Center is located on Daluuj, a world near Mon Calamari with unstable atmospheric conditions. When the Imperials attacked Mon Calamari shortly after the destruction of the first Death Star, Admiral Ackbar and his troops fled to Daluuj in life pods and were rescued by the *Falcon*. [GW]

Dantooine

☺ Dantooine, a remote planet far from the centers of civilization, once housed the base of operations for the Rebel Alliance. [SW]

Dark Force

See *Katana* fleet.

Dark Jedi

☺ The reborn Emperor envisions a new breed of Jedi Knights who are trained under the tenets of the dark side of the Force. These evil servants will be loyal to the Emperor, helping him spread the power of the dark side during the thousand years of rule the Emperor believes will be his. Evil Jedi Knights operating during the Clone Wars, a group of which threatened the Bpfassh system, were also called Dark Jedi. [DE, HE]

dark side, the

See the Force.

Dark Side Adepts

🌀 The members of the reborn Emperor's New Imperial Council are called Dark Side Adepts, and are drawn from the ranks of the Emperor's cohorts in the dark side of the Force. In the years prior to the Battle of Yavin, the Emperor used Byss as his private retreat. On this hidden world, he began to train men of great intelligence who demonstrated some ability to use the Force. He twisted them to the dark side, turning them into powerful Force users but always keeping them below his own level of power and ability. These Adepts serve the Emperor's will, and he eventually plans to disperse them throughout the galaxy to replace the old system of planetary governors. [DE]

Dark Side Compendium

🌀 The reborn Emperor calls the encyclopedia of dark side lore he is writing the *Dark Side Compendium.* He completed three volumes of his proposed several-hundred-volume set before he was defeated a second time by Luke Skywalker and Princess Leia. These completed books are *The Book of Anger, The Weakness of Inferiors,* and *The Creation of Monsters.* Luke Skywalker read all three while he was on Byss. [DE]

dart shooter

A dart shooter is a hand-held weapon that fires metal projectiles. These projectiles, or darts, are usually filled with toxins of varying strengths. Some toxins merely paralyze targets, others kill. [HLL]

Darth Vader (Lord Vader, Dark Lord of the Sith)

Darth Vader epitomized the Emperor's New Order. Standing two meters tall and dressed in flowing black robes and black body armor, Vader was a tangible evil and symbol of the Emperor's doctrine of rule through fear and terror.

Darth Vader

He was the servant and emissary of the Emperor, and later commanded the vast fleet charged with finding and destroying the Rebel Alliance.

Vader was once Anakin Skywalker, expert pilot, hero of the Clone Wars, and disciple of Obi-Wan Kenobi. Learning to use the Force by Kenobi's methods was too slow for the impatient Anakin. He wanted a quicker, less difficult path to the vast power he sensed all around him. Emperor Palpatine offered him just such a path—the dark side. All Anakin had to do was give in to his anger, fear, and aggression. Ambitious and headstrong, he stepped into the dark side's embrace and became Darth Vader.

According to the *Return of the Jedi* novel, when Kenobi saw what had become of his friend and student, Anakin Skywalker, he tried to draw him back from the dark side. But Vader wanted none of that. The two fought, and Vader fell into a molten pit. Though Kenobi thought him dead, Vader emerged from the pit. His shattered body, however, had to be sustained by life-supporting armor. When Kenobi learned that Vader lived, he helped Anakin's wife and newborn twins (whom Vader was not aware of) escape into hiding—Luke to Tatooine, and Leia and her mother to Alderaan.

Darth Vader, Dark Lord of the Sith, helped the Emperor hunt down and exterminate the Jedi Knights during the last days of the Old Republic and the opening moments of the Empire. Later, he was sent to help Governor Tarkin develop the original Death Star battle station. Once the Rebellion demonstrated that it posed a significant threat to the New Order, Lord Vader was put in charge of the Imperial fleet assigned to find and destroy the Alliance leaders. The mission took on personal significance when Vader discovered that the Rebel's newest ally was his own son, Luke Skywalker. Both the Emperor and Vader wanted to convert young Skywalker to the dark side, but Vader had his own agenda. He wanted himself and Luke to rule the galaxy side by side as father and son.

The first time that father and son met was on Cloud City. Luke rejected Vader's claims and offers, electing to fight him. But Vader was too powerful for the still-developing young Jedi. Luke barely escaped with his life, though he lost his right hand to his father's lightsaber.

Vader was confronted by his son a second time at Endor. Luke did not arrive as a half-trained apprentice Jedi this time, but as a full-fledged Jedi Knight. Luke's faith in his father's innate goodness won the day, bringing Anakin out of the darkness of Darth Vader and back into the light. He saved Luke and destroyed the Emperor, but at the cost of his own life. Vader's final act—as Anakin and not as the Dark Lord of the Sith—was to look upon his son and tell him that he was right. [SW, ESB, RJ]

Da Soocha

🌕 Da Soocha is an uncharted water world in the Cyax star system. The name means "Waking Planet" in Huttese, and the legends of the Hutts claim that the great ocean of Da Soocha is a single, conscious entity. The Mon Calamari evacuees hoped to reach this world and find a safe haven from Imperial forces. [DE]

data card

🌕 Data cards are thin plastic rectangles used to store information and programs for use in data pads and computers. These durable cards can be bent, dropped, and even exposed to weather without suffering undue damage. [TM, HE, HESB]

data pad

● A data pad is a palm-sized personal computer. It consists of a readout screen, input touch pad, data card slot, internal power source, and ports for coupling with droids or large computer terminals. It is used as a portable workstation, personal secretary, information organizer, data display, and storage unit by officers aboard capital ships, spaceport personnel, and anyone who needs to process, store, and retrieve information in this computer-dependent society. [TM, HE, HESB]

Deak

● Deak was a childhood friend of Luke Skywalker. He lives in Anchorhead, on the desert world of Tatooine. As teens, Luke and Deak would fly their skyhoppers in mock aerial duels and race through the many twisting canyons near their homes. [SW]

death mark

● A death mark is the term applied to individuals who have been singled out for execution. Han Solo had a death mark on his head when Jabba the Hutt offered a bounty for his capture—dead or alive. [ESB]

Death's Head

● The Imperial Star Destroyer *Death's Head*, commanded by Captain Harbid, served as part of Grand Admiral Thrawn's armada. [HE, DFR, LC]

Death Star, the

✪ The Death Star battle station was to be the ultimate weapon in the Empire's terrible arsenal. It was designed and constructed in secret as the answer to the Emperor's problems with the Senate and as a symbol of his New Order. Once it was fully operational, the Emperor ordered the Imperial Senate disbanded and declared that the Empire would keep local star systems in line through the use of fear—fear of the Imperial fleet and fear of the Death Star. The battle station, the size of a small moon and packed with more destructive power than the Imperial fleet, required a huge crew to operate. The armored shell housed the massive power plants needed to energize the battle station's primary weapon—a planet-destroying superlaser. In addition, the shell was covered with navigation trenches, docking bays, and turbolaser emplacements to fend off capital ship attacks. Artificial mountains and canyons were formed from rising docking ports and command complexes, and the bays held nearly endless squadrons of TIE fighters and other small craft. Though the Death Star showed its relentless power by destroying the planet Alderaan, Rebel agents were able to discover a weakness to exploit when they stole the technical readouts for the battle station. The Battle of Yavin ended with the destruction of the Death Star.

Three years later, as the second Death Star neared completion, another battle was waged to keep the massive weapon from being activated. Though never finished, the second Death Star was larger than the original. It measured approximately 160 kilometers in diameter and was armed with a superlaser that was more powerful and accurate than the original. It could be trained upon capital ships. The Rebels were able to destroy it at the Battle of Endor. [SW, RJ]

⚙ The original Death Star was the culmination of the Tarkin Doctrine, a plan and course of action proposed by Grand Moff Tarkin to the Emperor. The Tarkin Doctrine called for rule through the fear of force, using a battle station of such destructive magnitude that fear alone would keep the member worlds of the Empire in line. Imperial space station designer Bevel Lemelisk was charged with bringing Tarkin's terrible vision to fruition. Measuring 120 kilometers in diameter, the battle station was constructed over the penal colony world Despayre in the remote Horuz star system. The completed Death Star's personnel complement included twenty-seven thousand forty-eight officers, seven hundred seventy-four thousand five hundred seventy-six troops, pilots, and crewers, almost four hundred thousand support personnel, and more than twenty-five thousand stormtroopers. It carried assault shuttles, blast boats, strike cruisers, drop ships, land vehicles, and various support ships in its massive holds, along with seven thousand two hundred TIE fighters. Its surface was protected by ten thousand turbolaser batteries, two thousand five hundred laser cannons, two thousand five hundred ion cannons, over seven hundred tractor-beam projectors, and a superlaser. [DSTC]

Declaration of a New Republic

⚙ The textfile document known as the Declaration of a New Republic set forth the principles, goals, and ideals of the new galactic government formed by the Alliance after the Battle of Endor. The document was released one month after the battle ended. It was signed by Mon Mothma of Chandrila, Princess Leia Organa of Alderaan, Borsk Fey'lya of Kothlis, Admiral Ackbar of Mon Calamari, Sian Tevv of

Sullust, Doman Beruss of Corellia, Kerrithrarr of Kashyyyk, and Verrinnefra B'thog Indriummsegh of Elom. [HESB]

decoder

⊕ The device known as a decoder is one type of security deciphering mechanism. It works by analyzing and breaking the combinations on digitally encoded security locks. [HSR]

Deej

⊕ The Ewok warrior named Deej is the loving father of Weechee, Willy, Wicket, and Winda, and husband of Shodu. [ETV]

Deep Core haulers

⊕ The freighters licensed by the Empire to haul cargo to the Imperial systems in the Deep Core are called Deep Core haulers. [DE]

Deep Core Security Zone

⊕ The Deep Core Security Zone is made up of sealed-off sectors of the inner Galactic Core. The throne world Byss is hidden within the DCSZ. [DE]

Deep Galactic Core

🌀 Between the perimeter of the Galactic Core and the very center of the galaxy is the Deep Galactic Core, or Deep Core. This huge region of old stars and little interstellar matter features a black hole at its center, which is surrounded by masses of antimatter and dense stars. The reborn Emperor consolidated his forces in this region and planned to launch a final strike against his enemies. [DE]

Defeen

🌀 Defeen is a cunning, sharp-clawed humanoid who served as an Interrogator First Class at the Imperial Reprogramming Institute located in the Valley of Royalty on the planet Duro. His work helped get him promoted to the rank of Supreme Interrogator for the Dark Side Prophets on Space Station Scardia. [MMY, PDS]

Defel

🌀 Defel are an alien species that appear as large, red-eyed shadows under most lighting conditions. This has given rise to their common name: wraiths. Under ultraviolet light, Defels appear as stocky, fur-covered bipeds with protruding snouts and long, clawed, triple-jointed fingers. They stand about 1.3 meters tall, with shoulders as wide as 1.2 meters across. This species lives in underground cities on the planet Af'El, where most inhabitants make their living through mining and metallurgy. In the galaxy at large, Defel often find employment as hired muscle, spies, and assassins due to their shadowy forms. [GG4, DFRSB]

Defiance

🟢 The Mon Calamari warship *Defiance* replaced *Home One* as the flagship of the New Republic fleet and serves as Admiral Ackbar's personal vessel. [DE]

deflection tower

🔵 Deflection towers generate high-intensity deflection fields. The shields these towers project vary in intensity and shape to suit the needs of the user. They form the cornerstones of most planetary defense systems, making them highly protected locations. The original Death Star was equipped with deflection towers. [SW]

deflector shield

🔵 A deflector shield is one of two types of force field that repulses solid objects or absorbs energy, thus offering protection to everything under the shield. Ray shielding defends against energy such as radiation and blaster bolts; particle shielding prevents matter from penetrating the field. [SW, ESB, RJ]

Dellalt

🟢 The planet Dellalt, a member of the Tion Hegemony star group, was important in the time before the Old Republic known as the Expansionist Period. Now the world is mostly forgotten, far from the trade routes and major space lanes. Dellalt has two moons that orbit its watery surface. While the majority of the planet is covered by water, three main landmasses extend far enough above the waterline to provide living space for its humanoid and sauropteroid inhabitants. Histories and legends from the Expansionist Period claim that Dellalt was the site of Xim the Despot's colossal vaults, in which he supposedly stored the treasures he plundered from the surrounding star systems. [HLL]

Delta Source

See ch'hala tree.

Demma Moll

⬡ Demma Moll was a reserved, attractive woman in her mid-forties during the early days of the Empire. She owned a farm on the planet Annoo, though the Fromm gang desperately wanted to take possession of her property. She had a daughter named Kea, and she secretly led a band of freedom fighters working to destroy Fromm's weapons satellite, the *Trigon One*. R2-D2 and C-3PO met Demma during their adventures back in those days. [DTV]

Deneba

⬡ Deneba is a desert world that figures prominently in Jedi history. Thon delivered his message to ten thousand Jedi Masters here in the distant past. [DE]

Dengar

⬡ Dengar was one of the bounty hunters hired by the Empire to find and capture the *Millennium Falcon* and her crew

Dengar

immediately following the Battle of Hoth. Dengar, a human, wears assorted pieces of battle armor and carries a variety of weapons. [ESB]

🌀 The bounty hunter who confronted Mara Jade on the planet Rishi carried textdocs that identified him as Dengar. It is doubtful that the two are in any way related. Jade killed this Dengar to save herself and keep Karrde's organization from being found. [DFR]

Deppo

🌀 Deppo is a calibration engineer serving in an onboard factory within an Imperial World Devastator. [DE]

Derlin

See Major Derlin.

Derra IV

🔴 Derra IV was the site of a significant Rebel defeat leading up to the Battle of Hoth. An Alliance convoy on its way to Hoth with desperately needed supplies was ambushed by several squadrons of TIE fighters in the vicinity of the fourth planet in the Derra star system. The attack was brutal and swift. The convoy was destroyed and all Alliance personnel were killed. [ESBR]

detainment droid

🔴 Detainment droids float atop repulsorlift-generated fields and serve to secure and guard prisoners. These droids are equipped with binders on the ends of their four limbs which grasp and lock around the limbs of their prisoners. Imperial detention centers make extensive use of these droids. [DE]

Detention Block AA-23

🔴 Detention Block AA-23 was the location, deep within the Death Star battle station, where Princess Leia Organa was held captive by the Imperials. Specifically, she was imprisoned in Cell 2187. [SW]

Devaronian

🔴 The humanoid Devaronians come from the temperate world of Devaron. The males are hairless, with a pair of horns on the tops of their heads and sharp incisors filling their mouths. Many species feel uncomfortable in their presence, for they resemble the devils of a thousand different myths. The females are larger, with thick fur and no horns. The males suffer from wanderlust, and can be found in spaceports throughout the galaxy seeking passage to someplace else. The females prefer to remain at home and keep their advanced industries running. A Devaronian male can be seen briefly in the cantina scene in *Star Wars IV: A New Hope.* [GG1, GG4]

Devastator

The Imperial Star Destroyer *Devastator* captured Princess Leia's consular ship over the planet Tatooine. She was trying to smuggle the technical readouts of the original Death Star to Alliance High Command when the Star Destroyer intercepted her vessel. [SWR]

dewback

A dewback is a large reptile native to the planet Tatooine. On the desert world, these herbivores are used as beasts of burden by moisture farmers and as patrol animals by the local authorities and the military personnel assigned to the planet's Imperial garrison. The reptile is often used in place of mechanized vehicles due to its ability to withstand extremely high temperatures and the wear and tear of sand storms. [SW, SWR]

dianoga

A dianoga is an omnivorous creature that lives in shallow, stagnant pools and murky swamps. The creature grows to an average length of ten meters, and grabs prey with its seven tentacles. These tentacles also provide it with a means of locomotion. An eyestalk that emerges from the dianoga's trunk can be raised above the surface of the water to help the creature locate nearby prey. A dianoga somehow made its way into the waste disposals of the original Death Star battle station. It lived off the station's refuse, and almost made a meal of Luke Skywalker when he fell into its watery, garbage-filled lair. [SW]

digworm

Digworms are small creatures native to the planet Kamar. These worms burrow into solid rock by excreting acidic digestive juices. [HSR]

dinko

A dinko is a venomous, palm-sized creature known for its nasty disposition. With powerful rear legs covered with serrated spurs, twin pairs of grasping extremities jutting from its chest, and sharp, needlelike fangs, the dinko is quite formidable for such a small creature. The foul-smelling liquid it secretes to mark its territory is known to discourage even the largest predators. [HSE]

dipill

Dipill is a sedative used to relieve stress. [SME]

directional landing beacon

Directional landing beacons are found at most spaceports and other landing facilities. These devices transmit fixed signals which ships can use to orient themselves. The pulsed transmissions provide direction and distance information to a ship's nav computer. Landing beacons have a deceptively simple appearance. A cluster of blinking caution lights top a transponder globe, which is anchored by a tripod or unipod repulsorlift. The landing beacons located at official ports of call are listed in galactic navigation charts. [SME]

disruptor

⊙ The disruptor weapon fires a visible blast of energy that can shatter objects. When used against a living creature, the disruptor kills in a most painful and inhumane manner. Disruptors are illegal in most sectors of the galaxy. [HSE, HLL, HSR]

divto

⊙ A divto is a fearsome three-headed snake that grows to a length of three meters. These creatures hunt the night of Endor's moon, striking prey and delivering a numbing poison. Once the poison takes effect, the divto drags its prey into the deep forest to consume at its leisure. [DFRSB]

DJ-88 (Dee-Jay)

⊙ The powerful droid who serves as the caretaker and teacher in the Lost City of the Jedi, DJ-88 is white, with ruby eyes and a metal beard. He raised young Ken from the time the Jedi Prince was a small child, and Ken looks up to the droid as he would his own father. [LCJ, PDS]

Dobah

⊛ The female Phlog named Dobah is the mate of Zut and the mother of Hoom and Nahkee. [ETC]

Doc

⊛ Doc leads a band of outlaw techs who are wanted throughout Imperial space. Doc and his elusive techs specialize in making modifications (usually of an illegal nature) to space vehicles. Doc's daughter Jessa is a member of his band. [HSE]

Docking Bay 45

⊛ Docking Bay 45 is one of the holding bays in the spaceport on Etti IV, a planet in the Corporate Sector. Han Solo's *Millennium Falcon* illegally left the bay and escaped from Authority space by using the identification profile and name of another ship. [HSE]

Docking Bay 94

⊛ Docking Bay 94, in Tatooine's Mos Eisley docking facility, was where the *Millennium Falcon* waited to rendezvous with Ben Kenobi, Luke Skywalker, and the droids R2-D2 and C-3PO. Kenobi and Skywalker hired the ship and its pilots, Han Solo and Chewbacca, at one of Mos Eisley's cantinas. Docking Bay 94, like the rest of the bays at Mos Eisley, consists of an entrance ramp and a restraining wall that surrounds a shallow pit. The pit deflects and absorbs the blasts associated with starship takeoffs and landings, though by law those ships equipped with repulsorlifts must use them when entering and leaving the docking bays. [SW]

Doctor Cornelius

See Roofoo.

Doctor Evazan

See Roofoo.

Dodonna

See General Dodonna.

Domed City of Aquarius

⊕ Located in a giant bubble far below the Mon Calamari oceans, the Domed City of Aquarius is designed for use by both air- and water-breathing beings. Watery canals connect underwater dwellings, while markets and other structures are located in the air above the canals. [GDV]

Doonium

⊕ The heavy metal Doonium is one of the common materials used to build Imperial war machines. [GDV]

Dorja

See Captain Dorja.

dormo-shock

🔴 Traumatically injured individuals sometimes enter a natural healing sleep called dormo-shock. In this state, the body's regenerative and recuperative abilities work to heal the traumatized area or areas while the individual rests in a comalike sleep. [ESB]

D'rag

🔵 D'rag is a starshipwright from the planet Oslumpex V. [HSR]

Drang

🔵 Drang is one of two domesticated vornskrs that Talon Karrde employs as pets and guards. [HE, DFR, LC, HESB]

DRAPAC

🔵 DRAPAC stands for Defense Research and Planetary Assistance Center, an Alliance fortress built atop Dagobah's Mount Yoda. [MMY, QE]

Dr. Arakkus

🔵 Dr. Arakkus, a scientist and former head of an Imperial weapons development complex, was contaminated by a radiation experiment. He lived in an abandoned Imperial transport amid a graveyard of ships circling a collapsing star. An explosion killed Dr. Arakkus when Han Solo ignited a negatron charge to free the *Falcon* from the collapsing star's gravitational pull. [GW]

Dravis

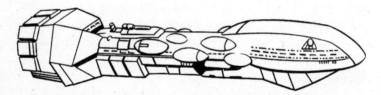 Dravis is a pilot in Talon Karrde's smuggling operation. [HE, DRF, LC]

Drayson

See Admiral Drayson.

Dreadnaught

Dreadnaught

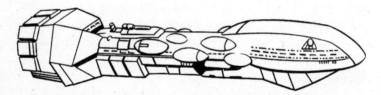 At one time, the Dreadnaught was the largest heavy star-cruiser class in service. Measuring 600 meters long, the Dreadnaught was first introduced before the start of the Clone Wars. By today's standards, this class of capital ship is slow, poorly shielded, and lightly armed. It requires massive crews, making little or no use of droid assistance. [ISB, HE, HESB, DFR, DFRSB]

driit

⚈ The monetary unit used on the planet Dellalt is the driit. [HLL]

droid

⚈ The automatons of the galaxy, droids are typically fashioned in the likenesses of their creators or in a utilitarian design that stresses function over appearance. Droids are equipped with artificial intelligence, though some are naturally created smarter than others depending on the function they are designed to serve. Many droids are programmed to understand Basic or the native language of their masters. Only those whose function is to regularly interact with organic beings are provided with a speech synthesizer. All others communicate via a program language that is unintelligible to most organic beings. (Some people who spend a lot of time working with or around droids do pick up the language—at least well enough to understand it.) Power is provided by rechargeable cells stored within a droid's body. Many organic cultures, including the Empire, treat droids as property and slaves, and many public areas are considered off-limits to droids.

There are five droid classifications, each assigned according to a particular droid's primary function. First-degree droids are skilled in physical, mathematical, and medical sciences. Second-degree droids are programmed in engineering and technical sciences. The social sciences and service areas (such as translation, spaceport control, diplomatic assistance, and tutoring) are the domain of third-degree droids. Fourth-degree droids are skilled in security and military applications. Menial labor and non-intelligence-intensive jobs (such as mining, salvage, transportation, and sanitation) are handled by fifth-degree droids. Most droids, regardless of their classification, have the capabilities of locomotion, logic, self-aware intelligence, communication, manipulation, and sensory reception. [SW]

droid harem

The droid harem was a huge castlelike structure on a plateau overlooking the Biitu farmlands. The Great Heep kept captured R2 units here, treating them to soothing oil baths and other droid luxuries before eventually consuming them. [TGH]

drone barge

A drone barge is a large space vessel used to ferry cargo or other supplies. Drone barges are controlled by droids or computers. They have no organic crews. [HSE]

Droopy McCool

Droopy McCool, a Kitonak, is a member of Max Rebo's Band. The chubby, comical musician plays a variety of wind instruments. [RJ]

drop shaft

See lift tube.

drop ship

🟦 Most massive capital warships cannot enter a planet's atmosphere, let alone make planetfall. To quickly transport troops or crew or cargo to a planet's surface, they employ fast-moving drop ships. Using powerful but short-burst drive units, drop ships plummet from orbit in barely controlled falls. When speed is not of the essence, shuttles and normal transports can be used. Drop ships mainly serve to deposit troops quickly into a battle zone. [DSTC, DFRSB]

Duinuogwuin

🟦 Duinuogwuins, or Star Dragons, are a sad, noble species with a habit of taking up lost causes. These huge, snakelike multipeds with gossamer wings average about ten meters long. Large, reptilian scales cover their bodies, though they have floppy, mammallike ears. Each body segment has a pair of legs, though the limbs attached to the forward segments have evolved into arms and hands. This ancient species comes from a secret, unknown world. They can be encountered on all types of worlds and even in deep space, where it seems they need no artificial protection. The Star Dragons have a deep-rooted sense of morality and honor, and most have at least some sensitivity to the Force. There are even tales that tell of an ancient time when Duinuogwuin served as Jedi Knights. [GG4, DFRSB]

dukha

🟦 In the clan-oriented culture of the Noghri, every clan has a village it calls home. At the center of each village is a dukha, around which all village life revolves. A dukha is a large, cylindrical building with a cone-shaped roof. The interior is a single open room featuring the clan high seat, used by the dynast (or clan leader) when he or she holds audiences. [DFR, DFRSB]

Dulok

The lanky, unkempt, bug-infested Duloks are distantly related to the Ewok species. In general, Duloks are nasty, bad-tempered, and untrustworthy. A large tribe of Duloks live in a village in the marsh lands of Endor's moon. The village is a cluster of rotted logs and swampy caves surrounding a stump-throne covered with the skins and skulls of small animals. [ETV]

Dune Sea, the

The Dune Sea stretches across the Tatooine wastes, a vast desert that once was a large inland sea. This inhospitable area suffers from extreme temperature variations and a lack of water. Ben Kenobi lived within the western portion of the area. [SW]

dungeon ship

A dungeon ship is a gigantic capital ship used to transport prisoners from one system to another via hyperspace. These massive vessels were originally designed during the Clone Wars to hold Jedi Knights. [DE]

Dunhausen

See Grand Moff Dunhausen.

Dunwell

See Captain Dunwell.

dura-armor

⚙ Heavy-grade dura-armor is made by compressing and binding together neutronium, lomite, and zersium molecules through the process of matrix acceleration. This industrial-strength armor is primarily used in military applications, as it has the ability to absorb and divert blaster energy. [HSE]

durasheet

⚙ While data pads are used for the majority of written documentation, the paperlike material called durasheet is sometimes employed. This material is reusable, as whatever is written upon it fades after a relatively short period of time. [HSR]

durasteel

⚙ Ultralightweight durasteel metal can withstand radical temperature extremes and severe stress from mechanical operations. Durasteel is used to build everything from aircraft and space vehicles to dwellings and simple machinery. [SW]

durkii

⊕ The durkii is a hideous, three-meter-tall creature with the face of a baboon and the body of a reptilian kangaroo. [DTV]

Duro

⊕ The planet Duro had a long and grand history—until the coming of the Empire. The world is now used as a dumping ground for toxic wastes produced by the Empire, and is the site of an Imperial Reprogramming Institute. Visitors to Duro rarely go down to the planet, as huge and well-stocked space stations abound. [MMY]

Duroon

⊕ Duroon is a planet within the Corporate Sector. The planet, which is capable of supporting life, has three moons. An active volcanolike fissure cuts across the planet's east-west axis. Hot springs, thermal vents, metal magma seepages, and radiation anomalies can be found over much of the planet's surface. Prior to his involvement with the Rebellion, Han Solo took on a job to deliver weapons to Duroon's disgruntled migrant workers, who were in the midst of revolting against their employer, the Corporate Sector Authority. [HSE]

Duros

⊕ The tall, thin species called Duros have large eyes, thin, slit mouths, and no noses. They come from the world of

Duro, and they have been traveling the space lanes for a very long time. This spacefaring race serves under an Imperial contract, hauling supplies and other cargo to Imperial installations. A group of Duros can be seen in the cantina during *Star Wars IV: A New Hope.* [GG4]

Dustangle

The alien archeologist named Dustangle has been in hiding in the underground caverns of Duro since the Empire subjugated the world. He is the cousin of Dustini. [MMY]

Dustini

The alien archeologist Dustini comes from the planet Duro. He decided to go on an off-world quest to appeal to the Alliance for help for his world. [MMY]

Dutch

Dutch was the lead pilot of a Y-wing starfighter squadron during the Battle of Yavin. According to the *Star Wars* novel, the squadron designation was Red Squadron. In the movie, it was called Gold Squadron. [SW]

Dyyz Nataz

The bounty hunter Dyyz Nataz, who often goes by the name of Megadeath, is a denizen of Nar Shaddaa. [DE]

E

E-wing starfighter

The E-wing is the newest starfighter serving in the New Republic fleet. A single pilot controls this craft and its advanced armament, and the new R7 series astromech droid provides able assistance. [DE]

elba beer

Elba beer is an ale brewed using elba grain on the planet Bonadan. [HSR]

Echo Base

Echo Base was the comm unit designation used by the secret Alliance command headquarters on the planet Hoth. [ESB]

Echo Station Three-Eight

Echo Station Three-Eight was one of the isolated Alliance outposts on the planet Hoth. Each sentry outpost used the comm unit designation "Echo Station" when transmitting and receiving communications from Echo Base. This particular outpost was destroyed by an Imperial probe droid as a prelude to the full-scale invasion that came to be known as the Battle of Hoth. [ESB]

Eclipse

⚫ The reborn Emperor ordered the construction of the *Eclipse*, a sixteen-kilometer-long Super Star Destroyer, to serve as his personal flagship. The huge, solid black vessel was designed to inspire dread and hopelessness in every opponent. [DE, DESB]

Egome Fass

⚫ Egome Fass is a member of the humanoid Houk species. Like all Houk, Fass has a square jaw and tiny, gleaming eyes set deep beneath his thick, bony brow. He worked for the outlaw twins J'uoch and R'all, and was known to rival the mighty Chewbacca the Wookiee in both height and strength. [HLL]

ejection seat

⚫ Small transport vehicles and most starfighters use ejection seats as a means of emergency escape. An ejection seat is jettisoned from a disabled ship, propelling the passenger away from dangers such as explosions or ship breakup. An ejection seat relies on the passenger using a full environment suit, and survival depends on a quick rescue. This escape system works best within a planet's atmosphere, where antigrav units can safely lower the seat to the ground. Most seats contain a twenty-four-hour oxygen recirculator and heating element that connects to a passenger's environment suit. [SWSB]

Elarles

⚙ Elarles was a waiter at a bar on Circarpous V. [SME]

electro-jabber

🌀 An electro-jabber is a high voltage prod used for crowd control. These devices are also called force pikes. [RJ]

electrobinoculars

🌀 The hand-held viewing devices called electrobinoculars allow users to observe distant objects in most light and dark conditions. The device's internal display provides the user with information regarding an object's range, relative and true azimuths, and elevation. With zoom capability, objects can be made to appear closer for detailed inspection or the depth of field can be widened for examination of the surrounding area. While electrobinoculars are sometimes called macrobinoculars, there is a substantial difference between the two viewing devices. Electrobinoculars process and enhance images through the use of sophisticated, built-in computers. Macrobinoculars do not offer these features. [SW, ESB]

electrorangefinder

🌀 An electrorangefinder calculates the distance between

the device and a target object. These devices are incorporated into electrobinoculars and macrobinoculars, and are essential components in the targeting and fire-control computers used by artillery and ship-mounted weapons systems. Electrorangefinders determine distances and calculate trajectories in an instant by projecting and receiving bursts of coherent light. [ESB]

electrotelescope

An electrotelescope is an electro-optical device that functions much like electrobinoculars, but has much greater power and resolution. [ESB]

Elom

The cold, barren world of Elom joined the Rebellion to combat the tyranny of the Empire and to free itself from enslavement. During the last years of the Galactic Civil War and well into the period of the New Republic, the Elomin people have tended to serve in units made up exclusively of their own species. The planet's principal export is the ore called lommite, and with it the Elomin are rebuilding their economy and stockpiling arms. Because of the world's location in the Borderland Regions, the Elomin fear reprisals from the reorganized Imperial forces. [HE, HESB]

Elomin

Tall, thin humanoids, the Elomin of the planet Elom have pointed ears and four hornlike protrusions emerging from the tops of their heads. They can also be recognized by their tusked noses, wide-set, protruding eyes, and the long hair behind their ears. With nothing more advanced than slug-throwers and combustion engines, the Elomin welcomed representatives from the Old Republic in years past. They accepted technological aid and soon joined the rest of the galaxy among the stars. Elomin admire order. They see other species as chaotic and unpredictable, and prefer to work with their own kind. During the height of the Empire, the Elomin and their world were placed under martial law. They were forced to labor for the Imperial effort, mining lommite for their Imperial masters. After the Battle of Endor, the Elomin took a place among the member worlds of the New Republic. [HE, HESB]

Emancipator

The Imperial Star Destroyer *Accuser* was one of two captured by the Alliance during the Battle of Endor. Lando Calrissian and Wedge Antilles commanded the renamed *Emancipator* during the Battle of Calamari. [DE, DESB]

emergency stud

X-wing starfighters come equipped with explosive bolts for jettisoning the pilot's canopy in an emergency situation. By depressing the emergency stud, the pilot blows the canopy away from the craft in order to make a quick exit. [SME]

Emperor, the (Palpatine)

The Emperor ruled the galaxy as the malevolent dictator of the Empire. As the man named Palpatine, he carved his Empire from the dying corpse of the Old Republic, using guile, fraud, astute political manipulations, and the dark side of the Force to forge his New Order.

As a senator in the Old Republic, Palpatine was an unassuming man serving at a time of widespread corruption and social injustice. The massive bureaucracy of the Republic had grown twisted and sickly over the span of generations. Like an immense tree with decaying roots, the Republic appeared strong but was slowly dying from within. To appease the member worlds who saw the galactic government as nothing more than a useless burden, the Senate offered up a promising young politician who seemed perfect for keeping the union together. Senator Palpatine appeared to lack drive and ambition, for he had remained apart from the political corruption that racked the Senate. Those who needed a stable government in place to continue their plundering believed they could use Palpatine as a figurehead, teaching him to smile obediently for the holo-

the Emperor

media. Those who genuinely wanted to save the Republic saw him as a compromise candidate who would serve as a puppet leader, following and implementing their plans to repair the system. Palpatine, however, had his own ideas.

Palpatine exceeded everyone's expectations after he was elected as head of the Senatorial Council and President of the Republic. He got the wheels of government turning again after long periods of inactivity. He stepped forward as a great leader who inspired trust and commitment. During the time of jubilation, promise, and hope that followed Palpatine's election, he slowly introduced the New Order and declared himself Emperor. The brief period of hope and light quickly turned dark as tyranny spread across the galaxy. The Empire was born.

The first real threat to the Emperor's rule appeared years later. Members of the Senate who had once tried to oppose him legally turned instead to rebellion and formed the Alliance to Restore the Republic. The Emperor was not concerned by this development; in fact, he welcomed it. A rebellion and the threat it represented gave him a motive to wipe away the last remnant of the Old Republic. He disbanded the Imperial Senate for the duration of the emergency and instituted the crowning policy of his New Order—rule by fear and force.

How the Emperor achieved his mastery of the dark side of the Force remains a mystery lost in the passage of time. Through his dark will, Darth Vader was created, the Jedi Knights were destroyed, the Old Republic was swept away, the Empire was forged, and the greatest military force ever assembled was unleashed upon the galaxy. He worked upon levels few could comprehend, forming plans within plans and manipulating his Empire the way a master gamesman manipulates the pieces on a holoboard. His grand schemes continued until a new player stepped to the table—Luke Skywalker.

From the moment that the Emperor learned of young Skywalker's existence, he knew he had to bring the young man into his fold. Like his father before him, Luke possessed nearly unlimited strength in the Force. The Emperor wanted that strength in his camp, under his tutelage. He wanted Luke turned to the dark side. In fact, the massive trap the Emperor set up in the Endor system was designed to finally achieve his desires concerning young Skywalker. That he also planned to destroy the Rebellion was a distant second. The Emperor craved power, and Luke Skywalker was a power for good that could not be allowed to remain free. Either Skywalker's power had to be turned to evil like his father's power before him, or he had to be destroyed. In the end, however, it was the Emperor who was destroyed. He died refusing to believe that good could actually find a way to triumph over evil. [SW, ESB, RJ]

🛈 Six years after his death over Endor's moon, the Emperor returned in a new clone body. This return led to the events depicted in the comic book series *Dark Empire*. In this account, the Emperor revealed that he had cloned himself many times before, discarding decaying, used-up bodies in favor of new, youthful clone bodies whenever the need arose. His second reign of terror ended due to the actions of Luke Skywalker and Princess Leia. [DE]

Emperor's Citadel, the

🛈 The Emperor's Citadel, located on the planet Byss, is a great black tower at the center of the throne city. After the Emperor was reborn into a new clone body six years after the Battle of Endor, he reigned from this hidden location. [DE]

Emperor's Hand

🌑 The Emperor's Hand was the codename used by Mara Jade when she served as one of the Emperor's elite operatives. Her job was to be the Emperor's eyes and ears throughout the galaxy, for she had enough control over the Force to communicate with him at great distances. She also carried out all of his orders, getting into and out of places to accomplish tasks other agents simply could not hope to realize. No one knows if there was more than one Emperor's Hand serving the Emperor, though Grand Admiral Thrawn's comments to Mara suggest that she was but one of several such operatives. [HE, DFR, LC]

Emperor's Inner Circle

🌑 The ministers and governors closest to the Emperor at the time of the Battle of Endor were collectively called the Emperor's Inner Circle. After the Emperor's death, this group unsuccessfully attempted to take control of the Empire. [DE]

Emperor's Throne Room

🌑 On the unfinished second Death Star, the Emperor oversaw the Battle of Endor from his specially constructed throne room. In addition to guard stations for the Imperial Royal Guard and huge viewports looking out into space, a massive throne dominated this area. [RJ]

🌑 Every *Imperial*-class or *Super*-class Star Destroyer, every Death Star battle station, and every other Imperial location that may be visited by the Emperor has a special throne room set aside for his specific and total use. From each throne room, the Emperor can take control of ship systems, monitor all activity, and contemplate the dark side of the Force and his own grand schemes. [DSTC]

Empire, the

🌀 Emperor Palpatine named his regime the Galactic Empire after he came to power. The regime was supposed to eradicate the corruption and social injustices of the previous government, but it soon became evident that the Emperor had no intention of returning the galaxy to a state of peace and justice. His government corrected the mistakes that made the Old Republic ineffective and unwieldy, but it also installed a program designed to subjugate as many planetary governments as possible for the personal glory and benefit of the Emperor. The Empire was a regime of tyranny and evil. Bolstered by a vast war machine and held together by the dark will of the Emperor, the Empire held sway over the galaxy for many years. Its iron hold was shattered by the Rebel Alliance at the Battle of Endor. [SW, ESB, RJ]

🌀 Since the Battle of Endor, the Empire has been reduced to a quarter of its size at the height of the Emperor's power. While it continues to rule a small portion of the galaxy and wages battles against the New Republic government, it is nothing more than a remnant, a pale shadow of its once darkly powerful self. In many ways, the Empire that exists five or more years after the Battle of Endor is much like the Rebel Alliance it once fought—disorganized, lacking in overbearing firepower, and engaged in a hit-and-run style of warfare. It showed some signs of its old glory under Grand Admiral Thrawn and the reborn Emperor, but the New Republic was able to win out against both of these threats. [HE, DFR, LC, DE]

Empress Teta

⊕ The star system called Empress Teta (or simply Teta) was named for the woman warlord who conquered it in the distant past. A prime source of carbonite exists in this system. According to the Jedi Holocron, terrible events occurred in this system approximately four thousand years ago. [DE]

Endor (Sanctuary Moon)

⊕ The Endor star system was selected as the construction site of the second Death Star battle station. The insignificant, out-of-the-way system had few planets and no major spaceports or travel routes, making it an ideal location for the secret Imperial project. It became famous later as the system in which the alliance finally won the Galactic Civil War by destroying the second Death Star, killing the Emperor, and scattering the remnants of the Imperial fleet. The system was named for its primary planet. Endor's moon is home to vast forests of giant trees, many predator species, and the tribal, tree-dwelling Ewoks. [RJ]

⊕ Three other planets orbit the system's ancient sun, but they are too far from its warm rays to support life. All three are rich in minerals and ores, and Imperial mining operations here once provided the materials necessary to build the second Death Star. By the time of the New Republic, only one mining operation remained active. It resides on the planet nearest Endor's moon, a large, dark orb designated Eloggi. A Sullustan company runs the operation under a charter granted by the New Republic. [DFRSB]

According to the Ewok animated television series,

Endor is a small moon that orbits around the planet Tana. A second, smaller moon also spins around Tana. Tana itself orbits a binary sun. [ETV]

energy battery

✪ Multiple turbolaser-gun and ion-cannon artillery emplacements set up in arrays, either on capital ships or protecting ground installations, are referred to as energy batteries. [SW]

energy call

✪ Portable power sources, energy cells (or power cells) come in a variety of sizes. Small energy cells fit in hand-held weapons such as blasters and lightsabers to provide the power needed to operate them. Larger cells fit in backpacks. On starships and capital ships, huge energy cells are linked in massive power cores. Energy cells are rechargeable. [SW]

energy gate

✪ An energy gate is a static, prepositioned force field operated from a distance and used to regulate the access routes of detention centers and other high-security areas. [SW]

Engret

✪ An associate of Rekkon and part of the group of infiltrators on Orron III, Engret, who was hardly more than a boy at the time, had a good heart and kindly temperament.

He and his companions sought the Authority Data Center on Orron III to learn the location of political prisoners being held by the Corporate Sector Authority. [HSE]

Ephant Mon

⬤ The alien Ephant Mon was an intelligent, bipedal pachydermoid who was a frequent associate of Jabba the Hutt. [RJ]

⬤ Ephant Mon was a Chevin, a rarely encountered pachydermoid species from the planet Vinsoth. He was not an official member of Jabba's organization, but he was the closest thing to a friend the crime lord admitted into his inner court. Ephant Mon was once a mercenary of some repute, but he turned to weapons-running after concluding that it was safer and more profitable to sell arms than to use them. He sold weapons to anyone, from pirates to outlaws to Rebels, though his most profitable ventures were with Jabba the Hutt. Unfortunately, he was aboard Jabba's sail barge when Luke Skywalker and his companions destroyed it during the rescue of Han Solo. [GG5]

Erpham Warrick

⬤ The legendary Ewok warrior Erpham Warrick built the great Ewok battle wagon. The Ewok hero named Wicket is his great-grandson. [ETV]

escape pod

⬤ An escape pod is a space capsule used by passengers and crew to abandon capital-class starships or small freighters in emergency situations. Escape pods range in size from small capsules barely large enough for two passengers to huge lifeboats capable of carrying many refugees. Some have limited ranges beyond simple planet drops, but few are as well-equipped or as powerful as true starships. Most escape pods feature stores of emergency supplies and have limited life-support, navigation, and propulsion units. These pods are not meant for long trips. The basic idea is to provide a safe and stable environment for a limited duration should the main ship have to be abandoned. With broadband distress beacons, pods are designed to float through space until a rescue vessel picks up the distress broadcast and arrives to provide aid. [SW]

escort carrier

To help fill the demand for TIE fighter combat support, the Empire developed the 500-meter-long escort carrier. The vessel augments the overall starfighter strength of whatever fleet it is attached to. It also provides a hyperspace platform for TIE fighters, giving the starfighters a method for quick travel via lightspeed. These boxlike, inelegant vessels carry entire TIE fighter wings in their cavernous bays. It is standard practice to have at least one squadron of TIE Interceptors in the mix. Additional smaller bays can carry up to six shuttles or other support craft. With only ten twin laser cannons, an escort carrier is not considered a combat vessel. It prefers to stay as far from the battle as possible, serving as a refueling and supply point for the TIEs it carries. [ISB]

escort frigate

The 300-meter-long Nebulon-B escort frigate class combat starship was originally built by the Kuat Drive Yards for the Empire. The Empire saw this vessel as the solution to its problems with Rebel raids on supply convoys. Standard equipment included twelve turbolaser batteries, twelve laser cannons, two tractor-beam projectors, two squadrons of TIE fighters in its bays, and powerful hyperdrives. The escort frigate proved a great deterrent to Rebel attacks. Fortunately, a significant number of these vessels either defected or were captured by the Rebellion and now serve in the Alliance fleet. The medical frigate seen at the end of *The Empire Strikes Back* is an escort frigate. [SWSB]

Espo

Espo is the slang term for the private security police employed by the Corporate Sector Authority. Espos are among the worst law-enforcement personnel in the galaxy. They follow no code of law or justice except for the Authority's edicts. They are the unquestioning bully-boys of the Authority, dressed in brown uniforms, combat armor, and black battle helmets, and armed with blaster rifles and riot guns. [HSE, HSR]

Etti IV

The hospitable planet Etti IV, on a major stellar trade route within Corporate Sector space, is home to many of the more affluent and influential Authority executives. The planet has no exportable resources, so it relies on its natural beauty and prime location to attract visitors and traders. [HSE]

EV-9D9 (Eve-Ninedenine)

The droid EV-9D9 was one of many droids in thrall to Jabba the Hutt. Ninedenine, with her female voice and gleefully sadistic attitude, was ideally suited to the job she held in Jabba's desert palace. The thin supervisor droid was in charge of cyborg operations, overseeing all of the droids in Jabba's crowded stables. [RJ]

baby Ewoks

Ewok

The curious, furred bipeds native to Endor's forest moon are called Ewoks. Standing about one meter tall, the tribal Ewoks have yet to advance beyond spears and bows, but their understanding of forest lore and survival skills cannot be matched by more-advanced species. These hunter-gatherers live in village clusters built high within the moon's giant trees. Easily startled, the Ewoks are nonetheless brave, alert, and loyal, and they can be fierce warriors when necessary. Dismissed as inconsequential by the Empire during the construction of the second Death Star, the Ewoks were one of the deciding factors in the Battle of

Endor. One tribe befriended Leia Organa and her companions in the Rebel strike force. With the help this tribe provided, the strike force was able to complete its mission to disable the shield generator protecting the Death Star. This allowed the Alliance fleet to engage the battle station directly and win the space battle that raged around the forest moon. [RJ]

🔰 The Ewok language is liquid and expressive, and most humans and other aliens can learn to speak it. Ewoks, conversely, can learn Basic, though they often mix in many words from their own language. During the day, Ewoks come down out of their tree villages to hunt and forage on the forest floor. At night, the forest belongs to huge carnivores, and even the youngest Ewoks know not to venture out after dark. The Ewok religion is centered around the giant trees of the forest moon. Legends refer to the trees as guardian spirits and even the parents of the people, which is why the Ewoks believe that the great trees are mighty, intelligent, long-lived beings. The Ewoks' mystical beliefs contain many references to the Force, though it is never named as such. They are a musical species, are overly curious, and are loyal to their tribes and friends. [SWSB]

Executor

🔰 *Executor* was Lord Darth Vader's personal flagship. The *Super*-class Star Destroyer was the first of a new type of ship. It was approximately five times larger than the *Imperial*-class Star Destroyer, measuring 8,000 meters from bow to stern. It was presented to the Dark Lord shortly after the Battle of Yavin and remained in service until its destruction at the Battle of Endor. [ESB, RJ]

⦿ The *Executor* was constructed shortly after the destruction of the first Death Star, at the starship yards on the world of Fondor. [GW]

Exozone

⦿ The insectoid bounty hunter Exozone often works with Boba Fett and Dengar. He recently helped the pair chase Han Solo and Princess Leia through the streets of Nar Shaddaa. [DE]

Expansion Region

⦿ The Expansion Region, once a center of manufacturing and heavy industry, started as an experiment in corporate-controlled space. When the residents demanded more freedom and change, the Old Republic turned control over to freely elected governments and sent the corporations elsewhere. (Years later, the Empire allowed for the creation of a Corporate Sector.) As much of the area's natural resources have been greatly diminished, the Expansion Region seeks to pull itself out of an economic slump by maintaining trade routes and portraying itself as an alternative to the crowded and expensive Core Worlds and Colonies regions. [SWRPG2]

F

Fadoop

🙂 Fadoop is the pilot and owner of the ship *Skybarge*. The green-furred, bandy-legged female is a Saheelindeeli, one of the intelligent primate species of the Tion Hegemony. She has an intense liking for chak-root, and once ran parts for Han Solo and Chewbacca during their adventures in and around Corporate Sector space. [HLL]

Fandar

🙂 The brilliant scientist Fandar, a member of the Chandra-Fan species, was the leader of Project Decoy. His goal was to create a lifelike human replica droid for the Alliance. The prototype his team developed was modeled to resemble Princess Leia. [QE]

feathers of light

🙂 Feathers of light are silver feathers awarded to young

Ewoks who complete the journey to the Tree of Light to feed it nourishing light dust. [ETV]

Festival of Hoods

🌑 The Festival of Hoods celebrates the coming of age of young Ewoks. When a young Ewok receives his or her hood, it is a symbol that the young one has made the transition from Wokling to pre-adolescent. [ETV]

Fidge

🌑 The ten-year-old Biituian named Fidge met R2-D2 and C-3PO during the droids' adventures in the early days of the Empire. Fidge had a pet reptile named Chubb, and he often traveled through the burrows Chubb liked to dig. [TGH]

Fifth Moon of Da Soocha

🌑 The Fifth Moon of Da Soocha was the location of the secret New Republic Command Center designated as Pinnacle Base. The intelligent species called Ixlls are native to Da Soocha Five. [DE]

Figrin D'an

🌑 The Bith musician named Figrin D'an leads the cantina band on Mos Eisley. [GG1]

Final Jump, the

🔰 The Final Jump is spacer slang for death. [HSR]

Fiolla of Lorrd

🔰 Fiolla, whose full name is Hart-and-Parn Gorra-Fiolla of Lorrd, hails from the planet and city of Lorrd. She was an aspiring Assistant Auditor General for the Corporate Sector Authority. During an undercover assignment to expose top Authority executives and Espo officials who were involved with an illegal slavery ring, Fiolla found herself unexpectedly teamed with Han Solo. Fiolla anticipated becoming a Senior Board Member if she remained with the Authority. [HSR]

firefolk

See Wistie.

Fire Rings of Fornax

🔰 The Fire Rings of Fornax are one of the unique wonders of the galaxy. The planet Fornax appears to be encircled by five rings of intense fire, which are really the solar prominences attracted to the planet due to its close proximity to its sun. [SW]

Fixer

🔰 Fixer was one of Luke Skywalker's companions on

162

Tatooine. The young man was an overbearing mechanic employed at the Tosche power station in Anchorhead. He was also the boyfriend of the young woman named Camie. [SW]

flameout

One of the more potent intoxicating beverages served around the galaxy is a drink called flameout. When prepared correctly, the drink has the unique properties of burning the tongue while freezing the throat. [HSR]

flechette cannister

Flechette cannister weapons hold clusters of tiny darts. The cannister is fired from a shoulder-mounted launcher. When the cannister hits its target it explodes, releasing its cloud of deadly darts. [HSR]

flechette missile

A flechette missile is a dart-shaped projectile about 110 millimeters in length. These missiles come in two power levels for use against different types of targets: antipersonnel and armor-piercing antivehicle varieties. [HSE, HLL]

flitter

Flitter is a common name for any type of one- or two-person airspeeder. [HSE]

floater

See landspeeder.

floating cities of Calamari

⊕ The floating cities of Calamari are huge, anchored metropolises that rest atop the oceans of the water planet and extend deep below the waves. These cities are home to the amphibious Mon Calamari and the Quarren. [SWSB, DE]

floating fortress

⊕ The Imperial floating fortress is a repulsorlift combat vehicle designed to augment ground assault and planetary occupation forces. The roughly cylindrical floating fortress is especially suitable for urban terrains, with its distinctive twin-turret heavy blaster cannon, well-armored body, and powerful repulsorlift engines. It is equipped with a sophisticated surveillance system that projects a thirty-meter-radius sensor probe around the vehicle, forming a target identification field. This field can be used to single out a specific target or to lock onto a large number of targets for elimination by the two top-mounted heavy blasters. A floating fortress requires a pilot, two gunners, and a sensor chief. It can also carry up to ten troopers. [ISB]

Fondor

⊕ After the destruction of the first Death Star, Darth Vader began work on his personal flagship, *Executor*, at the starship yards on the world of Fondor. [GW]

Force, the

🔴 The Force is an energy field generated by all living things. It surrounds and penetrates everything, binding the galaxy together. Like any energy field, the Force can be manipulated. Knowledge of these manipulation techniques gives the Jedi Knights their powers. There are two sides to the Force: the peace, knowledge, and serenity of the light side, and the anger, fear, and aggression of the dark side. Both sides of the Force are a part of the natural order, life-affirming and destructive. Through the Force, a Jedi Knight can see far-off places, perform amazing feats, and accomplish what would otherwise be impossible. [SW, ESB, RJ]

⚫ There are three known Force skills: control, sense, and alter. Only Force-sensitive beings can master Jedi skills and the techniques they control. The control skill is the ability of a Jedi to control his or her own inner Force. With this skill the Jedi learns to master the functions of his or her own body. The sense skill helps a Jedi sense the Force in things beyond and outside of themselves. A Jedi learns to feel the bonds that connect all things. The alter skill allows a Jedi to change the distribution and nature of the Force to create illusions, move objects, and change the perceptions of others. [SWRPG, SWRPG2]

Force lightning

⚫ The Force ability demonstrated by the Emperor aboard the second Death Star and directed against Luke Skywalker is called Force lightning. This corruption of the Force produces white or blue bolts of energy which fly from the user's fingertips toward a target. Force lightning flows into a target, causing great pain as it siphons off the living energy and eventually kills its victim. Jedi Knights would never employ this corrupted ability, but those who follow the dark side have no such reservations. Joruus C'baoth used Force lightning many times after he was recruited by Grand Admiral Thrawn. [HE, DFR, LC, HESB]

force pike

⚫ Force pikes are pole arms tipped with vibro-edged heads that can kill or stun with a single touch. Setting controls and power generators are located within the pike's grip. These weapons were particular favorites of the Emperor's Royal Guard. [HSE, SWSB]

Force sensitive

⚫ A Force-sensitive individual is more keenly attuned to the Force than most people, able to sense its presence and the presence of other Force sensitives. These individuals also run a greater risk of being drawn to the dark side because of their sensitivity. [SME, SWRPG2]

Force storm

⚫ A Force storm is a tornado of energy created by great disturbances in the Force. Dark Side Adepts have demonstrated limited control over the creation of these storms, while the reborn Emperor claims to be able to create and control Force storms at will. [DE]

Fortress of Tawntoom

🌀 The Fortress of Tawntoom was a city built into the interior walls of a volcanic crater in the Tawntoom colony of Roon. The Fortress was powered by the seething lava pit far below, and it served as the base of operations for Governor Koong. [DTV]

forward gun pod

🔴 A forward gun pod is a concealed blaster emplacement installed in the front section of certain starfighter and transport models. The forward gun pod on the *Millennium Falcon*, for example, extends from a hidden compartment in the ship's lower hull. Automatic cover plates slide open and shut on commands from the *Falcon*'s cockpit or automatically when the ship's anti-intruder system is triggered. The antipersonnel blaster is aimed and fired from the pilot's station. [ESBR]

forward tech station

🌀 The *Millennium Falcon*'s forward tech station serves as the transport's secondary command and control station. Located in the forward portion of the cargo hold, in the ship's passenger area, the station features consoles that monitor all ship systems. Data-bank hookups and droid ports provide accesses to the *Falcon*'s system and diagnostic computers. The ship's flight path can be monitored from this location while in automatic pilot mode, and can be controlled in emergency situations. [HSR]

4-LOM

The rogue droid 4-LOM, with its humanoid body and insectoid head, was among the bounty hunters contracted by Darth Vader to locate the *Millennium Falcon* after it escaped the Imperial assault on Hoth. [ESB]

Free-Flight Dance Dome, the

Travelers looking for a first-class nightclub on the planet Etti IV often visit the Free-Flight Dance Dome. The club is known for its variable-gravity-field dance floor, which accommodates not only adventurous fun-seekers, but also alien clients who need gravity alterations for maximum comfort. [HSR]

Freedom's Sons

During the Clone Wars, the group of insurgent patriots known as Freedom's Sons battled against tyrannical occupation forces which threatened the Republic. These freedom fighters from the conquered star systems helped the Jedi Knights reestablish law and order at the end of this war-torn period. [HSE]

Freerunner

The Freerunner is a particular model of armored repulsorlift speeder that falls under the category of combat assault vehicles (CAVs). Primarily used by the Alliance and private mercenary bands, the Freerunners get their name from the free-rotating gun platforms mounted atop them. With two anti-vehicle laser cannons and two anti-infantry blaster batteries, these speeders pack a terrific offensive punch. [RSB, DFR, DFRSB]

freeze-floating control

ⓤ The freeze-floating control, aboard atmosphere and space craft, is a computer-augmented system that works to counteract the effects of atmospheric turbulence in order to create a smoother flight. [SW]

freight droid

ⓒ Freight droids specialize in the retrieval and loading of cargo. Common droids of this class stand over 2.5 meters tall and are equipped with four extendable manipulators, crawler treads for locomotion, small lifting claws, and a gravity-shifting frame for dealing with unbalanced loads. [HLL]

Frija

ⓒ Frija was a humanoid-looking mechanical who rescued Luke Skywalker and C-3PO when they crash-landed on Hoth. She and her father were created by Imperial technicians to be used to decoy Rebels and allow time for the human Frija and her father, who was an Imperial Governor, to escape a Rebel attack. Unfortunately, the technicians programmed strong survival instincts into the mechanicals, and when the fighting began, they escaped and isolated themselves on Hoth. [GW]

fuel-ore processing plant

⊛ On the planet Biitu, the fuel-ore processing plant is a gigantic space factory/processing facility used by the Great Heep to mine fuel ore. The plant consists of a maze of pipes, conveyor belts, giant gears, cranes, furnaces, and other machinery. A moisture eater, a huge funnellike device that sucks in nearby clouds and moisture to create a tornadolike vortex, sits atop the plant. [TGH]

Fugo

⊛ Fugo, a member of the Chadra-Fan species, was a colleague of the brilliant scientist named Fandar. After Fandar suffered grievous injuries, Fugo carried on the work of the Alliance's Project Decoy. [QE]

fungus of the Rokna tree

⊛ The deadly blue fungus of the Rokna tree is prevalent in the forests of Endor's moon. The sharp points protruding from the fungus cause memory loss, rapid aging, and eventually death in those who come in contact with them. [ETV]

fusion furnace

⊛ The fusion furnace power-generating device produces heat and light, and serves as the power source for recharging the energy cells of vehicles, droids, and weapons. These furnaces range in size from huge spaceport models for powering capital ships to small, portable models for recharging energy cells on the move. [ESB]

fusioncutter

Fusioncutters are industrial tools that produce wide-dispersion laser beams. These tools are used in construction, mining, and metal work. A hand-held version can be found among the tools all starships and field workers carry. [SW]

Fuzzum

Members of the Fuzzum species look like balls of fuzz with long, thin legs. They use nothing more technologically advanced than their ever-present spears. [DTV]

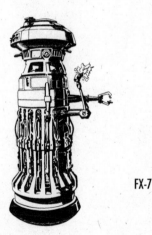

FX-7

FX-7

The sturdy FX-7 medical assistant droid aids both droid and organic surgeons with sophisticated appendages and specialized medical diagnostic and procedural programming. Considered antiquated by current standards, this droid model can mostly be found far from the galaxy's Core Worlds and in service to the Rebel Alliance. [ESB]

G

gaderffii

The traditional weapon of Tatooine's Sand People (or Tusken Raiders) is the double-edged gaderffii, or gaffi stick. This deadly, axelike weapon is fashioned from metal scavenged from wrecked or abandoned vehicles and spaceships that wind up in the Tatooine wastes. [SW]

Gaff

Gaff was the aide-de-camp of Governor Koong during the early days of the Empire. Gaff was a Kobok, a green, fuzzy insectoid with deadly stingers on his forearms and three eyes. One of these eyes was located in the back of his head. [DTV]

Galactic Civil War, the

The Rebellion started at the instant the Empire replaced the Old Republic and tyranny gripped the galaxy. Years later, the scattered Rebels were organized into the Alliance to Restore the Republic, and the galaxy shuddered on the edge of civil war. The exact moment when the Galactic Civil War began cannot be pinpointed with certainty, but by the time of the Battle of Yavin it was in full swing. Star system after star system slipped through the Empire's clenched fist to join the Alliance, and civil war rocked the galaxy from the settlements of the Outer Rim Territories to the majestic spires of Imperial City. The Battle of Endor marked the end of the civil war as the Alliance destroyed the second Death Star and routed the Imperial fleet. [SW, ESB, RJ]

⚙ The war was slow in grinding to a halt, though, as the remnants of the Empire continued to struggle with the emerging New Republic. While the civil war may have ended, more than five years after Endor the conflict continues, with the Empire still trying to destroy the New Republic. [HE, DFR, LC, DE]

Galactic Constitution

⚙ The Galactic Constitution is the ancient foundation document of the democratic Old Republic. [DE]

Galactic Core

⚙ The bulging central region of the galaxy is called the Galactic Core. The term is also used in reference to the heavily inhabited region surrounding the Deep Galactic Core. This region was the original location of the ruling Republic, and later, the ruling Imperial star systems. From the Core systems, the first galactic government spread outward like the spokes of a wheel. [SWSB, HESB, SWRPG2, DE]

Gallandro

⊕ In Corporate Sector space and the systems surrounding it, there was once an amoral blaster-for-hire named Gallandro. Those who knew of him feared him, for he was lightning-fast and deathly accurate. In his last years, he was one of the most trusted operatives working for the Corporate Sector Authority. His orders came directly from the regional administrator, Odumin. Tall and lean, Gallandro always wore expensive, impeccable clothing. He had graying, close-cropped hair and a long mustache decorated with golden beads. His blaster holster was slung low, and his white scarf hung like a badge of office.

Han Solo crossed the gunman's path twice in those years prior to his involvement in the Rebellion. The first time, Solo won out by evening the odds. He tricked Gallandro into grabbing hold of a rigged security case that sent a bolt of paralyzing energy through both men's right arms. Faced with drawing against the ambidextrous Solo with his off hand, Gallandro opted for surrender. The second time, the two faced each other in the lost vaults of Xim the Despot with no tricks or incredible displays of luck between them. Instead, it was just skill against skill. The older Gallandro's speed-draw was a blur of ruthless economy that moved his right arm and hand and nothing else. Solo's mechanics incorporated shoulder and knee movements with a slight dip and partial twist. To Solo's credit, he came closer to beating Gallandro in a fair fight than anyone else in a long time. But Gallandro's blaster bolts struck Solo's shoulder and forearm before Solo's own blaster could finish its ascent. The antiweapon defenses of Xim's treasure vaults zeroed in on the gunman, however, and a dozen lethal blasts reduced him to a blackened corpse. [HLL, HSR]

gameboard

Any holographic projection table used primarily for amusement purposes is called a gameboard. On the gameboard's surface, three-dimensional holograms compete at the directions of the players. Players control the holograms by tapping commands into one of four or more attached keypads. The *Millennium Falcon* has a gameboard installed for the recreational use of its crew. [SW]

Gamorrean

Gamorreans are a brutish, porcine species known for their great strength and violent tendencies. Green skinned, with piglike snouts, small horns, and tusks, Gamorreans stand approximately 1.8 meters tall. Their size and temperament make them excellent heavy laborers and mercenaries.

Gamorrean guard

A number of Gamorreans served as guards in Jabba the Hutt's desert palace. [RJ]

While Gamorreans can understand most alien tongues, their own vocal apparatus makes it impossible to produce the sounds necessary to converse in other languages. They are native to the pleasant world of Gamorr, which has a wide variety of temperatures and terrains. Gamorreans love to hack and slash, and their world's history is marked by almost constant war. In Gamorrean culture, females handle all of the productive work. They farm, hunt, manufacture items, and run businesses while the males spend all their time training for and fighting wars.

Gamorreans live in clans that are headed by matrons. The matrons order the males to battle at the beginning of the campaign season. Wielding primitive melee weapons with expert savagery, the males fight from early spring to late fall. While they have adapted to technological weapons, they do not use blaster and power arms in their planet-bound campaigns. Technological weapons are saved for off-planet use.

When Gamorr was discovered by traders (who lost seven trading vessels before they sent a heavily armed ship to "finish" negotiations), its people were turned into slaves. In addition to serving as slaves, some Gamorreans have managed to sell their contracts on the open market, finding employment as guards, mercenaries, professional soldiers, and even bounty hunters. Unfortunately, Gamorreans do not consider a deal binding unless it is sealed in blood. They do not believe in working for anyone who cannot best them in hand-to-hand combat. [SWSB]

Gamorr

The home planet of the Gamorrean species. [SWSB]

Gamor Run, the

The Gamor Run is a legendary long-haul smuggling route plagued by hijackers and pirates. [DE]

Gank Killers

Gank Killers are members of the alien species considered the bodyguards of choice by many Hutt crime lords. They can be seen in the presence of Hutts on the streets of Nar Shaddaa, as well as in other places frequented by the sluglike Hutt species. [DE]

Gargan

Gargan was the six-breasted dancing girl in Jabba the Hutt's court. [RJ]

Gargon

The planet Gargon was the site of one of Han Solo's more memorable exploits. Han and his Wookiee partner Chewbacca received double payment to go to the planet, break into some huge, well-guarded vaults, avoid the notorious gangster who owned the facilities, steal the hoard of spice stored there, and return to their employer with the precious cargo. [RJ]

Garindan

The long-snooted alien who followed Luke Skywalker

and Ben Kenobi around Mos Eisley was Garindan, a Kubaz spy who works for the highest bidders—including the Empire and Jabba the Hutt. [GG1]

Garm Bel Iblis

Garm Bel Iblis, a Senator from the Corellian system, helped start the Rebellion when the threats of the Empire originally surfaced. When the Alliance emerged to fight the Empire, Bel Iblis went into hiding and began his own private war against the New Order. Bel Iblis and Mon Mothma never got along. He had worked with her and Bail Organa in the Rebellion's formative years. It was Bel Iblis who convinced three of the biggest resistance groups to join forces and form the Alliance. The results of that meeting became known as the Corellian Treaty, but what should have been Bel Iblis's finest hour turned out to be Mon

Garm Bel Iblis

Mothma's. For she had the gift of inspiration, and she became the true symbol of the Alliance. When Bail Organa died with Alderaan, Bel Iblis left to form his own private army. He feared that Mon Mothma was only seeking to overthrow the Emperor in order to set herself up in his place. He waited for that to happen, but it never did. In the intervening years, his pride kept him away. Bel Iblis hoped to build a fleet and return with dignity and respect, but the best he could create was a strike force. Still, after Bel Iblis and his strike force provided some badly needed assistance to Han Solo at the hidden location of the *Katana* fleet, Princess Leia officially invited them to join the New Republic. Now Bel Iblis uses his military strategies and tactics to help direct the New Republic fleet. [DFR, DFRSB, LC]

Gee Long

Gee Long was one of the members of Auren Yomm's famous racing team which competed in the Roon Colonial Games. [DTV]

General Covell

The young Imperial officer named General Covell was placed in charge of the Empire's ground troops with the return of Grand Admiral Thrawn. Thrawn wanted his soldiers ready for the inevitable subjugation of planets which would come under his plan for the galaxy, and Covell was ordered to train his young and inexperienced troops for such battles. He was among the most experienced of the remaining Imperial officers when Grand Admiral Thrawn took command of the remnants. He had learned from the legendary General Veers, who saw Covell as a younger version of himself. In fact, Covell served as Veers's first officer during the Battle of Hoth. Captain Pellaeon promoted him to major general in charge of *Chimaera*'s ground troops after the Battle of Endor. Thrawn gave him the rank of general when he returned, and he immediately began training his troops for real battle. Raids on places like the planet Myrkr were good training exercises for his troops, but Covell yearned to take back the Core Worlds, such as Coruscant, from the New Republic. He never got to fulfill his dreams, for he died on the planet Wayland after Joruus C'baoth destroyed his mind. [DFR, LC, DFRSB]

General Dodonna

✦ General Jan Dodonna was the Alliance officer who planned and coordinated the assault on the first Death Star at the Battle of Yavin. [SW]

✦ General Dodonna was presumed to have died on Yavin Four. Since his health was failing, he decided to remain behind after the Rebel fleet left. He then set off concussion charges in the main buildings, stopping a wave of Imperial bombers attacking the base and giving the Alliance more time to evacuate. Dodonna reappeared during the events of the Battle of Calimari as an elder statesman of the New Republic. [GW, DESB]

General Madine

✦ General Crix Madine of the Alliance, a young Corellian with strict military discipline, was one of Mon Mothma's most important military advisers during the Galactic Civil War. His most notable efforts were expended during the period leading up to the Battle of Endor. A covert operations specialist, Madine planned and executed the procurement of an Imperial shuttle. Then he trained and assembled the strike team that accompanied Han Solo to Endor's moon to destroy the shield generators protecting the new Death Star. [RJ]

⚙ Crix Madine joined the Alliance shortly after the Battle of Yavin. He was an honored and decorated Imperial officer before defecting to the Alliance, serving as commander of an elite commando unit. Rumors persist that his last Imperial assignment was so criminal in nature that Madine refused to complete it—even though the orders came from the Emperor himself. When Madine came to the Alliance, others who had defected before him vouched for his integrity and commitment. Mon Mothma accepted him into the ranks, and he quickly proved himself one of her top military advisers. While Admiral Ackbar developed space combat tactics, Madine was charged with developing the Alliance's ground tactics. In the New Republic, Madine still commands a top military position, though he refused a seat on the Provisional Council. "I'm a warrior, not a politician," was the answer he gave Mon Mothma when she offered him a Council seat. [GG5, DFR, DFRSB]

General Rieekan

⚙ General Rieekan was the Alliance officer charged with the command of all Rebel ground and fleet forces in the Hoth star system. [ESB]

General Tagge

⚙ General Tagge was one of the senior Imperial officers serving under Grand Moff Tarkin on the original Death Star battle station. [SW]

General Veers

General Veers commanded the Imperial ground troops assigned to Lord Darth Vader's special armada. When the armada tracked the Rebels to Hoth, Vader commanded Veers to personally supervise the invasion force. This force consisted of AT-AT walkers and waves of Imperial snowtroopers. [ESB]

Ghent

The young man named Ghent serves as the chief slicer for Talon Karrde's smuggling operation. Besides maintaining computer and droid programming, Ghent can break most encrypt codes and computer-security measures with relative ease. He is barely out of his teens, and his great wealth of knowledge and bright-eyed optimism create a wall around him that allows very little through; only computers and the programs that run them can keep his attention for long. It was Ghent who helped the New Republic break a number of Imperial encrypt codes, including the ones that led to false accusations against Ackbar and that were transmitting intelligence information out of Coruscant for the spy called Delta Source. [HE, DFR, LC, HESB, DFRSB]

Gillespee

The slightly-less-than-honorable Samuel Thomas Gillespee is an old friend of Talon Karrde. He retired from the smuggling trade to set up house on the planet Ukio. When Grand Admiral Thrawn took control of that world, Gillespee left in search of a smuggling operation willing to employ him and his men. He signed on with Talon Karrde to indirectly (and for a profit) help the New Republic against the Empire. He often travels the space lanes in the ship *Kern's Pride*. [LC]

gimer stick

A gimer stick is an edible twig from plants that grow throughout the swamps of Dagobah. The gimer plant produces a succulent juice that gathers in sacs on the bark. The sticks can be chewed for their flavor and to quench thirst. Yoda, the Jedi Master, was fond of chewing gimer sticks. [ESB]

Givin

The Givin species look much like animated skeletons. Unlike most vertebrates, they carry their skeletons on the exterior of their bodies. Large, triangular eye sockets dominate their skull-like faces, giving them a perpetual expression of sadness. The Givin come from the planet Yag'Dhul, where they deal in precise thoughts and measurements. They are expert mathematicians who see those species with more subjective outlooks as lazy and slovenly. Most have a phobia concerning exposed flesh, often going to great lengths to avoid the sight of it in other species. A Givin makes a brief appearance during the cantina scene of *Star Wars IV: A New Hope*. [GG4]

gladiator droid

During the most decadent and lawless periods of the Old Republic, many droid models with less-than-beneficial primary programming were put into service. Gladiator droids, for example, were designed for close-quarters combat and used in violent sporting events involving other droids or even living beings and creatures. [HSE]

glow rod

🌀 The general term "glow rod" refers to any device designed to provide a portable light source. Most are long, thin tubes that cast brilliant spheres of light through chemical phosphorescents. These rods are controlled by an activation-intensity switch. Other glow rods are power cells attached to lamp bulbs. Glow rods can be carried, clamped to clothing or equipment, or placed on a stable surface. [HLL, SWSB, HESB]

Golden Sun

🌀 Golden Sun is a living, communal intelligence made up of thousands of tiny polyps that inhabit the coral reefs of the planet Sedri. These coral dwellers have an affinity for the Force, though they refer to it as "the universal energy." Through the Force and the connection of thousands of minds, the Golden Sun produces a nearly limitless supply of energy. This energy is so intense that it effects the gravity readings of the planet, registering it as a small sun and causing hyperdrive safety cutoffs to activate. The native Sedrians of the planet worship the Golden Sun, and their Force-sensitive high priests actually hear the voices of the communal polyps as dreams and visions. Force users can detect thousands of minds in the Golden Sun, all connected in maddening, joyous communion. [BGS, GG4]

Gold Five

See Red Five.

Gold Leader

✪ Gold Leader was the comm unit designation for Lando Calrissian and the *Millennium Falcon* (which served as Lando's combat craft) during the Battle of Endor. It was Lando's responsibility to lead the Alliance starfighters against the second Death Star. The designation came from military parlance, where Gold Leader refers to the officer who serves as master of ceremonies for important events. For the Alliance, there was no more important event than the assault on the uncompleted battle station.

Lando's accurate assessments, clear perceptions, and quick decision-making in the midst of battle helped defeat the Imperial fleet and bring about the end of the Galactic Civil War. Gold Leader and Red Leader (Wedge Antilles) were personally responsible for destroying the Death Star's power core which, in turn, destroyed the entire battle station. [RJ]

Gold Two

See Red Two.

Gold Wing

✪ Gold Wing was the Alliance starfighter battle group under the command of Gold Leader during the Battle of Endor. [RJ]

Goldenrod

✪ Han Solo often referred to C-3PO by the nickname "Goldenrod." [RJ]

Gorax

✪ The huge giant called Gorax lived in an underground cavern on Endor's forest moon. The giant was covered with thick, matted fur, had pointy ears, and a jutting lower jaw filled with nasty teeth. Gorax was killed during the rescue of Jeremitt and Catarine Towani. The pair was captured by the giant, and their children, Mace and Chindel, along with a few Ewok friends, braved Gorax's lair to free them. [EA]

Gorm the Dissolver

✪ The ugly, armored bounty hunter known as Gorm the Dissolver resides in Nar Shaddaa, the vertical city. [DE]

Gornash

See Prophet Gornash.

Gorneesh

✪ King Gorneesh is the sly, foul-tempered leader of the Duloks, who inhabit the swamps of Endor's moon. [ETV]

Gotal

⊙ A Gotal is any member of the intelligent, technologically advanced, bipedal species from the moon called Antar Four. They have two cone-shaped growths rising from their heads, flat noses, protruding brows, and shaggy gray fur. The head cones serve as additional sensory organs, able to pick up and distinguish different forms of energy waves. Most other species feel uncomfortable around Gotals because of their additional senses. For their part, Gotals do not like droids due to the high-energy output they give off, which tends to overload the Gotals' senses. They have a hard time interpreting the emotions of other alien species, often mistaking affection for love and anger for hatred. They make excellent scouts, bounty hunters, trackers, and mercenaries, though they tend to try to remain neutral in the galactic conflict. [GG4, DFRSB]

Governor Bin Essada

See Bin Essada.

Governor Tarkin

See Grand Moff Tarkin.

Grammel

See Captain-Supervisor Grammel.

Grand Admiral Thrawn

Grand Admiral Thrawn

During the height of the Empire, twelve Grand Admirals served as the Emperor's military commanders. Five years after the Battle of Endor, at a time when the New Republic thought that all of these leaders had been destroyed, one returned to command the remnants of the Empire: Grand Admiral Thrawn. Thrawn was a tall man of regal bearing, whose features hinted at a non-human origin. He had shimmering blue-black hair, pale blue skin, and glowing red eyes. He spent much of his career in the Unknown Regions, earning the right to wear the white uniform of a Grand Admiral. Like the other Grand Admirals, Thrawn was a military genius. He had a habit of pulling stunning victories out of certain defeat. His passion for art was not simple diversion, for he believed that by studying an opponent's art he could discover a way to defeat him. As the only non-human to receive the rank of Grand Admiral, which in itself was a remarkable feat considering the Emperor's dislike of alien species, Thrawn constantly had to prove his worth and ability to lesser officers when he was first promoted. This changed after a short period of time, for Thrawn proved again and again that he was the equal or better of every other officer in the New Order.

He returned from an extended mission in the Unknown Regions to discover that the Emperor was dead and the Imperial fleet was in ruins. He rallied the remnants of the Empire and set in motion a plan to destroy the New Republic (which he refused to call anything other than the Rebellion) that included the use of Force-inhibiting ysalamiri, a Dark Jedi Master, and two items from the Emperor's hidden storehouse in Mount Tantiss: a working cloaking device and a set of Spaarti cloning cylinders. Through the use of hit-and-run attacks, political schemes, spies, and superior planning, Thrawn almost destroyed the New Republic. But the Republic held fast, its heroes rallied, and Thrawn's personal bodyguard Rukh betrayed him, ending the Grand Admiral's threat to the New Republic forever. [HE, DFR, LC, HESB, DFRSB]

Grand Moff Dunhausen

🌑 Grand Moff Dunhausen is lean and crafty. He always wears his trademark laser-pistol-shaped earrings. [GDV]

Grand Moff Hissa

🌑 Grand Moff Hissa obviously has a bit of alien blood running through his veins, as he has slightly pointed ears and spear-pointed teeth. Of all the Grand Moffs still active after the Battle of Endor, Hissa is the one Trioculus trusts the most. He was eventually given command of the Empire's Central Committee of Grand Moffs. Due to a mishap with toxic waste on the planet Duro, Hissa lost his arms and legs. He gets around in a repulsorlift chair, and his arms have been replaced with limbs taken from an assassin droid. [GDV, MMY, PDS]

Grand Moff Muzzer

The brash and easily excitable Grand Moff Muzzer is plump and round-faced. [GDV]

Grand Moff Tarkin

Grand Moff Tarkin was the Imperial governor charged with overseeing a large section of the Outer Rim Territories. As one of the Emperor's most loyal administrators, Tarkin devised and implemented the construction of the first Death Star battle station. His concepts led to the Empire's doctrine of rule by fear and helped the Emperor disband the Imperial Senate. He died in the Battle of Yavin after refusing to evacuate the Death Star prior to its destruction by Rebel forces. [SW]

Grand Moff Thistleborn

The authoritative Grand Moff Thistleborn has bushy eyebrows which frame his dark, penetrating eyes. His loyalty to the Empire's Central Committee of Grand Moffs is absolute and above question. [GDV]

gravel-maggots

🜨 Gravel-maggot worms feed upon rotting flesh and aid rapid decomposition. These creatures can be found in the hills and rocky badlands of the planet Tatooine. [SW]

gravel storm

🜨 The planet Tatooine is subject to frequent and turbulent atmospheric conditions. One of the worst results in the phenomenon of the gravel storm. During these terrible storms, strong winds whip rocks, sand, and loose debris through the air with deadly force. [SW]

gravity well projector

🜨 Gravity well projectors are connected to massive gravity well generators on ships such as the *Interdictor*-class cruiser. The projectors emit waves of energy that disrupt the mass lines of realspace, simulating the presence of a true stellar body. This displacement of mass lines serves two purposes: first, ships within the sphere of influence of a gravity well cannot engage their hyperdrives; second, ships that come in contact with the resulting gravity shadow while traveling through hyperspace must drop back into realspace when their hyperdrive cutoffs kick in. [ISB, SH]

gravsled

🜨 Convenient, cheap, and fast, gravsled vehicles provide transportation via antigrav or repulsorlift engines. A gravsled is a flying platform with no exterior shell. A windshroud offers some protection to up to three passengers. [HSR]

Gray Leader

(☻) Gray Leader was the comm unit designation for the commander of Gray Wing, one of the four main Rebel starfighter battle groups active during the Battle of Endor. Gray Leader and his Gray Wing fell during the early moments of the battle. [RJ]

Gray Wing

(☻) One of the four main Rebel starfighter battle groups participating in the Battle of Endor. [RJ]

Great Heep, the

(☻) The Great Heep was an enormous, grotesque droid employed by the Empire to mine fuel ore on the planet Biitu. With a body composed of various droid parts and tubing, the Great Heep operated a huge processing plant during the early days of the Empire. One side of the Great Heep was filled with visible pistons that bounced up and down in terrible rhythm, while one of his arms was chopped off at the elbow. Grinder blades filled his awful maw, and tiny robots lived on his hull like mechanical parasites. Two crazed humans were always near the Great Heep, busy shoveling fuel into his massive boilers. [TGH]

Great Pit of Carkoon

✪ Located within the Dune Sea on the planet Tatooine, the Great Pit of Carkoon is a large depression that serves as the resting place for the creature known as the Sarlacc. [RJ]

Greedo the Rodian

Greedo

✪ Greedo, a member of the Rodian species, was one of many bounty hunters hired by Jabba the Hutt to apprehend or dispose of Han Solo after Solo failed to complete a smuggling job for the crime lord. Greedo, with his multifaceted eyes, skull-ridge spines, and tapirlike snout, caught up with Solo at a cantina in Mos Eisley Spaceport. Solo was forced to dispose of the bounty hunter in order to save his own life. [SW]

Green Leader

✤ Green Leader was the comm unit designation for the commander of Green Wing, one of the four main Rebel starfighter battle groups active during the Battle of Endor. Green Leader and his group fired the last blaster salvo that caused the disabled Super Star Destroyer to crash into the unfinished Death Star. Green Leader died completing this assault. [RJ]

Green Squadron

✤ The B-wings and Y-wings of the Green Squadron starfighter battle group fought in the Battle of Calamari. [DE]

Green Wing

✤ Green Wing was one of the four main Rebel starfighter battle groups participating in the Battle of Endor. It was also the comm unit designation for Green Leader's second-in-command, who accompanied Red Leader (Wedge Antilles), Gold Leader (Lando Calrissian), and Blue Leader in an assault on an Imperial communications ship. He lost his life in the effort, but gave the others the opportunity to destroy the enemy vessel. [RJ]

Greenies

See Mimbanite.

Gribbet

⊙ A small fishlike alien, Gribbet is a bounty hunter who works with Skorr. Skorr and Gribbet nearly captured Han Solo on the planet Ord Mantell. [GW]

Griff

See Admiral Griff.

Grigmin

⊙ Grigmin operated a one-man traveling air show. As a stunt pilot and rumored aerial combat champion, Grigmin made a living by displaying his talents to paying customers on backwater worlds. He employed Han Solo and Chewbacca for a brief time before the pair became involved in the Galactic Civil War. [HLL]

Guardian patrol ship

⊙ The Empire's *Guardian*-class patrol ships are recent additions to the Imperial fleet, coming into service after the Battle of Endor. Two common models are the XL-3 and XL-5. [DE]

gundark

⊙ The wild, four-armed gundark anthropoid grows to a height of 1.5 meters and is known for its fearlessness and amazing strength. This animal species has given the galaxy the phrase, "you look like you could pull the ears off a gundark," which means that an individual appears healthy and strong. [ESB]

Gupin

A Gupin is any of the small, elflike species who live in a large volcanic structure on the moon of Endor. The structure sits in the center of a vast grassland and is filled with flowers, waterfalls, and terraced plants. The Gupins can change into other forms, though this ability is dependent on the beliefs of others. [ETV]

Gwig

The young male Ewok named Gwig recently passed from babyhood and now seeks to join the older Ewoks on their many adventures. [ETV]

Gyndine

The planet Gyndine is the territorial administrative world where Governor Bin Essada maintains a residence. [SME]

gyro-balance circuitry

Gyro-balance circuitry gives machines three-dimensional direction-sensing capabilities. These devices are found in vehicles and droids, helping the machines achieve stability in all three planes whether at rest or in motion. [HSE]

H

Halla

⊕ Halla, an old woman with a limited use of the Force, lives on the planet Mimban. Shortly after the Battle of Yavin, Halla enlisted Leia Organa and Luke Skywalker to help her find the ancient Kaiburr Crystal. [SME]

Hammerhead

See Ithorian.

hanadak

⊕ A hanadak is a ferocious beast that dwells in the forest of Endor's moon. It is a big, powerful creature that looks like a cross between a grizzly bear and a baboon. [ETV]

hang glider

✪ A hang glider is a primitive mode of transportation that employs a light framework covered with animal skins to travel on natural currents of air. The Ewoks of Endor's moon use hang gliders to travel across the vast valleys of their homeworld. [RJ]

Han Solo

Han Solo

✪ Many tags can be applied to the Corellian-born Han Solo: starship pilot, smuggler, pirate, and even Rebel hero. He became involved in the Galactic Civil War when he took on a simple transport job in a cantina in Tatooine's Mos Eisley Spaceport. After jettisoning Jabba the Hutt's cargo of spice to avoid an Imperial blockade, Han needed to raise enough credits to reimburse the crime lord. For seventeen thousand credits, he agreed to ferry Ben Kenobi, Luke

Skywalker, and two droids to Alderaan in his stocklight freighter, the *Millennium Falcon* (which he won from Lando Calrissian in a high-stakes sabacc game). The adventures that followed saw Solo help rescue Princess Leia Organa from the depths of the Death Star, and then provide covering fire for Luke's shot which destroyed the huge battle station. He became one of the Heroes of Yavin, and spent the next three years helping the Alliance avoid the growing number of Imperial hunters searching them out. Solo received more than enough credits from Princess Leia to pay off Jabba, but he and his longtime partner, Chewbacca the Wookiee, got drawn into the Rebellion, and the debt to Jabba remained unpaid. When Solo finally decided the time was right to return to Tatooine, Jabba had already put a death mark on the Corellian's head. Bounty hunters from all over the galaxy were looking for Solo, his ship, and his Wookiee companion. On Ord Mantell, a pair of hunters came close to collecting the bounty, but Solo managed to evade them. As the finishing touches were being made to the new Rebel base on Hoth, Solo saw his departure opportunity come and go. Before he could get away, the Empire again caught up with the Rebels. One notorious hunter, Boba Fett, tracked Solo to Bespin and led the Empire right to him. After encasing Solo in carbonite, Darth Vader turned his frozen form over to Boba Fett for delivery to Jabba. Solo's friends would not give the smuggler-turned Rebel up so easily, however, and they launched a rescue mission that saw Jabba and his criminal organization destroyed and Boba Fett lost to the Great Pit of Carkoon.

On his return, Solo agreed to lead the Alliance strike team to Endor's moon as the prelude to the Battle of Endor.

Solo has great skills as a pilot and blasterslinger. His reputation among other smugglers is almost as large as his own ego, and he adds his own boastful tales to those already in circulation. He is arrogant, extremely lucky, and possessed of a sharp wit and biting sense of humor. Once Chewbacca and the *Millennium Falcon* were the only constants in his life, but now he has an extended family, a group to belong to, and a cause worthy of his talents. Luke Skywalker is the younger brother and friend he never had. Princess Leia is the love of his life, and their affections for each other have grown over the course of their adventures. Lando Calrissian, his onetime friend and associate, has returned to round out this group of companions. A natural gambler, Solo is brave to a fault, impulsive, and willing to risk everything to win. [SW, ESB, RJ]

🔰 After growing up in the Corellian star system, Han enrolled in the Imperial Academy. He graduated with honors and was on his way to a brilliant career in the Imperial Navy when his conscience got in the way. He decided to rescue a Wookiee from slavers, which earned him a dishonorable discharge and the lifelong gratitude of the Wookiee. As Wookiees were an enslaved species under Imperial law, it was not Han's place to interfere with the slavers, but he could not stand by and watch the Wookiee be mistreated. That Wookiee was Chewbacca, and this choice was to influence the rest of Han Solo's life. After being discharged, Solo wandered the galaxy with little purpose. He took on a number of unsavory jobs, and all the while Chewbacca remained at his side—even though Han tried repeatedly to get him to leave. A Wookiee's life debt is not something taken lightly, and Chewbacca stayed until Han finally acknowledged his presence. They became partners and then fast friends. [HSR, HLL, HSE SWSB]

During the six years following the Battle of Endor, Han Solo married Princess Leia and became the father of three potential Jedi Knights: Jacen and Jaina, twins, and Anakin. He continues to take on missions for the New Republic, though he long ago gave up any official rank or title. [HE, DFR, LC, DE]

Hasti Troujow

🔰 Hasti Troujow is the young, beautiful ex–mining camp laborer who helped Han Solo and Badure reach the secret treasure vaults of Xim the Despot. This expedition took place shortly before Solo became involved in the Galactic Civil War. [HLL]

haul jets

🔰 "Haul jets" is a spacer expression for a quick departure, similar in tone and meaning to the phrase "Let's get out of here." [SWR]

HC-100

🔰 The homework-correction droid HC-100 is humanoid in shape, with silver skin and glowing blue photoreceptor eyes. Designed and built by DJ-88, HC-100's primary function is to correct and grade young Ken's educational assignments. He walks in perfect step, much like a soldier on the march, and his speech patterns match that of an Academy drill instructor. [LCJ, PDS]

Headquarters Frigate, the

See *Home One*.

heads-up display

🔰 Most starfighters come equipped with heads-up display

units. These holographic projectors show all of the tactical and diagnostic information pilots need to be aware of at all times. The information is displayed at eye level in transparent holograms and holographs so that pilots can stay focused on the space in front of them without needing to look down at instrumentation panels. [HSE, SWSB]

Heater

🔴 Heater was one of Jabba the Hutt's gunmen and lieutenants. [SWR]

herd ship

🔵 Ithorian herd ships travel the space lanes like great caravans, bringing unusual merchandise from one end of the galaxy to the other. Designed for Ithorian comfort, they are built to duplicate the tropical environment of the Ithor planet, full of indoor jungles, artificial storms, wildlife, and vast expanses of lush vegetation. [SWSB, GA]

Herglic

🔵 Herglics come from the planet Giju. These huge bipeds apparently evolved from water-dwelling mammals. They stand about 1.9 meters tall, have extremely wide bodies (more than twice the width of two humans), and have smooth, hairless skin that ranges from shades of light blue to nearly black in coloration. Fins and flukes have been replaced by arms and legs, though they still breathe through blow holes in the tops of their heads. This species is known for its explorers and merchants, who were among the first members of the Old Republic. The manufacturing centers of Giju were the earliest to be taken over by the Empire, and after a brief and bloody struggle, the pragmatic species surrendered completely to the Empire's will. This allowed them to live fairly comfortably as they labored for Imperial masters. By the time of the New Republic, the Herglic were treated neutrally—neither trusted nor ignored. They bounced back faster than did those on worlds that refused to submit to the Empire, like Kashyyyk and Mon Calamari, because their manufacturing centers were never destroyed, and many species believe them to be traitors to the rest of the galaxy. Herglics tend to overindulge in gambling, and they are very self-conscious about their size. [DFR, DFRSB]

Hermi Odle

✪ Hermi Odle, one of the aliens in Jabba the Hutt's desert palace, served the crime lord faithfully until the organization was toppled by Luke Skywalker and his companions. A huge bipedal of unknown origin, Hermi wore a tattered robe. [RJ]

hibernation sickness

✪ When a person is brought out of suspended animation, hibernation sickness can result. This medical condition is characterized by temporary blindness, disorientation, muscle stiffness and weakness, hypersensitivity, and occasionally madness. Han Solo suffered from a mild case of hibernation sickness after he was released from his carbonite prison by Princess Leia. [RJ]

Hideaz Quill-Face

⚙ Hideaz Quill-Face is a massive, three-meter-tall smuggler of an unidentified alien species. He works with Spog, his partner, and the pair can often be found in the Byss Bistro. [DE]

High Council of Alderaan, The

✪ The High Council of Alderaan was the legislative body that ruled over the planetary government. [SWR]

High Court of Alderaan

✪ The High Court of Alderaan was the royal house that presided over the planet's High Council. [SWR]

High Prophet Jedgar

✪ High Prophet Jedgar is a 2.3-meter-tall human with a bald head, bearded chin, and hooded eyes. Like the other mysterious Prophets of the Dark Side, he wears black robes that seem to glitter with the light of inner stars. Kadann, the Supreme Prophet of the Dark Side, relies upon Jedgar to help him gain command of the Empire. [MMY, PDS]

Hija

See Lieutenant Hija.

Hin

⊕ Hin was one of the two Yuzzem miners who aided Luke Skywalker and Princess Leia during their adventures on Mimban. Hin met the Rebels in Captain-Supervisor Grammel's prison and helped them escape. He later rescued Luke at the Temple of Pomojema. [SME]

Hirken

⊕ Viceprex Hirken was the administrator of the Corporate Sector Authority's installation on Mytus VII, otherwise known as Stars' End. He was a tall, handsome, patriarchal figure who always wore impeccable top-exec attire. [HSE]

Hissa

See Grand Moff Hissa.

Hissal

⊕ Hissal was a scholar and academician from the University of Rudrig, who brought guidance and aid from the institution to his home planet Brigia. The tall, purple-skinned humanoid temporarily employed Han Solo and Chewbacca prior to the pair's involvement in the Galactic Civil War. [HLL]

H'kig

⊕ H'kig was a religious leader on the Core World of Galand several centuries ago. He preached a message of strict morals and goodness, which angered the royal families of Galand. The Viceroy of Galand finally put H'kig to death, but this only served to launch his religion. Seventy years ago, the H'kig faithful purchased two colony ships and fled the religious persecution of Galand's decadent society. They settled on Rishii, establishing a theocratic government whose laws are based on the teachings of H'kig. Even so, they are very tolerant of other faiths. [DFRSB]

Hobbie

☮ Hobbie was one of the veteran Rebel pilots assigned to Luke Skywalker's Rogue Squadron on the ice planet Hoth. Hobbie's comm unit designation was Rogue Four. [ESB]

Ho'Din

⊕ The Ho'Din are a gentle humanoid race from the planet Moltok. They prefer nature to technology, and their natural medicine techniques are recognized throughout the galaxy. The name Ho'Din means "walking flower," which roughly describes this species. Their flesh is rubbery and their forms lanky. A typical Ho'Din grows to a height of three meters. Thick, snakelike tresses sprout from their heads. These ever-moving modified hairs are covered with gleaming red and violet scales. The Ho'Din are nature worshippers who dislike processes and policies that harm ecosystems. [GG4, LCJ, HESB, LC]

holocomm

⊙ A holocomm, or HoloNet comm unit, allows owners to transmit and receive messages over the HoloNet. [ISB, DFRSB]

Holocron

See Jedi Holocron.

holocube

⊙ Holocubes are hand-sized, six-sided objects that hold three-dimensional holo images. By moving the cube around, one can see all aspects of a given image. [HSE]

hologram

⊙ Holograms are moving three-dimensional images. These images can be broadcast in real time as part of comm-unit communications, or via the galaxy-wide HoloNet. [SW]

Hologram Fun World

⊙ The theme park called Hologram Fun World is located in a glowing, transparent dome that floats inside a blue cloud of gas hanging suspended in outer space. The promotions declare that the park is "a world of dreams come true." Lando Calrissian served as Baron Administrator of Hologram Fun World for a time after the Battle of Endor. [QE, PDS]

holograph

Holographs are static three-dimensional images. [SWR]

holographic recording mode

This is a recording process for capturing images and sounds in a three-dimensional format. Devices featuring holographic recording mode can store high-resolution images as both holograms and holographs. These images can be contained on a holotape. R2 astromech droids have this capability. [SWR]

holomonster

Holomonsters are animated holograms in the form of fantastic creatures taken from the myths and legends of the galactic community. These three-dimensional images are projected onto hologameboards for use as playing pieces in various hologames. [SW]

HoloNet

The Old Republic Senate commissioned the construction of a galaxy-wide HoloNet to provide a free flow of hologrammic communications between the member worlds. Before the HoloNet, communications were handled face-to-face via hyperspace travel (which was usually faster than subspace comm transmissions) or by subspace planetary relays. Subspace relays are still the easiest and cheapest way to send transmissions within systems or between neighboring systems. For communication over longer distances, the

HoloNet uses hundreds of thousands of non-mass transceivers, which are connected through a vast matrix of coordinated hyperspace simutunnels and routed through massive computer sorters and decoders. Relays sent through the hyperspace matrix reach their targets nearly instantaneously, providing a real-time exchange of news, ideas, and information. When the Emperor came to power, he shut down large portions of the HoloNet. It remained active in the Core Worlds and was used as a military communications medium for keeping the Imperial fleet in contact, but all of the outer systems were cut off to isolate them and keep the Emperor's practices regarding them from reaching the major metropolitan worlds. [ISB, DFRSB]

holoprojector

🌑 Holoprojectors transmit moving, three-dimensional images. These devices use modulasers to broadcast real-time or recorded holograms. [HSE, DFRSB]

Home One

🌑 *Home One* is the Mon Calamari–designed starship that served as Admiral Ackbar's personal flagship during the Battle of Endor. The vessel, also referred to as the Headquarters Frigate, was the command ship from which Ackbar directed the Alliance armada against the second Death Star and the Imperial fleet. Like all Mon Cal vessels, *Home One* is cylindrical and organically artistic, with no hard angles to mar its fluidlike surface. Armed for war, *Home One* has twenty-nine turbolaser batteries, thirty-six mini-ion cannon emplacements, multiple shield and tractor-beam projectors, and twenty hangar bays to house its complement of ten starfighter squadrons and other craft. [RJ]

homing beacon

See directional landing beacon.

Honoghr

Seven planets fill the Honoghr star system. Tiny Logru spins closest to the sun with its oceans of boiling lava. Distant Kuthul, the frozen giant, rests in the system's farthest orbit. The fourth world, Honoghr, is the only one capable of supporting life. Even at its height, Honoghr's hold on life was tenuous at best. It was not a world of abundant resources, but it was the most this system had to offer. The Noghri, savage hunters turned into killers by the Empire, were born on this world. Little of the planet is still fit for habitation. The small area called the Clean Land, with the major city of Nystao and clusters of small villages, is all that remains of a once vibrant world.

A disaster befell the world a few decades back: two combating starships chose this world's orbit as the site of their battle. The resulting clash was like something out of the primitive Noghri's legends. Two gods fought high in the sky, using lightning the likes of which the Noghri had never seen. One of the great warships crashed into the planet, triggering massive earthquakes and releasing toxic chemicals into the air. The Noghri clans migrated to the traditional truce ground, the one place on the planet spared the full brunt of the disaster. It was in this Clean Land that Darth Vader found the Noghri. He provided medicine, food, tools, and decon droids to clean the land. The Noghri bowed down to this black-clad savior, and Vader became their master. Of course, this was all part of a grand deception. Vader and the Empire were not repairing the land, they were keeping the world in such a state that the Noghri would always be dependent on them. Princess Leia uncovered the deception and told the Noghri that their world should have been cleansed in a few short years. She has restored their freedom and released them from Imperial bondage. [DFR, DFRSB]

Hoom

⊛ Hoom is a massive Phlog youngster, the son of Zut and Dobah, and the brother of Nahkee. [ETV]

Hoona

⊛ Hoona is an adolescent Phlog female who once fell in love with the Ewok Wicket because of a magic potion administered by a Dulok shaman. [ETV]

Hoover

⊛ Hoover is a quadriped alien with a long, disproportionate snout and large eyes. He was a member of Jabba the Hutt's court until the crime lord was killed and his organization shattered by Princess Leia Organa and Luke Skywalker. Hoover's alien species has yet to be identified, and it is not known if Hoover survived the carnage inflicted upon Jabba's organization. [RJ]

horizontal booster

⊛ On the stock freighter *Millennium Falcon*, the horizontal booster is a hyperdrive subsystem that provides energy to the ionization chamber to cause ignition. [ESB]

Hoth

(�) Hoth is the sixth planet in an out-of-the-way star system of the same name. The frozen world of wind, snow, and ice was the location of the primary Rebel Alliance base three years after the Battle of Yavin. The secret Echo Base was discovered by the Empire, and the ice planet became the site of a terrible engagement known as the Battle of Hoth. While daytime temperatures across the planet are tolerable for humans wearing proper clothing, the night brings such cold that to travel or even leave protected shelters is tantamount to suicide. The extreme cold even affects vehicles and machinery, and all of the Alliance equipment had to be modified to withstand the weather. For a time, the Rebels had to employ specially adapted tauntauns as mounts until their airspeeders were converted to operate in the cold and snow. During the Alliance's brief exploration of the planet, only one life-form was discovered—the wampa ice creature. Its size and need for food suggests that other creatures live in the frozen wastes, but they have not yet been identified or cataloged. [ESB]

(�) Since being conquered by the Empire, Hoth has been the location of an Imperial garrison and detention center. [PDS]

House Glayyd

See Ammuud Clans.

House Reesbon

See Ammuud Clans.

hoverscout

⚙ By combining hover engines with repulsorlifts, a hoverscout can handle most terrain types with little trouble. The Empire's primary hoverscout is the Mekuun Swift Assault Five, which operates effectively as a small unit reconnaissance craft, an offensive point vehicle, and even an infantry and armor support craft. In this capacity, hoverscouts sometimes work in conjunction with AT-AT walkers. The Swift Assault requires a crew of four to make use of all its systems. It is armed with a heavy blaster cannon, a light laser cannon, and a concussion missile launcher. [ISB, DFRSB]

howlrunner

⚙ The wild, omnivorous howlrunner inhabits the planet Kamar. These animals have heads that resemble human skulls, though overall howlrunners appear canine. [HSR]

human-droid relations specialist

✪ A human-droid relations specialist is a droid programmed to provide an interface between humans and other droids (or other self-aware mechanicals, such as ship computers). Language interpretation and diplomatic programming make up this classification's primary functions. C-3PO was designed and programmed into this classification, though he has gained other talents and abilities over the long years, as he has not been subjected to memory wipes. [SW]

human replica droid

⊕ The innovative human replica droid was designed by Fandra and the scientists of the Alliance's Project Decoy. These lifelike droids are designed to look like a specific person in order to fool the enemy. [QE, PDS]

humming peeper

⊕ A humming peeper is a small flying creature found in the swamps near the Dulok villages on the moon of Endor. The hypnotic humming sound produced by these creatures in large numbers causes listeners to fall asleep. [ETV]

Hunter-Killer probot

⊕ The Hunter-Killer probot is a capital-ship-sized droid modeled after the Imperial probe droid. Designed for pursuit and police actions against isolated quarries, the fully automated droid ship has a full offensive and defensive armament, graphicscan recognition codes for identifying targets, and an interior holding bay that can detain captured freighters. [DE, DESB]

Hurcha

⊕ Hurcha is the eighth planet in the Churba star system and is so far from its sun that it is much too cold to support life. [DFR, DFRSB]

hurlothrumbic generator

⊕ The hurlothrumbic generator produces energy waves that stimulate the base of the brain to cause varying levels of fear. At low power, the waves cause mild anxiety. Turned up high, they send even the strongest, bravest individuals running in terror. The Imperial Moff Bandor experimented with the device on the planet Questal. Rebel agents were able to disable it and convince the Empire to abandon the project. [GCQ]

Hutt

⊕ A Hutt is any of the intelligent species from the planet Varl, a dying world orbiting a dwarf star named Ardos. A Hutt has a huge, bulbous head, a wide, blubbery body, a tapering, muscular tail, and speaks Huttese. They can reach lengths of up to five meters. Hutts have no legs, but they do have short, swollen arms. Two enormous, reptilian eyes emerge from the folds of flesh covering the head, and a lipless mouth slices across the wide face. Most Hutts are megalomaniacs who believe themselves the equals of any gods. They are tough and thoroughly immoral, given to taking and exercising power over others. As a long-lived species— some Hutts claim to be as old as one thousand years—many Hutts have left their homeworld to set up colonies or to mingle with the other races in the galaxy. Jabba the Hutt, for example, established a criminal organization and set up his base on the desert planet Tatooine. [GG4]

Hutt caravel

⊕ A Hutt caravel is a short-range space transport. Hutt

crime lords use these vessels to travel between the Hutt planet Nal Hutta and its spaceport moon Nar Shaddaa. [DE]

Hutt floater

⊕ Hutt floaters are repulsorlift platforms used by members of the Hutt species to move their bloated, nearly limbless bodies from place to place. [DE]

hydrospanner

⊕ A hydrospanner is a power tool similar to a wrench. [ESB]

Hyllyard City

⊕ The major population center on the planet Myrkr is Hyllyard City. It is a frontier town, consisting of ship landing pits and a close-packed collection of makeshift structures. The city is inhabited by a few settlers, and serves as a haven for smugglers and fugitives from other worlds. [HE, HESB]

hyperdrive

⊕ The starship engine and its interrelated systems that propel space vessels to supralight speeds and into hyperspace is called the hyperdrive. [ESB]

⊕ Powered by incredibly efficient fusion generators, hyperdrive engines hurl ships into hyperspace, a dimension of space-time that can only be reached by faster-than-light speeds. Hyperdrives work with astrogation computers to assure safe and dependable hyperspace travel. To protect ships from hyperspace gravity shadows, most hyperdrives come equipped with an automatic cutoff. If a gravity shadow is scanned along the route ahead, the cutoff dumps the ship back into realspace. Even with cutoffs, ships that fly too close to gravity shadows while traveling through hyperspace can sustain massive—and sometimes fatal—amounts of damage. [SWSB, HESB]

hyperdrive motivator

The hyperdrive motivator is the primary lightspeed thrust initiator in the hyperdrive engine system. It is connected to a vessel's main computer system to monitor and collect sensor and navigation data in order to determine jump thrusts, adjust engine performance in hyperspace, and calibrate safe returns to normal space. [ESBR]

hyperspace

Galactic travel took an amazing leap forward with the discovery of hyperspace. With the use of a hyperdrive, a starship can exceed the speed of light and enter a dimension that takes advantage of the wrinkles in the fabric of "normal," or "real," space. [SW]

Hyperspace is a dimension of space-time that can only be reached by traveling at lightspeed. Hyperspace is coterminous with realspace, which means that every point in realspace is associated with a unique point in hyperspace. If a ship travels in a specific direction in realspace prior to jumping to hyperspace, then it continues to travel in that direction through hyperspace. In addition, objects in realspace cast "shadows" into hyperspace which must be plotted and avoided in order to ensure a safe trip. A star in realspace casts a shadow of itself which exists in the corresponding hyperspace location. This makes current astrogation charts and careful jump calculations especially important to those who use hyperspace to travel the space lanes. [SWRPG, SWRPG2, SWSB]

hyperspace commo

☺ Faster-than-lightspeed communications are called hyperspace commos. [HSE]

hyperspace compass

☺ A hyperspace compass is a device used by starships to navigate. Hyperspace compasses are oriented on the center of the galaxy, and work in realspace and in hyperspace. [DE]

Hyperspace Marauder

☺ The *Hyperspace Marauder* is the starship owned and operated by the smuggler Lo Khan. [DE]

hyperspace transponder

☺ The hyperspace transponder, the heart of all hyperspace communications systems, produces the weak signals that send comm messages through hyperspace. Since hyperspace transponders are not always reliable or effective, the New

Republic has been pouring a huge amount of resources into designing and building more effective versions. [DE]

hyperspace wormhole

A hyperspace wormhole is an unpredictable natural phenomenon that suddenly connects distant points of the galaxy by creating hyperspace tunnels. These wormholes produce vast amounts of energy in the form of violent storms. Great disturbances in the Force can sometimes trigger a wormhole. [DE]

I

I-7 attack ship (Howlrunner)

⚙ Incom's I-7 attack ship is a newly commissioned Imperial starfighter that was introduced during the period marked by the rebirth of the Emperor. These crafts are commonly called Howlrunners by their pilots, after the wild omnivores from the planet Kamar. [DE]

ID profile

⚙ A ship's ID profile is broadcast from its telesponder (or transponder). This electronic signal contains all relevant information about the ship, including its name, registration number, current owner, home port, classification, armament and power plant ratings, and any restrictions that apply to it, its cargo, and its owner. Ship telesponders are activated by queries from sources with interrogator modules, such as military vessels and spaceport control towers. ID profiles can be altered, but the process is extremely difficult and highly illegal. [HSE, FG]

Ido

🏛️ Ido is the sister of the Mor Glaydd of the planet Ammuud. [HSR]

IG-88

IG-88 (Phlutdroid)

✴️ The battered war droid IG-88 was among the bounty hunters commissioned by Lord Darth Vader to hunt down and capture the *Millennium Falcon* and its crew after the Battle of Hoth. [ESB]

Ilic

🏛️ Ilic, on the planet New Cov, is one of eight walled cities clustered in the great jungles, which are so rich with biomolecule-producing plants. Ships and shuttles must enter the city through vents near the top of the silver-skinned dome. The Bothan named Borsk Fey'lya has numerous business interests in Ilic, and it was here that he often contacted Garm Bel Iblis and his private army. Professional greeters welcome visitors with data-card maps and guides to the many markets and the recreational, administrative, living, and processing sections of the city. While the city and corporate-controlled planetary government consider themselves to be part of the New Republic, they make periodic tributes to the Empire to keep from incurring Imperial wrath. [DFR, DFRSB]

ILKO

⊗ ILKO was one of the master encrypt codes the Empire used for transferring data between Coruscant and the original Death Star construction facility at Horuz. It took twelve-year-old Ghent (Talon Karrde's slicer) nearly two months to crack at the time, while the combined resources of the fledgling Alliance needed a month to accomplish the same thing. [LC]

illuminescences

⊗ Illuminescences is the name of an organic clothing material with the unique property of glowing in the dark. Processed from dried swamp hemp cultivated on Oshetti IV and spun into fine cloth, the material's glow comes from bacteria that lives in the hemp. Different bacterial strains produce different colored glows. [HSE]

Ilthmar Gambit

⊙ The Ilthmar Gambit is a hologram boardgame move used to gain a tactical advantage over an opponent's guarded position. The player employing the Ilthmar Gambit uses a single playing piece as bait to draw out his opponent's defended pieces. After capturing the piece, the rest of the opponent's forces are left open to the player's follow-up attack. [HSR]

ilum crystals

See Adegan crystals.

Imperial Charter

⊙ The Imperial Charter contains the rules and agreements set forth by the Empire which govern the rights and responsibilities of all Imperial worlds and star systems. The charter granted to each member system features provisions concerning resource usage, rights of passage, military protection, tributes, and colonization. [SME]

Imperial City

⊙ Imperial City, on the planet Coruscant, has changed allegiance a few times in its long history. During the days of the Old Republic, it served as the capital of the galactic union and the permanent headquarters of the Senate. When the Emperor came to power, the city was named Imperial City and became the ruling seat of the New Order. After the Battle of Endor, Imperial City was declared the command base of the New Republic. This cosmopolitan city is always crowded. When the Old Republic was in charge, every known intelligent species in the galaxy was drawn to the bright lights of this beautiful city. The Emperor, of course, closed the city to nonhumans—alien species were only permitted at the sides of their human masters.

The ancient Senate Hall fills part of the city. Its carved stone pillars surround seemingly endless tiers of benches. The massive Imperial Palace looms over the hall, tapered spires and fragile-looking towers jutting from every surface. These glowing towers stretch out to blend with the rest of the city's architecture, giving the impression of one endless structure that reaches from the base of the Manarai Mountains to cover a huge portion of the planet's main continent.

At the time of the Emperor's rebirth, the city came under siege by the reorganized forces of the Imperial fleet. Great portions were destroyed in the resulting battles. [HE, DFR, LC, DE]

Imperial customs vessel

The Empire normally uses light corvettes as customs vessels. These 180-meter-long ships patrol Imperial space and perform spot inspections of merchant vessels to look for contraband or other undeclared cargo. Armed with six turbolaser batteries, these ships can handle most of the smuggler vessels they can catch up with. [GG6]

Imperial Freight Complex

The Imperial Freight Complex, which orbits the planet Byss, is a huge docking tower and spaceport. Licensed independent haulers bring cargo to this facility for unloading. [DE]

Imperial garrison

⊙ Dark, ominous, prefabricated structures that can be set up quickly on any planet, Imperial garrisons are the visible presence of the Empire on distant worlds. A garrison base serves a number of functions. These bases are scientific, diplomatic, and military strongholds for the Empire, and they are displays of force that can quickly cow even the most rebellious planet. Carried aboard Star Destroyers for immediate deployment, Imperial garrisons are charged with the subjugation and protection of planets within the Empire. Garrisons are employed to enforce martial law, squelch uprisings, support local governments loyal to the Empire, and deter piracy. With the aid of extensive environmental control units, garrisons can be set up anywhere. The typical personnel assigned to an Imperial garrison feature a staff of three thousand, including eight hundred stormtroopers and various support personnel, assorted ground-assault vehicles, and forty TIE fighters. [SWSB]

Imperial gunner

⊙ Imperial gunners are part of a special sub-unit of the Imperial pilot corps. All Imperial ships larger than TIE starfighters that are equipped with high-tech arms employ these highly trained weapons masters. Gunners are selected based upon keen eyesight, superior reflexes, and a rapport with gunnery weapons. Gunners can be recognized by their specialized computer helmets (usually black). In addition to providing protection from the high-energy output produced by laser batteries, the helmets are equipped with macrobinocular viewplates and sensor arrays to assist with targeting fast-moving fighter craft. In the films, Imperial gunners were seen at the controls of the Death Star's superlaser. [ISB]

Imperial Hyperspace Security Net

The hyperspace lanes that connect to the secure systems of the Deep Galactic Core are continuously monitored for unauthorized space traffic by the Imperial Hyperspace Security Net, a new technology that integrates hyperspace commo principles with intensified cross-channel radiation. [DE]

Imperial Intelligence

Imperial Intelligence is the military counterpart of the civilian-controlled Imperial Security Bureau (ISB). It consists of four distinct divisions: the Ubiqtorate, the Internal Organization Bureau, the Analysis Bureau, and the Bureau of Operations. During the time of the New Republic, this was one of the best-trained and professional portions of the Empire to survive the Battle of Endor and its consequences. It gladly gave its full support to Grand Admiral Thrawn's war effort. [ISB, DFRSB]

Imperial Royal Guard

The Imperial Royal Guard is a unit of specially selected Imperial soldiers who serve as the Emperor's personal guards. Only the most promising soldiers who fall within the required size, strength, intelligence, and loyalty ranges are chosen for this duty. They are trained in the use of a

Imperial Royal Guard

wide range of weapons and unarmed combat styles, and conditioned to obey the Emperor's will and protect him with their very lives. Imperial Royal Guards wear flowing red robes, helmets, and full body armor. [RJ]

Imperial Sovereign Protectors

The highest-ranking members of the Imperial Royal Guard are called Imperial Sovereign Protectors. Like other Royal Guards, they serve as the Emperor's personal body guards. Rumors abound that these elite soldiers are empowered by the dark side of the Force. At least one Sovereign Protector is at the Emperor's side at all times. After the Emperor's rebirth, the Sovereign Protectors were charged to guard the clone vats on Byss. [DE]

Imperial Star Destroyer

See Star Destroyer.

Imperial stormtrooper

See stormtrooper.

Imperial walker

See All Terrain Armored Transport.

Imperialization

⊛ The process of galactic conquest as set forth by the Empire is called Imperialization. Imperialization focuses on the conquest of star systems, the regulation of commerce, and the taxation and appropriation of goods and services for the benefit of the Empire and its objectives. [SW]

Incom skyhopper T-16

See skyhopper.

Incom T-65

See X-wing starfighter.

Ingey

⊛ Ingey was the cherished pet of young Prince Coby of Tazzum-an. This small, rare creature was a tesselated arboreal binjinphant—a sort of kangaroo-ferret cross. [DTV]

Ingo

⊛ Ingo is a desolate world of salt flats and craters. Its inhabitants, mostly human colonists, work hard to keep food on the table and their high-tech tools and equipment in good repair. [DTV]

Inner Council

⊛ The ruling body of the New Republic's Provisional Council is the Inner Council, whose members include Mon Mothma, Admiral Ackbar, Leia Organa Solo, and Borsk Fey'lya. These individuals and their associate members decide the true course of the New Republic through heated debate and compromise. Before becoming architects of a new galactic government, most of the members of the Inner Council were the leaders of the Rebellion. [HE, HESB]

Inner Rim Territories

⊛ Originally known as the Rim, the area now called the Inner Rim Territories was once thought to mark the end of galactic expansion. This diverse region is nearly as civilized as the Core Worlds, though it benefits from being newer and less crowded. As the Empire demanded more and more of the planets of this region, disgruntled colonists struck out to find better environs in the Outer Rim Territories. [SWRPG2]

insignia of the New Republic

insignia of the New Republic

The seal adopted by the Provisional Council as the insignia of the New Republic is based upon the symbol of the Alliance that preceded it. The blue crest of the Alliance, itself taken from the seal of the Old Republic, is set within a circle of stars that represent the galactic community. The circle is trimmed in gold, symbolizing the right of the people to govern themselves. [HESB]

Inspector Keek

Inspector Keek was the chief of the planet Brigia's Internal Security Police. This pompous, quasi-militaristic individual wore numerous decorations on his oversized uniform. [HLL]

Interdictor-class cruiser

Using the shell of a 600-meter-long heavy star cruiser, the Interdictor-class cruiser was designed to serve a specific purpose in the Imperial fleet. The core of this vessel is a massive gravity-well generator and its four gravity-well projectors. The projectors emit waves of energy that disrupt the mass lines of realspace, simulating the presence of a true stellar body. This displacement of mass lines serves two purposes: first, ships within the sphere of influence of a gravity well cannot engage their hyperdrives; and second, ships traveling through hyperspace that come in contact with the resulting gravity shadow must drop back into realspace when their hyperdrive cutoffs kick in. Thus, Interdictors prevent lightspeed escapes by enemy ships, and ambush those ships traveling the hyperspace lanes by forcing them to shift back into realspace so that an Imperial armada can pounce on them. [ISB, HE, HESB]

Internal Organization Bureau

⬤ A division of Imperial Intelligence, the Internal Organization Bureau (or IntOrg) protects the rest of Intelligence from both internal and external threats. Its agents police other divisions to verify loyalty and reliability. While some of its agents operate in a covert fashion, most have high visibility and appear to be civilized political appointees. They can be extremely ruthless, however, as many enemies of the Empire can attest. [ISB]

interrogator

⬤ An interrogator is a device that sends out an electronic high-frequency signal in order to activate a starship's ID-profile transponder. All military ships and spaceports are equipped with interrogators so that authorities can identify and screen approaching vessels. [HSE]

interrogator droid

👊 Interrogator droids are terrifying mechanicals designed by the Empire to question prisoners using a variety of techniques, including torture and chemical injection. These dark, globe-shaped droids possess multiple appendages tipped with tools of their pain-inducing trade. Interrogator droids come equipped with repulsorlift engines for movement. [SW]

interruptor template

🏛 The metal panels on the *Millennium Falcon* that help prevent accidental damage from the ship's own weapons are called interruptor templates. These panels automatically slide into position to keep the *Falcon*'s lower quad-laser battery from shooting the landing gear or entry ramp when the ship is in landing configuration. [HSE]

ion cannon

👊 An ion cannon fires bursts of ionized energy that cause damage to a target's mechanical and computer systems by overloading and fusing circuitry. Unlike blaster bolts, ion bursts cause no structural damage. They do, however, neutralize ship weapons, shields, engines, and other vital systems. Ship-mounted ion cannons come in a variety of low power ratings, while those designed to serve as planetary defenses have the highest power ratings available. Planetary ion cannons are mounted in multistory, spherical towers that have their own power supplies. These tower cannons hurl devastating bursts of ionized energy into space to ward off hostile vessels. One of these weapons protected the Rebel base on Hoth from orbital assault. [ESB]

ion engine

🔴 The ion engine is the most common sublight drive in use throughout the galaxy. Ships achieve great speeds in normal space by employing these engines. An ion engine produces sublight speed thrusts by hurling charged particles through an exhaust port. [SW]

IRD

🔴 IRDs are starfighters used by Corporate Sector Authority police. These starfighters are extremely fast, but not very maneuverable. [HSE]

Irenez

🔴 As a member of Senator Garm Bel Iblis's private army at Peregrine's Nest, the woman-warrior named Irenez served as chief of security, intelligence coordinator, pilot, and bodyguard for Sena and Iblis. When the senator agreed to join the New Republic, she went along as well. [DFR, DFRSB]

irradiator

🔴 Spaceports use irradiator lighting systems to decontaminate arriving ships. Irradiators emit narrow bands of light that kill most disease-carrying organisms without harming vessels or more advanced life-forms. [HLL]

Ishi Tib

☢ Ishi Tib was one of Jabba the Hutt's alien subordinates. Bipedal, with bulbous eyes and a beaklike mouth common to his species, Ishi Tib was slightly more than 1.5 meters tall. While it has not been confirmed, it is believed that Ishi Tib died with the rest of Jabba's entourage aboard the crime lord's sail barge. [RJ]

☢ Though the alien who worked for Jabba the Hutt was called Ishi Tib, that is the name of his species. The Ishi Tib race comes from the planet Tibrin, where they live in cities built atop carefully cultivated coral reefs. They are meticulous planners, and many intergalactic corporations seek them out as managers and technicians. [GG4]

Ithor

☢ Ithor is the fourth planet in the Ottega star system and home to the race called Ithorians, or Hammerheads. This lush, tropical world teems with plant and animal life. Some of the planet has been tamed by the Ithorians, but large regions remain wild and unexplored. Nature and technology co-exist on this world, and both work together to support the Ithorians' peaceful civilization based upon sound ecological principles. Ithors live in great "herd" city ships which float above the surface of the world and migrate around the planet's three "civilized" continents. Each herd is a several-level-high, disk-shaped repulsorlift complex that serves as a center of industry, commerce, and culture. [SWSB]

Ithorian

⚫ The species name for the aliens commonly referred to as Hammerheads is Ithorian. Their common name comes from their T-shaped heads, which rest atop long, curved necks. Ithroians come from the Ottega star system, in the Lesser Plooriod Cluster. They speak Basic with a strange twist due to their two mouths, each located on one side of their necks. This generates a stereo effect, which produces one of the most beautiful and difficult native languages in the galaxy. Ithor, the fourth planet in the Ottega system, is a jungle world that the Ithorians have learned to respect and even worship. The ecologically minded species believes that only their eco-priests should ever set foot upon the ground of the great Mother Jungles. The rest live within great floating herd cities. Herbivores, Ithorians never take more than they need from their planet, and they practice a system of planting two trees for every one they are required to take from the jungles.

Some herd cities have been converted to starships and equipped with hyperdrives. In this way, Ithorian caravans travel the space lanes, bringing unusual merchandise from place to place. The herd ships are built to mimic the environment the Ithorians know, complete with indoor jungles, artificial storms, examples of Ithorian wildlife, and vast corridors of lush vegetation.

Ithorians are a gentle, peace-loving species. They have great respect for all forms of life. They are a gregarious and curious people, who enjoy their roles as space merchants almost as much as ecological preservers. In the Outer Rim Territories, the arrival of a herd ship is cause for celebration. [SWSB]

Ixll

⊕ Ixll is the species name of the small, intelligent flying beings that inhabit the Fifth Moon of Da Soocha. These beings speak a language, comprised of chirps and whistles, which has many similarities to the language of R-series astromech droids. Mischievous Ixll sometimes emit sounds that affect a droid's programming. In their native environment, Ixll are hunted by creatures called Tumnors. Ixll have a friendly relationship with the New Republic's Pinnacle Base personnel. They often guide Republic ships through the dangerous peaks of the moon. [DE]

Izrina

⊕ Izrina is the queen of the Wisties, the glowing, flying species of Endor's moon. [EA, ETV]

J

Jabba the Hutt

🌑 Jabba the Hutt, the notorious crime lord who ran his organization from the planet Tatooine, was one of the major kingpins in the Outer Rim Territories. His organization was into a wide variety of illegal activities. From smuggling to spice dealing, slave trading to murder, loan sharking to protection, Jabba the Hutt had his bloated fingers in all the underworld's pies. Like others of his race, Jabba was a legless, sluglike being with reptilian eyes and gross mannerisms. Approximately four meters long, Jabba was huge even among his own kind. His desert palace on Tatooine was full of all kinds of decadent luxuries, an army of alien and human criminals, droid slaves, and fawning servants. Among Jabba's most prized possessions were the rancor and the sail barge. Every smuggler, bounty hunter, pirate, and thief in the Outer Rim Territories eventually took on a job for Jabba, including Han Solo and his partner Chewbacca.

In fact, it was because of a job Solo botched that Jabba ultimately met his end. After Solo dumped a shipment of spice to avoid an Imperial blockade, Jabba gave the smug-

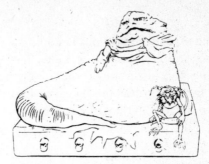

Jabba the Hutt

gler a limited time to make good on the shipment's worth. When Solo failed to return to Tatooine to pay off his debt—he was off helping the Rebellion—Jabba put a price on his head. Boba Fett eventually collected the bounty, but Solo's Rebel companions came to rescue him. Among this group was Luke Skywalker. Although Skywalker's Jedi "mind tricks" did not work against Jabba, his other abilities made short work of the crime lord's men. It was Princess Leia, however, who actually killed Jabba. Since that time, other criminal organizations have been attempting to fill the void left by Jabba the Hutt's sudden and unexpected demise. [SW, ESB, RJ]

Jacen Solo

Jacen Solo is the son of Han Solo and Leia Organa Solo. Like his mother and Uncle Luke, Jacen is strong in the Force. He and his twin sister Jaina were born approximately five years after the Battle of Endor, during the events surrounding the return of the Empire's Grand Admiral Thrawn. [HE, DFR, LC]

Jaina Solo

⚙ Jaina Solo is the daughter of Han Solo and Leia Organa Solo. Like her mother and Uncle Luke, Jaina is strong in the Force. She and her twin brother Jacen were born approximately five years after the Battle of Endor, during the events surrounding the return of the Empire's Grand Admiral Thrawn. [HE, DFR, LC]

Jak Sazz

⚙ The smuggler Jak Sazz frequents the Byss Bistro. [DE]

Janson

🔆 Janson was a young Rebel serving with the forces of Echo Base on the ice planet Hoth. He was gunner on the snowspeeder piloted by Rogue Three. [ESBR]

Jawa

Jawa

🔆 Jawas, the meter-tall scavenger race native to Tatooine, are rodentlike beings with offensive odors and jabbering speech. Jawas remain hidden within coarse cloaks, with only their small, glowing eyes visible in the shadowy folds of their hoods. Jawas travel in bands, searching for discarded hardware to collect, wrecked ships to salvage, or unattended vehicles to steal. They clean and repair these items, selling and trading them with Tatooine's settlers and those passing through Mos Eisley Spaceport. Jawas nest within huge vehicles called sandcrawlers and rumble across the desert wastes in these massive but slow transports. [SW]

Jedgar

See High Prophet Jedgar.

Jedi Code, the

💮 The Jedi Code is the philosophy that sums up the beliefs of the Jedi Knights: "There is no emotion; there is peace. There is no ignorance; there is knowledge. There is no passion; there is serenity. There is no death; there is the Force." A Jedi does not act for personal power or wealth but seeks knowledge and enlightenment. A Jedi never acts from hatred, anger, fear, or aggression but acts when calm and at peace with the Force. [SWRPG, SWRPG2]

Jedi Holocron

💮 The Jedi Holocron is a legendary artifact that appears as a small, palm-sized glowing cube of crystalline formations and hardware. Curious designs etched into its technological components hint at the artifact's great age. Through the use of primitive hologrammic technology, Jedi teachings were stored within it centuries ago. These teachings can be accessed by true Jedi Knights, who are able to interact with the embedded images. [DE]

Jedi Knights

When the Old Republic first came into existence, the Jedi Knights were there to protect it. They were the guardians of justice and freedom, the most respected and powerful force for good for over a thousand generations. While the Jedi were known for their supernatural skills with lightsabers, their real power came from their ability to tap into and manipulate the Force. Jedi Knights defended the Old Republic from all threats, including the proponents of the Clone Wars, but there was one threat they could not stand against—internal corruption. First the Republic itself fell to the corruption of its leaders, and the Empire was born. Then, before the Knights could move against him, the Emperor used one of their own to destroy the Jedi. Through treachery, deception, and the actions of the corrupted Jedi Knight called Darth Vader, the Jedi Knighthood was exterminated. Presumably, only Vader, Obi-Wan Kenobi, and the Jedi Master named Yoda survived the Emperor's eradication of the Jedis. It was Kenobi and Yoda who trained young Luke Skywalker to become the first of a new line of Jedi Knights. [SW, ESB, RJ]

Jedi Master

The most powerful Jedi Knights eventually evolve into Jedi Masters. Jedi Masters are teachers and miracle-workers of extreme power and ability. Jedi Masters have moved beyond the need for weapons such as lightsabers, preferring to depend solely on the Force to give them strength. The Jedi Master Yoda trained Luke Skywalker after the death of Obi-Wan Kenobi. [ESB]

Jenet

🌀 Jenet are a scavenging species with pale pink skin, red eyes, and sparse white fur. They come from the planet Garban in the Tau Sakar system. They have incredible memories and are considered quarrelsome by other species. After developing starships, they quickly colonized the other worlds in their star system. During the Galactic Civil War, these colonies were turned into labor camps by the Empire. [GG4, ZHR]

Jeremitt Towani

🌀 Jeremitt Towani and his family were shipwrecked on Endor's forest moon for a time, where they became good friends with Wicket and his Ewok tribe. Jeremitt's wife is Catarine, and his children are Mace and Cindel. [EA, BFE]

Jerjerrod

See Moff Jerjerrod.

Jessa

🌀 Jessa was the daughter of Doc, leader of a band of out-law techs operating in and around Corporate Sector space. Jessa was Doc's second-in-command and an accomplished technician herself. She was a tall, shapely woman with curly-blond hair and freckles. Her friends and close associates called her Jess. [HSE]

Jhoff

See Controller Jhoff.

Jindas

☺ The gypsylike Jinda tribe wanders Endor's forest moon. It makes its living by trading with Ewok tribes and putting on shows. The tribe and its members have a talent for getting lost. [ETV]

jizz-wailer

☺ A jizz-wailer is a musician who plays a fast, contemporary, upbeat style of music. [RJ]

Jodo Kast

☺ The ruthless, cunning bounty hunter Jodo Kast wears the same type of battle armor favored by Boba Fett, though it is unknown if the two have some connection dating back to the Mandalore warriors of the Clone Wars or if they just picked up the same armor somewhere. Kast often works with the alien Puggles Trodd and the female named Zardra. [TM]

John D

See Blue Six.

Jomark

⊛ The planet Jomark came to prominence when rumors circulated that a Jedi Master had been hiding on the world since before the rise of the Emperor. This was the world on which the clone Joruus C'baoth chose to set his trap for Luke Skywalker. It is the second of six worlds in the system, and the only capable of supporting life. The colony world has had little contact with the rest of the galaxy since its last star-chart update fifteen Standard years ago. The planet is mostly ocean, with one small continent called Kalish and thousands of small islands. When Joruus C'baoth arrived on the world, he quickly took it over. He ruled from a structure called High Castle, an artifact of a nonhuman species that had disappeared from the world long before the human colonists arrived. The colonists came to Jomark during one of the Old Republic expansions a few thousand years before the events of *Star Wars IV: A New Hope*. As with many of the colonies of the time, Jomark was forgotten. Its inhabitants slowly descended to a more primitive, superstitious state as power cells failed and knowledge was forgotten. Now they stay away from the relics left behind by the long-gone alien species, for they believe these strange sites to be haunted. The colonists (which is what they call themselves, though few know what the term means) live by fishing and sea farming. They have no interest in the events happening elsewhere in the galaxy, and they were very happy to see Joruus leave after his plan to capture Skywalker failed. [HE, DFR, HESB, DFRSB]

Jord Dusat

⊛ Jord Dusat came from the planet Ingo, where he learned to race landspeeders over desolate, crater-studded acid salt flats. He was the best friend and main race competitor of Thall Joben. Jord was a bit of a rebel and a troublemaker, though he dreamed of becoming a professional speeder racer. R2-D2 and C-3PO encountered him during their adventures, which took place in the early days of the Empire. [DTV]

Jorus C'baoth

The human Jedi Master Jorus C'baoth was born on the planet Bortras in Reithcas Sector, back in the days of the Old Republic. His interests in the Jedi Knighthood and his innate abilities in the Force led him to join the Jedi Training Center on Kamparas. After four years and a period of private training with an unknown Jedi Master, he became a Jedi Knight. Twelve years later, he assumed the title of Jedi Master. His service to the galaxy included participating in the demilitarization observation group sent to Ando as representatives of the Old Republic, membership in the Senate Interspecies Advisory Committee, and being personal adviser to Senator Palpatine on matters pertaining to the Jedi. He was part of the Jedi Knight task force sent to Bpfassh to deal with the Dark Jedi insurrection. He led the delegation sent to Alderaan to determine which royal family should receive the title of viceroy, and helped rule in favor of the Organa family. He also assisted the Jedi Master Tra's M'ins to mediate a peaceful end to the Duinuogwuin-Gotal conflict. When the Outbound Flight Project to search for life outside the known galaxy was proposed, Jorus was one of six Jedi Masters on the exploration ship launched from Yaga Minor. This was the last recorded appearance of Jorus C'baoth, as the Outbound Flight Project never returned. [HE, DFR, DFRSB, LC]

Joruus C'baoth

Joruus C'baoth

Joruus C'baoth was the clone of the famed Jedi Master Jorus C'baoth. Grand Admiral Thrawn found Joruus on the planet Wayland, where he was guarding one of the Emperor's hidden storehouses. He was confused about his origin and past, hindered by shattered memories and periods of insanity brought on by clone madness (a malady afflicting most of the early clones, who were grown too quickly). Joruus appeared as an old, white-haired man with a long beard. His eyes seemed bright and alert, and his body was strong and lean. Joruus, however, was insane, though he nonetheless wielded great powers forged in the dark side of the Force. He believed that all lesser beings hate the Jedi because of their power and knowledge, and that it was the duty of the Jedi to rule over the lesser beings to keep the galaxy safe. Thrawn entered into an uneasy alliance with

Joruus in order to reestablish the New Order, promising to turn Luke Skywalker, Leia Organa Solo, and Leia's unborn twins over to the mad Jedi Master. For his part, Joruus planned to reshape these Force users into his own image, starting a new society of Dark Jedi with which to rule the galaxy. Joruus eventually turned on Thrawn in order to advance his own plans. Although Luke Skywalker tried to heal the madness which corrupted Joruus, in the end he was forced to destroy him. [HE, DFR, DFRSB, LC]

Jovan Station

⚙ Jovan Station was the name of the command center for the Imperial blockade of Yavin Four. [GW]

juggernaut

⚙ The juggernaut heavy assault vehicle is an old-style wheeled craft that still sees service with the Imperial forces assigned to the Outer Rim Territories. These hulking, cumbersome vehicles are dangerous and look about as powerful as they truly are. Five sets of massive wheels help the juggernaut lumber across most terrain types. The front and rear wheels turn independently of each other, allowing it to navigate fairly effectively for a non-repulsor vehicle. Resembling a wheeled AT-AT, the juggernaut has a scanning tower, thick armor, and powerful weapons, including three heavy laser cannons, one medium blaster cannon, and two concussion grenade launchers. [ISB]

J'uoch

⚙ J'uoch and her fraternal twin brother R'all own and operate a mine on the planet Dellalt. She is an unscrupulous woman with an almost malevolent nature. Her thick, straight brown hair falls around her pale face, out of which peer her large black eyes. J'uoch and her brother competed with Han Solo to be the first to discover the lost treasures of Xim the Despot back before Solo became involved with the Rebellion. [HLL]

jubilee wheel

A jubilee wheel is a popular betting game found in casinos throughout the galaxy. [HLL]

Judicator

The Imperial Star Destroyer *Judicator*, commanded by Captain Brandei, served as part of Grand Admiral Thrawn's personal armada. [HE, DFR, LC]

jump

See hyperspace.

Jundland Wastes

The Jundland Wastes is a rocky, dry, and extremely hot canyon and mesa region on the planet Tatooine. It borders the Dune Sea, and is inhabited by Tatooine's nomadic Sand People. [SW]

Junkfort Station

⊕ Junkfort Station is a spaceport where ships can be modified and fitted with illegal equipment. [GW]

Jyn Obah

⊕ The tall humanoid named Jyn Obah was first mate to the pirate captain Kybo Ren back in the early days of the Empire. He was distinguished by his long red hair, his protruding lower teeth, and the ring he wore through his nose. He also wore the upper portion of a stormtrooper's helmet on his head, as well as a stormtrooper's chest plate for protection and as a fashion statement. [DTV]

K

Kabal

🌐 Kabal is a neutral world and the site of the Conference of Uncommitted Worlds, which was held just after the destruction of the first Death Star. [GW]

Kabe

🌐 The Chadra-fan named Kabe was abandoned by slavers on Tatooine, where she now makes a living as a skilled thief and street beggar. She gets into all sorts of trouble, but benefits from the protection of her large friend Muftak the Talz. [GG1]

Kadann

🌐 Kadann, the Supreme Prophet of the Dark Side, is a human dwarf with a black beard. Those who wished to lead the Empire after the Battle of Endor sought Kadann's dark

Kadaan

blessing to make their rule legitimate. He often issues mysterious prophecies made up of nonrhyming, four-line verses to Imperial leaders. The Alliance studies these prophecies for insights into what the Empire might be planning. Kadann assumed leadership of the Empire for a brief time after the Battle of Endor. [LCJ, PDS]

Kaiburr Crystal

The Kaiburr Crystal, a deep crimson gem, rests within the Temple of Pomojema. Legends describe the crystal as a Force-enhancing artifact, capable of strengthening the abilities of those who wield the Force. The priests of the temple are rumored to have mysterious healing powers, which could be Force techniques enhanced by the crystal's natural properties. [SME]

Kaink

The elderly Kaink is an Ewok priestess who serves as guardian of the Soul Trees and the village legend-keeper. [ETV]

Kalla

The planet Kalla, located within Corporate Sector space, houses a number of well-known institutions of higher education. Those with the best reputations specialize in the technological, commercial, and administrative fields. [HSE]

Kamar

Kamar, a hot, desert planet, orbits a white sun in a star system just outside Corporate Sector space. Many stranded locals have survived there by sucking water out of the roots of the native Miser plant, which collects moisture from the arid atmosphere. [HSR]

Kamarian

Kamarians inhabit the planet Kamar. These insectile beings have two sets of arms, spherical skulls, thick, segmented prehensile tails, and light-colored exterior chitin. Han Solo ran a brief business venture for the Kamarians who lived in the arid Badlands region of the planet. These Badlanders were smaller in size and had lighter chitin than typical Kamarians. After the Badlanders turned Solo's holovid theater into a religious experience, the smuggler was forced to pack up and hastily leave the planet. [HSR]

Kane Griggs

⊕ Kane Griggs was the navigator aboard the New Republic Star Destroyer *Emancipator*, which had been captured from the Empire, during the Battle of Calamari. [DE]

Kanz Disorders

⊕ The Kanz Disorders were a series of violent uprisings back in the time of the Old Republic. During this period, the Lorrdian people were held captive. Eventually, Old Republic forces and the Jedi Knights liberated these people, but the Kanz Disorders are considered the turning point on the Lorrdian people's long road to freedom. [HSR]

Karrde

See Talon Karrde.

Kasarax

⊕ Kasarax, a sauropteroid on the planet Dellalt, provided aid to Han Solo and his companions during the quest to find the lost treasures of Xim the Despot. [HLL]

Kashyyyk

⊕ The planet Kashyyyk is the homeworld of the Wookiee

species. This jungle world is full of natural wonders and amazing sights. Its huge trees form an extensive ecosystem which is divided into several horizontal levels. The Wookiees and various flying creatures live in the uppermost level. Increasingly more hostile life-forms are encountered as one descends through the lower ecosystems toward the planet's surface far below.

🟦 The massive Wookiee cities are built hundreds of meters above the ground, in the highest branches of the jungle trees. The cities integrate modern technology with natural beauty to create some of the true wonders of the galaxy. Under the Empire, Kashyyyk and its inhabitants were guarded by a fleet of ships and numerous garrisons. The Wookiees were enslaved, forced to use their great strength to serve the Empire. By Imperial decree, free Wookiees were illegal. Those found off-planet or outside Imperial work camps were considered outlaws. After the Battle of Endor, Kashyyyk was liberated, and it is now a full member world of the New Republic. [HE, HESB, SWWS]

Katana fleet

🟦 The *Katana* fleet, or the Dark Force, consisted of two hundred Dreadnaught heavy star cruisers. The fleet's flagship, the *Katana*, was considered to be the finest starship of its time. The entire fleet was fitted with full-rig slave circuits to significantly decrease the size of the crew needed to run the ships. The fleet's unofficial name came from the dark gray hull surfacing of the Dreadnaughts.

With the Clone Wars still years away, the *Katana* fleet was launched to a massive Old Republic public-relations drive. Unfortunately, the crews were infected with a hive virus that drove them all mad. In their insanity, they slaved the ships together and the whole fleet jumped to lightspeed—to disappear for decades. Grand Admiral Thrawn located the dormant fleet and turned them against the New Republic five years after the Battle of Endor. [DFR, DFRSB]

Katarn Commandos

See Page's Commandos.

Kea Moll

⚫ Kea Moll was a beautiful seventeen-year-old young woman when C-3PO and R2-D2 first met her during their adventures in the early days of the Empire. Kea lived on her mother's farm complex on the planet Annoo. She was brave and athletic, able to handle both spacecraft and landspeeders with an expert's touch. [DTV]

Kee

⚫ Kee was a Yuzzem miner on the planet Mimban. He helped Luke Skywalker, Princess Leia, and the old woman Halla retrieve the legendary Kaiburr Crystal from the Temple of Pomojema. [SME]

Keeheen

⚫ Keeheen was the mate of Atuarre, the female Trianii who accompanied Han Solo to Stars' End. [HSE]

Ken

⬢ Twelve-year-old Ken was brought to the Lost City of the Jedi when he was a baby. An unidentified Jedi Knight placed him there for safekeeping, giving him into the care of the droid DJ-88. Dee-Jay was instructed to raise Ken and educate him. Initially, Ken did not know where he came from or who his parents were. He has reason to believe that he may be a Jedi Prince, and he wears a strange birthstone around his neck on a silver chain. Certain Jedi abilities come naturally to Ken. These include the abilities to cloud perceptions, read minds, and move small objects through the power of the Force. Except for the books, data files, and droids of the Lost City and Zeebo, his pet Mooka, Ken grew up alone. He eventually left the city to follow his hero, Luke Skywalker, and join the Alliance. Near the end of his first series of adventures, Ken discovered that Triclops is his father. [LCJ, ZHR, PDS]

Kendalina

⬢ The Jedi Princess named Kendalina was forced to serve as a nurse in an Imperial insane asylum located deep within the spice mines of Kessel. [PDS]

Kessel

⬢ The planet Kessel is a world of oppression and opportunity. The oppression comes from the planet-wide Imperial correctional facility, infamous for its forced labor camps and impenetrable defenses. The opportunity takes the form of one of the planet's primary products, the controlled commodity called "spice." For smugglers brave enough or desperate enough to risk capture and imprisonment in Kessel's labor camps, there is a secret space route to and from the planet. Known as the Kessel Run, this route serves as the main path for smuggling spice off-planet. Smuggler pilots also use the Kessel Run to determine who has the fastest ship and best flying skills among their peers by logging how long it takes a ship to successfully make the run. [SW]

Kessel Run

See Kessel.

kete

🌀 A kete is a large winged creature that looks much like a giant dragonfly. These creatures live in spiral mounds made out of a sticky, marshmallowlike substance. [ETV]

Kez-Iban

See Mon Julpa.

Khabarakh

🌀 The Noghri named Khabarakh was a member of the Death Commando squad sent to capture Princess Leia from her hiding place on Kashyyyk. He was the only member of his squad to survive, and he was captured by Chewbacca the Wookiee. It was Khabarakh who recognized Leia as the

Khabarakh the Noghri

daughter of Darth Vader and therefore the heir to Vader's hold over the Noghri people. After Leia earned his trust, Khabarakh was an instrumental voice in helping her gain the aid of the Noghri. [HE, HESB, DFR, LC]

kholm-grass

Once true kholm-grass grew across the world of Honoghr. Now only the Empire's bioengineered version of the plant grows over much of the planet. It is a uniformly brown, hybrid strain of the original plant, which kills other forms of plant life and keeps the world from recovering. Only animals capable of eating the kholm-grass have survived outside the small area of Clean Land, so the Noghri who inhabit Honoghr must rely on imported supplies. [HE, DFR, LC]

Khuiumin

🌑 The Khuiumin system was the base of operations for the notorious Eyttyrmin Batiiv pirates until the Empire made a concerted effort to destroy the group during the early days of the New Order. The pirates amassed an armada of small- and medium-sized starships, gathering approximately one hundred and forty vessels to defend themselves against the approaching Imperial fleet. Two *Victory*-class Star Destroyers were deployed by the Empire. *Bombard* and *Crusader* used superior tactics to outfight and outwit the pirates, eventually destroying not only their armada, but their defended ground base as well. [SWSB]

King Gorneesh

See Gorneesh.

Kir

🌑 Kir is a planet deep within the heart of the Corporate Sector, where crystals are mined and refined for use as crystalline vertex, the Corporate Sector currency. [HSE]

Kirdo

🌑 The planet Kirdo is the homeworld of the alien Kitonak race. [GG4]

Kitonak

🌀 Kitonaks are a species of pudgy, yeast-colored beings with tough, leathery hides. They come from the planet Kirdo, where their ability to draw in upon themselves and seal vulnerable body openings in folds of flesh protects them from the world's harsh desert environment. They are a patient race, whom many consider to be plodding. Droopy McCool, a member of Max Rebo's jizz-wailer band, was a Kitonak. [GG4]

Klaatu

🌀 Klaatu was one of the Nikto skiff guards employed by Jabba the Hutt. Like other members of his race, Klaatu has olive-colored reptilian skin and small horns around his face. [RJ]

kleex

🌀 Kleex are large, flealike parasites that infest the tails of the huge creatures called durkii. Though the durkii is normally a docile beast, it can become a raging monster due to the discomfort caused by kleex infestation. [DTV]

Klev

See Commander Klev.

Koong

🏛 Governor Koong was a burly, unshaven man in his mid-fifties during the early days of the Empire. He led a band of criminals in the Tawntoom region of Roon. He used political intrigue, theft, and hijacking to increase his personal power in the Roon system. [DTV]

Kowakian monkey-lizard

🏛 Monkey-lizards are rare animals from the planet Kowak. These creatures are extremely silly and stupid, and the surest way to insult someone across the galaxy is to call that being a Kowakian monkey-lizard. [QE]

Kraaken

🏛 Kraaken, a humanoid with long pointed ears, was Commander Silver Fyre's second-in-command. He was a traitor who attempted to kill Luke Skywalker and steal a data card carrying secret information vital to the Alliance. [GW]

Krath, the

🏛 The Krath was an ancient magical sect that ruled the Empress Teta star system approximately four thousand years before the events of *Star Wars IV: A New Hope*. Formed by the experiments of the Tetan elite, this group received its power from the dark side of the Force and its name from an evil, magical god prevalent in the legends of the region. Princess Leia learned their story while accessing the knowledge stored in the Jedi Holocron. [DE]

krayt dragon

⟐ Krayt dragons are large, carnivorous reptiles that live in the mountains surrounding Tatooine's Jundland Wastes. [SW]

kroyie

⟐ The kroyie, a species of huge bird native to the Wookiee planet of Kashyyyk, are hunted for food and are considered delicious by the Wookiees. The kroyie inhabit the upper branches of the planet's giant trees. Kroyie are attracted to bright lights, and Wookiees use search beams to hunt the great birds. [HE, HESB]

KT-10

⟐ KT-10 was an R2 unit with a female personality program. She and R2-D2 became romantically interested in each other while both were in the Great Heep's droid harem back in the early days of the Empire. [TGH]

KT-18

⟐ The droid KT-18 is a pearl-colored housekeeping mechanical with a female personality program. The droid's familiar name is Kate. Luke Skywalker purchased Kate from Tatooine Jawas as a gift for Han Solo. [ZHR]

Kuari Princess

The *Kuari Princess* is a Mon Calamari luxury spaceliner famous for its state rooms, bazaar deck, and slafcourses (a popular recreational sport in which participants navigate an obstacle course atop fast-moving repulsor sleds). [RM]

Kubaz

The humanoid Kubaz species stands 1.8 meters tall and has short, prehensile trunks where other species have noses. They have rough-textured, green-black skin and large, sensitive eyes. On many worlds, Kubaz must wear special goggles to protect their eyes from harsh light. They are a cultured species who place a high value on tradition, art, and music. Their homeworld of Kubindi is famous for its cuisine—at least among those with a taste for insects. A Kubaz is seen following Luke and Ben around Mos Eisley in *Star Wars IV: A New Hope*. [GG1, GG4]

Kybo Ren

The infamous pirate captain Gir Kybo Ren-Cha, or simply Kybo Ren, was a short, overweight human who operated during the early days of the Empire. He was distinguished by his long, dangling mustache and a small goatee. [DTV]

L

Laakteen Depot

⚛ Laakteen Depot was the Rebel outpost Darth Vader destroyed on the *Executor*'s maiden voyage. [GW]

Labria

⚛ Labria the Devaronian is an information broker who sells knowledge to anyone willing to pay for it. He currently operates at the Mos Eisley spaceport on Tatooine. [TM, GG1]

Lady Luck

⚛ The modified pleasure space yacht named *Lady Luck* belongs to Lando Calrissian. He bought it and has been working on its modifications since setting up his mining operation on Nkllon. While *Lady Luck* already exceeds the manufacturer's performance standards, Lando still plans additional upgrades and improvements. The fifty-meter-long space yacht has a hyperdrive engine, combat shields, and a laser cannon. [HE, HESB, DFRSB]

Lady of Mindor

🌀 *Lady of Mindor*, a commercial starship, travels throughout Corporate Sector space ferrying passengers from planet to planet and star system to star system. It makes no stops in any restricted areas. Han Solo and Fiolla of Lorrd once booked passage on the starship from Bonadan to Ammuud in order to evade Espos and slavers who were searching for them. [HSR]

Lafra

🌀 Lafra, a planet situated near Corporate Sector space, is the home of a race of intelligent, gray-skinned humanoids. These beings were once winged flyers, though they lost this ability over eons of evolutionary change. All that remains to remind them of their airborne past are small, nonfunctional soaring membranes. [HSE]

Lake Spirit of Mimban

🌀 The Lake Spirit of Mimban inhabits the subterranean waterways of the planet Mimban. It appears as an amorphous, translucent, and phosphorescent creature. [SME]

Lambda-class shuttle

☸ Of all the space shuttles operating in the Imperial fleet, perhaps the most distinctive is the *Lambda*-class shuttle. The three-winged shuttle resembles an inverted Y in flight. The two lower wings fold upward when it lands. This type of shuttle carries up to twenty passengers (usually stormtroopers or high-level Imperial officials) and their gear, or the equivalent amount of material, plus the command crew (who operate the shuttle from the cockpit). Passengers and crew enter and exit the shuttle through a lower hatch which drops open when the craft has landed. [RJ]

Lancer-class frigate

The 250-meter-long *Lancer*-class frigate was introduced into the Imperial fleet after the Battle of Yavin as a counter-measure against Rebel starfighters. Armed with twenty quad laser cannons mounted on towers, it more than holds its own against enemy starfighters. However, it has few defenses against other capital ships. [ISB, DFRSB]

landing claw

Space vessels employ landing claws to attach themselves to most surfaces, regardless of their orientation. Most landing claws use either magnetic or mechanical grips to adhere to a surface. They form a solid connection between a ship and another ship, a space dock, or another landing or parking surface. [ESB]

Landing Zone, The

The Landing Zone is a popular bar on the planet Bonadan. It can be found in the planet's Alien Quarter. [HSR]

Lando Calrissian

Lando Calrissian, soldier-of-fortune and master gambler, turned "respectable" after winning stewardship of Bespin's Cloud City in a game of sabacc. As Baron Administrator of Cloud City and its Tibanna-gas mining operation, he proved to be adept at keeping the outpost on an even keel and turning a handsome profit. In fact, things were going so well that Calrissian should have realized his luck was about to change. Imperial forces under the command of Lord Darth Vader arrived at Cloud City and "persuaded" Calrissian to assist them. The Dark Lord made Lando an offer he could not refuse—a deal to keep the Empire out of Bespin system forever. All Lando had to do was betray his old friend, associate, and sometime-rival Han Solo.

After escaping from Imperial forces in the Hoth system, Han Solo brought his damaged *Millennium Falcon* to Cloud City for repairs. Lando, who once owned the *Falcon* until

Lando Calrissian

he lost it to Solo in a sabacc game, welcomed Solo and his companions to the facility, promising to get his techs right to work on the *Falcon*'s troublesome hyperdrive. While he played the cordial and dashing host, Lando was setting Solo up for a fall—though the fall that came was not the one Lando had agreed to. He went along with Vader because the Dark Lord had claimed to be after someone named Skywalker. Solo, Leia, Chewbacca, and C-3PO were nothing more than bait, the Dark Lord had claimed, explaining that after the trap had been sprung, the four could remain on Bespin. The Empire's promise to leave Cloud City to its own devices and the large number of heavily armed stormtroopers at Vader's side had convinced Lando to go along with the deal. When he discovered that Vader was changing the terms to suit his own purposes and that his beloved Cloud City was about to become an armed camp, Lando finally decided to help Han. He ordered the evacuation of Cloud City, but was too late to rescue Han Solo from the bounty hunter Boba Fett. Instead, he helped Leia and Chewbacca escape in the *Falcon*, and even managed to help save Luke Skywalker from the very bottom of the floating city.

Later, Lando took part in the mission to rescue Han Solo from the clutches of Jabba the Hutt. His role in that mission was one of deceit, for he disguised himself as one of Jabba's guards and worked his way into Jabba's court so that he could watch, listen, and wait for an opportunity to make a move. After saving Solo and helping to destroy Jabba the Hutt, Lando decided to take a commission in the Rebel Alliance. Due to his reputation as a soldier-of-fortune, especially for his role in the Battle of Taanab, Lando was given the rank of general. He then volunteered to lead the starfighter assault on the second Death Star, a job that was made much easier by Solo's generous offer of the *Millennium Falcon*. At the helm of the *Falcon*, Lando's daring, expertise, and quick thinking were pivotal in the great space battle that took place above Endor's forest moon. In fact, he accompanied Wedge Antilles on the run to destroy the Death Star's power core. In the end, Lando was decorated as a hero alongside Luke Skywalker, Han Solo, and Princess Leia. [ESB, RJ]

⚙ Before losing the *Millennium Falcon* to Han Solo, before becoming Baron Administrator of Cloud City, and before signing on to help the Alliance, Lando Calrissian engaged in a number of adventures that helped build his reputation. At the helm of the *Falcon*, Calrissian took a year-long trip during which he went to the planets of the Rafa system in search of ancient alien treasure, was stalked by a series of enemies because of his habit of winning high-stakes games of chance, and helped a persecuted alien species called the Oswaft. During this period, Lando was accompanied by a five-armed astrogation/pilot droid named Vuffi Raa. Lando had won the droid, like most of his other possessions, in a game of sabacc. [LCM, LCF, LCS]

After the Battle of Endor, Lando resigned his commission and returned to the private sector. His dealings with the Alliance led to the New Republic's offer to finance his new venture in the Athega system. Without realizing it, Lando became an upstanding citizen—war hero, honest businessman, and responsible administrator. He established a mining company on the planet Nkllon, and supplied a steady flow of raw materials to the New Republic. He was drawn back into the everlasting galactic conflict when the mole miners used in his operation were stolen by the Emperor for use in the Imperial assault on Sluis Van. He wound up suspending his business dealings to help Han Solo and the New Republic deal with the threat posed by Grand Admiral Thrawn. After the defeat of Thrawn, Lando rejoined the Republic to assist in its continuing struggle against the Empire. He helped command the Republic forces at the Battle of Calamari. [HE, DFR, LC, DE]

landspeeder

landspeeder

🌀 A landspeeder is any type of surface transport vehicle that employs repulsorlift propulsion engines. Even when parked, a landspeeder remains suspended about a meter off the ground as an aftereffect of the repulsor field generated by the engine. [SW]

🌀 The most popular landspeeders currently on the market include Bespin Motors' Void Spider TX-3, the Ubrickkian 9000 Z001, the Mobquet Deluxe, and the new SoroSuub XP-38. Landspeeders are sometimes referred to as floaters or skimmers. [SWSB]

Lanni Troujow

🌀 Lanni Troujow, the sister of Hasti Troujow, discovered a log recorder from the legendary starship *Queen of Ranroon*. With the information stored in the recorder, Hasti was able to locate the ancient ship's lost treasures. She had the help of Han Solo and Chewbacca the Wookiee in this endeavor. Lanni was killed by competing treasure-seekers J'uoch and R'all and their agents, but not before she was able to pass along information to her sister, Hasti Troujow. [HLL]

lantern bird

⚛ A lantern bird is a large, beautiful flying creature that lives in shimmering nests high in the trees of Endor's forest moon. These birds have incandescent tail feathers. Logray sometimes uses the tail feathers to create medicinal potions. [ETV]

lantern of sacred light

⚛ The lantern of sacred light is an Ewok holy item. As long as its flame remains lit, the Ewok villages are protected from the Night Spirit and its worshipers. [ETV]

laser cannon

⚛ A laser cannon is a more powerful version of a blaster weapon. Usually ship- or vehicle-mounted, laser cannons shoot visible bolts of coherent light in rapid fire. They are prone to overheating and rely on internal cooling systems to keep them functioning throughout an extended battle. [SWSB]

Latara

⚛ Latara is a pretty, mischievous young female Ewok who loves to play pranks. She also loves to play her flute. She is a good friend to Kneesaa. [ETV]

Leeni

⚛ Leeni is a female Ewok baby, or a Wokling. [ETV]

Princess Leia

Leia Organa

Leia Organa, Princess and Senator from the planet Alderaan, became involved with the Rebel Alliance and soon was one of its most popular and influential cell leaders. While Leia has some memories of her natural mother, the parents she knew best were the Organas, the foster parents who took her into their family while she was still an infant. Her foster father, Bail Organa of the Royal Family of Alderaan, raised her as though she were his own daughter, providing her with love and caring. She was raised as befits a princess, learning the principles of justice and honor along with her other studies. As she grew older, she became a political leader on Alderaan, eventually winning a seat on the Imperial Senate at a young age. But while she fought for reforms on the Senate floor, she also went to work for the Alliance to Restore the Republic. It was while on a two-fold mission for the Alliance and her foster father that she became involved in the events that would lead her into the company of Luke Skywalker and Han Solo.

At Bail Organa's insistence, Leia was heading for Tatooine to find General Obi-Wan Kenobi and recruit him for the Rebellion. On the way, she received plans for the Death Star battle station, which had been stolen by Rebel

273

spies and transmitted to her ship. Before she could reach Obi-Wan, her consular ship *Tantive IV* was intercepted by an Imperial Star Destroyer under the command of Lord Darth Vader. She barely had time to hide the plans in the memory banks of an astromech droid and order it to find Obi-Wan Kenobi before she was captured. As a prisoner of Vader, Leia underwent terrible interrogation sessions as the Imperials sought to discover the location of the main Rebel base as well as the whereabouts of the stolen technical plans. She withstood everything they used upon her, giving them only the name of an abandoned base for their trouble. Worse, though, she was forced to watch as her beloved adopted homeworld was destroyed in an awesome display of the Death Star's power. Shortly thereafter, Luke Skywalker and Han Solo rescued her from the battle station and ferried her and the technical plans to the real Rebel base on Yavin Four. Due to Leia's efforts and the help of her new companions, the first Death Star was eventually destroyed.

With Alderaan gone, Luke, Han, and Chewbacca became Leia's new family, and she threw herself into her work with the Alliance. During the three years that followed the Battle of Yavin, Leia grew to love her companions. The group had numerous adventures, becoming heroes and the inspiration for the struggling Alliance. When Han Solo was captured, Leia was among the small team that went to bring him back. She pretended to be the Ubese bounty hunter Boushh in order to get into Jabba the Hutt's stronghold. Her identity was discovered, however, and Leia had to endure the humiliation of being Jabba's slave for a time. But she paid back the crime lord, strangling him with the very chain that held her captive. Finally, Leia was part of the strike force that went to the forest moon at the start of the Battle of Endor. Her diplomatic skills helped convince the native Ewoks to aid the Rebellion, thus bringing an end to the Galactic Civil War.

During the Battle of Endor, Leia learned that Luke Skywalker was her twin brother. The two had been separated at birth and placed in hiding by Obi-Wan Kenobi to keep them safe. It was believed that the twins, with their latent abilities in the Force, would be the last hope for the galaxy, provided they could be kept secret from the Emperor long enough to realize their potential. [SW, ESB, RJ]

⊛ While Leia refused to accept a seat of power in the Alliance, since the end of the Battle of Endor she has taken her place as the leader of Alderaan's survivors and accepted a post in the New Republic's Provisional Government. She serves on both the Provisional and Inner Councils. As for her personal life, she accepted Han Solo's proposal of marriage. Now she is Leia Organa Solo, princess, councillor, wife, mother, and Jedi-Knight-in-training. Her first children, the twins Jacen and Jaina, were born during the events surrounding the return of the Empire's Grand Admiral Thrawn. Her third child, Anakin, was born a year later, after the events surrounding the rebirth of the Emperor. In addition to her governmental duties, Leia tries to find time to learn the ways of the Force from her brother Luke. She is becoming fairly competent with the lightsaber. [HE, DFR, LC, DE]

Lesser Plooriod Cluster

⊛ The twelve star systems that comprise the Lesser Plooriod Cluster are far from the hub of Imperial activity. After leaving Corporate Sector space, Han Solo and Chewbacca attempted a military-scrip exchange scam in the Cluster. It failed miserably and left them among the ranks of the needy for a time. [HLL]

Leth universal energy cage

🌀 The floating confinement cell called the Leth universal energy cage was created by Umak Leth for the Empire. It was designed to hold even the most powerful prisoners. [DE]

Leviathor

🌀 The ancient Leviathor is leader of the Whaladons. Known as a great and wise ruler, Leviathor has helped many of his species to remain free by outsmarting those who would hunt them. It is said that Leviathor knows the entire history of his species, and it is believed that he is the last great white Whaladon still alive. [GDV]

Lianna

🌀 Lianna is an industrial, urbanized world in the heart of the Allied Tion sector. The world is home to many starship engineering corporations, including Santhe/Sienar Technologies, the parent company of Sienar Fleet Systems, which manufactured the Imperial TIE fighter. [ML]

Liberator

🌀 One of two Imperial Star Destroyers captured by the Alliance during the Battle of Endor, the *Adjucator* was renamed the *Liberator* and placed under the command of Luke Skywalker. After Coruscant was recaptured by the Empire, *Liberator* crashed into Imperial City as the result of damage sustained during combat. Luke's skillful deployment of the Star Destroyer's shields and repulsorlifts prevented the death of the crew. [DE, DESB]

Liberty

(⊕) The alliance star cruiser *Liberty* was the first Rebel casualty of the Battle of Endor. The ship and its entire crew were vaporized by the second Death Star's primary weapon. [RJ]

Lieutenant Hija

(⊕) Lieutenant Hija was the Imperial chief gunnery officer aboard the Star Destroyer *Devastator*. He was at his post when the *Devastator* overtook and captured the *Tantive IV* in the Tatooine star system. [SW]

Lieutenant Page

(⊕) The New Republic officer named Lieutenant Page hails from the planet of Corulag. He grew up as the pampered son of a corrupt Imperial Senator, but was never influenced by his father's moral deficiencies. In fact, he idolized the Jedi Knights of old and dedicated himself to their ideals. He was forced into the Academy, eventually graduating and being assigned to General Veers's ground-assault command. While on leave, he heard Senator Leia Organa speak on the subject of galactic rights. She inspired him to defect and join the Alliance. He became part of General Madine's and Major Derlin's commando units, and was eventually offered command of his own squad. He decided to keep the rank of lieutenant, following after the example of others he admired like Luke Skywalker and Han Solo, who both gave up their ranks but continued to aid the Republic. He is a nondescript-looking man of medium height and build—the perfect undercover operative. Now, five years after the Battle of Endor, his special missions team takes on the assignments few others can handle. [HE, HESB]

Lieutenant Tschel

⊕ Lieutenant Tschel is a young officer aboard the Imperial Star Destroyer *Chimaera*. He served as a member of the bridge crew under Captain Pellaeon and Grand Admiral Thrawn during Thrawn's campaign to destroy the New Republic five years after the Battle of Endor. [HE, DFR, LC]

life debt

See Wookiee life debt.

lift tube

⊕ A cylindrical shaft that extends vertically and horizontally through buildings, ships, and space stations for the express purpose of transporting people and objects is called a lift tube. Of all the mechanical and antigravitational systems used to accomplish this, repulsor fields are the most commonly employed. [SW]

light dust

⊕ Light dust is a sacred powder that nourishes the Tree of Light on Endor's forest moon. [ETV]

lighter

🌀 Small space vessels used primarily for loading, unloading, and moving cargo between huge space freighters and planets or space stations are called lighters. Lighters must be employed when the huge space freighters cannot get close to their destination due to their size or other restrictions. [HSE, HLL]

Light Festival

🌀 The Light Festival is an Ewok celebration honoring the periodic rejuvenation of the Tree of Light. [ETV]

lightsaber

lightsaber

🔵 The lightsaber is the elegant weapon of the Jedi Knights. These power swords project blades of pure energy capable of cutting through most materials—except the blade of another lightsaber. The design seems simple from the outside: a handgrip with several switches ends in a mirror-like, concave metal disk. Inside the handgrip, power cells and variously shaped crystals are activated to produce the narrow beam of meter-long light that gives the lightsaber its name. When activated, a lightsaber hums with power. Considered archaic when compared to blasters and other modern weapons, lightsabers are nonetheless impressive and powerful personal weapons that require extensive training to use effectively. Tradition dictates that lightsabers be constructed by their Jedi owners as part of the knighthood training. [SW, ESB, RJ]

⊙ The lightsaber is a compact technological wonder built into a handle from twenty-four to thirty centimeters long. A single power cell produces a tremendous charge of energy which flows through a series of multifaceted jewels within the handle's interior. The jewels focus the energy into a tight beam that can be emitted from the concave disk atop the handle. Sabers with a single jewel have a fixed amplitude and blade length. Those with multiple jewels (usually no more than three) can alter their amplitude and change the length of the light blade. This is accomplished by rotating an exterior control that varies the distance between the jewels. The emitted beam arcs back from its positively charged continuous energy lens to a negatively charged high-energy flux aperture set in the disk atop the handle. The power amplitude determines the point at which the beam arcs back, setting the blade's length. The lightsaber's blade emits no heat, though it does fluoresce. [SWSB, HESB]

lightspeed engine

See hyperdrive.

Light Spirit

The Light Spirit is a benign entity worshiped by the Ewoks. It protects them and guides them in all they do. [ETV]

light table

A light table is a holoprojector array commonly employed in command centers throughout the galaxy. These flat, circular devices display both holograms and holographs via the parabolic holoprojector at the center of the table's top. Numerous data displays surround the projector, offering plenty of room for information readouts. All of the displays and three-dimensional projections can be manipulated from touchboards around the table's edge. [RJ]

Lisstik

Lisstik was the leader of the Kamarian Badlanders who traded with Han Solo and Chewbacca the Wookiee during their stay on the planet Kamar. [HSR]

l'lahsh

L'lahsh was a traditional food dish made on the planet Alderaan. [SWR]

Lobot

On Cloud City, Lando Calrissian's administrative aid was the cyborg named Lobot. Through the use of a brain-enhancing device that he wore around his head, Lobot was able to remain in constant contact with Cloud City's central computers. [ESB]

locomotor

A locomotor is a servomechanism that gives droids and other automatons the ability to move from place to place. [SW]

Logray

The medicine man of the Ewok tribe that befriended Princess Leia and her companions is named Logray. This tan-striped Ewok wears the half skull of a great forest bird atop his head. A single feather adorns its crest. He wields a staff of power decorated with the spine of a great enemy. In his youth he was a great warrior, but now he is revered for his great wisdom. He aids his tribe with a variety of magic spells and potions. [RJ]

Lo Khan

The old smuggler Lo Khan, owner and operator of the *Hyperspace Marauder*, assisted Salla Zend and Shug Ninx during their visit to Byss. His partner and first mate is Luwingo, the Yaka cyborg. [DE]

lommite

The mineral lommite, found primarily on the planet

Elom, is a major component in the manufacture of transparisteel. [HESB]

Lord of the Sith

See Darth Vader.

Lord Tion

☪ The Imperial noble and soldier named Lord Tion served the Emperor as a task force commander. He was charged with identifying and eradicating all Alliance personnel and Rebel sympathizers on the planet Ralltiir. Lord Tion played an instrumental role in providing the location of the plans for the original Death Star battle station to Bail Organa. [SWR]

Lorrdian

✪ The human inhabitants of the planet Lorrd call themselves Lorrdians. They are renowned throughout the Empire as superlative mimes and mimics. This mimicry was originally developed as a form of communication, called "kenetic communication," during the Kanz Disorders. During this period, the Lorrdians were forbidden by those who conquered them to communicate in any way while they were busy at their slave labor. To get around this, they worked out an intricate and subtle system of facial expressions, hand movements, and slight body signals to pass along ideas and information to one another. Because of the period of servitude they had to endure until freed by Jedi Knights and forces of the Old Republic, most Lorrdians have no tolerance for slavers or slavekeepers. [HSR]

Lost City of the Jedi

🌑 An ancient city built long ago by Jedi Knights, the Lost City of the Jedi is located deep below the surface of Yavin Four. Droids have cared for the city and its hidden secrets for untold ages. A few Imperials are aware of the rumors concerning the city's existence, but none know its true location. [LCJ, PDS]

Luke Skywalker

🌑 Luke Skywalker is the Tatooine farm boy who went on to become a Rebel hero and Jedi Knight. He was raised by Owen and Beru Lars, who he believed were his uncle and aunt. During his eighteenth year, as boredom and the need to finally leave the desert planet were suffocating him, he saw signs of a space battle in the skies over Tatooine. He did not know it at the time, but this was more than a real engagement happening in Tatooine's orbit—it was a sign that his whole life was about to change, and that the destiny he was born to fulfill was ready to begin.

When Luke's Uncle Owen purchased a pair of droids from a group of Jawa merchants, Luke became wrapped up in the smaller droid's quest. For little R2-D2 had come to Tatooine to locate Obi-Wan Kenobi and present him with an important message. That message propelled Luke Skywalker on a journey to rescue Princess Leia and learn the skills of the Jedi Knights. Obi-Wan, whom Luke knew as Old Ben, explained that Luke's father had been a Jedi Knight who had been betrayed and murdered by Kenobi's student, Darth Vader. He gave Luke his father's lightsaber, promising to teach the young man the ways of the Force.

Unfortunately, the Empire was meanwhile searching for the pair of droids. Stormtroopers tracked the droids to the

Jawas and from them to Owen and Beru Lars, killing them all in their desire to leave no witnesses behind. With the help of Han Solo and Chewbacca the Wookiee, Luke, Obi-Wan, and the droids escaped from Tatooine and eventually rescued Princess Leia from the Death Star, though Obi-Wan was killed by Darth Vader during the campaign. But the Force was strong in Luke Skywalker, and he fired the shot that destroyed the Death Star to end the Battle of Yavin.

Over the next three years, Luke became a prominent member of the Rebel Alliance. He achieved the rank of commander and took charge of the X-wing squadron known as Rogue Squadron. While on Hoth, Luke was led by a vision of Obi-Wan Kenobi to the swamp planet Dagobah, where he was to find a Jedi Master named Yoda to complete his training. Luke learned much from the wizened old Yoda, but he cut his training short to help his friends at Cloud City. This was the site of Luke's first confrontation with Darth Vader. He lost three things in this meeting, and almost lost a fourth—his life. Vader sliced off Luke's right hand, sending it and his lightsaber heirloom into the bowels

Luke Skywalker

of Cloud City. Then Luke lost his innocence, for Vader told him that Kenobi had lied: Vader had not killed Luke's father. He *was* Luke's father. With the help of Princess Leia and Lando Calrissian, Luke barely escaped with his life.

After being fitted for a prosthetic hand, Luke traveled to Tatooine to rescue Han Solo from Jabba the Hutt. When Jabba refused to simply hand over Solo and let them all go free, Luke was forced to destroy the crime lord and his entire operation. He then returned to Dagobah to finish his training and discover the truth of Vader's words. But he found a dying Yoda, who confirmed his worst fears and explained that his training was complete. All he had to do to become a full Jedi was to confront Vader a second time. He also learned, from Ben Kenobi's spirit form, that Leia was his sister—another Skywalker strong in the Force, kept hidden to one day battle against the Emperor. At Endor, Luke decided to meet Vader, not in battle, but to free the good in him and return his father Anakin from the dark side. Even as the Emperor worked to corrupt Luke, Luke managed to reach the small spark of good buried deep within the darkness and armor of Vader, and Anakin Skywalker reemerged. Anakin then killed the Emperor and sacrificed his own life to save his son. Luke returned to his friends and family as the Galactic Civil War came to an end. [SW, ESB, RJ]

⚙ Five years after the Battle of Endor, Luke continued to assist the New Republic as a sort of goodwill ambassador and Jedi Knight at large. In the intervening years, he had begun training Princess Leia, but had not progressed very far. He was instrumental in putting a stop to Grand Admiral Thrawn's campaign to destroy the New Republic through the use of cloned warriors and the mad Jedi Master named Joruus C'baoth. During this period, he withstood the threats of Mara Jade and eventually convinced her to join the New Republic (or at least sign on so that he could help her learn to use her Force abilities).

One year later, Luke decided that the best way to defeat the reborn Emperor and resolve the galactic conflict was by learning the Emperor's darkest secrets as his protégé. In the end, he was forced to battle a young clone of the Emperor filled with the undying evil of the ancient Palpatine. The Emperor defeated him in lightsaber combat, but Leia came to her brother's aid. Luke learned that the way of the Jedi is not a solitary path. With the power of luminous beings, the brother and sister unleashed the Force upon the dark nexus that was Palpatine—together conquering his evil with a Jedi fire that outshone the dark side. Now it falls to Luke to help the Jedi order rise again. [HE, DFR, LC, DE]

Lumat

🔘 The Ewok warrior Lumat also serves as the tribe's woodcutter. He is the father of Latara, Nippet, and Wiley. His mate is Zephee. [ETV]

lumni-spice

🔘 Lumni-spice is the rarest form of spice in the galaxy. It grows deep in the caverns on Hoth and is fiercely protected by the dragon-slug, which feeds on the spice. [GW]

Lur

🔘 Turbulent winds, rain, sleet, and snow constantly pummel the surface of the planet Lur. The world, which lies in a star system close to the Corporate Sector, is partially covered by huge glacial fields. The intelligent inhabitants of the planet are called Lurrians. These small, bipedal hominids have fine white fur and large blue-green eyes. [HSR]

Luuke Skywalker

⊕ Luuke Skywalker was the clone of Luke Skywalker, created from cells taken from the hand Luke lost in his lightsaber duel with Darth Vader at Cloud City. The Jedi Master Joruus C'baoth, himself a clone, ordered the creation of Luuke from the Emperor's prized souvenir: sample B-2332-54. He wanted a Jedi student of his own, and if he could not have the real Skywalker he would settle for the specially created clone. Using Luke's lightsaber, lost along with his hand, the clone nearly destroyed the true Jedi during their confrontation on Wayland. Mara Jade killed Luuke Skywalker during the fray, fulfilling the powerful last command thrust upon her years before by the dying Emperor. [LC]

Luwingo

⊕ Luwingo is the first mate on the *Hyperspace Marauder* and partner to Lo Khan, the ship's owner. He is a Yaka cyborg, possessing brain implants like the other members of his race. Though he appears brutish, Luwingo regularly beats the L7 logician droid in hologames. [DE]

Lwyll

⊕ Lwyll, the wife of the smuggler Roa, is a striking woman with masses of wavy, white-blond hair and an elegant face. She knows Han Solo from the time when Solo worked for her husband. [HSR]

M

Mace Towani

The young teenage boy named Mace Towani is part of a human family that became shipwrecked on Endor's forest moon for a time. He, his sister Cindel, and his parents Jeremitt and Catarine had a number of amazing adventures with the Ewoks they befriended. [EA, BFE]

macrobinoculars

Macrobinoculars are hand-held viewing devices that magnify distant objects, providing both day and night vision through built-in light and dark scopes. Readouts within the viewplate give information on the viewed object's true and relative azimuth, its elevation, and its range. [SW]

macrofuser

The macrofuser is a miniature welding tool. It is designed and calibrated for heavy-duty repairs of complex metals, like those found in starships. [ESB]

Madine

See General Madine.

Magg

⊙ The slave trader Magg posed as Fiolla of Lorrd's personal assistant in order to keep tabs on her investigations in Corporate Sector space. [HSR]

main drive

⊙ A starship's main drive is its primary propulsion unit and most powerful onboard engine. In the case of hyperspace-capable ships, the main drive is usually the hyperdrive. [SWR]

maintenance hauler

⊙ When starships break down, a specific type of star tug called a maintenance hauler provides towing services back to the nearest spaceport. Major space lanes have small fleets of haulers at the ready to quickly clear wrecks so that sublight and hyperspace travel can continue uninterrupted through the area. [HLL]

maitrakh

⊙ Maitrakh is the Noghri word for the female ruler of a clan. The word is used as a title, full of reverence, respect, and tradition, and once it is applied to a Noghri it almost becomes a name as well. One particular maitrakh, the woman who leads clan Kihm'bar, provided help to Princess Leia and was influential in convincing the Noghri to turn away from the Empire. [DFR, DFRSB, LC]

Major Derlin

Major Derlin was an Alliance field officer assigned to the Rebel base on Hoth at the time of the battle which rocked that system. [ESB]

makants

Makants are large, playful insects that appear to be crosses of mantises and crickets. They live in the forests of Endor's moon. [ETV]

Maker, the

The Maker is a reference to the One Who Creates. Many droids use this expression in an almost-religious context. C-3PO, for example, often uses the phrase "Thank the Maker!" when something good happens to him or his friends. [SW]

Mako Spince

The grizzled old Corellian smuggler named Mako Spince was Han Solo's classmate at the Academy. He is now a traffic controller at the spaceport moon Nar Shaddaa. [DE]

Malani

⊛ The young Ewok named Malani is Teebo's little sister. She has a huge crush on Wicket. [ETV]

Mal'ary'ush

⊛ Mal'ary'ush is the Noghri title applied to Leia Organa Solo. It identifies her as the daughter of Lord Darth Vader and heir to the debt the Noghri believe they owe him. [HE, DFR, LC]

Malkite Poisoner

⊛ A Malkite Poisoner is any of a secret order of elite assassins who learned their deadly craft on the planet Malkii. The world is a haven for all manner of terrorists and mercenaries, though the Poisoners are by far the most infamous. These assassins carry small vials of lethal toxins in specialized kits, which fit into hiding places within the assassins' clothing. They live by a special code that demands that members of the elite order never allow themselves to be captured alive. [HSR]

Malorm Family

⊛ The crimes of the Malorm Family are among the most infamous of those ever to occur in Corporate Sector space. These human psychopathic killers hijacked the luxury spaceliner *Galaxy Wanderer* as it passed through the Corporate Sector. During the incident, the Malorm family dropped more than thirty passengers out of the spaceliner into deep space, ransacked the ship's vaults, and held Authority Espo forces at bay. The three men (Shalla, Rek and Jez), and two women (Sheyna and Star) who made up the Malorm Family escaped but were tracked to the Authority planet Matra VI. The Corporate Sector Authority Counterterrorist Security Team set up an ambush and eventually brought the group to justice. [HLL]

Manarai Mountains

The snow-covered peaks of the Manarai Mountains rise above Imperial City, covering a significant area of the planet Coruscant's main continent. [HE, HESB]

Mandalore warriors

The Mandalore warriors were defeated by the Jedi Knights during the Clone Wars. [ESB]

mantigrue

The mantigrue is a hideous, dragonlike creature with leathery wings, sharp claws, and a long, pointed beak. These beasts can be found on Endor's forest moon. One of the creatures is the slave or Morag, the Tulgah witch. [ETV]

manumitting

When a droid's obedience-rationale functions are reprogrammed with an incentive for extraordinary services, it is called manumitting. This incentive takes the form of a reward of freedom, allowing a droid to find its own preferred work and activities if it meets the incentive requirements. [HSR]

Mara Jade

🌀 Mara Jade once served as the Emperor's Hand, an extension of the Emperor's will that could go anywhere in the galaxy to advance his evil. Her limited abilities in the Force made her a perfect agent; she could hear her master's call over vast distances. She had prestige, power, purpose and respect—until Luke Skywalker caused the Emperor's death. She blames herself for that event, for she was on Tatooine, undercover in Jabba the Hutt's court, when Skywalker arrived to rescue Han Solo. She was unable to work her way onto Jabba's sail barge, however, so Skywalker eluded her and eventually went to Endor's moon for the confrontation with her master. Since the death of the Emperor, the woman with the dancer's figure, green eyes, and red-gold hair has been consumed by deep hatred for Skywalker. In fact, the last message her master sent to her was an order to kill Luke Skywalker.

After Endor, Mara could not go to the Imperial remnants, for her identity was a secret. She had worked outside the normal chain of command and protocol, a shadow controlled by the Emperor and unknown to the rest of the bureaucracy. Besides, the Empire was dying and she did not want to be part of its funeral. Still, she had no identity, no contacts, no resources. She was forced to take whatever jobs she could find, all the while planning the many ways she would kill Skywalker. She eventually hooked up with Talon Karrde's organization, and her abilities and training earned her the rank of his second-in-command.

Her powers began to return in response to the emergence of the Jedi Master Joruus C'baoth. On Myrkr, she

Mara Jade

was forced to help Luke Skywalker in order to save Karrde and his organization. This pattern repeated itself a number of times during the events surrounding the return of Grand Admiral Thrawn. In the end, Mara continued to help Skywalker, and he in turn helped her. She was able to quench her hatred by slaying the clone of Luke Skywalker created by Joruus C'baoth, and may even take up Luke's offer to stay with the New Republic and become a Jedi Knight. [HE, DFR, LC, HESB, DFRSB]

Marauders

The Marauders are a species of barbaric, two-meter-plus-tall humanoids who prey upon the more peaceful inhabitants of Endor's forest moon. These beings have scaly, monkeylike faces, and wear ragged clothing adorned with scavenged items. The Marauders weave a path of death and destruction in their search for an elusive entity they call "the power." They inhabit a gloomy, moat-surrounded fortress in the middle of a desolate plain. [BFE]

Mark II Reactor Drone

✦ Mark II Reactor Drones are utility droids built and programmed for menial labor. Heavily shielded outer casings protect their sensitive internal circuitry and give these droids a lumbering, cumbersome appearance. [SWR]

Mark X Executioner

✦ The droid model Mark X Executioner is designated a gladiator droid. Its basic function is to perform as an entertainment droid specializing in combat sports. To defend itself and to provide an offensive punch when matched against living creatures and other droids, the Mark X has built-in flame projectors, flechette missile launchers, and blasters. Two crawler threads provide it with locomotion. [HSE]

Marso

✦ Marso is the leader of a group of mercenary pilots called the Demons. [HLL]

Massassi

✦ The ancient Massassi site on Yavin's fourth moon holds a number of huge temples whose origin remains a mystery to this day. One of these temples was converted into a secret Rebel base. The base was evacuated after the Battle of Yavin. [SW]

The Massassi left a creature known as the night beast to protect their homeland against enemy takeover. During the time the ancient ruins housed the Rebel base, the night beast was awakened when a TIE fighter crashed. Luke Skywalker was able to lure the beast into a supply ship and send it off in the direction the Massassi people had taken when they departed. [GW]

Master Control Signal

The Master Control Signal is a transmission beamed through hyperspace to the Empire's new World Devastators. Originating on the hidden world of Byss, this signal guides and controls the war machines. [DE]

Master Thon

The alien Jedi Master, Thon of Ambria, lived approximately four thousand years before the time of the New Republic. As the teachings of the Krath sect were gaining prominence, Master Thon addressed a great assembly of ten thousand Jedi Masters who had gathered on Mount Meru on the desert world of Deneba. He spoke eloquently against straying from the light side, hoping to convince his peers of the dangers of the Krath philosophy. [DE]

Max Rebo

The Ortolan musician named Max Rebo is leader of a jizz-wailer band. This blue, flop-eared being was a favorite of Jabba the Hutt. His band often played exclusive concerts for the crime lord at Jabba's desert palace on Tatooine. [RJ]

Max Rebo Band

(✺) The Max Rebo Band, an odd collection of alien jizz-wailers, often performed exclusive engagements for the crimelord Jabba the Hutt. The band was made up of Max Rebo, Droopy McCool, and the singer Sy Snootles. [RJ]

Mazzic

(✺) The smuggler chief Mazzic runs an operation that is much more militaristic than Talon Karrde's. In addition to freighters of all descriptions, his fleet includes a number of customized combat starships, like the *Skyclaw* and the *Raptor*, which he is not afraid to send into the thick of battle. He travels in his personal transport, the *Distant Rainbow*. The woman named Shada, his deceptively decorative bodyguard, is never far from his side. Mazzic is among the smuggler chiefs Karrde convinced to join forces to indirectly (and for a profit) help the New Republic against the Empire during the time of Grand Admiral Thrawn's campaign. [LC]

medical cocoon

(✺) A medical cocoon is a portable enclosure for moving the sick and injured from one environment to another. A medical cocoon is totally self-sufficient, equipped with its own miniature power generator, regulators, and monitoring bank. The regulators control the cocoon's temperature and humidity level, as well as the circulation of precious fluids and gases throughout the cocoon. A patient can be cared for and sustained within a medical cocoon until transported to a medical facility. [SME]

medical droid

⚓ A medical droid is any mechanical whose primary function is to diagnose or treat illness and injury, perform or assist with surgical procedures, or provide care for the infirm. [ESBR]

✴ Medical droids are common fixtures in hospitals and clinics throughout the galaxy. Many models are non-mobile, tethered to huge diagnostic and treatment analysis computers. The MD series of medical droids are the models that have seen the widest service. From the MD-Os (Emdee-Ohs), diagnostic droids who assist physicians with patient examinations, to the MD-5s (Emdee-fives), general-practitioner droids who are considered the "country doctors" of space, the MD series is versatile, competent, and affordable. The older 21B and FX series droids can still be found among the Alliance and on frontier worlds. [SWSB]

medical frigate

⚓ A medical frigate is any small star cruiser devoted exclusively to the transportation and care of the wounded and convalescent, and staffed primarily by medical personnel. These ships also carry medical supplies and facilities for treating and caring for the sick and injured. [ESB]

meditation chamber

⚓ In Lord Darth Vader's private chambers aboard the Super Star Destroyer *Executor*, his personal meditation chamber served as his sanctum from the world. This spherical enclosure split open to permit exit and entry, its top and bottom halves separating like the maw of some dark beast. The interior consisted of a comfortable, reclining chair, a comlink and visual display, and a mechanical device for quickly removing and replacing Vader's helmet and breath mask. The pressurized sphere kept Vader comfortable even when his helmet was not in place. [ESB]

medpac

A medpac (or medipak) is a compact first aid kit complete with everything necessary to treat wounds when a medical facility is unavailable. Each medpac contains a synth-flesh dispenser, vibroscalpel, flexclamp, pain killers, disinfectant pads, and precious fluid and gas cartridges. No set of survival gear would be complete without at least one medpac. [HSE, HLL, HSR, SWRPG2]

Meerian Hammerhead

Meerian Hammerhead is a member of an alien species of humanoids called Ithorians which have flat heads and curved necks. [SWR]

Megadeath

See Dyyz Nataz.

memory flush

A memory flush, or memory wipe, is used to erase all of the accumulated data stored in a computer system or droid data bank. Most droids dread this procedure. [SW]

Mid Rim

The huge expanse of space between the Inner Rim and Outer Rim Territories is called the Mid Rim. It is a less wealthy and less populated region, with fewer natural resources, than the regions around it. As an undeveloped area, much of the Mid Rim remains either unexplored or the domain of fringe society groups like smugglers and pirates. [SWRPG2]

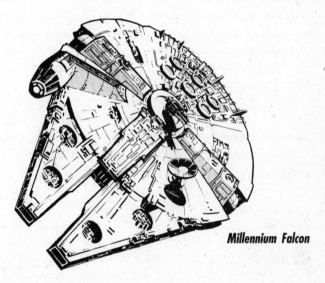

Millennium Falcon

Millennium Falcon

The *Millennium Falcon* is an old, battered, and reconstructed stock light freighter of Corellian design, approximately twenty-seven meters in length. Currently it serves as the personal transport and means of income of Han Solo and his partner, Chewbacca the Wookiee. In the past, it also belonged to Lando Calrissian and assorted others. Under Solo's guidance and Chewbacca's careful and loving administration, the *Falcon* has undergone major overhauls, refittings, and modifications that make all but its external appearance vastly different from the manufacturer's specifications. Some of the modifications include custom security mechanisms, computer-assisted targeting consoles, and boosted deflector shields; it also has a more powerful hyperdrive, armored hull, and weapons system than allowed for a ship of its class, size, and designation. The *Falcon* is armed with two quad laser cannons (one each in top and bottom turrets), two concussion missile launchers, and a retractable light laser cannon. With the addition of falsified ID profiles and hidden cargo holds, the *Falcon* is a perfect smuggling vessel. During much of the Galactic Civil War, the *Falcon* suffered from a rash of minor problems that required almost constant periods of repair. Still, it was one of the best ships in service to the Alliance. It participated in the destruction of both Death Star battle stations, ran through Imperial blockades with apparent ease, and ferried Princess Leia Organa on many of her most important missions during those dark years. [SW, ESB, RJ]

Mimban

Mimban was the name the locals gave to the planet Circarpous V. The world lies under a perpetual cloud of rain storms and is composed of moist and misty jungles. [SME]

Mimbanite

A Mimbanite is a native inhabitant of Circarpous V. The humans who live and work on the planet call these surface dwellers "greenies," a derogatory term. Other nonhuman species living on a Mimban include the Coway and the Thrella. [SME]

Minos Cluster

🌀 The Minos Cluster is located on the edge of the known galaxy, beyond which there are no star charts, no Empire, and no Rebellion. The worlds of the Cluster have only recently been colonized, and the entire area is behind the times and out of touch. It is an area where the fringe society holds sway—smugglers, pirates, and outlaw types readily head to the Cluster in the hopes of earning (or stealing) a fortune. [GG6]

missile tube

🌀 A missile tube is a mobile, fixed, or portable canister that carries and fires long- or short-range missiles (usually of either the proton or concussion type). [HSR]

mobile command base

🌀 The tread-driven mobile command base gives Imperial field commanders a protected, mobile base of operations from which they can lead their ground forces. The armored outer hull is almost one meter thick and covered in reflective shielding. The interior command pod is encased within a second shell or armor, creating a secure cocoon from which field commanders can view ground actions. It can hold up to seven passengers, as well as its crew of three. A sophisticated sensor array gathers battlefield data for analysis by onboard computers to help the command personnel devise tactics and constantly update strategies. Each mobile command base has a heavy laser cannon, but this is more for defense than for offense. The vehicle is not supposed to engage in direct combat, but to provide a secure platform for battlesite observation and planning. [ISB]

Moff Jerjerrod

(✦) Moff Jerjerrod was the commander in charge of overseeing the construction of the second Death Star battle station. [RJ]

Moff Tarkin

See Grand Moff Tarkin.

mogo

(✦) A mogo is a massive black-furred creature with a camellike head and an undulating body. Mogos are used for transportation on the planet Roon. [DTV]

moisture farm

(✦) Moisture farms extract water from the atmosphere for profitable use on dry, desert worlds. The moisture farms of Tatooine, for example, use vaporators to pull water from the air. This water is then used by the farmers for drinking and to irrigate subterranean produce farms; sometimes the precious liquid is sold to other inhabitants. Luke Skywalker grew up on one of Tatooine's moisture farms. [SW]

mole miner

⊙ A mole miner is a utility craft specially designed to operate in space, on asteroids, and on worlds with hostile or no atmospheres. As the name implies, a mole miner digs ore out of locations that are normally out of the reach of most humans and humanoid species. It does not have the range or storage capacity to function as an independent craft. Instead, it operates from a base or headquarters ship, leaving its dock to perform its function and then returning at the end of a work shift. The two-man mole miner looks like a cone that has had its point chopped off. It can be operated by a crew or controlled by a remote comm unit using the craft's integrated slave circuits.

Using its bottom-mounted plasma jets to slice through solid rock, the mole miner gathers the precious minerals and ores into storage bins through a series of vacuum shafts and grinders. Though once in widespread use, mole miners have largely been replaced by mining droids. Lando Calrissian employed mole miners at his operation on the planet Nkllon until a large number of the craft were stolen by Grand Admiral Thrawn. The Empire used the mole miners at the Battle of Sluis Van to burrow into capital ships so that Imperial crews could hijack the vessels. [HE, HESB]

Moltok

⊙ Moltok is the homeworld of the Ho'Din species. [GG4, LCJ]

Momaw Nadon

⊙ The Ithorian (or Hammerhead) named Momaw Nadon

lives on the planet Tatooine, an exile from his native Ithor because he spoke out against the Empire and called for his peaceful species to fight against the tyranny. He aids the Alliance in whatever way he can, providing information and sheltering Rebel agents when the opportunity arises. [GG1]

Mon Calamari

🔴 The bipedal amphibious species known as the Mon Calamari come from the planet of the same name. This gentle race became strong supporters of the Rebellion after the Empire invaded their world. The Mon Calamari watched many of their cities crumble under the onslaught of the Empire in response to their refusal to toil as slaves to help build the Imperial war machine. The capricious destruction was intended to be a clear message as to the fate of all those who oppose the Emperor's New Order. Instead, it turned the peaceful Mon Calamari into a formidable fighting force and the soul of the Rebel Alliance. In addition to their numbers, the Mon Calamari brought with them badly needed capital starships and the leadership of Ackbar. [RJ]

🔴 The Mon Calamari are a race of shore-dwellers with an affinity for water. They developed a symbiotic relationship with the water-dwelling Quarren who also inhabit their world, and this joining led to the planet's golden age. With the Quarren to mine ore from the ocean floor and the Mon Calamari to design practical uses for the metal, the great floating cities of Mon Calamari were built. These cities extend above and below the water, and the technology was eventually used to create orbiting space platforms. The Mon Calamari see space as an endless ocean of stars, and they were tempted to explore those depths from the earliest periods of their civilization. First they colonized their own star system; then they discovered the secret of the hyperdrive. But before they could reach out to find the galactic community they dreamed of, they met the Empire. The Empire did not want to share anything with the Calamarians; they wanted to use the gentle folk and their technology to further their own war effort. When the Mon Calamarians refused to become slaves, the Empire destroyed a number of floating cities. It was the Empire's opinion that such a display of destruction would cow the peaceful people. Instead, they learned to fight back. After repelling the Imperial forces, the Mon Calamarians discovered the Alliance to Restore the Republic. They joined with this group, pledging to fight for the dream of freedom until the Empire was finally destroyed.

Six years after the Battle of Endor, as the New Republic was solidifying its position in the galaxy, the Empire began a new campaign to reassert its power and dominance. The water world of Calamari was the first planet attacked by the reborn Emperor's World Devastators in the Battle of Calamari. The world suffered great amounts of damage, but the new Imperial war machines were eventually stopped thanks to the actions of Luke Skywalker. [SWSB, DE]

Mon Calamari star cruiser

Each Mon Calamari star cruiser is handcrafted by dedicated technicians and engineers. These capital ships are treated as works of art, not simply as weapons of war. In fact, they were originally spaceliners that were converted into combat starships when the Mon Calamari joined the Alliance. One of the first models to be converted was the MC80, a 1,200-meter-long cylindrical ship covered with pods, bulges, and bumps arranged in a seemingly haphazard fashion. Mon Calamari ships look more organic than technological, but they are considered to be among the finest vessels traveling the space lanes. These vessels are built with many redundant systems, making them difficult to service but extremely reliable in combat situations. [SWSB]

Mon Julpa

Mon Julpa was the crown prince of the planet Tammuz-an during the early days of the Empire. The evil vizier Zatec-Cha stripped Mon Julpa of his title and his memory, and for a time he wandered the planet as the tall, frail, simpleminded Kez-Iban. [DTV]

Mon Mothma

Mon Mothma had been the senior Senator of the Old Republic when Palpatine rose to power. She remained a part of the Senate for as long as she thought there was still a way to repair the system from within. When Palpatine declared himself Emperor and the Senate lost all but the most rudimentary powers, Mon Mothma went underground to help

Mon Mothma

form the Alliance to Restore the Republic. She organized cells of resistance across the galaxy, using her own beliefs in freedom and the rights of all beings to inspire others to action. As the Empire's tyranny became more apparent, her movement gained momentum and spread rapidly. Soon whole planets were throwing in with the Alliance, and Mon Mothma was elected as its leader. Her initial plan never wavered: by engaging the Empire in hit-and-run skirmishes, the Alliance would publicize its existence to the galaxy and show that the Empire was not all-powerful. Over time, she worked to organize the forces necessary for a final military confrontation to determine the fate of the galaxy. That confrontation took place in a tiny system, in the shadow of a forest moon—the Battle of Endor. [RJ]

⬤ Mon Mothma's family background prepared her for her role in the Rebel Alliance. Her father was an arbiter-general for the Old Republic who was called upon to settle disputes between the various member species. Her mother was a planetary governor, who taught her daughter how to administer, to organize, and to lead. Chandrila, her homeworld, elected her to the Republic Senate at an early age (she was the youngest Senator to serve until the election of Leia Organa of Alderaan). She served with vigor and integrity, despite the fact that the Republic was already crumbling from internal corruption. She distrusted her colleague Senator Palpatine from the start, and was at the forefront of those opposing his New Order when he was elected President of the Senate. She strived to work within the law, upholding the principles of the Republic even as the Empire was being formed. She was the last Senator to gain the title of Senior Senator, but she relinquished this post when it appeared that the Senate was to be disbanded. Going into hiding, she used her skills as a diplomat to bring the various rebellious groups together as the Alliance to Restore the Republic. In this capacity, she was selected to lead the Alliance in its quest to restore freedom and justice to the galaxy. [SWSB]

Since the end of the Galactic Civil War, Mon Mothma has been working to build a new government called the New Republic. She has aged noticeably in the five years since the Battle of Endor, but her mind remains sharp and her commitment total. Through her efforts, the new republic may well become as true in form as it is in name. [HE, DFR, LC]

Mookiee

🌑 Mookiee is a female baby Ewok, or Wokling. [ETV]

Mooth

🌑 Mooth is the elderly trader who operates a trading post on Endor's forest moon. This fast-talking character resembles a humanoid anteater. He wears a primitive gambler's visor on his head, and an abacus strapped across his chest. [ETV]

Morag

🌑 Morag is a powerful Tulgah witch who lives on the forest moon of Endor. With a shriveled, stooped body and a mandrill's face, she is thoroughly evil. Her skills in magic and medicine rival even Logray's. She lives in a castlelike formation set into the side of the active volcano called Mount Thunderstone. Spear-wielding Yuzzums patrol her home atop rakazzak beasts. [ETV]

morrt

Parasites about the size of field mice, morrts are native to the planet Gamorr. These bloodsuckers feed on living organisms, staying with a single host throughout their long lives. Gamorreans consider morrts to be friendly, cuddly, and loyal. They keep these parasites as pets and status symbols. They are the only creatures to which Gamorreans display open signs of affection, and the more morrts attached to a Gamorrean, the more status the Gamorrean has in the eyes of his fellows. Matrons and clan warlords regularly have in excess of twenty morrts covering their bodies, growing fat on their bodily liquids. [SWSB]

Mor Glayyd

Mor Glayyd is the patriarch of the Glayyd family on the planet Ammuud. "Mor" is a title of respect that is bestowed upon the current clan patriarch. The given name of the Mor Glayyd when Han Solo visited the planet, prior to his involvement in the Rebellion, was Ewwen. [HSR]

Mos Eisley

Mos Eisley is the spaceport city on the Outer Rim world of Tatooine. The city attracts interstellar commerce as well as all sorts of spacers looking for rest and relaxation after a long haul. The vast number of aliens and humans constantly moving through the spaceport, and its distance from the centers of Imperial activity, make Mos Eisley a haven for all types of thieves, pirates, and smugglers. Even now, without the influence of Jabba the Hutt and his criminal organization, the city remains a "hive of scum and villainy." The city's old central section is laid out like a wheel, while the newer sections are formed into straight blocks of half-buried buildings (to protect them from the heat of the twin suns). Instead of having a central landing area, the entire city is the spaceport, with craterlike docking bays scattered throughout Mos Eisley. [SW]

motivator

A motivator is the primary device within a droid that converts energy into mechanical motion. Without a motivator, a droid would not be capable of locomotion. [SW]

Motti

See Admiral Motti.

Mount Tantiss

Mount Tantiss, on the planet Wayland, was used by the Emperor as a private storehouse for those items he deemed important to his long-range plans. The storehouse was a combination trophy room and equipment dump, built within the hollowed-out mountain. The multiple levels included vast chambers of art, captured souvenirs, and experimental devices, as well as royal suites and a throne room for the Emperor. Among the treasures hidden within Mount Tantiss's vaults were a working prototype for a cloaking device and tiers upon tiers of spaarti cloning cylinders. [HE, DFR, LC, HESB, DFRSB]

Mount Yoda

⊕ Mount Yoda, a mountain on the planet Dagobah, was named in honor of the famed Jedi Master after the Battle of Endor. The Alliance established a base on the mountain. [MMY, PDS]

mudmen

⊕ Mudmen are creatures made entirely of mud which live on the planet Roon. They love to tickle victims until they are completely helpless and then rob them of all their shiny objects. Mudmen explode into small blobs if they are sprayed with water, though they then regenerate into more mudmen. [DTV]

Muftak

⊕ Muftak the Talz grew up in the streets of Mos Eisley, where he continues to make a living doing odd jobs and even begging. He hangs out with the Chadra-fan named Kabe. [GG1]

Mungo Baobob

⊕ Mungo Baobob, who loved to travel and seek new treasures, was a member of the family that owned the Baobob Merchant Fleet during the early days of the Empire. His home planet was Manda. He frequently disregarded safety precautions and careful planning while pursuing reckless adventure. He was sent to the planet Biitu to establish a trading post and fuel-ore mining operation.

Murgoob, The Great

🌑 The Great Murgoob (or Murgoob the Cranky) is the aged and nasty oracle of the Duloks. He is over six hundred years old. [ETV]

Muskov

See Chief Muskov.

Muzzer

See Grand Moff Muzzer.

Myneyrsh

🌑 Myneyrsh inhabit the planet Wayland. Like the Psadan, the Myneyrsh were present on the world when the first human colonists arrived centuries ago. The Myneyrsh are tall, thin humanoids with four arms and a smooth layer of blue crystal flesh that makes them seem to be beings of glass. They stand about 1.9 meters tall. The Myneyrsh use bows and arrows and animals instead of blasters and repulsors, and they have held an uneasy peace with the other inhabitants of Wayland after years of warfare. [HE, HESB, LC]

mynock

🌑 A mynock is a parasitic creature that feeds on energy. These black, leathery flying creatures attach themselves with specialized suction organs to passing starships. They

mynock

typically travel in packs, and a common specimen can grow as large as 1.6 meters with a wingspan of 1.25 meters. [ESB]

Mynocks are a silicon-based life-form that evolved in the vacuum of space. They are nourished by stellar radiation and absorb silicon and other minerals from asteroids and other space debris. When they absorb enough extra material, they reproduce by dividing in two. As they are extremely energy-tropic, they often attach themselves to passing starships. They not only seek the energy spillage these ships give off, but they absorb the minerals from the hulls in order to reproduce themselves. This causes untold damage to the ships if their presence is not discovered in time. Although they once came from a single system, mynocks have migrated throughout the galaxy as unwanted passengers aboard unsuspecting starships. [SWSB]

Myrkr

The isolated world called Myrkr lies within the Borderland Regions of space that separate New Republic territory from what remains of the Empire. The temperate planet once served as the private base of operations for Talon

Karrde's smuggling ring. He was forced to abandon the base after Grand Admiral Thrawn invaded the planet in search of Luke Skywalker. Myrkr has some unique features. Its tall trees have a high metal content which blocks sensor sweeps, and one of its native species, the creatures called ysalamiri, have the ability to push back the Force. While Luke Skywalker was visiting the planet, he recalled stories from his youth that invoked frightening images of fortresses inhabited by evil beings that had trees growing through them. His memories of the dark tales were incomplete, and all he could remember were feelings of danger, helplessness, and fear. [HE, HESB]

Mystra

A professional killer, Mystra carries a wrist blaster and wears a helmet with cybervision that gives her perfect aim on any target. [GW]

Mytus VII

Mytus VII, a planet located deep within Corporate Sector space, was the site of the Authority's secret prison facility called Stars' End. This rocky, airless planet orbits at the edge of its solar system. Two small moons spin around it. [HSE]

N

Nahkee

🌀 The baby Phlog (or Phlogling) named Nahkee stands more than two meters tall. Despite his great size, he displays all of the trust, innocence, and curiosity of all children his age. [ETV]

Nal Hutta

🌀 Nal Hutta, which means "Glorious Jewel" in Huttese, is one of the systems colonized by the Hutts. The infamous Jabba the Hutt was born in this system. [DE]

NaQuoit Bandits

🌀 The outlaw group of nonhumans known as the NaQuoit Bandits operate in the Ottega system, where they prey upon local space traffic. [DE]

Narra

See Commander Narra.

Nar Shaddaa

Nar Shaddaa is the spaceport moon that orbits the planet Nal Hutta. Untold smuggling operations are based here, and many Corellian pirates use the place as a refuge. In addition, all manner of galactic dregs, both alien and human, fill the streets of the vertical city. [DE]

nashtah

Nashtah are six-legged hunting creatures native to the planet Dra III. These bloodthirsty reptilians are vicious and tenacious. Once they have a prey's scent, they stay on its track until they catch it. With triple rows of jagged teeth and diamond-hard claws, they can easily back up their aggressive tendencies. Green color, sleek hide, and a long barbed tail add to the nashtah's physical impressiveness. [HSR]

nav computer

A nav computer is a specialized processing unit that calculates lightspeed jumps, plots hyperspace and realspace trajectories, and suggests routes based upon available time and energy fuel. Nav computers also display astrogation charts and work in conjunction with a ship's navigational sensors. These devices are sometimes called navicomputers. [SWRPG, SWSB]

Needa

See Captain Needa.

Neema

🌀 Neema is the daughter of the Jedi Knight Vima-Da-Boda. [DE]

nek battle dog

neks

🌀 Nek battle dogs are bred in the Cyborrean system for sale on the galactic black market. These vicious creatures are fitted with armor and attack stimulators. [DE]

nerf

✊ Nerfs are domesticated herbivores, cared for by tenders called nerf herders. These animals are grown as a meat source, though their pelts have a variety of uses. [ESB]

nergon 14

⊕ Nergon 14 is an unstable, explosive element. It is one of the primary components in Imperial-made proton torpedoes. A pulsating blue color when inert, nergon 14 changes to bright red and then white before it explodes. [DTV]

Neva

See Captain Neva.

New Alderaan

⊕ A colony planet established by the Rebel Alliance, New Alderaan is home for those Alderaanians who were off-world when Moff Tarkin ordered the peace-loving planet destroyed. Mon Mothma's disabled daughter lives on this planet. [DE]

New Cov

⊕ The planet New Cov is the third world in the Churba star system. It has no indigenous intelligent life, but its vast jungles teem with abundant natural resources. Eight walled cities, including the city of Ilic, have been built on New Cov by the New Cov Biomolecule Company to serve as work colonies. The sentient plants of the world are a great source of biomolecules—an important manufacturing component that cannot be synthesized. These biomolecules are used to create medicines and in partially organic industrial processes. The Covies harvest the biomolecules, process them, and then prepare them for shipment to heavy-industry planets. Of course, the dangerous plants eat as many harvesters as they can, and the armored city walls are designed to keep out plants and their spores. The planet is allied with the New Republic, but it makes periodic tributes to the Empire in the form of sanctioned Imperial raids. The Empire comes in, takes however many refined biomolecules it needs, then leaves the world to its own devices. In this way, the Covies stay on good terms with both governments. [DFR, DFRSB]

New Order, the

The New Order is the name of the Emperor's tyrannical regime. [SW]

New Republic, the

The New Republic is the name of the democratic government established by the Alliance to Restore the Republic after the Battle of Endor. It is based on the tenets and principles that marked the best years of the Old Republic. [HE, DFR, LC, DE]

Nien Nunb

Nien Nunb, a Rebel pilot from the planet Sullust, served as Lando Calrissian's copilot aboard the *Millennium Falcon* during the Battle of Endor. Like others of his species, Nien Nunb is a jowled, mouse-eyed humanoid. He stands slightly over 1.5 meters tall. [RJ]

night beast

night beast

🔴 When the Massassi departed Yavin Four, they left the night beast as a guardian to protect their homeland against enemy takeover until they returned. When an Imperial TIE fighter crashed into the Massassi ruins, the night beast emerged and ravaged the Rebel base hidden there. With the aid of the Force and R2-D2, Luke Skywalker was able to lure the night beast into a Rebel supply ship and send it off to follow its original masters. [GW]

nightcrawler

🔵 Nightcrawlers are small nocturnal insects native to the planet Tatooine. [SW]

Night Spirit

The Night Spirit is an evil entity whom the Ewoks fear and the Duloks (and other evil inhabitants of Endor's moon) worship. It sometimes manifests as ghostly apparitions. [ETV]

Nikto

The humanoid species known as the Nikto have flat faces with multiple nostrils. Four small horns protrude from their foreheads. Several Nikto were employed by Jabba the Hutt as skiff guards and hired muscle. [RJ]

Niles Ferrier

The large human named Niles Ferrier has dark hair, wears a beard, and dresses in ornate tunics. He smokes long, thin cigarras, and the distinctive aroma of carababba tabac and armundu spice hangs around him. This jack-of-all-trades is best known as a starship thief. When Grand Admiral Thrawn placed a bounty of twenty percent over current market value for capital ships, Niles could not pass up the chance to make some quick credits. He works with a small gang of five humans, a Verpine, and a Defel. Though Lando Calrissian and Luke Skywalker foiled Niles Ferrier's plans to steal a few ships from the Sluis Van Shipyards, he was able to provide Thrawn with an even greater prize—the location of the legendary *Katana* fleet. [DFR, DFRSB, LC]

Nilz Yomm

☻ Nilz Yomm was the father of Auren Yomm. In the early days of the Empire, Nilz ran a trading post and was a very respected physician in the Roon colonies. [DTV]

Ninedenine

See EV-9D9.

Nippett

☻ Nippett is an infant Ewok on Endor's forest moon. [RJ]

Nkllon

☻ A planet in the Athega system, Nkllon is a super-hot world rich in ores and other raw materials. It orbits very close to its sun, and ships that approach without the protection of accompanying shieldships risk having their hulls melted away. The planet has a very slow rotation, however, and this allowed Lando Calrissian to set up a mining operation on the planet. Since the dark side of the world is relatively safe to work on, Calrissian built a moving city to serve as a base and processing plant. Called Nomad City, the base moves in order to always stay on the planet's dark side. [HE, HESB]

Noa

☻ The old man named Noa has been stranded on Endor's

moon for many years. He arrived there by star cruiser while conducting a survey expedition, but his ship crashed. He has a gruff exterior but a kind heart. He has a long white beard, piercing eyes, and an ample belly. He befriended Cindel Towani and Wicket the Ewok mostly at the urging of his companion Teek. [BFE]

Noghri

🔘 Lord Darth Vader discovered the Noghri species on the planet Honoghr sometime before the formation of the Rebel Alliance. The Empire tended to ignore nonhuman primitives unless they could somehow be exploited, and the Noghri were ripe for exploitation. Through a massive deception and planet-toxification program, Vader convinced the Noghri that they were indebted to him and the Empire. They became the Emperor's personal Death Commandos, serving as Imperial assassins until Princess Leia revealed the deception during the events instigated by Grand Admiral Thrawn.

Noghri are small, compact killing machines. They are intelligent predators, natural hunters with deadly skills. They have large eyes, protruding tooth-filled jaws, gray skin, and thin, powerful muscles. With their enhanced sense of smell, they can identify individuals by scent alone. These 1.3-meter-tall beings have a strong code of honor not unlike that displayed by the Wookiees of Kashyyyk. With long arms and sharp claws, they developed an unarmed combat style that is among the most deadly in the galaxy.

The Emperor kept the Noghri a secret, using them as clandestine warriors. They bowed to Lord Vader as their savior, extending the same respect to Princess Leia when she eventually met these beings and convinced them that she was Vader's daughter. Grand Admiral Thrawn kept a

Noghri as his personal bodyguard and sent squads of the Death Commandos to capture Leia and her unborn twins. Since Thrawn's defeat, the Noghri have left the service of the Empire and are working with the New Republic. [HE, HESB, DFR, DFRSB, LC]

Nomad City

⊕ Nomad City is a mobile mining base on the planet Nkllon. It is owned and operated by Lando Calrissian, who established the business after the Battle of Endor. The city is a huge, humpbacked structure that uses the planet's shadow to protect itself from the intense heat of the system's sun. It lumbers along like a slow, living creature, covered with thousands of lights and surrounded by tiny support craft including shuttles and pilot craft that help direct the mobile city. Built from scavenged vessels such as an old *Dreadnaught*-class cruiser and over forty captured AT-AT walkers, Nomad City was designed based upon plans for a rolling mining center Calrissian had found among the personal belongings of Cloud City's founder, Ecclessis Figg. The Empire later attacked Nomad City, stealing over fifty of the operation's mine molers for use in its attack on Sluis Van. Nomad City was disabled by an attack during the latter period of Thrawn's command. The city had to be evacuated and was incinerated by Nkllon's blazing sun. [HE, HESB, LC]

normal space

See realspace.

Norvall II

⊙ Norval II, a planet in the system of the same name, joined the New Republic after its citizens overthrew the government that was loyal to the Empire. The people of Norval II are among the best pilots now serving the New Republic. [DE]

Norvanian grog

⊙ The expensive and potent liquid intoxicant from the planet Ban-Satir II is called Norvanian grog. It is produced and marketed from the isle of N'van in the planet's northern hemisphere. [HSE]

Nunurra

⊙ The city Nunurra on the planet Roon is the site of the Roon Colonial Games. [DTV]

O

Obi-Wan Kenobi

See Ben (Obi-Wan) Kenobi.

Obroan

⊕ An inhabitant of the planet Obroa-skai is called an Obroan. Their world is terrestrial in nature, with frozen deserts and oceans and tall, jagged mountains. The world is primarily known for its massive library computers. [HE, HESB]

Obroa-skai

⊕ Obroa-skai system is located in the Borderland Regions of the galaxy. The system occupies a strategic position between those portions of space controlled by the remnants of the Empire and the New Republic. It is a neutral star system, though its inhabitants have shown some favoritism toward the New Republic. The system is renowned for its massive library, located on the primary planet (also named

Obroa-skai). The reputation that has developed over the centuries is that the complete knowledge of the galaxy has been gathered within the computers of Obroa-skai's information repositories. It was from these library computers that Grand Admiral Thrawn pulled the astrogation coordinates of the planet Wayland. [HE, HESB]

Odumin

See Spray of Tynna.

Old Republic, the

Ⓐ The Old Republic was a democratic galactic government that spanned time as well as distance. For over a thousand generations, this government spread justice and freedom from star system to star system. Elected senators and administrators from all the member worlds participated in the governing process, and the noble Jedi Knights served as the Republic's protectors and defenders. In the years prior to the current era, corruption, greed, and internal strife began to destroy the Old Republic from within. Special-interest groups and power-hungry individuals accomplished what no outside threat ever could—they weakened the galactic government and gave rise to apathy, social injustice, ineffectiveness, and chaos. To reverse this destructive trend, or at least give the impression that something was being done, both sides elected a compromise candidate to serve as president of the Senate.

For all his promises and plans, the newly elected Senator Palpatine quickly named himself Emperor, abolished the Republic, and began a reign of terror and even greater social injustice based upon his dark vision of a New Order. The Old Republic passed away, and the Empire was born. [SW]

Omega Signal

When a member of the Alliance Battle Staff issues the code Omega Signal, all Rebel warriors are ordered to disengage from combat and retreat. [ESBR]

Oola

Oola was one of the slave girls serving in Jabba the Hutt's court. She was of the same alien Twi'lek species as Bib Fortuna, a pretty humanoid with twin head-tails. Her primary function was to dance for the entertainment of Jabba and his entourage. When she failed to obey one of Jabba's orders, the crime lord had her killed while his court laughed in appreciation. [RJ]

orbital gun platform

An orbital gun platform is any vessel or fortification that can launch an attack from space upon the planet it orbits. [SWR]

orbit dock

Orbit docks spin in space above planets, providing landing and maintenance facilities and other services to spacers and their ships. Some docks handle large capital ships with connecting boarding tubes. Others have landing bays for small freighters. A few can even administer to the needs of the gigantic container ships that ply the space lanes. Large orbit docks have multiple docking facilities and operate like small space stations. With one or two capital-ship dry docks, hangar bays, and multiple docking tubes, these facilities can cater to vehicles ranging in size from stock light freighters to large capital ships. These multidocks are usually constructed around multiple-level entertainment areas. Services often include motel cubes, space-stop cafés and cantinas, holovid and live entertainment, and even dock markets. Sluis Van has an extensive collection of orbit docks in its shipyard facilities. [HE, HESB]

Orbiting Shipyard Alpha

Orbiting Shipyard Alpha is a spaceship repair dock high above the planet Duro. [MMY]

Ord Mantell

On the planet Ord Mantell, Han Solo met up with and escaped from a pair of bounty hunters who were after the reward placed on him by Jabba the Hutt. [ESB]

Ord Pardron

The planet Ord Pardron, in the star system of the same name, was a member of the New Republic during the time of Grand Admiral Thrawn's campaign to rebuild the Empire. The planet houses the main Republic military forces for the surrounding systems, with its base serving as the primary defense for Ando, Filve, Crondre, and other planets in the Abrion and Dufilvian sectors. Thrawn's forces hit several targets at once, reducing Ord Pardron's own defenses to the bare minimum as it tried to send assistance to the other worlds. It was severely damaged when Imperial ships arrived to attack it, and the base was subsequently unable to send help to Ukio—which had been Thrawn's true target all along. [LC]

Organa

See Leia Organa. See Bail Organa.

Orlock

See Commander Orlock.

Orron III

⊕ The agricultural world of Orron III in Corporate Sector space has ideal conditions for good crop production due to its stable seasons, which are the result of the planet's slight axial tilt. An Authority Data Center is located on this world. [HSE]

Ortolan

⊕ Ortolans are heavy, squat bipeds with long trunks and dark, beady eyes. They have floppy ears, small mouths, short, chubby fingers, and thick, baggy, blue-furred hides. They come from the planet Orto, a cold world in the system of the same name. Ortolans love to eat, often giving up other activities to indulge themselves with a second or third helping of food. Max Rebo, the jizz-wailer from Jabba's palace, is an Ortolan. [GG4]

Ossus

⊙ The planet Ossus, in the Adegan system, was the site of an important Jedi stronghold in the ancient past. While some scholars have speculated that the order of the Jedi Knights started here, that has never been determined. The cities were mysteriously abandoned about four thousand years prior to the events of *Star Wars IV: A New Hope*, though the ruins remain to this day. A gentle, primitive people now occupy the planet. [DE]

Oswaft

⊙ The Oswaft are a species of intelligent mantra-ray/jellyfishlike beings who inhabit the water planet of ThonBoka. They are broad and streamlined, with powerful wings and a sleek, muscle-covered dorsal surface. They have tentacular ribbons hanging from their ventral side, and their entire bodies have a glasslike transparency with hints and flashes of inner color. Though extremely intelligent, the Oswaft are not remarkably imaginative. They are a long-lived species, with a patient and conservative outlook on life. [LCS]

otherspace

⊙ The technologically advanced inhabitants of the galaxy know of realspace and hyperspace, and a select few have learned of a place that seems to exist apart from both of these dimensions. Termed "otherspace," this region is full of dead, lifeless planets. This void appears as a storm-gray expanse of nothingness, with some small swirls of colored gases and stars that look like shining holes of darkness.

Only a few of the Charon's biologically engineered ships float in this dead void, seeking any last vestiges of life to slaughter as sacrifices to the Charon cult of death. [OS]

Ottega

⦿ Ottega, a star system in the Outer Rim Territories, has an unusual number of inhabited worlds and moons. The 75 planets and 622 moons combine to make the entire system a popular tourist region. [DE]

Outbound Flight Project

⦿ The Jedi Master Jorus C'baoth was influential in convincing the Old Republic Senate to authorize and fund the Outbound Flight Project. The goal of the project was to search for and contact intelligent life outside the known galaxy. Jorus was one of six Jedi Masters attached to the project, which was launched from Yaga Minor. The ship, its crew, and the six Jedi Masters never returned from the search, and nothing was ever heard from them after the initial launch. [HE, DFR, LC]

Outer Rim Territories

⦿ The star systems located on the farthest edge of Imperial space are collectively known as the Outer Rim Territories. The desert world of Tatooine lies within one of these distant systems. [SW]

⦿ This region has been considered the galaxy's frontier since it was originally opened for settlement during the time of the Old Republic. When the Empire controlled all of known space, it was considered a backwater area good for nothing but exploitation. The worlds of the Rim are still recovering from the pillaging promoted by the Empire, for it was from this region that the Empire got most of its slaves and resources. Because the Emperor was free to conduct his most terrible atrocities here, away from the eyes of the Core worlds, the planets and species of the Rim Territories tended to support the Rebellion. [HESB, SWRPG2]

outlaw tech

🌑 An outlaw tech is a member of a band of well-equipped and highly trained technicians who operate in and around Corporate Sector space. These techs make a living by illegally modifying and repairing space vessels. Their clients include criminal organizations, fugitives, the Rebellion, and other groups politically opposed to the Empire and/or the Corporate Sector Authority. Outlaw techs specialize in upgrading ship armaments, engines, sensor capability, hull codes, and shielding, and often strive to make these changes with as few noticeable modifications as possible. The techs keep the location of their bases secret, often moving at a moment's notice in order to stay ahead of Authority security patrols and Imperial agents. [HSE]

Outpost Beta

🌑 The isolated sentry station called Outpost Beta served as an advance lookout point for the Rebel Alliance base on Hoth. The soldiers assigned to this station were the first to spot the Imperial invaders at the start of the Battle of Hoth. They watched the drop ships land beyond the base's defensive shields and saw the lumbering Imperial AT-ATs start their relentless march toward the base and its shield generators. Their warning provided the base with some small measure of extra time before the devastating attack began. [ESBR]

Owen Lars

✪ Owen Lars was a moisture farmer on the planet Tatooine. He and his wife, Beru, were the guardians of Luke Skywalker. Luke believed that Owen was his natural uncle, but in fact the man was Ben Kenobi's brother. Kenobi gave Luke into Owen's care right after Luke was born. Owen and his wife were killed by Imperial stormtroopers as they searched for R2-D2 and the secret data stored in the droid's memory. [SW, RJ]

owriss

🌑 An owriss is a large, harmless, bloblike creature that inhabits the forests of Endor's moon. [ETV]

Ozzel

See Admiral Ozzel.

P

Page

See Lieutenant Page.

Page's Commandos

⊕ Lieutenant Page of the New Republic heads a special-missions team called the Katarn Commandos. The unit, named for a predator from the Wookiee homeworld Kashyyyk, consists of twelve of the best-trained soldiers serving the Republic. Officially, the special-forces unit is attached to the office of the Commander-in-Chief, but in practice it often operates independently for weeks or months at a time. It is a rogue team, like Wedge Antilles's Rogue Squadron, with no set mission profile but the capability to handle most assignments. It operates either as a single unit or broken up into smaller elements, and all members are trained to work in any environment. Each soldier is a jack-of-all-trades as well as a specialist in a single field. The team currently consists of Lilla Dade, the pathfinder or scout; Gottu and Idow, urban combat specialists; Frorral the Wookiee, wilderness fighter; Mian Hoob of

Sullust and Korren of Alderaan, team technicians; the Bothan Kasck, infiltrator and shadow; Vandro, heavy weapons and repulsorlift specialist; Syla Tors, ex-Corellian pirate and pilot; and Jortan and Bri'vin, medical technicians. [HE, HESB]

Pakka

🌑 The Trianii named Pakka, son of Atuarre and Keeheen, helped Han Solo infiltrate the Corporate Sector Authority's prison facility at Stars' End. The young Trianii was struck mute after his father Keeheen was taken captive by Authority agents. [HSE]

palmgun

🌑 A palmgun is a small blaster pistol designed for close-range combat. Due to its size, a palmgun is easily concealable. These weapons are also called holdout blasters. [HSR]

Palpatine

See Emperor.

Pantolomin

🌑 The primary planet in the Panto star system is Pantolomin. Two other planets also orbit the sun: Toloran, a colder, harsher world, and distant Atloran. The entire system operates as a resort for galactic travelers. From the tropical climes of Pantolomin to the wintery wonderland of Toloran, from the zero-G campgrounds of Atloran to the deep-space station of Panto Prime, the system features vacation packages for every taste and species. Pantolomin is an ocean world with a tropical and semitropical environment. The three continents and five major islands are jungle paradises, and the underwater coral reefs are renowned for their great beauty. A popular attraction is the subocean cruise ships, like the *Coral Vanda*, which take leisurely tours through the ocean depths. The amphibious Lomins and the Tolos of Toloran share duties and responsibilities on the system's governing tourist board. [DFR, DFRSB]

Paploo

Paploo

🏵 Paploo is a member of the Ewok tribe that befriended Princess Leia and the Rebel strike team sent to the forest moon at the start of the Battle of Endor. Known for his brazen actions and nearly foolhardy bravery, Paploo was the Ewok who stole the speeder bike and distracted the attention of the guards watching over the secret Imperial facility on Endor's moon. Paploo's distraction provided the Rebel strike team an opportunity to penetrate the Imperial base. [RJ]

Paradise

🌑 Paradise system is a massive star system that has been turned into a space junkyard. The system is controlled and operated by the Ugors, though the scavenger Squibs seek to capture it for themselves. All of the planets that once filled the system have been broken up by the Ugors to form the basis of their glorious junkyard. [SH]

paralight system

🌑 A starship's paralight system is a combination of mechanical and opto-electronic subsystems found in a hyperdrive. It is responsible for translating a pilot's manual commands into a set of corresponding reactions within the hyperdrive power plants. [ESB]

Par'tah

🌑 The Ho'Din named Par'tah controls one of the smuggling groups operating in the Borderland Region between Imperial and New Republic space. Hers is a marginal operation which puts on the illusion of wealth and abundant success. Her base is hidden on a hot jungle planet off the major space lanes. She collects technological items, often rummaging through her clients' cargo for new additions before completing a delivery. She dislikes Brasck, who is a poor businessman and often beats her to contracts, but she has a good relationship with Talon Karrde, who sometimes directs her to new pieces for her collection. She prefers to deal with the New Republic, but needs the large payoffs the Empire offers. [HE, HESB, LC]

particle shielding

⚓ Particle shielding is a defensive force field that repels matter of any form. This type of deflector shield is usually used in conjunction with ray shielding to provide full protection to starships and planetary installations. [SW]

passenger liner

⚙ Passenger liners, or spaceliners, are the basic mode of transport used by most galactic travelers. These vessels range in size from small in-system ships to giant interstellar luxury liners complete with multiple decks of entertainment facilities. [SWSB]

Pellaeon

See Captain Pellaeon.

pelvic servomotor

⚓ Pelvic servomotors provide bipedal droids with the means to produce mechanical movements in their legs. Without these power units, bipedal droids (or legged droids of any sort) would not be able to move their legs to walk or otherwise get around. [SW]

Peregrine

⚙ One of the six Dreadnaughts from the legendary *Katana* fleet that makes up Garm Bel Iblis's private strike force is his flagship, the *Peregrine*. [DFR]

Peregrine's Nest

Peregrine's Nest was Garm Bel Iblis's last hidden base before his strike force returned to join the New Republic. The base was constructed of bi-state memory plastic for quick break-down and set-up. It was protected by anti-infantry, anti-vehicle, and anti-orbital artillery, and featured a large cache of personal armaments. [DFR]

Permondiri Explorer

The survey starship *Permondiri Explorer* is now a ship of legend among spacers across the galaxy. With its crew of 112, it was sent on a mission to explore and chart a new star system. After its initial departure, all contact with the ship ceased and it was declared lost in space. Several massive expeditions have been organized to locate the *Explorer*, but none were able to locate the ship or discover what may have happened to it. [HSR]

Phlog

Phlogs are a giant, brutish species that live in the desert land of Simoom on Endor's moon. This area is many kilometers from the Ewok forest villages. The Phlogs are usually calm and peaceful, but they can become dangerous when disturbed. [ETV]

Phlutdroid

See IG-88.

phobium

⊙ The metal alloy phobium was used to coat the power core of both Death Star battle stations. [GDV]

Pho Ph'eahian

⊙ Pho Ph'eahians are members of the intelligent humanoid species native to the planet Pho Ph'eah. Members of this species have four arms and blue fur. [HSR]

photoreceptor

⊛ Photoreceptors are devices that capture light rays and convert them into electronic signals for processing by video computers. Among their many uses, these devices serve as eyes in most droid models. [SW]

phototropic shielding

⊛ The process of phototropic shielding turns transparent materials into light filters while retaining their transparency. When the process is applied to glass, transparisteel, and other see-through materials, intense light rays are toned down to a level acceptable to most intelligent species. [SW]

Piett

See Captain Piett.

Piggy

See Blue Four.

pinnace

⊛ Small ships called pinnaces are carried aboard large space vessels for defensive purposes. These ships are built for speed, equipped with propulsion drives capable of hurling them to close to lightspeed. Heavily armed and highly maneuverable, pinnaces come close to combat starfighters in terms of performance and utility. Pinnaces are sometimes referred to as battle boats. [HSR]

Pinnacle Base

⊛ The New Republic High Command Center on Da Soocha's Fifth Moon is designated as Pinnacle Base. High Command was transferred to this location after Imperial forces invaded Coruscant. [DE]

plastoid

☥ Plastoids are any type of thermoformed substances, such as many forms of battle armor. [SW]

Platform 327

☥ The landing pad on Bespin's Cloud City where the *Millennium Falcon* was moored on its visit to the outpost after the Battle of Hoth was designated platform 327. [ESB]

Ploovo Two-For-One

One of the galaxy's infamous crime lords, Ploovo Two-For-One is an unscrupulous and portly humanoid from the Cron Drift. Among his many endeavors, Ploovo is a con man, a loan shark, a thief, a smash-and-grab man, and a bunko steerer. Han Solo sometimes worked for Ploovo, and for a time he owed the crime lord a good amount of credits. Since Solo also caused Ploovo to lose face on a number of occasions, the crime lord ordered Solo's termination back in the days before the smuggler became involved in the Rebellion. [HSE]

pocket cruiser

A pocket cruiser is an obsolete class of capital ship that saw extensive service during the end phase of the Clone Wars. This class is small compared to modern capital ships, but it was easy to manufacture and was on par with most of the other war ships of the day. Those still in use are considered to be relics, though they can still be found as training platforms, pirate ships, and even among the arsenals of local military forces. [HLL]

Point 5

Point 5 is a gambling game that is played in many casinos throughout the galaxy. [HSR]

Ponda Baba

The Aqualish known as Ponda Baba was the companion

of the thug Roofoo (also known as Doctor Evazan and Doctor Cornelius). [GG1]

Pops

✪ According to the *Star Wars* novel, Pops was the name of the veteran Rebel Y-wing pilot. His comm unit designation during the Battle of Yavin was Red Five. In the movie, his designation was Gold Five. [SW]

Porkins

See Blue Four.

Pote Snitkin

✪ Pote Snitkin was a Nikto who worked as a helmsman for Jabba the Hutt. He piloted one of Jabba's skiffs and was among those killed during Luke Skywalker's rescue of Han Solo and Princess Leia from the Hutt's vile clutches. [RJ]

power converter

✪ A power converter is the ignition system for a starship. It routes energy from a ship's primary power source (or furnace) to its propulsion units to achieve thrust. [ESB]

power coupling

✪ In starships, a power coupling device handles the large amounts of energy flowing through paralight systems. It directs power to the hyperdrive motivator, which then acti-vates the hyperdrive engine to achieve the jump to lightspeed. [ESB]

power droid

✪ A power droid is an ambulatory power generator. The box-shaped droid moves about on two thick, articulated legs, carrying an energy-producing generator in its body. The primary function of this service droid is to provide for the energy requirements of fellow droids, ships, vehicles, and other mechanical devices. [SWR]

power gem

✪ The aura radiated by the rare artifacts called power gems disrupted magnetic defense shields, enabling pirates to raid other ships. The gems lost power over time. The very last gem had just enough power left to enable Vrad Dodonna to ram his ship into the *Executor*, shattering its forward shields. [GW]

power prybar

✪ Like other power tools, a power prybar uses its own en-ergy source to apply leverage, thus making it easier and more efficient to use. [HLL]

power terminal

✪ A power terminal is an energy distribution station. Ve-hicles, ships, and droids can be brought to a power terminal for recharging. [SW]

preducor

⊕ One of the true monsters of Endor's moon is the terrible beast called the preducor. A preducor stands on four powerful, clawed legs, reaching heights of four meters and growing five meters long. A preducor's head is surrounded by a mane of razor-sharp hair, and a long, spiked tail stretches behind it. Its protruding maw is full of fearsome teeth, and its eyes glow with evil light as it hunts the forest's night. The great folds of skin on its back are vestiges of wings that no longer function. Docile during the day, at night they hunt and roam where they please. [DFRSB]

pressor

⊕ Pressors are small repulsor projectors used to control and induce pitch in a starship. In starfighters, pilots activate pressors via their control sticks. In larger vessels, activators are found on helm control consoles. [SW]

Priests of Ninn

⊕ The Priests of Ninn inhabit the religious haven of Ninn, a planet-wide retreat where they practice the tenets of their beliefs. These tenets incorporate formalistic abstinence. Priests of Ninn normally dress in green vestments. [HSR]

Princess Leia Organa

See Leia Organa.

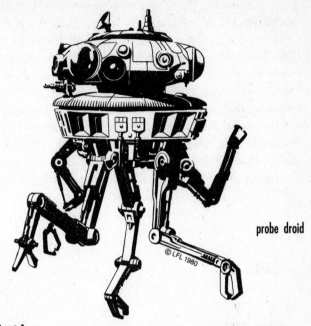

probe droid

probe droid

🔴 Probe droids, or probots, are designed to perform reconnaissance missions, gathering data and transmitting it back to their masters. As sophisticated surveillance and tracking droids, probots have a wide variety of scientific and military applications. Tenacious hunters and searchers, probots are equipped with an array of sensors, including electromagnetic, motive, acoustic, seismic, and olfactory measuring devices. Military probots typically receive offensive and defensive weaponry. Designed to withstand the rigors of space and hostile planetary environments, these droids are extremely tough and durable, and have a variety of specialized tools connected to many mechanical appendages.

Most probots are launched in one-way pods which get the droids to their target locations. Once there, they must complete their missions and report back to their bases of origin. If feasible, the bases may provide a means for the droids' return; otherwise, they are on their own. If the missions call for it, probots are provided with orbital ships that allow them to perform their missions from space and then return to their bases. Most models use repulsors to provide locomotion once they reach their destination. The Empire employed a large number of these droids to search for the hidden Rebel base after the Battle of Yavin. One finally tracked the Rebels to the ice planet Hoth. After broadcasting its findings back to its command ship, the probot self-destructed in order to avoid capture. [ESB]

probot

See probe droid.

program trap

�️ Even the most innocuous droids can become lethal weapons through the use of program traps. An internal command is placed in a droid's primary performance banks to cause a power overload in response to a predetermined event, signal, or time. This power overload, whose potential the reprogrammed droid is usually totally unaware of, has the explosive capability of a moderate-sized bomb. [SW]

Project Decoy

🔘 Project Decoy was the secret Alliance program headed by the Chadra-Fan scientist Pandar. The goal of the program was to create a human replica droid. [QE]

Prophet Gornash

⚙ The Prophet of the Dark Side called Gornash coordinates spy activities from the group's space station headquarters, Scardia. [PDS]

Prophets of the Dark Side

⚙ The Imperial group known as the Prophets of the Dark Side pose as great mystics who are strong in the Force's negative aspects. In truth, they are an investigation bureau with a vast network of spies. Led by the Supreme Prophet Kadann, these false mystics wield much power in the Empire. They retain control by making their prophecies come true through whatever means are necessary—including bribery, force, and even murder. [LCJ]

prosthetic replacements

⚙ Since the end of the Clone Wars, medical science has made great advances in the field of prosthetic replacements. Modern galactic medicine can now replace lost limbs and organs with effective and lifelike prosthetic parts. Those who receive biomedical prosthetics can see through artificial eyes, feel and grip with artificial hands, and run with artificial legs. Mechanical hearts pump blood through living bodies, and other replacement organs handle other important bodily functions. Most prosthetics do not enhance normal body abilities. They employ synthenet neural interfaces to give recipients full control of replaced limbs. Synth-flesh covers biomechanical replacement parts, giving them the look and feel of natural body parts. As there is a natural prejudice against droids and cybernetics, those who have re-placement parts usually keep the fact to themselves. Luke Skywalker has a prosthetic hand that replaces the one he lost in his first battle with Darth Vader. [HESB]

Proto One

☻ The ancient droid called Proto One had been fitted with so many diverse replacement parts that he looked like a strange mixture of many different droid types. He was the proprietor of the spaceship scrapyard on the planet Boonta during the early days of the Empire. R2-D2 and C-3PO met Proto One during their adventures in those times. [DTV]

protocol droid

☮ A protocol droid's primary programming includes lan-guages, interpretation, cultures, and diplomacy, all geared toward helping it fulfill its usual function as an administra-tive assistant, diplomatic aide, and companion for high-level individuals. C-3PO is a protocol droid. [SW]

proton grenade

☻ A proton grenade is a small concussion weapon capable of damaging a small starfighter. [GW]

proton torpedo

☮ A proton torpedo is a projectile weapon that must be launched from a specialized delivery system. Both starfighters and capital ships can be outfitted to deliver these weapons, and there are even smaller versions which can be fired from a shoulder- or back-mounted launcher. These concussion weapons carry a proton-scattering energy warhead. Complete particle shielding will deflect proton torpedoes. Proton torpedoes were used to destroy both Death Star battle stations. [SW, RJ]

Provisional Council

🌀 The Provisional Council was established by the Provisional Government of the New Republic. Its main job, besides providing leadership and direction for the new government, is to work toward the formal reestablishment of the principles and laws of the Old Republic. Its ruling body is the Inner Council, whose members include Mon Mothma, Admiral Ackbar, and Leia Organa Solo. [HE, HESB]

Psadan

🌀 The Psadan are a short, stocky humanoid species that inhabits the long-forgotten world of Wayland. Thick, stonelike scales cover their bodies, forming irregular, lumpy shells over their backs. These shells start over the ridge of the brow, sweep across the head, and fall down the back. Smaller, closer-packed plates cover the rest of their bodies. The Psadan share their world with the Myneyrsh and human colonists. All three have engaged in open hostilities at various times in the planet's history. Like the Myneyrsh, the Psadan have a primitive society. Bows and arrows are their primary weapons, and animals serve as transportation and beasts of burden. [HE, HESB, LC]

pterosaur

💮 A pterosaur is a carnivorous flying reptile found on the planet Ammudd. [HSR]

Puggles Trodd

💮 The one-meter-tall, rodentlike alien named Puggles Trodd makes his living as a bounty hunter, often teaming up with Jodo Kast and Zardra to complete high-paying contracts. He fears the other bounty hunters, but he knows that together they can make more credits than if they work alone. He is pessimistic, unpleasant, and brooding, though he loves to watch things explode. [TM]

Pui-ui

💮 The small, sentient beings called Pui-ui are natives of the planet Kyryll's World. A Pui-ui measures about 1.25 meters tall, appearing as two spherical bodies connected by a short neck. Cilia growing out of the base of the bottom sphere provide these beings with locomotive capabilities. The Pui-ui language is made up of a wide range of shrill sounds. [HLL]

Q

Quamar Messenger

🌀 The luxury spaceliner *Quamar Messenger* carries up to 600 passengers and is serviced by a crew of 45. The vessel has a hyperdrive engine, allowing it to travel at lightspeed. [HLL]

quarrel

🌀 The Wookiee bowcaster fires energy projectiles called quarrels, which explode upon impact with a target. [RJ]

Quarren (Squid Head)

🌀 Quarren is the species name for the aliens who are commonly called Squid Heads by the galaxy's general populace. These amphibious beings share the world of Calamari with the Mon Calamari race, though the Quarren prefer the depths of the floating cities to the upper reaches the Mon Cals call home. The Quarren are more practical and con-

servative than their idealistic world-mates. Whereas the
Mon Calamari have adopted Basic as their language of
choice, the Quarren have kept their oceanic tongue. The
Quarren are sea dwellers, able to live out of the water but
preferring the security of the ocean depths. These pragmatic
people are unwilling to trust new ideas. They do not dream
of brighter tomorrows like the Mon Cals, but instead hold
fast to the reality of yesterdays. While they profess that the
two races should remain in the sea, they have followed the
Mon Cals into their floating cities and out among the stars.
They have become dependent on the Calamarians, and this
dependency has led to resentment and even outright hatred.
Rumors persist that it was a small number of Quarren who
helped the Empire originally invade the planet. In the face
of invading forces, the Quarren cooperated with the Mon
Calamari to repel the Imperials. But since that day, many
Quarren have fled the planet to seek a life elsewhere in the
galaxy. They seem to have purposely remained apart from
both the Alliance and the Empire, preferring to find a place
on the fringes of society. Quarren can often be found working with pirates, slavers, crime lords, smugglers, and other
unsavory sorts. [SWSB]

Queen of Ranroon

⬙ The cargo vessel *Queen of Ranroon* carried the spoils
gathered during the interstellar conquests of Xim the Despot. The now-legendary ship never reached port on its last
run; it was either lost or destroyed with its cargo stored
deep in its many holds and bays. Whether it was lost or destroyed, the ship became the subject of wild spacer stories.
It even reached the level of ghost ship, with reported sightings occurring every so often to a spacer making a run. To
a spacer, the name symbolizes wealth beyond measure, and

many have tried to discover its whereabouts over the centuries. Even Han Solo participated in a quest for the vessel prior to his involvement in the Rebellion. [HSR, HLL]

Queen Rana

Queen Rana is the ancient ruler of the planet Duro. A huge monument dedicated to the queen fills the Valley of Royalty on Duro. [MMY]

quickclay

Quickclay is a viscous, gray-green soil that covers many areas on the planet Circarpous V. Like quicksand, the soft, shifting mass of quickclay yields easily to pressure and tends to suck objects down into it. [SME]

R

R2-D2 (Artoo-Detoo)

✦ The astromech droid R2-D2 (or Artoo-Detoo) hooked up with Luke Skywalker at the beginning of the events that led to the Battle of Yavin and has been at his side ever since. Like other astromech droids, R2-D2 is a starship utility droid. His domed head can rotate a full three hundred and sixty degrees, and his short, squat, cylindrical body is full of instruments, sensors, and devices designed to help him perform his primary functions. R2-D2 stands upright on two legs that end in treaded rollers. A third leg drops from a

R2-D2

compartment in his lower body to provide him with added stability when moving across irregular terrain.

Artoo-Detoo and his counterpart, See-Threepio (C-3PO), were aboard Princess Leia's consular ship when it was overtaken and boarded by Imperial forces. The Princess placed the technical readouts for the Death Star in Artoo's memory banks, then ordered the little droid to find Obi-Wan Kenobi. Since that time, Artoo has served as Luke's companion and aide, assisting from his socket in Luke's X-wing, accompanying him to Dagobah, and helping to save the day on Endor's forest moon. Artoo understands Basic, but communicates in his own expressive language of beeps and whistles, which Threepio must often translate for their human (and Wookiee) companions. [SW, ESB, RJ]

R2 unit

One of the most popular astromech droid models in service is the R2 unit. R2-D2, Luke Skywalker's droid, is an R2 unit. Like other astromech droids, R2 units are designed to operate in hostile environments, especially deep space. By plugging into terminals or ship-interface sockets, R2 units can augment and enhance the computer capabilities of starships. These droids assist with piloting and navigation and serve as onboard repair and maintenance technicians. Through the use of infrared receptors, auditory receivers, computer linkups, and a variety of sensor packages, these droids can interact with the world around them. A holographic recorder/projector located in the domed head allows these units to record and play visual images which occur within their sight range. A number of retractable maintenance appendages are hidden within the cylindrical bodies. These include firefighting apparatus, information storage/retrieval jacks, grasping claws, laser welders, and circular saws. R2 units stand 1.05 meters tall. [SW, ESB, RJ]

R5-D4

See R5 unit.

R5 unit

☺ Like the popular R2 series, an R5 unit is an astromech droid. Owen Lars originally purchased an R5 unit (R5-D4) from the Jawa traders. Luke convinced him to take R2-D2 instead when the R5 unit displayed signs of damage. [SWR]

R7 unit

☺ The R7 unit is the newest series of astromech droids. R7 units were specifically designed to interface with the new E-wing starfighters. [DE]

rakazzak beast

☺ A rakazzak beast is any of the three-meter-tall, spider-like creatures that inhabit the forests of Endor's moon. Yuzzum warriors often ride rakazzak mounts. Rakazzaks can spin thick, sticky webs that they use to trap their enemies. [ETV]

Rakrir

See Sabador.

Ra-Lee

⚙ Ra-Lee was the pretty, tan-furred Ewok who is the wife of Chief Chirpa. She died defending her daughters, Kneesaa and Asha. [ETV]

R'all

⚙ R'all, the fraternal twin brother of J'uoch, runs a mining concern on the planet Dellalt with his sibling. For a human, the unscrupulous R'all has an unusual appearance. His straight brown hair, widow's peaks, and pale skin are set off by his black-irised eyes. Along with his twin sister, R'all competed with Han Solo to be the first to find the lost treasures of the legendary ship *Queen of Ranroon*. [HLL]

R'alla mineral water

⚙ R'alla mineral water comes from springs in the underground caverns of the mountain town of R'alla. Located on the planet of the same name, R'alla mineral water is known for its purity and medicinal benefits. It is also a main ingredient in certain bootleg intoxicants. Smugglers make substantial profits by trafficking this commodity to other worlds. Han Solo and Chewbacca once made a living smuggling the mineral water to the planet Rampa. [HSR, HLL]

Ralltiir

⚙ The planet Ralltiir was one of the Rebel Alliance's first supporters. When its ties and allegiances were discovered, it was subjugated by Imperial forces. [SWR]

Ralrra

⚙ The tall, powerfully built Wookiee named Ralrra (short for Ralrracheen) wears a gold-threaded tan balric. A speech impediment allows Ralrra to actually speak Basic. Before the Empire, he was an ambassador to the Old Republic. As a slave to the Empire, he was used by his Imperial masters to communicate with the rest of his species. He originally attempted to resist the Imperial occupation forces, but forced himself to comply after they executed a dozen women and children from his family unit. Afterward, his proximity to Imperial officers provided him with information vital to the Alliance's efforts to free Kashyyyk. Now, like most Wookiees, he feels he owes a life debt to the Alliance for its efforts. When Chewbacca brought Princess Leia to Kashyyyk to keep her safe from Grand Admiral Thrawn's Noghri Death Commandos, Ralrra was one of two Wookiees assigned to protect her. [HE, HESB]

Rampa

⚙ The inhabitants of the industrial planet Rampa have destroyed much of their world's ecosystem to build and maintain their industrial base. On Rampa, the air is unfit to breathe, the water is too polluted to drink, and the land has been made too barren to support even the most rudimentary farm produce. The world's population has been herded into small areas, and most make do with synthetic nutrients instead of real food. Due to the vast amount of industry, Rampa's spaceports are always busy. Smugglers make huge profits bringing water to the planet illegally. So much water comes through the planet's approach corridors that spacers have nicknamed the route the "Rampa Rapids." [HSR, HLL]

Ranats

⚙ The ratlike species called Ranats are small and cunning, with sharp teeth and long tails. In their native tongue they call themselves Con Queecon, or "the conquerors." Most other species find this very laughable, since the one-meter-tall beings appear harmless. They are savage killers, however, with a taste for other intelligent beings. Since Jabba the Hutt's death, a group of these aliens have taken over the crime lord's desert palace. [GG4, ZHR]

rancor

⚙ The terrible beast called the rancor was a five-meter-tall carnivore that walked on two legs and was reptilian in appearance. With long, out-of-proportion arms, huge fangs, and long, sharp claws, the rancor was a fearsome sight. While some believe that the rancor was a unique creature, others contend that an entire world of the powerful beasts is just waiting to be discovered. The only known specimen was kept in a special pit in Jabba the Hutt's desert palace on Tatooine. The crime lord used the creature as a source of entertainment and as a method for getting rid of employees and others who failed him. The pit was below Jabba's court, providing an excellent view as victims struggled to fend off the huge creature. Luke Skywalker was forced to kill the beast when Jabba dropped him into the pit in an effort to destroy the Jedi Knight. [RJ]

Rand Ecliptic

⚙ The space freighter *Rand Ecliptic* was Biggs Darklighter's first assignment after he graduated from the Academy.

He served as first mate until he jumped ship to join the Rebellion. [SW]

Raskar

🌀 Raskar was a former space pirate and owner of the last power gem. He staged arena fights between all who wanted the gem, and made a fortune betting on the fights. Chewbacca was able to beat the best fighter, and he and Han Solo left with the gem. Later, Raskar's ship was near Hoth when the *Falcon* landed at the newly established Rebel base. When Luke and Solo tried to scare Raskar's ship away from Hoth, Raskar attempted to get Solo's reward for rescuing Leia in exchange for not turning him over to Jabba the Hutt. Solo unknowingly led Raskar to a deep cavern on Hoth containing a huge deposit of lumni-spice, but the protective dragon-slug forced them to leave. Raskar redeemed himself on Ord Mantell when he rescued Han Solo and Luke Skywalker from the bounty hunter Skorr. [GW]

ray shielding

☾ Ray shielding is a force field designed to block and absorb energy fire. It is an essential part of every starfighter and capital ship's defensive systems. [SW]

reactivate switch

☾ A reactivate switch is a droid's master circuit breaker, used to turn the mechanicals on and off. [SWR]

realspace

🌑 Realspace, or normal space, is the dimension in which all residents of the galaxy live. Realspace has distance and volume, as it encompasses all stars, planets, and the space in between. Travel within realspace is slow compared to traveling through the shadow-dimension called hyperspace. [SWRPG, SWRPG2]

Rebel Alliance insignia

Rebel Alliance, the

🏵 The popular name for the Alliance to Restore the Republic is the Rebel Alliance. Opposed to the tyranny of the Empire and its New Order, star systems, single worlds, and even factions and individuals from otherwise neutral or Empire-aligned planets united to bring justice and freedom back to the galaxy. The Alliance's opposition ranged from subversive activities to military actions, culminating in the massive Battle of Endor. In most cases, the term "Rebel" was used by the Empire. The Alliance rarely applied the term to themselves. [SW, ESB, RJ]

Rebellion, the

🏵 The opposition fostered by the Alliance to Restore the Republic was commonly called the Rebellion, especially by the Empire. [SW, ESB, RJ]

Rebels

(logo) Rebels was the term applied by the Empire to members of the Alliance to Restore the Republic. [SW, ESB, RJ]

Rebel Star

(logo) The New Republic escort frigate *Rebel Star* was one of the ships that participated in the rescue of the downed *Liberator* and its crew. [DE]

recording rod

(logo) Recording rods are long, clear, cylindrical tubes used to record and play back audio and visual images. Recorded material appears as a two-dimensional image on a rod's surface. Activation switches are located on each end of a recording rod. [SME]

Red Five

(logo) According to the *Star Wars* novel, Red Five was the comm-unit designation for veteran Rebel pilot Pops' Y-wing during the Battle of Yavin. Pops perished during the assault on the Death Star. In the movie, his designation was Gold Five. [SW]

Red Leader

(logo) According to the *Star Wars* novel, Red Leader was the comm-unit designation for Rebel pilot Dutch's Y-wing during the Battle of Yavin. He led his squadron on the first assault wave against the Death Star battle station. In the movie, his designation was Gold Leader. [SW]

During the Battle of Endor, Red Leader was the comm-unit designation for Rebel pilot Wedge Antilles' X-wing. He commanded the Red Wing attack element that took on the Imperial fleet and the second Death Star battle station. [RJ]

Red Two

(✷) According to the *Star Wars* novel, Red Two was the comm-unit designation for Rebel pilot Tiree's Y-wing during the Battle of Yavin. In the movie, his designation was Gold Two. [SW]

Red Wing

(✷) Red Wing was one of the four main Rebel starfighter battle groups participating in the Battle of Endor. It was also the comm-unit designation for Red Leader's second-in-command. [RJ]

Ree-Yees

(✷) Ree-Yees was the name of the three-eyed, goat-faced alien who was a member of Jabba the Hutt's court. [RJ]

Rekkon

(✷) Rekkon is a black university professor from the planet Kalla. He left his post to find his nephew, a suspected activist who supposedly worked to oppose the Corporate Sector

Authority. The broad-shouldered, tall, and bearded Rekkon gathered together a group of others who were searching for missing friends, relatives, and loved ones who had somehow run afoul of the Authority. As their leader, Rekkon enlisted the aid of Han Solo in the search, which eventually led to a place called Stars' End. [HSE]

Relentless

During the period of the Galactic Civil War that followed the Battle of Yavin, the Imperial Star Destroyer *Relentless* was under the command of Captain Parlan. One of his major missions was to locate and capture the brilliant Old Republic naval officer Adar Tallon on Tatooine before he could be recruited by the Rebellion. Parlan failed, and was summarily executed by Lord Darth Vader. The ship was then turned over to Captain Westen, who commanded it for a time until he, too, disappointed Lord Vader. [TM, OS]

The Imperial Star Destroyer *Relentless*, under the command of Captain Dorja, failed to capture Han Solo and Luke Skywalker at New Cov during the events surrounding the return of Grand Admiral Thrawn five years after the Battle of Endor. [DFR].

remote

A remote is any owner-programmable automaton that can perform its primary functions without constant supervision and instruction. Unlike true droids, remotes can only do what they are told to do. They possess no capability for independent initiative. An example of a remote is the floating sphere that Luke uses to practice his lightsaber skills aboard the *Millennium Falcon*. [SW]

Renegade Flight

✪ The Rebel pilots charged with escorting an Alliance supply convoy to the planet Hoth were codenamed Renegade Flight. The convoy carried badly needed supplies for the Rebel base on Hoth, and Renegade Flight was assigned to protect the shipment. [ESBR]

Renegade Leader

✪ Renegade Leader was the comm-unit designation for Narra, the Alliance starfighter pilot in charge of Renegade Flight. [ESBR]

Renegades

✪ Renegades are the onetime-loyal citizens of Coruscant who have turned to pillaging and thievery to survive since the collapse of the planet's social order. The Renegades live among the ruins of Imperial City, competing with the Scavs for survival. [DE]

repulsor

✪ A repulsor is an antigravitational propulsion unit. Also called repulsorlift engines, repulsors are the most popular propulsion systems used in land and atmospheric vehicles throughout the galaxy. By producing a repulsor field that pushes against a planet's gravity, repulsors provide the thrust that makes landspeeders, airspeeders, and speeder bikes move. Repulsorlift engines are also used in starfighters and small starships as supplementary propulsion systems and for docking and atmospheric flight. [SW, ESB, RJ]

repulsorlift engine

See repulsor.

restraining bolt

🔴 A small, cylindrical device, a restraining bolt fits in a special socket on the exterior of a droid. When inserted, a restraining bolt keeps a droid from wandering off, and also forces it to respond immediately to signals produced by a hand-held summoning device keyed to a specific bolt or series of bolts. [SW]

Rethin Sea

⚫ The liquid metal core of the gas giant Bespin is called the Rethin Sea. [GG2, ZHR]

retinal print

⚫ Retinal prints are used to identify individuals by comparing the retinal patterns of a person in question with the prints stored within a security computer. [SME]

reversion

🔴 Reversion is the act of returning to realspace from hyperspace. [SWR]

Rieekan

See General Rieekan.

Rishi

⚙ The planet Rishi, which orbits the sun called Rish, is a hot, moist world of mountains, valleys, and swamps. Human and alien colonists live in the deep valleys; the native Rishii live in the high mountains. The colonists are part of a fundamentalist religious sect called the H'kig. They follow strict standards of propriety concerning clothing, length of hair, and social mores. As long as visitors do not break any of the religious laws or disturb the colonists, they are free to come and go as they please. Many underworld organizations have established bases in Rishi's city-vales, including Talon Karrde. The colonists export minerals, ores, and primitive fuels, and H'kig missionaries from the planet spread the tenets of the faith in spaceports throughout the galaxy. [DFR, DFRSB]

Rishii

⚙ Rishii are small avians who live in tribal clusters atop the mountains of the planet Rishi. They have feathered wings that allow them to fly, and humanlike hands that have helped them develop into primitive tool users. Each tribal cluster, or nest, is composed of a number of family groups. These nests live in peace with the neighboring nests and even with the human colonists who live in the city-vales. The Rishii do not understand why anyone would want to live in the hot lowlands, but they do not object to the colonists' presence and even trade with them sometimes. The Rishii are especially interested in the "shiny rocks" that allow the wingless colonists to fly. They have a knack for languages, which they learn by mimicking the sounds made by newcomers. They use slings to hunt, and have very little interest in items of advanced technology. [DFRSB]

Roa

🌀 The former smuggler and blockade runner named Roa gave Han Solo his first fringe job and took him on his first Kessel Run. Now a respectable and successful entrepreneur, Roa owns one of the largest import-export firms serving the systems of Roonadan and Bonadan. [HSR]

robot starfighters

🌀 The Empire has designed robot starfighters called TIE/D's, which are operated by remote computer control or onboard droid brains. [DE, DESB]

Roche Asteroid Field

🌀 The Roche Asteroid Field is a cluster of rocks locked into orbit in the Roche star system. The Verpine species lives among these asteroids. It was here, at the asteroid designated Research Station Shantipole, that the Verpine techs helped Admiral Ackbar design and build the B-wing starfighter. [SFS]

Rodian

The Rodians of the planet Rodia in the Tyrius star system have multifaceted eyes, tapirlike snouts, and rough, green skin. A ridge of spines crests a Rodian's skull, and their long, flexible fingers end in suction cups. These beings are natural bounty hunters, for on their planet they learn to hunt for sport. They take on contracts as part of grand games and contests, caring nothing for the concept of law enforcement. Greedo, who worked for Jabba the Hutt in *Star Wars IV: A New Hope*, is a Rodian. [GG1, GG4]

Rogue Flight

Rogue Flight was the code name for the Rebel starfighter pilots charged with the protection of evacuating forces during the Imperial assault on Hoth. [ESBR]

Rogue Four

Rogue Four was the comm-unit designation for Rebel pilot Hobbie's snowspeeder during the Battle of Hoth. [ESB]

Rogue Leader

Rogue Leader was the comm-unit designation for Rebel pilot Luke Skywalker's snowspeeder during the Battle of Hoth. [ESB]

Rogue Squadron

The X-wing starfighter squadron that took on the original Death Star and included such pilots as Luke Skywalker, Biggs Darklighter, and Wedge Antilles eventually came to be known as Rogue Squadron. Luke took command of the group and designed the concept of a squadron without a set mission profile. Without standing orders, his "Rogue Squadron" could take on any and all missions that came its way. He combined the best pilots with the best fighters and taught them to work as a single unit. When Luke finally resigned to spend more time with his Jedi studies, Wedge took charge of the squadron. Twelve X-wings and their pilots and astromech droids comprise Rogue Squadron. [GG3, HE, DFR, LC, HESB]

Rogue Three

Rogue Three was the comm-unit designation for Rebel pilot Wedge Antilles' snowspeeder during the Battle of Hoth. [ESB]

Rogue Two

Rogue Two was the comm-unit designation for Rebel pilot Zev's snowspeeder during the Battle of Hoth. [ESB]

Rokur Gepta

Rokur Gepta, the last of the fabled sorcerers of the planet Tund, was responsible for utterly obliterating every living thing from the surface of the world. He did this partially to preserve the secret of the powerful magic he wielded, and partially out of sheer malice. He was an empty being, and his emptiness required an endless amount of power to fill. He dreamed of ruling the small wedge of the galaxy once controlled by the Old Republic, and eventually moving on to take control of whatever lay beyond. He had searched out his ancient mentors, the original sorcerers of Tund, and had exterminated them. Descriptions of Rokur Gepta varied. To some, he was a malignant dwarf; to others, he was a frightening giant nearly three meters tall. All accounts agree that he was perpetually wrapped in cloaks of ashy gray. He wore a turbanlike headdress that wound around his face, obscuring all features except his eyes, which were twin pools of whirling, insatiable, merciless voracity. Lando Calrissian was forced to battle the sorcerer near the end of his year-long trek as owner and captain of the *Millennium Falcon*. He was able to defeat the sorcerer, discovering that Rokur was actually a Croke—a small, snail-like being with hairy black legs. This vicious species uses camouflage and illusion to make its way in the galaxy at large. Lando took the small creature that had been Rokur Gepta and squeezed until his gloves were covered with greasy slime, making sure that no Sorcerer of Tund would ever rule the galaxy. [LCS]

Romort Raort

🌀 The Irith spice-jacker named Romort Raort, a denizen of Nar Shaddaa, is not popular among underworld society. His popularity aside, he is left alone because of his association with a gang of thieves who make a habit of taking swift vengeance on those who cross them. Romort and his gang have made a number of deals with the Hutts that allow them to operate along most of the major galactic spice routes. [DE]

Roofoo

Roofoo was one of the aliases used by the humanoid thug who assaulted Luke Skywalker in the Mos Eisley cantina. He claimed to have the death sentence in twelve star systems before Ben Kenobi was forced to subdue him. [GG1]

Other aliases for this person include Doctor Evazan and Doctor Cornelius. His Aqualish companion was known as Ponda Baba. [SWR, GG1]

Roon

Roon is a mysterious planet surrounded by a belt of moonlets, asteroids, and other cosmic debris. Half of Roon is spectacular, with emerald continents and sapphire oceans. The other half of the planet is dark and cold, trapped in perpetual night. According to spacer legends, its star system (which shares the same name) holds untold treasures. [DTV]

Roonadan

Roonadan, the planetary neighbor of Bonadan, was the world from which Han Solo and Fiolla of Lorrd boarded the spaceliner *Lady of Mindor*. [HSR]

Royal Guard

See Imperial Royal Guard.

Rudrig

The planet Rudrig, in the Tion Hegemony, serves as a university world, with many campuses, housing complexes, and recreational facilities. All advanced students in the Tion Hegemony travel to Rudrig for higher-education training. The university also sends aid to developing worlds throughout the Tion Hegemony, as it is the only seat of advanced knowledge in this area of the galaxy. [HLL]

Rukh

Rukh is a member of the Noghri species. Like the rest of his race, he served as one of the Emperor's Death Commandos. When Grand Admiral Thrawn returned from the Unknown Regions, he took charge of the Noghri and selected Rukh to be his personal bodyguard. Rukh was never far from the Grand Admiral's side, hiding in the shadows until his particular talents were called for. When the truth of how the Empire kept the Noghri in line was revealed by Princess Leia, Rukh waited for the best opportunity to take his revenge on Thrawn. [HE, DFR, LC, HESB]

Ruuria

The planet Ruuria is home to the insectoid species called Ruurians. The world's society is made up of one hundred and forty-three colonies, and every Ruurian belongs to a single colony for life. [HLL]

Ruurian

🌀 The insectoid species from the planet Ruuria, Ruurians are slightly longer than one meter. Bands of reddish brown decorate their wooly coats. Eight pairs of short limbs jut from their bodies, each limb ending in four digits. Feathery antennae emerge from a Ruurian's head, protruding from above multifaceted red eyes, a tiny mouth, and small nostrils. This alien species goes through three main life cycles: larva, chrysalis, and chroma-wing stages. With their great natural linguistic abilities, Ruurians often go into diplomatic and scholarly fields. [HLL]

Rwookrrorro

🌀 The Wookiee city Rwookrrorro, nestled high atop a tight ring of giant wroshyr trees, is considered one of Kashyyyk's most beautiful metropolitan centers. The city covers more than a square kilometer, with wide, straight avenues and multileveled buildings. The branches of the trees grow together to form the foundation of the city. Houses and shops are built directly into the tree trunks, with many entrances open to empty space. Only the natural climbing abilities of the Wookiees allow them to get into and out of these openings. The city served as a hiding place for Princess Leia while she was pregnant with the twins Jacen and Jaina. There Chewbacca and other Wookiees defended the princess from a Noghri commando squad. [HE, HESB]

rycrit

🌀 The rycrit is a cowlike animal raised by the Twi'leks on the planet Ryloth. [SWSB]

ryll

⚫ The mineral ryll, mined on the planet Ryloth, is used to create a number of medicines used throughout the galaxy. It is also smuggled into the Corporate Sector for illegal sale to the workers under contract to the Authority. As a recreational substance, ryll is highly addictive and extremely dangerous. [SWSB]

Ryloth

⚫ The principle planet of Ryloth, in the Outer Rim star system of the same name, is home to the Twi'lek species. This dry, rocky world of shadowy valleys and mist-covered peaks has a thin but breathable atmosphere. The planet orbits its sun in such a way that one side of the world bakes under perpetual daylight while the other side is plunged into constant night. Most of the world's inhabitants live in this darkness, including the Twi'leks. The dark side would be nothing more than frozen rock if not for the swirling currents of hot air that blow in from the sun-swept regions. These heat storms are dry twisters that provide the warmth necessary to support the dark side's ecology. The Twi'leks live within massive catacombs built directly into the rocky outcroppings and cliff sides that cover the planet's dark side. On this primitive industrial world, the inhabitants use windmills and air-spun turbines to turn the hot winds into power for the city complexes' heat, air circulation, lights, and minor industries. The Twi'leks' chief export is the medicinal mineral known as ryll, which has illegal uses in addition to its legitimate applications. [SWSB]

S

S-foil

🜨 The wing section assembly of an X-wing starfighter is called an S-foil. The double-layered wings spread apart for attack, forming the X that gives the craft its name. Each wing section is connected to the diagonal wing section opposite it. [SW, RJ]

sabacc

🜨 Sabacc is the card game Lando Calrissian and Han Solo are both fond of playing. In fact, Han won the *Millennium Falcon* from Lando in a sabacc game the two played many years ago. [ESB]

🜨 Sabacc is played with an electronic deck of seventy-six card-chips whose values change randomly in response to electronic impulses. There are four suits in a sabacc deck: sabers, staves, flasks, and coins. Each suit consists of eleven numbered cards (one to eleven) and four ranked cards (twelve to fifteen). The ranked cards are the Commander, the Mistress, the Master, and the Ace. There are also sixteen face cards. When a hand is dealt, the dealer presses a button on the sabacc table to send out a series of random pulses that shift the values and pictures shown on the card-chips. Through several rounds of bluffing and betting, players watch and wait for their card-chips to shift. They can lock any or all of their card-chip values by placing them in the table's interference field, which blocks the pulses and stops the card-chips from changing. To win at sabacc, a player must get a "pure sabacc" which totals exactly twenty-three, or an "idiot's array" which consists of an idiot face card (value zero), a two value card, and a three value card—a literal twenty-three. Some players cheat by using a skifter, a card-chip rigged to change its value when the player presses the corner of the card. [CCC, HESB]

Sabador

⊙ Sabador owns a pet store on the planet Etti IV. A Rakririan from the planet Rakrir, Sabador has a short, segmented, tubular body, five pairs of limbs, two eyestalks, an olfactory cluster, and a vocal organ that is located in the center of his midsection. He stands upright on the lowest two sets of limbs. [HSE]

Saheelindeel

⊙ The planet Saheelindeel, in the Tion Hegemony, is home to an intelligent simianlike species. The world is technologically slow and backward, far below the galactic norm. A queen rules Saheelindeeli society, and she is in the midst of forging a modernization campaign. [HLL]

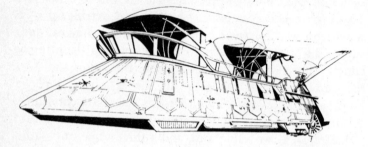

sail barge

sail barge

⊛ A sail barge is a huge repulsorlift vehicle that can be used over either water or sand. Jabba the Hutt had one such vehicle. The huge, armor-hulled sail barge served as his personal transport for traveling across the desert wastes of Tatooine. His associates often used the vessel to stage raids, for it boasted an impressive amount of offensive weaponry. Its blaster deckguns were notably formidable. Though the sail barge was equipped with a powerful thrust engine, the crew normally used the barge's main sails to catch the desert winds and propel the ship over the shifting sands. Jabba's sail barge was destroyed by Luke Skywalker and his companions during the rescue of Han Solo. [RJ]

Salacious Crumb

⊛ The small Kowakian monkey-lizard named Salacious

Crumb was a member of Jabba the Hutt's court. In fact, Crumb held a favored position in the court, always sitting close to his bloated lord and master. When Jabba spilled food and drink, Crumb was there to catch it and consume it himself. Known for his taunting cackle and his habit of mimicking everything said around him, Salacious Crumb was an annoying and disgusting being. He died along with many of Jabba's associates during Han Solo's rescue and escape. [RJ]

Salla Zend

Salla Zend

⊛ Salla Zend is a tough female smuggler and the former girlfriend of Han Solo. Salla built the *Starlight Intruder* transport ship. [DE]

Salporin

⊛ Salporin the Wookiee, Chewbacca's childhood friend,

was one of two Wookiees charged with protecting Princess Leia during her stay on Kashyyyk while Grand Admiral Thrawn's Noghri Death Commandos were searching for her. He was a master of the ryyyk blade, often wielding two of the wicked-looking knives simultaneously. Salporin grew up with Chewbacca, though he remained on Kashyyyk after wanderlust gripped Chewbacca and sent him traveling to the stars. Salporin fell in love with the Wookiee maiden Gorrlyn, and the two started a life together high in Kashyyyk's trees. Unfortunately, this left him on the planet when the Imperial troops arrived. He was forced into slavery, toiling for many long years until Alliance special forces set up secret bases in the lower jungles. Then Salporin escaped his chains and joined the freedom fighters. With his help and the help of other escaped Wookiees, the Alliance was able to set Kashyyyk free. Salporin survived Imperial slavery and the great war of freedom that followed the Battle of Endor, but he could not survive a Noghri attack. He died protecting Princess Leia. [HE, HESB]

Sanctuary Moon (Endor)

Sanctuary Moon was one of the names given to the forest moon of Endor. [RJ]

sandcrawler

A sandcrawler is a huge, multistoried land vehicle that travels on giant treads. The Jawas of Tatooine live, work, and travel within sandcrawlers. The interiors, which have been described as warrenlike, are filled with all of the items the Jawas salvage in their wanderings. [SW]

Tusken Raider

Sand People (Tusken Raiders)

🔴 The Sand People of Tatooine, also called the Tusken Raiders, are a nomadic species with violent tendencies. To protect themselves from the harsh desert environment, Sand People wear heavy robes and strips of cloth, breath masks, and eye protectors. The very aggressive Sand People live in an uneasy peace with Tatooine's moisture farmers. They have been known to attack settlements from time to time. Traveling in small tribes atop their banthas, these nomads are experts at desert survival. Their traditional weapon is the gaderffi stick. [SW]

sand skimmer

🌑 A sand skimmer is a one-person repulsorlift vehicle that consists of a disk to stand on. A large sail extends from the rear of a sand skimmer, helping it travel over sand flats and similar terrain types. [DTV]

sand sloth

🌑 A sand sloth is a beast of burden that resembles a cross between a rhinoceros and a musk ox. Demma Moll uses these creatures on her farm complex on the planet Annoo. [DTV]

sandwhirl

🔴 One type of desert storm that occasionally ravages Tatooine is called a sandwhirl. [SW]

Sarlacc

🔴 The Sarlacc is a terrible creature that lives in the wastes of Tatooine's Dune Sea. This omnivorous, multitentacled beast lives at the bottom of a deep sand pit called the Great Pit of Carkoon. Its large mouth, measuring more than 2.5 meters in diameter, waits at the bottom of the pit. The mouth is lined with three rows of needle-sharp teeth, all pointing inward to keep food trapped within. It prefers its food alive, and uses its tentacles to snatch passing creatures and drag them into its mucous-coated maw. Local belief is that victims caught in the Sarlacc's gut die slow, pain-filled deaths, as the creature's digestive juices require one thousand years to break down food. Jabba the Hutt often used the Sarlacc as a means of eliminating opponents. He made the mistake of banishing Han Solo and Luke Skywalker to the Sarlacc's pit, but they escaped its hungry maw. The bounty hunter named Boba Fett, along with a few of Jabba's henchmen, were not so lucky. [RJ]

⚙ Six years after the Battle of Endor, Boba Fett appeared again to harass Han Solo. Boba Fett had escaped from the Great Pit of Carkoon sometime during the intervening years to show up on Nar Shaddaa, claiming that the Sarlacc found him to be "somewhat indigestible." [DE]

Sate Pestage

✺ Sate Pestage was the Emperor's Grand Vizier. [ESB]

Sauropteroid

⚙ The intelligent aquatic reptiles of the planet Dellalt are called Sauropteroids. Ranging in size from ten to fifteen meters in length, Sauropteroids constantly swim the world's oceans, keeping their heads held above the water on long, muscular necks. Their humanoid heads feature blowholes, and their hides range from light gray in color to greenish black. [HLL]

scan grid

✺ A scan grid is a device used to measure and analyze the magnetic and thermal properties of metals. This is accomplished by applying electrical surges to the metal and examining the effects with specialized sensors. Darth Vader used a scan grid to torture Han Solo on Cloud City. [ESB]

Scardia

⊙ Scardia is the space-station headquarters of the Prophets of the Dark Side. [PDS]

Scardia Voyager

⊙ The golden starship *Scardia Voyager* is used exclusively by the Prophets of the Dark Side. [MMY, PDS]

Scavs

⊙ Scavs are junk traders who gather their wares from battlefields, often looting these areas while the combat is in progress. They employ armored and wheeled transports, neks, and weapons droids to protect themselves. [DE]

Scimitar assault bomber

⊙ When Grand Admiral Thrawn returned to take command of the Imperial remnants five years after the Battle of Endor, he ordered the construction of new ships. One of the first of these was the Scimitar assault bomber, which combined the best features of the TIE Interceptor, the TIE bomber, and Alliance starfighters to create a dedicated assault bomber. With an ion thrust sublight engine and two interlocked repulsorlift generators, the Scimitar is a very fast, very maneuverable atmospheric craft. It carries twin racks of concussion missiles beneath its wings, and has two laser cannons for additional defense. [DFR, DFRSB]

scout trooper

See stormtrooper.

scout walker

See All Terrain Scout Transport.

Screed

See Admiral Screed.

sector

A sector is a cluster of star systems gathered together for economic and political reasons. The Old Republic originally began the practice of combining linked star systems into sectors. At first, a sector was made up of as many star systems as it took to give it approximately fifty habitable (or already inhabited) planets. This definition became less binding as the Republic continued, and in its later days most sectors were vast and unmanageable. When the Emperor introduced his New Order, he reinvented sectors to better control and administer his Empire. Under the Empire, a Moff controls a sector. All of the planetary governors within the sector answer to the Moff (who may also serve as a governor of a favorite world). Each Moff has a military sector group under his command, and uses these forces to secure the possibly hundreds of systems within his sector. To deal with rebellious or otherwise difficult systems, the Emperor appointed Grand Moffs to oversee priority sectors. A priority sector is a sector consisting of systems in which unrest is chronic or recently on the rise. A priority sector often crosses the boundaries of standard sectors, containing the worlds of a dozen or more sectors. [ISB]

Sedrian

🌑 Sedrians are sleek, aquatic mammals that grow to about three meters in length. A fine, slick fur covers their bodies from head to fluke. These seal-men are a combination seal and humanoid, with the head and lower body of a seal and the torso and arms of a humanoid. They inhabit the water planet Sedri. While they can breathe air and live outside water for brief periods of time, they prefer their watery environs. They are peaceful, reflective beings who live in underwater cities. They worship the living coral called Golden Sun, which also provides them with a unique source of power. [BGS, GG4]

See-Threepio

See C-3PO.

seeker

🌑 A seeker is a type of remote. A small, fist-sized metal ball covered with an array of fine sensors, a seeker serves as a training tool for security and military personnel. As a training tool, seekers are programmed to fire low-powered, nonlethal blaster bolts. Miniature repulsors hold the seeker aloft and allow it to make rapid altitude and position changes. Obi-Wan Kenobi and Yoda used seekers to train Luke Skywalker in the use of the lightsaber. A military model can be fitted to fire high-powered lethal blaster bolts and programmed to track and terminate specific targets. The Empire sometimes uses seekers for this purpose. [SW, SWR, ESB]

Seggor Tels

⚙ The Quarren named Seggor Tels has claimed to be the one who betrayed all of the inhabitants of Mon Calamari when he lowered the planetary shields, allowing the Empire to invade and enslave the world. By his own admission, he also helped organize his people to stand with the Calamarians to repel the invaders. In the wake of these events, he decided to remain on his world while most of his brethren departed. He hates the Calamarians for their dreams, yet he feels shame for his actions. He hopes to find his own dream on the world of his birth. [SWSB]

Sena Leikvold Midanyl

⚙ Sena Leikvold Midanyl is Senator Garm Bel Iblis's chief aide and adviser. She once served as his unofficial ambassador-at-large for Peregrine's Nest. [DFR]

Senate, Imperial

⚙ The Imperial Senate was the last holdover from the days of the Old Republic. It was originally just the Senate, becoming the Imperial Senate after the Empire was established. All member worlds of the Empire, and the Old Republic before it, sent elected politicians to the Senate to create laws, pacts, and treaties to help in governing the galactic union. In an Empire that was becoming more and more dictatorial and tyrannical, the democratically elected members of the Senate were an anomaly from another age. It was the Imperial Senate's job to select the course of the galactic government and administer to the many member systems in a way that benefited everyone they represented. The leader of the forum was the President of the Senate, who was elected by the other Senators to serve as a roving ambassador, arbiter, policy maker, and planner. Once the Death Star battle station was declared ready, the Emperor "suspended" the Senate for the "duration of the galactic emergency," instituting his doctrine of rule through fear. [SW]

Senator Palpatine

See Emperor.

sensor

⚙ Sensors assist ships and their crews to analyze the galaxy around them. They work by scanning an area and forming composite images of the information they receive. Passive-mode sensors gather information about the immediate area around a ship as it comes to the sensor array. Scan-mode sensors send out pulses in all directions, actively gathering information in a much wider area. Search-mode sensors actively seek out information in a specific direction. Focus-mode sensors closely examine a specific portion of space. [SWRPG2]

sensor suite

All of the major systems and subsystems, both hardware and software, associated with complex sensor arrays are collectively called the sensor suite. [HSE]

sensory plug-in

Astromechs and other droids have sensory plug-in devices that allow them to interface with computers, sensors, monitors, and data systems via a direct connection. [SME]

sentient tank

See tank droid.

Sentinel

A Sentinel is one of the massive guards employed to protect the reborn Emperor's citadel on the planet Byss. Their origin is unknown, but some believe that they are giant aliens, cyborgs, or droids. [DE, DESB]

Serpent Masters

The Serpent Masters rode winged serpents controlled by ultrasonic signals emitted from a medallion the Supreme Master wore. R2-D2 was able to duplicate the ultrasonic sig-

Serpent Master

nals, enabling Luke Skywalker to ride a serpent and defeat the Serpent Masters to free Tanith Shire's people from slavery. [GW]

servo-grip

⊛ The servodriven hands of a droid are called servo-grips. [HLL]

servodriver

⊛ A servodriver is a powered hand tool used to tighten and loosen bolts, screws, and fasteners. It is also the name of a device that produces motions when it receives signals from a controller. [SW]

Shada

The deceptively decorative Shada is a female mercenary from a mysterious militaristic order of female warriors. Most recently, she has been serving as the bodyguard for the smuggler chief Mazzic. In this role, she appears with plaited hair and a blank expression—until trouble starts. Then she is all business, throwing enameled needles with lethal accuracy and using her more-than-adequate combat skills to protect the smuggler chief. [LC]

Shannador's Revenge

Shannador's Revenge is an *Invincible*-class capital ship that flies under the banner of the Corporate Sector Authority. [HSE]

Shazeen

Shazeen is the name of the Sauropteroid who helped Han Solo and his party on the planet Dellalt during their quest for the lost treasures of Xim the Despot. Obviously a veteran of many conflicts, Shazeen has a nearly black hide and notched and bitten flippers, and is missing an eye. [HLL]

shield

See deflector shield.

shield generator

⊛ Shield generators produce the power needed to create and maintain deflector shields, then focus those shields around a given object, be it ship, building, or even parts of an entire planet. [RJ]

shieldship

⊛ When Lando Calrissian needed a way to move transports safely into the interior of the Athega star system, he designed a unique, heat-resistant escort vessel called a shieldship. The mining operation he planned to set up on the planet Nkllon, the closest world to Athega's hot sun, required transports to bring in supplies and take mined ore off to market. The intense rays of the sun make travel dangerous even for powerful Star Destroyers, for the heat burns away hulls, shielding, and even sensor arrays.

Calrissian presented his design for the shieldship to the newly created Republic Engineering Corporation and commissioned it to build the vessels he envisioned. A shieldship resembles a massive flying umbrella. A curved, 800-meter-wide dish provides protection against Athega's intense rays, while its underside contains tubes, fins, and cooling apparatus that circulates coolant to keep the dish from melting during the trip in-system. A cylindrical, 400-meter-long pylon stretches perpendicularly beneath the dish, with a tug at its center to drive the massive shieldship. The shieldships start at one of the depots stationed at the outer rim of the system. Here a shieldship takes command of a visiting freighter's slave circuits and makes the short jump into the system's hot interior, safely towing the freighter in its cool, artificial shadow. Shieldships require constant maintenance, and coolant and cooling gear must be replaced after every trip. [HE, HESB]

shimmersilk

Shimmersilk is a very sheer and lustrous fabric used to create high-fashion articles throughout the more advanced regions of the galaxy. [HSR, HSE]

Shistavanen

The intelligent species called the Shistavanen, or Wolfmen, are fur-covered bipeds with wolflike faces, sharp claws and teeth, and glowing eyes. A Shistavanen appears during the cantina scene in *Star Wars IV: A New Hope*. [GG1, GG4]

shock-ball

Shock-ball is an outdoor team sport whose object is for one team to stun the other into unconsciousness by employing a charged orb. Team members use insulated mitts to handle the orb and scoops to fling and catch it. After the specified game length expires, the team with the most conscious members wins the match. [HLL]

short-term memory enhancement

Through the use of this Force control technique, a Jedi Knight can replay recent events in his or her mind to carefully examine images and peripheral happenings. This allows the Jedi to recall a particular detail that was observed but not consciously remembered. [DFRSB]

Shrag Brothers

⊕ The Shrag Brothers live and operate in Nar Shaddaa's vertical city. These sneak-thieves often strip Hutt caravels for quick credits. [DE]

Shug Ninx

⊕ Shug Ninx is the half-Corellian master mechanic who operates a large ship repair facility on Nar Shaddaa. He is a friend of Han Solo's from the smuggler-turned-hero's wild youth. [DE]

Sic-six

⊕ Sic-six are an intelligent arachnid species. They are black in color, with tri-sectioned bodies ranging in length from 1.2 to 2.1 meters and hard, chitinous carapaces. They have eight 6-jointed legs, eight eyes, and posterior spinnerets. Sic-six live on the planet Sisk, where these patient web lingerers have become intelligent hunters who use advanced technology to capture prey. [GG4]

Silencer-7

⊕ The *Silencer-7* was one of the Imperial World Devastators participating in the Battle of Calamari. [DE]

Silver Fyre

See Commander Silver Fyre.

Silver Speeder

⊛ *Silver Speeder* was the name of the sleek racing landspeeder once owned by the bounty hunter Boba Fett. The speeder was loaded with nasty gadgets for eliminating opponents: cutting lasers, magnetic harpoons, and a terrible chainsaw shredder. [DTV]

Simoom

⊛ Simoon is a great desert land on the far side of Endor's moon. It is inhabited by the Phlogs. [ETV]

Sise Fromm

⊛ The old yet powerful crime boss named Sise Fromm operated out of a stronghold on the planet Annoo during the early days of the Empire. This member of the Annoo-dat species considered himself to be the "crown king of crime." His legitimate import/export business was actually a front for extortion, kidnapping, and blaster running. He had a son, Tig, who was also in the business. [DTV]

Sith, the

⊛ The mysterious and as-yet-unrevealed group called the Sith causes great fear in those who know of them. They are sometimes called the Dark Lords of the Sith, and Darth Vader has been identified as one of their number. [SW]

Skandits

⊕ Skandits are a chittering, squirrellike species that inhabit the forests of Endor's moon. They have furry black masks and wield slingshots and whips. They love to ambush unsuspecting caravans traveling the forests. [ETV]

skiff

skiff

⊕ A skiff is a surface utility vehicle that employs repulsors to float and move about. Jabba the Hutt used 9.2-meter-long skiffs as companion craft to his giant sail barge. Each skiff was operated by a single driver, who guided it with two directional steering vanes. [RJ]

skimmer

See landspeeder.

Skipray blastboat

⊕ Blastboats fill the gap between starfighters and capital

ships, combining some of the best of both vessel classifications into one ship. They have the speed of starfighters and the armament of capital ships. The most popular model currently in use, Sienar Fleet Systems' GAT-12j Skipray, operates equally well in atmosphere and deep space. While it was designed for point missions and patrol assignments for the Imperial fleet, it never replaced the TIE fighter. Consequently, blastboats were dumped on the open market. Since then, they have found their way into local defense fleets, smuggler camps, and mercenary forces. With hyperdrives and power-boosted armaments, blastboats are formidable ships. They are considered to be capital ships not because of their size (a mere twenty-five meters long), but because of the power rating of their weapons systems. The Skipray performs exceptionally well within a planet's atmosphere, outclassed only by high-performance airspeeders. In deep space, it has low maneuverability and so relies on speed and a devastating first strike. Its weapons include three medium ion cannons, one twin laser cannon turret, one proton torpedo launcher, and one concussion missile launcher. [ISB, HE, HESB]

Skorr

🔘 The bounty hunter Skorr nearly captured Han Solo on the planet Ord Mantell. [GW]

Skyhook

🔘 Skyhook was the codename used to identify the secret Alliance operation that sent the *Tantive IV* to retrieve the technical readouts for the original Death Star battle station. [SWR]

skyhopper

The T-16 Incom skyhopper is a pleasure and utility airspeeder. This model's cockpit and controls are laid out in a similar fashion to those found in the X-wing starfighter. The pilot's compartment and engine is located in the center of trihedral wings. Luke Skywalker learned to fly a skyhopper during his youth on Tatooine. [SW]

Skynx

The insectoid scholar named Skynx comes from the planet Ruuria, where he belongs to the K'zagg Colony. He accompanied Han Solo on the quest to find the lost treasures of the *Queen of Ranroon*. As the leading expert on the pre-Republic era at the University of Ruuria, he studied and deciphered documents from that time. [HLL]

Slave I

Slave I

🔰 *Slave I* is the starship owned and operated by the bounty hunter named Boba Fett. [ESB]

Slave II

🔰 The hyper-modern attack vessel *Slave II* is the bounty hunter Boba Fett's new ship. He has been seen with the vessel since his escape from the Great Pit of Carkoon. [DE]

slave circuit

🔰 Most starships are equipped with at least limited slave circuits. These mechanisms allow for remote control of a starship, usually by a spaceport control tower to assist with landing, or by the ship's owner when he or she wishes to remotely power up the ship. Fully rigged slave circuits create totally controlled vessels that require few crew members and sometimes only a single pilot. [HE, DFR, LC]

sleeper bomb

🔰 A sleeper bomb is an explosive device that remains inert until a preset signal activates it. In its inert state, a sleeper bomb can be attached to a target with little danger of it being detected. Once activated, it draws energy from a nearby power source until a sufficient charge has been gathered to release its explosive energy. [HSR]

Slick

⦿ Han Solo once went by the nickname Slick. It was given to him by his friend and former instructor, Badure. [HLL]

Sljee

⦿ The intelligent multitentacled Sljee, from the planet of the same name, have low, slab-shaped bodies and specialized organs called olfactory stalks. These stalks, composed of concentrated olfactory antennae, give the Sljee a keen sense of smell. In fact, they identify and categorize all objects of odor. [HSR]

Sluis Van

⦿ Sluis Van is the primary planet and central star system in the Sluis sector. As a participating member of the New Republic, the system receives the protection and support of the new galactic government. The system occupies a major spot along active space lanes, and its extensive deep-space shipyard facilities are the best and largest in the area. The facilities are made up of dozens upon dozens of orbit docks. Shuttles constantly travel from the docks to Sluis Van and back again, ferrying spacers throughout the shipyards and to the planet they orbit. Huge armored defense platforms protect the shipyards from pirate raids and smugglers, but larger forces require the intervention of the New Republic fleet.

Grand Admiral Thrawn's first real strike against the New Republic occurred in the Sluis Van shipyards. In response to the Empire's attack on Bpfassh system and its neighbors in the Sluis sector, the New Republic was forced to send combat starships to the area to help with relief efforts. As the ships gathered around Sluis Van, Thrawn and his armada arrived. The Grand Admiral hoped to capture the warships intact to increase the size of his fleet. The plan would have worked out in the Empire's favor if not for the actions of Luke Skywalker, Han Solo, and Lando Calrissian. [HE, HESB]

Sluissi

🌑 The technologically advanced Sluissi of the planet Sluis Van appear as humanoids from the waist up, though their lower bodies end in a snakelike tail. They are renowned for their expertise with starships, and the Sluis Van Shipyards are considered one of the best places to go for repairs or maintenance. Longtime members of the Old Republic, the Sluissi people readily joined the New Republic after the Battle of Endor. These beings are methodical and somewhat plodding; they take their time in everything they do. Jobs may take longer, but they turn out to be very well done. Nothing ever seems to excite or disturb a Sluissi, for they are even-tempered and very calm. They consider themselves to be mechanical artists, and all artists know that great art cannot be rushed. [DFRSB]

smuggling guilds

🌑 The smuggling groups that control various sectors on the spaceport moon of Nar Shaddaa are unofficially called smuggling guilds. [DE]

Snaggletooth

The alien called Snaggletooth belongs to an as-yet-unidentified species of bipeds. He can easily be identified by his widely spaced eyes, large nostrils, and wide, grinning mouth. His mouth contains a handful of teeth, all in the middle of the lower jaw, with one pointed tooth sticking up on the right side. Snaggletooth appeared briefly in the cantina scene of *Star Wars IV: A New Hope*. [SW]

snowspeeder

The Incom T-47 airspeeders specially adapted to the hostile environment of the ice planet Hoth were called snowspeeders. These small, wedge-shaped airspeeders were heavily armored and highly maneuverable, redesigned to provide air protection to the Rebel base on Hoth. A forward-sitting pilot and rear-facing gunner crewed each snowspeeder, employing two forward heavy laser cannons and a rear-mounted harpoon cannon. [ESB]

snowtrooper

A snowtrooper is the name applied to specialized stormtroopers trained and equipped to operate in frozen conditions. [SWSB]

snubfighter

See X-wing starfighter.

Snunb

See Captain Syob Snunb.

Solo

See Han Solo.

Sonniod

🔰 The former smuggler and bootlegger named Sonniod is an acquaintance of Han Solo and Chewbacca the Wookiee. When Solo last met up with the compact, gray-haired little man, Sonniod was running a legitimate holofeature loan service. His current activities are unknown. [HSR]

Soul Tree

🔰 A Soul Tree is a special tree planted at the time an Ewok baby is born. Ewoks feel a great kinship toward their individual Soul Trees, and they care for them throughout their lives. When an Ewok dies, a hood is tied around the trunk of his or her Soul Tree to signify the sad event. [ETV]

Sovereign Protectors

See Imperial Royal Guard.

Spaarti cloning cylinder

🔰 Spaarti cloning cylinders are a remnant of the terrible

Clone Wars. In these machines, clones were grown to maturity. A full growth cycle required a year's time, for anything less led to clone madness. Many of the earliest clones suffered from this malady, since the process and technique took many years to develop and perfect. The Emperor kept a large number of Spaarti cloning cylinders hidden in his private storehouses, which were scattered around the galaxy. Grand Admiral Thrawn discovered one such storehouse on the planet Wayland, and he used the cylinders he found there to grow clone soldiers and crews to fill his forces. He even managed to accelerate the growth process by using ysalamiri. It was determined that rapid clone growth was hampered by the natural properties of the Force, which surrounds all living things. By using the ysalamiri to form bubbles devoid of the Force around the Spaarti cylinders, Thrawn was able to grow perfect clones in as little as twenty days. [HE, DFR, LC]

space barge

Space barges operate within systems to keep commerce moving. These heavy-duty short-range vessels have powerful engines and good-sized cargo bays to move goods quickly and efficiently among larger hyperdrive-equipped cargo ships, orbiting storage holds, and planetary spaceports. They are also used to unload massive container ships, which cannot penetrate too deeply into a system due to their great size. [SWSB]

spacer

Spacer is the term applied to those who make a living by traveling the space lanes, either in their own ships or as part of a crew. [SW]

Spacers' Garage

Spacers' Garage is the huge starship repair facility on Nar Shaddaa. It is owned and operated by Shug Ninx, an old friend of Han Solo. [DE]

space slug

Space slugs are colossal, wormlike creatures that live within asteroids. Their metabolisms allow them to survive in airless vacuums and subsist on minerals. These strange creatures grow to lengths as great as 900 meters. [ESB]

Like mynocks, space slugs are silicon-based life-forms. They prey upon mynocks, as well as on anything else moving around asteroids. Space-slug flesh has a number of commercial uses, and some spacers make a living hunting them. Space slugs reproduce through fission, splitting into two separate creatures. [SWSB]

Space Station Kwenn

Space Station Kwenn is considered the last fuel and supply stop before entering the Outer Rim Territories. The citylike station features everything the weary spacer might need and desire after a long voyage. The station is built atop an extensive docking platform consisting of scores of individual, modular space docks, and hangar bays. Still farther below the station is the massive dry dock gridwork, used for parking, overhauling, refitting, or otherwise repairing capital-class chips. [TM, SF]

Space Station Scardia

The cube-shaped Space Station Scardia is headquarters for the Prophets of the Dark Side. [LCJ, PDS]

spacing

Spacing is a form of execution in which the victim is cast into space without any kind of protective gear. [HLL]

speeder

See airspeeder, landspeeder, snowspeeder.

speeder bike

Small, one-person repulsor land vehicles, speeder bikes move at incredible rates, making them perfect for use as

speeder bike

scout and reconnaissance craft. Four directional steering vanes extend from the front of a speeder bike on twin outriggers, providing a high degree of maneuverability. The pilot directs the bike with elevation and maneuver controls located in the handgrips. Two rocker-pivoted foot pads regulate speed, while controls at the forward end of the saddle are for parking, weaponry, communications, and energy recharging. Military speeder bikes, like those used by the Empire's scout troopers, have armor plating and are armed with blaster cannons. [RJ]

speeder transport

Speeder transports are large shuttlecraft used by the New Republic to move V-wing airspeeders from capital ships to launch points within a planet's atmosphere. [DE]

spice

A product of the labor mines of Kessel, spice is a controlled commodity. It makes a popular cargo for smugglers because of its high profit-to-volume margin. [SW]

Spirit Tree

The Spirit Tree of Endor's moon is considered to be the original tree of the forest. The Ewoks believe that all life started with this tree, and that all life must eventually return to it. [ETV]

Spray of Tynna

⊕ Spray of Tynna is the name used by a short, bipedal skip tracer employed by Interstellar Collections Ltd. A member of a species of intelligent sea otters, Spray is actually Odumin, a powerful and influential territorial sector manager for the Corporate Sector Authority. [HSR]

Spurch Goa

⊕ The bounty hunter Spurch Goa, also known as Warhog, has a nasty temperament. He lives on the spaceport moon Nar Shaddaa. [DE]

Squeak

⊕ Squeak is a Tin-Tin Dwarf who works for Big Bunji as a messenger and gopher. [HSE]

Squib

⊕ Squibs are small, furry bipeds with tufted ears, large eyes, short muzzles, and black noses. Their fur ranges in color from deep red to brilliant blue. They come from the world of Skor II, which orbits the Squab star. These fearless nomads roam the galaxy in reclamation ships, using tractor beams to salvage junk (which they consider treasure). The Squibs have an intense rivalry going with the Ugors, as both try to claim salvage before the other. Squibs are overconfident and curious, overbearing and uppity. They love to haggle, a practice that they have turned into an art form. The more complicated and convoluted a deal a Squib can strike, the better the level of satisfaction and success. [SH, GG4]

Squid Head

🌙 The alien species commonly called Squid Heads are characterized by the four tentacles that protrude from their jaws, their leathery skin, their suction-cupped fingers, and their turquoise eyes. One of these beings was a frequent guest (or perhaps an employee) in the court of Jabba the Hutt. [RJ]

✪ Squid Heads call themselves Quarren. They come from the planet Mon Calamari, which they share with the Calamarian species. [SWSB]

ST 321

🌙 The comm unit designation for Darth Vader's personal *Lambda*-class shuttle was ST 321. [RJ]

Standard Time Part

🌙 The basic unit used to measure time throughout the Empire is called the Standard Time Part. [SW]

stang

✪ Stang is an Alderaanian swearword. [SME]

star cruiser

🏵 A star cruiser is a particular class of capital ship. [SW, ESB, RJ]

Star Destroyer

🏵 The colossal, wedge-shaped capital starships called Star Destroyers are perhaps the most-feared and most instantly recognizable vessels roaming the space lanes. The two newest classes of Star Destroyers, the *Imperial* class and the *Super* class, are found exclusively in the Imperial fleet. An older model, the *Victory* class, dates back to the end of the Clone Wars and can be found in service among system defense and large corporate constabulary fleets.

The *Imperial*-class Star Destroyer is 1.6 kilometers long and bristles with offensive weaponry. Turbolasers and ion cannon batteries create wide-ranging fields of fire around the wedge, and a complement of TIE starfighters are carried within its hangar bays to add even more punch. Defensive shield generators, tractor-beam projectors, and sophisticated sensor arrays round out this capital ship's exterior emplacements. An Imperial Star Destroyer also carries drop ships, landing barges, shuttles, repair vessels, deep-space probes, an assortment of specialized droids, field artillery weapons, walkers, ground assault vehicles, modular building units, soldiers, and Imperial stormtroopers.

The *Super*-class Star Destroyer, the newest model in the fleet, is eight kilometers long, dwarfing even the massive Imperial Star Destroyers. Though the Super Star Destroyer is approximately five times as powerful as its smaller predecessor, the few currently in service are not primarily used as combat starships. Instead, these vessels are used as command ships, guiding fleets and serving as headquarters from which to conduct planetary assaults and space battles. Lord Darth Vader's *Executor* was a Super Star Destroyer. [SW, ESB, RJ]

☻ Lira Wessex, daughter of the engineer who designed the earlier Victory Star Destroyer, was the driving force behind the Imperial model. Bristling with sixty turbolaser batteries, sixty ion cannon batteries, ten tractor beam projectors, and a full wing of TIE fighters (seventy-two starfighters) in its hangar bays, the Imperial Star Destroyer is a flying weapons platform. While the Empire cannot hope to garrison every system in its control, it can project its might anywhere within a short period of time by using combat starships such as the Imperial Star Destroyer. [SWSB]

An even newer *Super*-class Star Destroyer was built to serve as the reborn Emperor's flagship six years after the Battle of Endor. This solid-black model is sixteen kilometers long and covered with weapons and defenses. [DE]

Star Galleon

☻ The 300-meter-long Imperial Star Galleon is designed to combine the cargo space of a bulk freighter with the armament of a combat starship. With ten turbolaser batteries and concussion missiles, the Star Galleon can carry cargo and defend itself, thus eliminating the need to have separate freighters and escort craft. The interior is designed to hamper boarding parties, with fortresslike emplacements in the corridors, force fields, heavy blast doors, and a complement of three hundred troopers. The cargo-hold pod, located in the very center of the ship, has an added level of protection: it can be jettisoned from the vessel when its computers automatically activate a small hyperdrive and send it on a prearranged lightspeed jump. [ISB, DFRSB]

Starhunter Intergalactic Menagerie

The Starhunter Intergalactic Menagerie was a traveling sideshow that toured the galaxy during the early days of the Empire. The main attractions were rare and usually illegally acquired creatures from many different worlds, and it moved from system to system in a huge cruiser. The sideshow and ship were owned and operated by the sleazy Captain Stroon. Stroon's first mate and assistant was the lizardlike humanoid called Mr. Slarm. [DTV]

Starlight Intruder

The transport *Starlight Intruder* is a hotrod junkheap of a ship. It was built by its owner, the smuggler Salla Zend. The *Intruder* is equipped with a hyperdrive and has holds big enough to carry immense loads of cargo. [DE]

Star Runner

The star cruiser owned and operated by young Kea Moll was called the *Star Runner*. [DTV]

Stars' End

Stars' End is a secret Corporate Sector Authority penal colony on the planet Mytus VII. The name refers to the location of the Mytus star system, which sits at the end of a faint wisp of stars at the edge of Corporate Sector space. [HSE]

starshipwright

A person skilled in the craft of building and repairing starships is called a starshipwright. [HSR]

Stenness

The Stenness star system contains seven mining worlds that were discovered four thousand years before the events of *Star Wars IV: A New Hope*. The resources of these mines were exhausted long ago, but the inhabitants continue to live on the wealth they have inherited from their ancestors' time of plenty. The 'Nessies, as these inhabitants are called, are known for their stinginess and their powerful addiction to spice. [DE]

stim-shot

A main component of medpacs, the stim-shot is a stimulant administered with a pneumatic dispenser. [ESBR]

stock light freighter

Corellian-built stock light freighters are among the most common small trading vessels operating in the known galaxy. At one time, this class of ship was the backbone of intergalactic trade. While stock light freighters are still in use, many companies have turned to large bulk freighters and container ships to move their wares. These vessels come in a variety of shapes and sizes, but all are built around the basic design of a command pod, storage holds, and engines.

The *Millennium Falcon* is a modified stock light freighter, a model YT-1300 Corellian transport. [SWSB]

Stokhli spray stick

Stokhli spray sticks are long-range stun weapons developed by the Stokhli people of the planet Manress. Wielders of these weapons can release a spraynet mist from a nozzle atop the stick. The spraynet mist can be shot at targets up to 200 meters away, and is charged with a powerful stun current. Originally developed as a tool for large-game hunters, Stokhli spray sticks have found applications as both defensive and offensive personal weapons. The stick is activated by depressing a thumb trigger. [HE, HESB]

stormtrooper

The Imperial shock troops who are totally loyal to the Emperor are called stormtroopers. Unlike regular Imperial soldiers, stormtroopers wear white-and-black armored spacesuits over black body gloves. They are deployed to neutralize resistance to the New Order, and placed aboard Imperial vessels to be used as first-strike forces and to make sure lower officers stay true to the Emperor's vision. Trained to obey orders, stormtroopers will rush into combat without a thought for their own safety. If the Emperor issues an order, stormtroopers will drop everything else to obey it. Their armored spacesuits provide limited protection against blaster fire. The eighteen pieces that make up the outer shell create an enclosed, self-sustaining environment. The two-piece body glove controls body temperature. Stormtrooper officers wear shoulder poltroons. [SW, ESB, RJ]

stormtrooper

Totally loyal to the Empire, stormtroopers cannot be bribed, seduced, or blackmailed into betraying their Emperor. They live in a totally disciplined, totally militaristic world where obedience is paramount and the will of the Emperor is absolute. In addition to the main stormtrooper legions, a number of special units have been assembled to operate on the varied worlds and climates of the Empire. To deal with problems on ice-covered worlds, cold-assault troopers are elite frozen-environment combatants. Also called snowtroopers, these Imperial soldiers wear the basic white-and-black armor equipped with powerful heating and personal environment units, terrain-grip boots, and breathing masks.

Second only to the Royal Guard, the elite zero-g

stormtroopers, or spacetroopers, are trained to operate exclusively in space. When the Empire needs to launch an assault on a spacefaring vessel, spacetroopers are sent in to do the job. Each trooper wears full body armor capable of withstanding the rigors of hard vacuum. This armor functions as a personal spacecraft and attack vehicle. With sensor arrays, magnetic couplers for adhering to ships, repulsorlift propulsion units, and a wide assortment of weaponry, spacetrooper armor makes these troopers fearsome to behold. Two meters tall and twice as wide as a normal stormtrooper, spacetroopers can unleash a devastating barrage on their targets. Concussion, gas, and stun grenades, miniature proton torpedoes, blaster cannons, and laser cutters are standard ordnance. Specially designed assault shuttles carry spacetroopers into combat. [SWSB, HE, HESB]

Scout troopers are lightly armored, highly mobile stormtroopers who are usually assigned to Imperial garrisons. They use speeder bikes to patrol perimeters, perform reconnaissance missions, and scout enemy locations. To assist them when traveling at the high speeds speeder bikes reach, scout troopers wear specialized helmets equipped with built-in macrobinocular viewplates and sensor arrays. These feed into computers that analyze terrain features instantaneously to help the scouts navigate at high speeds. They also map the areas they explore, producing a continuous record of each mission they participate in. Scout troopers wear lightweight armor and padding over a black body glove, and carry small automatic blasters. [SWSB]

Strike-class medium cruiser

The 450-meter-long Imperial *Strike*-class medium star cruiser was designed to be mass-produced in a short span of time. This triumph of the Empire's modular design philosophy is made up of prefabricated component sections. Introduced near the end of the Galactic Civil War, the *Strike*-class cruiser continues to serve an important role in the remnants of the Imperial fleet under the command of Grand Admiral Thrawn. It is one of the few vessels that can still be turned out with regularity by the Empire's remaining construction centers. Thanks to their modular design, the cruisers' interiors can be configured to accommodate specific mission profiles. Some have room to carry a ground assault company, including troops, two AT-STs, one AT-AT, and a limited number of support speeders. Others are modified to make room for a complete squadron of TIE fighters. Other configurations include prefab garrison deployers, troop transports, and planet assault cruisers packed with five AT-ATs for surgical deployment. Strike cruisers normally carry twenty turbolasers, ten turbolaser batteries, ten ion cannons, and ten tractor-beam projectors. [ISB, HESB]

Strum

🌑 Strum is one of two domesticated vornskrs Talon Karrde employs as pets and guards. [HE, DFR, LC, HESB]

Subjugator

🌑 The *Victory*-class Star Destroyer *Subjugator*, under the command of Captain Kolaff, was targeted by a Rebel Mon Calamari strike force codenamed Task Force Starfall. The task force, made up of Mon Cal star cruisers, met the Star Destroyer in mortal combat and managed to destroy it. [SF]

sublight drive

⊕ Sublight drives move starships through realspace. A number of different types of sublight drives exist, but the most popular is the Hoersch-Kessel ion drive. Through fusion reaction the H-K produces charged particles that hurl ships forward when released. Since the mildly radioactive discharge is illegal on most populated worlds, starships with H-K sublight drives employ repulsorlifts for travel within a planet's atmosphere. [SWSB]

Sullust

⊕ The star system of Sullust, with its primary planet of the same name, threw its support to the Rebel Alliance after the Rebel victory at Yavin. It was in this star system that the Alliance armada gathered prior to the Battle of Endor. The assault on the second Death Star was planned and launched from this location. Nien Nunb, Lando Calrissian's copilot during the assault, is a native of the planet Sullust. [RJ]

⊕ The people of Sullust, called Sullustans, are jowled, mouse-eared humanoids with large, round eyes. They live in the vast subterranean caverns beneath the surface of their harsh, volcanic world. While the small species can venture to the surface for limited periods of time, they find the cooler caves to be much more to their liking. The natural caverns have been turned into beautiful underground cities, and visitors come from all over the galaxy to see the sights and shop in the remarkable marketplaces. The planet is also the headquarters of the vast intergalactic conglomerate SoroSuub Corporation. This leading mineral-processing company has subdivisions that handle energy, space mining, food packaging, and technological products. During the height of the Galactic Civil War, SoroSuub Corporation dissolved the planetary government and proclaimed the tenets of the New Order as the ruling authority for the world. This situation lasted until shortly before the Battle of Endor, when pro-Alliance factions took control away from SoroSuub. [SWSB]

Sunfighter Franchise, The

The Sunfighter Franchise is one of the false names and registrations used by Han Solo for the *Millennium Falcon*. He hasn't used this particular ID profile since his days evading Corporate Sector Authority patrols. [HSE]

sungwas

Sungwas are massive doglike creatures native to the bog moon Bodgen. They are a nightmarish cross of wolf and weasel. [DTV]

Super Star Destroyer

See Star Destroyer.

Supreme Commander Skywalker

Luke Skywalker was given the title of Supreme Commander by the reborn Emperor after he agreed to become the Emperor's apprentice and protégé. [DE]

Supreme Prophet

See Kadaan.

Survivors

🌀 The Survivors are the descendants of the early space explorers who wound up on the planet Dellalt. Extreme isolationists, they hate other Dellaltians, weaving this hatred into their barbaric religion. It is believed that these humans are the descendants of the spacers marooned when the legendary starship *Queen of Ranroon* crashed. As generations passed, they forgot their true origins and turned the customs and technology of their ancestors into myths and legends. The technological artifacts salvaged from the crash became sacred talismans and implements for use in their religious practices. The major ritual of the Survivors seems to be based upon the actions undertaken by marooned spacers—setting up an emergency beacon and calling for rescue. Powered by sacrifices, the Survivors hope that the "signals" of their prayers will be "received" and lead to their "deliverance" (or rescue). [HLL]

swamp crawler

🌀 A swamp crawler is a land vehicle used for traveling across marshy terrain. The inhabitants of the planet Mimban make ample use of these vehicles. A swamp crawler features a multiwheel transmission system, six balloon tires, and a central spherical wheel. This global wheel can be used to execute quick ninety- and one-hundred-eighty-degree turns when required to traverse the challenging topography. [SME]

swoop

A swoop is an airspeeder equivalent to a surface-hugging speeder bike. Basically an engine with a seat, swoops are fast and highly maneuverable. All controls are located in the swoop's handlebars and saddle, and a wind fairing provides stabilization and direction shifts. Swoop racing is a very popular sport in the Galactic Core and throughout the civilized regions of the galaxy. The sport requires huge domed arenas called swoop tracks, which enclose tens of thousands of viewing seats, circular flight paths, obstacle courses, and massive concession booths. Some outlaw bands in the Outer Rim Territories use swoops, and swoop gangs like the Nova Demons and Dark Star Hellions have gained infamy for their crimes. Han Solo once raced swoops professionally. [HSR, HLL, SWSB, DFRSB]

Swimmer

See Swimming People.

Swimming People

The Sauropteroids of Dellalt are called the Swimming People. A single Sauropteroid is referred to as a Swimmer. [HLL]

Sy Snootles

The alien Sy Snootles was the lead singer for Max Rebo's jizz-wailing band of musicians. Bipedal, with spotted

Droopy/Rebo/Sy Snootles

yellow-green skin and long, thin limbs, Sy sang through a mouth that was positioned at the end of a foot-long protrusion extending from the lower portion of her face. Sy and the rest of the band performed for Jabba the Hutt's court just prior to the crime lord's death. [RJ]

S'ybll

After the escape from Yavin, the *Falcon*, with Luke Skywalker, Han Solo, and C-3PO aboard, developed problems and landed on a paradiselike planet for repairs. Luke encountered S'ybll, a mind witch who could change shapes. S'ybll tried to entice Luke to abandon his friends and stay with her. [GW]

synth-flesh

Synth-flesh is a translucent gel derived from the cellular regeneration medium called bacta. When applied to superficial wounds, synth-flesh seals the skin and promotes rapid healing of damaged tissue. After the gel dries, it slowly flakes off to reveal new, scarless tissue where the wound used to be. Synth-flesh is often found among the supplies in a medpac. [HSE]

system patrol craft

Several popular models of patrol craft operate within star systems as the first line of defense against pirates, smugglers, and hostile alien forces. Because of their mission profile, system patrol craft usually have powerful sublight engines but no hyperdrives. They also perform custom inspection duties and watch for disabled ships that require assistance. [ISB, DFRSB]

Syub Snunb

See Captain Syub Snunb.

T

T-16

See skyhopper.

T-47

See snowspeeder.

Taanab

See Battle of Taanab.

Tagge

See General Tagge.

talkdroid

Talkdroid is another name for a protocol droid, used primarily by alien species from less developed worlds. [RJ]

Talon Karrde

Talon Karrde

Talon Karrde is one of the top operators in the galaxy's fringe community since the death of Jabba the Hutt. A human, Karrde does not flaunt his position or accomplishments. He is a slender, thin-faced man with short, dark hair and pale blue eyes. His main business is smuggling, though he is also an information broker of no small reputation. His base and home on the planet Myrkr had to be deserted after the Empire and New Republic agents clashed there, forcing him to give up the place he had grown to love. His operations extend deeply into both Imperial and New Republic space, so he tries to remain neutral in his dealings with both. He is considered honest in his dealings, as well as coldly calculating and even mercenary. He believes very strongly in his associates, and their debts are his debts—as are their credits. He refuses to have anything to do with slave running or kidnapping. During the events surrounding the return of Grand Admiral Thrawn, Talon Karrde was unwillingly dragged into the emerging struggle between the

Empire and New Republic. He eventually decided it would be good business to assist the New Republic, and the aid his organization provided helped it foil Thrawn's plans. [HE, DFR, LC, HESB, DFRSB]

Talz

⚙ The large, strong beings from Alzoc III are called Talz. These white-furred beings stand about two meters tall and have four eyes: two large ones and two small ones. Though they appear fierce, they have gentle personalities. Their world is not technologically advanced, and the Empire subjugated it to use its inhabitants as slave laborers. A Talz appears in the cantina scene in *Star Wars IV: A New Hope*. [GG4]

Tammuz-an

⚙ The planet Tammuz-an is noted for the double rings that surround it. [DTV]

Tanith Shire

⚙ A supply tug operator at the starship yards on Fondor, Tanith Shire stole drone barges and sent them crashing on a planet where they were salvaged by the Serpent Masters, who kept Shire's people in slavery. Luke Skywalker and Tanith Shire escaped Fondor on one of these barges. After crash landing, Luke defeated the Serpent Masters and freed Shire's people. [GW]

tank droid

⚛ The advanced Imperial combat droid (Arakyd XR-85) called a tank droid, or sentient tank, combines the properties of an armored vehicle weapon with the intelligence and programming of a droid. These weapons played a significant role in the invasion of Imperial City, which occurred six years after the Battle of Endor. [DE, DESB]

Tantive IV

☘ *Tantive IV* was the name of Princess Leia Organa's consular ship. It was captured in the Tatooine star system after intercepting the technical plans for the original Death Star battle station. The capture of this ship was the start of the events that led to the Battle of Yavin. [SWR]

Targeter

⚛ Targeter was Winter's codename during her time of service with Alliance Procurement and Supply. Her mission profile was to enter Imperial installations, use her perfect memory to gather intelligence and create detailed maps, and then pass the information along to Rebel agents so that they could procure supplies for the Rebellion from Imperial stockpiles. [DFRSB, LC]

targeting computer

☘ A targeting computer is a sophisticated piece of equipment used aboard starfighters and other military starships to assist in combat. Working in cooperation with a starship's nav computer and sensor array, a targeting computer acquires hostile targets for the ship's weapons systems. By calculating trajectories and attack and intercept courses, targeting computers help pilots and gunners track and fire at fast-moving enemy ships. [SW]

target remote

See remote and seeker.

Tarkin

See Grand Moff Tarkin.

Tarrik

(☸) Tarrik was one of Bail Organa's most-trusted servants on the planet Alderaan. [SWR]

Tarrin

(☸) Tarrin was a Rebel Alliance pilot serving in Luke Skywalker's X-wing squadron during the period marked by the Battle of Hoth. [ESBR]

Tatoo I, Tatoo II

(☸) The twin suns of the Tatooine system are the binary stars Tatoo I and Tatoo II. [SW]

Tatooine

⚙ Tatooine, the primary planet in the star system of the same name, is a desert world far from the bright center of the galaxy. Located in the region of space called the Outer Rim Territories, Tatooine is the world on which Luke Skywalker grew up. Twin suns beat down upon this sand-covered world, burning the great expanses of desert and all those who dwell there. The planet is home to Jawas, Sand People, banthas, Krayt dragons, human settlers, and assorted aliens who populate Mos Eisley Spaceport. The human settlers, most of whom make a living as moisture farmers, live in communities like Anchorhead. Many members of the galaxy's fringe society, such as smugglers, mercenaries, and bounty hunters, use Tatooine as a base because of its distance from the watchful eyes of the Empire and other galactic governments. [SW]

tauntaun

⚙ Tauntauns roam the frozen wastes of the ice planet Hoth. Easily domesticated, tauntauns were used as mounts and pack animals by the Alliance during its stay on Hoth. Thick gray fur protects tauntauns from Hoth's extreme temperatures, though they cannot survive the brutal nights without finding shelter. Swift and sure-footed, herds of these creatures can be seen running across the plains of snow and ice during the daylight hours. [ESB]

Tav Breil'lya

⚙ The Bothan named Tav Breil'lya serves as a top aide to the New Republic's Councilor Borsk Fey'lya. He never goes anywhere without wearing an ornate neckpiece—his family's lineage crest. As a Council-Aide, he is extremely loyal to Fey'lya, and is often assigned to the most important fact-finding missions. Like most Bothans, Breil'lya plays games of politics in such a way that the game is more important than the outcome. Lacking Fey'lya's subtlety, he plays the game with a heavy, obvious hand.

As part of his regular duties, Tav Breil'lya traveled to the planet New Cov to meet with Garm Bel Iblis. The Bothan hoped to convince the ex–Old Republic Senator to join the New Republic as an ally of Fey'lya's political faction. That, of course, did not work out in the Bothans' favor, for the nature of the games they were engaged in was revealed to the rest of the Provisional Council. [DFR, DFRSB]

Tawntoom

⊕ The colony Tawntoom is a frontier settlement on the frozen, dark side of the planet Roon. The colony served as a base for Governor Koong and his band of thieves during the early days of the Empire. [DTV]

tech dome

☮ On Tatooine and other settlement worlds, the garage/ workshops that extend off houses are called tech domes. [SWR]

Teebo

☮ Teebo is one of the leaders of the tribe of Ewoks that befriended Princess Leia and the Alliance strike team on

Endor's forest moon. Teebo's striped fur alternates between light and dark gray. He wears a horned half skull decorated with feathers atop his head, and carries his weapon of choice—a stone hatchet. [RJ]

(symbol) Teebo is a dreamer and a poet. He has a mystical ability to communicate with nature. [ETV]

Teek

(symbol) The scruffy, furry Endor creature named Teek has close-set eyes and buck teeth. He is very mischievous. His lightning-quick speed allows him to dart from place to place in the blink of an eye. [BFE]

telesponder

(symbol) A telesponder automatically broadcasts a ship's ID profile in response to signals sent by spaceports and military authorities. [HSE]

Temple of Pomojema

(symbol) The Temple of Pomojema, located on the planet Mimban, is a shrine to the Mimbanite god Pomojema. The legendary Kaiburr Crystal was kept in this structure. A stone ziggurat, the temple is supported by obsidian pillars, and a stone icon representing the god is displayed for all the faithful to see. Pomojema is depicted as a winged humanoid with talons and a faceless head. [SME]

tentacle bush

⚙ The tentacle bush is a low-lying plant found on the planet Arzid. Its grasping tentacles snatch small creatures and deliver them to the bush for digestion. [PDS]

Terak

⚙ Terak is the cruel and evil king of the Marauders who prey upon the inhabitants of Endor's forest moon. He is obsessed with finding "the power," and the witch Charal assists him in his search. [BFE]

terrain-following sensor

⚙ Terrain-following sensors (TFS) allow ships to fly parallel to the ground at a fixed height, as selected and activated by the pilot. Interfacing with a ship's propulsion and flight-control systems, terrain-following sensors automatically adjust the ship's course to avoid obstacles and compensate for changing terrain features. [HSE, HSR]

Tetan Elite

⚙ According to the histories stored in the Jedi Holocron, a group of young aristocrats from the Empress Teta system turned to the dark side of the Force approximately four thousand years before the events of *Star Wars IV: A New Hope*. The self-indulgent Tetan elite dabbled in primitive magics as a means of amusement, eventually tapping into the Force's dark side. The first of the group to fall was Satal Keto, who organized his cohorts into a secret society called the Krath. [DE]

Teta

See Empress Teta.

Thall Joben

⊕ Thall Joben grew up on the planet Ingo with his best friend and rival, Jord Dusat. Thall had a passion for building and racing landspeeders. When he was seventeen years old, during the Empire's early days, he encountered the droids R2-D2 and C-3PO. [DTV]

Theelin

⊕ The Theelin are a now-extinct, near-human species. Shug Ninx of Nar Shaddaa has Theelin blood, for his mother was one of the last of that species. [DE]

thermal cape

⊕ The lightweight metal-foil and spider-silk-composite ponchos called thermal capes retain the wearer's body heat, providing protection from the cold. Thermal capes, also called thermal wraps, are usually standard equipment in survival gear packs. [SME]

thermal coil

See condenser unit.

thermal detonator

(U) The powerful explosive called a thermal detonator comes in the form of a small, metal ball. When the detonator is activated, a fusion reaction causes an explosion. Princess Leia, disguised as the bounty hunter named Boushh, threatened Jabba the Hutt's court with a thermal detonator to demonstrate Boushh's nerve and impress the crime lord. [RJ]

thermosuit

(O) A thermosuit is a thin, lightweight coverall worn over normal clothing to protect the wearer from temperature extremes. [HSR, SME]

Third Battle of Vontor, The

(O) The Third Battle of Vontor was the last in a series of major conflicts directed against the pre-Republic tyrant known as Xim the Despot. In this battle, Xim the Despot was finally defeated by the forces that opposed his rule. [HLL]

Thisleborn

See Grand Moff Thistleborn.

Thon

(☸) Thon was a continent on the planet Alderaan. [SWR]

Thrawn

See Grand Admiral Thrawn.

Thrella Well

(☺) A Thrella Well is any of a series of shafts that lead from the surface of Circarpous V to the network of caverns that extends deep within the planet's crust. These wells are located all over the planet's surface, and are said to be the work of the legendary race known as the Thrella. [SME]

Tibanna gas

(☸) The rare gas extracted from Bespin's atmosphere and processed at Cloud City is called Tibanna gas. [ESB]

(☺) Hot air rises through Cloud City's unipod, sucking in the gases that float in Bespin's atmosphere—including tibanna gas. Tibanna gas is processed and spin-sealed in carbonite for transport off-planet. When cohesive light passes through Tibanna gas, its energy output is multiplied fourfold. In this way, blasters and other energy weapons produce greater energy yields (and therefore greater amounts of damage) when Tibanna gas is used as a conducting agent. Personal weapons cannot withstand this extra yield, but ship-mounted blasters benefit greatly from the use of Tibanna gas. [GG2]

Tibor

⟨❂⟩ The bounty hunter Tibor is a member of the Barabel species. This vicious, bipedal reptiloid frequents the Mos Eisley cantina and is a regular employee of Zorba the Hutt. [ZHR]

Tibrin

⟨❂⟩ Tibrin is the planet homeworld of the alien Ishi Tib race. The Ishi Tib cities are built on Tibrin atop carefully cultivated coral reefs. [GG4]

TIE crawler

⟨❂⟩ A TIE (Santhe/Sienar Technologies Century Tank) crawler is a cheap, expendable ground-assault vehicle modeled after the TIE interceptor. Huge wheels replace the solar-panel wings on either side of the infamous cockpit sphere, allowing these tanklike craft to traverse a wide variety of terrain. [DE, DESB]

TIE fighter

⟨❂⟩ The main combat starfighter used by the Empire is the TIE fighter. Fast, maneuverable, and apparently endless in number, TIE fighters are deployed from bases and capital ships, as they have neither the range nor the capability to travel great distances on their own. As short-range patrol and attack craft, TIEs serve the Imperial fleet very well. Twin ion engines provide the propulsion for these fighters, which are controlled by a single pilot. At the height of the

TIE fighter

Empire's military buildup, when resources were plentiful and supplies were nearly unlimited, the need was felt for a deep-space starfighter that was cheap to make, quick to produce, and relatively powerful—especially in large numbers. The TIE fighter was the result. Armed with two laser cannons but lacking any sort of combat shields, TIEs were designed for use as reconnaissance craft, perimeter defense ships, and ship-to-ship combat vehicles. The distinctive hexagonal solar-panel "wings" that jut from the spherical command pod gather light and convert it into energy that

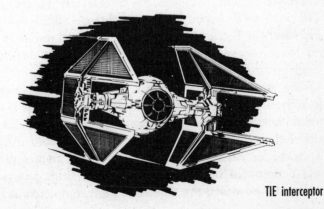

TIE interceptor

powers the propulsion and weapons systems. In addition to the basic TIE fighter design, a bent-wing interceptor and a double-pod bomber model are also found in Imperial service. Darth Vader even had his own custom-built TIE for the occasions when he wanted to engage in ship-to-ship combat with the rest of his forces. [SW, ESB, RJ]

⊛ Designed and built by Sienar Fleet Systems, the TIE fighter comes in a variety of special-assignment models. The original TIE starfighter was developed while SFS was still Republic Sienar Systems. The upgraded TIE was produced after the company came under the direct control of the Imperial Navy. The TIE/ln is the standard fleet-based TIE fighter. It carries a separate power generator for its laser cannons. The TIE/rc is equipped with extensive sensor and long-range communications packages to assist it with its reconnaissance duties. Built for fire-control duty, the TIE/fc transmits precise targeting information back to its fleet. Finally, the TIE/gt features an enlarged hull for carrying torpedoes and bombs. It is usually used as a ground-support vehicle, though it is gradually being replaced by the TIE bomber. Every Star Destroyer carries a complete wing of TIE fighters. A wing is made up of six squadrons, and squadrons are divided into three flights of two ships each. Therefore, a TIE squadron has twelve starfighters, and a TIE wing totals seventy-two starfighters. [SWSB]

After the Battle of Endor, when Imperial resources were no longer as vast and limitless as they were during the height of the Emperor's rule, the Imperial remnants began adding shields to TIE fighters. The starfighters were no longer expendable. For the Empire to continue as a viable force, it had to conserve its weapons of war much the way the Rebellion had once done. Under Grand Admiral Thrawn, for example, the success of a TIE fighter mission was determined by how many of these ships returned as well as by how well the objectives were completed. [HESB]

Tig Fromm

The Annoo-dat named Tig Fromm also went by the names of Baby-Face Fromm and Junior Fromm. He was the son of Sise Fromm, and like his father, he was a gangster of some repute. Based on the planet Ingo, he led his own gang of outlaws, though he often worked in cooperation with his father. Unlike his father, who liked to keep things old-fashioned, Tig was fascinated by modern technology. During the early days of the Empire, his project to build the weapons satellite called *Trigon One* was shut down by R2-D2, C-3PO, and their companions at the time. Kea Moll was among these companions. [DTV]

t'ill

The t'ill was a flowering plant that grew on the planet Alderaan. [SWR]

Tin-Tin Dwarf

The Tin-Tin Dwarf is an intelligent, rodentlike species. Members of this alien species are bipedal and stand less than a meter tall. [SWR]

Tion

See Lord Tion.

Tion Hegemony

The Tion Hegemony is a remote cluster of star systems near Corporate Sector space but far from the heavily populated galactic core. Twenty-seven star systems make up the Hegemony. [HSR, HLL]

Tiree

See Red Two.

Toda

Toda, or Lord Toda, ruled over a major portion of the planet Tammuz-an during the early days of the Empire. He called himself the "overlord of the outer territories." He was a gruff and surly individual who dressed as did his warrior tribesmates, in a combination of rough canvas and organic armor. [DTV]

Togorian

Togorians are a bipedal, feline species from the planet Togoria in the Thanos star system. These tall, slender beings grow to heights of three meters. They are covered with fur and have long, thin muscles of great strength. To outsiders, they seem aloof and very suspicious. [GG4]

Tonnika sisters

A pair of female con artists who operate in the galactic

fringe, Brea and Senni Tonnika use their natural charms to manipulate people and earn credits. They call themselves the Tonnika sisters, though some believe that that is only part of their deception. The Tonnika sisters can be seen in the cantina during *Star Wars IV: A New Hope*. [GG1]

Too-Onebee (2-1B)

The medical droid Too-Onebee, in service to the Rebel Alliance, is a skilled surgeon and field medic. This droid treated Luke Skywalker twice during the time of the Battle of Hoth, including performing an operation to replace Luke's severed hand with a mechanical replacement. Like other droids of Too-Onebee's class, the droid has surgical manipulation appendages, a medical diagnostic computer, and a treatment analysis computer. [ESB]

Toprawa

The planet Toprawa served as the Alliance's initial hiding place for the Death Star's technical readouts. These plans were stolen by Rebel forces during a raid on an Imperial convoy that was taking them to a secret Imperial storage base. [SWR]

Torm

Torm, a tall, brawny man with red hair and blue eyes, was part of the secret civilian group organized by Rekkon to locate missing friends and relatives who were suspected prisoners of the Corporate Sector Authority. Torm served as second-in-command of the group's mission to infiltrate an Authority Data Center on Orron III. The group hoped to learn the location of the Authority's illegal detention center in order to rescue the political prisoners. Torm comes from a wealthy family on the planet Kail. [HSE]

torpedo sphere

A torpedo sphere is a dedicated siege platform designed to knock out planetary shields. Even partial shields can protect a planet from orbital assault, making it necessary to launch a complicated and expensive ground-assault action. To open a world to the destructive power of the Imperial fleet, the Empire created the massive, 1,900-meter-diameter torpedo sphere. This forerunner to the Death Star battle station is covered with thousands of dedicated energy receptors designed to analyze shield emissions to find weak points in the shields. With five hundred proton torpedo tubes arranged in an inverted conical formation, the torpedo sphere can rain a massive salvo onto a small area (usually six meters square). The resulting hole that opens for a few brief microseconds, provided the emission analysis was successful, provides a window through which the sphere's turbolasers can target the shield generators. If there is a mistake in calculations or the gunnery crews are even slightly off, the process of analysis, bombardment, and targeting must start all over again. [ISB]

Torve

The human named Fynn Torve is a member of Talon Karrde's smuggling organization. He is among the best of Karrde's freighter pilots. Though not as flashy as Han Solo or as sophisticated as Lando Calrissian, Torve usually handles the most important and difficult runs for his boss. [HE, DFR, LC]

Tosche Station

The power and distribution station named Tosche Station is located near the town of Anchorhead on the planet Tatooine. From its inception, the station has served as a gathering place for Anchorhead's young people. Luke Skywalker and his friends frequented the place during his youth. [SW]

tracomp

The portion of shipboard sensor arrays charged with ground referencing is called the tracomp. This device locates a planet's axial and magnetic poles, places the ship within a spherical coordinate lattice, and locks onto any transmitting navigational beacons within range. [SME]

tractor beam

A tractor beam is a modified force field that can immobilize and move objects caught within its influence. An emitting tower, called a tractor-beam projector, produces the beams, though range and strength are determined by the power source that runs it. Tractor beams serve a number of important functions. In spaceports and hangar bays, tractor beams help guide ships to a safe landing. Salvage vessels, cargo haulers, emergency craft, and engineering ventures all employ tractor beams to assist them in their jobs. On military ships, tractor beams can be used to capture enemy vessels or simply hold them in place while offensive weaponry can be brought to bear. [SW, ESB, RJ]

transfer register

Throughout the galaxy, transfer registers are used to document the sale or trade of property and merchandise. An electro-optical device records the thumbprints of buyers and sellers, officially registering the transaction. [SWR]

transparisteel

The malleable metal called transparisteel can be pressed and formed into thin, transparent sheets that retain nearly all of the metal's strength and durability. This see-through metal is used in place of glass on starships and other structures that require visibility while maintaining protective strength. [HSE]

transport ship

The Rebel Alliance often converted spaceliners into transport ships. As transport ships, these starships were redesigned to move materials and personnel from system to system. An outer hull protects cargo containers and passenger pods that can be fastened to or removed from the open inner hull very quickly. These vessels carry little or no armament, relying instead upon escort ships and starfighters to protect them. They are equipped with hyperdrives, however, which allow them to traverse vast distances in short amounts of time. The command crew of a Rebel transport operates out of a small, cramped pod located toward the rear of the vessel and atop the outer hull. Transport ships were used extensively during the evacuation of the Rebel base on Hoth. [ESB]

treaded neutron torches (TNTs)

🌑 Treaded neutron torches, or TNTs, are ground vehicles designed to blast through rock with their fireball-shooting cannons. TNTs were created for use in the Kessel spice mines as a means for opening up new shafts. Since their introduction, other uses have been discovered for the vehicles, including jungle and forest clearing. [LCJ]

treadwell robot

🔴 A treadwell robot is a wheeled, multipurpose, six-limbed droid that can be programmed to perform many forms of menial labor. [SW]

Tree of Light

🌑 The Tree of Light is a mystical tree in the forest of Endor's moon. A bright, beautiful glow surrounds this tree. The glow keeps the Night Spirit from using its powers during the day. According to tradition, a group of young Ewo must periodically travel to the tree and feed it the s dust that rejuvenates its strength. [ETV]

Tregga

🌑 Tregga is an old acquaintance of H bacca the Wookiee. He was captured i contraband and sentenced to lif planet Akrit'tar's penal colony. [

Trianii

The Trianii are an intelligent species of humanoid felines native to the planet Trian. As a spacefaring civilization, the Trianii have established many off-world colonies. The Corporate Sector Authority claimed many of the older Trianii colony worlds even before its charter over that sector of space was granted. The Trianii who lived on these worlds were forced to leave, though some were retained to labor for the Authority. [HSE]

Trianii Ranger

The elite members of Trian's law enforcement legion are called Trianii Rangers. [HSE]

Triclops

Triclops is the true son of Emperor Palpatine. He appears human, though he has a third eye in the back of his

Triclops

head. The Empire considers Triclops insane, and most officials fear that disaster would result should he become Emperor. Few outside the Imperial leaders know of Triclops's existence, as he has spent most of his life hidden in an Imperial insane asylum. Rumors of the Emperor's three-eyed son are whispered throughout the galaxy, however, no matter how hard the Imperials strive to maintain the secret. Despite the shock-treatment scars that mar his temples and his white, jagged, unkempt hair, Triclops appears serene and peaceful. He possesses a quiet, iron determination. Though he professes to believe in peace, his subconscious mind invents terrible weapons of destruction while he sleeps. It was eventually revealed that Triclops is the father of the young Jedi Prince named Ken. [LCJ, MMY, QE, PDS]

Trioculus

Trioculus, the Supreme Slavelord of the spice mines of Kessel, came forward after the Emperor's death to claim that he was Palpatine's banished son. He appears as a handsome human with a third eye on his forehead. He became Emperor for a time due to the support of the Grand Moffs, though his claim held no substance. In truth, Trioculus is an imposter and a liar. [GDV, ZHR, MMY, PDS]

trompa

Three meters tall and massive, a trompa is a bipedal creature with long arms and sharp-clawed paws. Its thick fur covers powerful muscles, and two spiral horns curve out of its head. The trompa is extremely ferocious and more than a little deadly. [GCQ]

Tschel

See Lieutenant Tschel.

Tulgah

⊙ The Tulgah folk are a rare species of troll-like beings who have an extensive knowledge of magic. Some Tulgah are great healers. Others, like Morag, have twisted their knowledge to evil and wield powers of black magic. [ETV]

tumnor

⊙ A tumnor is a flying creature that lives in the upper atmosphere of Da Soocha and its moons. These predators stalk Ixlls, hunting the intelligent species as a source of food. [DE]

Tund

⊙ The planet Tund, in the system of the same name, is far from the centers of galactic civilization. It is a legendary place, rumored for ten thousand years and more to be the home of subtle and powerful magis. The name Tund conjures up images of fear, and few even dare whisper it so as not to invoke its malevolent attention. Now the world is sterile, devoid of native life. Its surface has been roasted to a fine, gray, powdered ash, all hints of evergreen forests, tropical jungles, and endless prairies wiped away by the magic that destroyed the world. The planet glows in the dark with a ghostly greenish residue of energies as yet unknown to the rest of the galaxy. It is the home of the last of the fabled sorcerers of Tund, Rokur Gepta. [LCS]

turbolaser

🔴 A turbolaser fires supercharged bolts of energy, usually from the desk of a capital ship or a surface-based defense installation. Turbolasers are more powerful than regular laser cannons, discharging hotter and more concentrated energy bolts. These weapons require constant temperature regulation from built-in cryogenic cooling units. [SW]

Tusken Raider

See Sand People.

Twi'lek

🔵 Twi'lek is the species name of the humanoid aliens with twin head tentacles. Bib Fortuna and Oola, of Jabba the Hutt's court, are Twi'leks. They come from the planet Ryloth, located in a system in the Outer Rim. The Twi'lek language combines verbal components with subtle head-tail movements. With the meanings provided by the head-tail movements, Twi'leks can carry on private conversations in the midst of other species.

Twi'leks are omnivorous. On their homeworld, they cultivate edible molds and fungi, and raise cowlike rycrits for their meat and hides. These beings are nonviolent, preferring to use cunning and slyness instead of force. Twi'leks live in vast city complexes located on their planet's dark side. Each complex is autonomous, governed by a head clan of five Twi'leks who jointly oversee production, trade, and other daily endeavors. These leaders are born into their positions, and they serve until one of their number dies. At this time, the remaining members of the head clan are driven from their complex to die in the Bright Lands of the planet's light side. This makes room for the head clan of the next generation.

As the technology level of Ryloth does not support spacefaring capabilities, the Twi'leks must depend on neighboring systems (such as Tatooine), pirates, smugglers, and merchants for their contact with the rest of the galaxy. They attract these ships with their chief export, ryll. The mineral ryll has legitimate medicinal uses, but it is also a popular and dangerously addictive recreational substance used in the Corporate Sector. One hazard that the Twi'leks face on a regular basis is slavers, who come to their world to fill their ships with Twi'lek slaves. [SWSB]

Tydirium

Tydirium was the name of the *Lambda*-class Imperial shuttle used by Han Solo's Rebel strike team to covertly

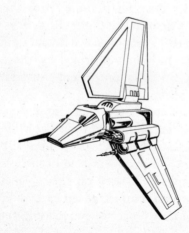

shuttle *Tydirium*

454

reach Endor's forest moon. The shuttle had been captured prior to the mission for use as the setup to the Battle of Endor. [RJ]

Tynna

The cold, arboreal world of Tynna was the home planet of the skip tracer named Spray. [HSR]

Tyrann

Tyrann was the Supreme Master of the Serpent Masters. [GW]

U

U-33

⚙ The U-33 class of orbital space boats are sublight-speed loadlifters used to shuttle personnel and material between planetary spaceports and orbiting space stations. This old ship model has been replaced by a number of newer, more efficient classes, though U-33s can still be found working in frontier systems and on developing worlds. A few are even used as training ships by the Academy. [HLL]

Ubese

✦ The bounty hunter Boushh spoke Ubese, a language typified by its metallic sounds. [RJ]

Ubiqtorate

⚙ A division of Imperial Intelligence, the Ubiqtorate oversees all of the activities of the agency at the highest levels. It is considered the true center of Imperial Intelligence by most operatives and military leaders. The Ubiqtorate formulates strategies for the entire agency, passing these along as goals to the other divisions. Ubiqtorate members are anonymous, often unknown to their subordinates. [ISB]

Ugnaught

Ugnaughts are a species of humanoid-porcine beings who live and work on Bespin's Cloud City. They are usually found in the Tibanna-gas processing plants, or as general laborers in the bowels of the floating city. [ESB]

Ugor

Ugors are a species of intelligent unicellular protozoans that grow to the size of one meter in diameter. They can extrude up to thirty pseudopodia at a time, some of which contain visual and other sensory organlike growths, or even openings and membranes that allow them to communicate via speech. Ugor move by oozing from place to place or by controlling specialized environment suits built to humanoid specifications (two arms and legs). They come from a star system they call Paradise, a junk-filled asteroid field that they administer. To them, garbage is holy. Every piece of junk is a religious relic. They have an exclusive contract with the Empire to collect garbage jettisoned from Imperial fleet ships and store it in their garbage-dump system. Gambling, bargaining, and cheating are the high moral standards the Ugors live up to. Other scavenger species, like the Squib, are considered business rivals to be crushed and eliminated. [SH, GG4]

Ukio

⚙ The planet Ukio, the primary world in the system of the same name, is an agricultural world that serves as one of the top five producers of foodstuffs for the New Republic. During Grand Admiral Thrawn's military campaign against the New Republic, Ukio was forced to surrender to the Empire after Thrawn demonstrated a powerful new weapon. To those on the planet's surface, it appeared that the Empire had developed turbolasers capable of firing through planetary shields. This was actually accomplished by an elaborate illusion. While Thrawn's Star Destroyer fired bolts of energy at the shield, cloaked Dreadnaughts hiding invisibly beneath the shield fired matching bolts with uncanny timing. The Ukian Overliege, fearing the destructive power of such a weapon, was forced to surrender to the Empire. For the rest of Thrawn's campaign, the Ukian food distribution and processing facilities and the vast farming and livestock grazing regions were under Imperial control. [LC]

Ulic Qel-Droma

⚙ Ulic Qel-Droma was a great Jedi who lived approximately four thousand years before the events that took place in *Star Wars IV: A New Hope*. Princess Leia learned of Ulic while accessing the histories stored within the Jedi Holocron. [DE]

Umak Leth

⚙ The Imperial engineer Umak Leth is the creator of many destructive tools for the Empire. Among his creations are the Leth Universal Energy Cage and the terrible war machines called the World Devastators. [DE]

Umboo

⊕ Umboo is a colony in the Roon star system. It was the home of Auren Yomm and her parents. A lightstation in space guides ships through the treacherous dust cloud that surrounds the system. [DTV]

Umwak

⊕ The true name of the Dulok shaman is Umwak. He often travels in disguise to trick the Ewoks. [ETV]

Unknown Regions

⊕ The Unknown Regions are the parts of the galaxy and beyond that remain unexplored. Certain regions within the borders of known space are also called Unknown due to the fact that they appear on no official astrogation charts. Some of these places are known to the Empire, the Rebellion, and even fringe society groups, but they remain hidden from the galaxy at large. [HE, HESB, SWRPG2]

Uplands, the

⊕ The Uplands was a pastoral region on the continent of Thon, which was located on the now-destroyed planet of Alderaan. [SWR]

urchin

⚫ An urchin, or dandelion warrior, is a strange plantlike creature with heads that resemble dandelion tufts but are actually spiked balls. These creatures can hurl sharp quills from their heads. Urchins with peculiar starred patterns are valuable for medicinal applications. [ETV]

Urdur

⚫ The planet Urdur was the site of one of the secret bases used by the outlaw techs operating in and around Corporate Sector space. The band of outlaws that used the base was led by Doc and Jessa. [HSE]

Uul-Rha-Shan

⚫ Uul-Rha-Shan was the bodyguard of Viceprex Hirken of the Corporate Sector Authority. Uul-Rha-Shan was a member of an intelligent reptilian species. He was bipedal, with red-and-white-patterned green scales, black eyes, a darting tongue, and sinister-looking fangs. [HSE]

V

V-wing airspeeder

🔵 The atmospheric attack craft called V-wing airspeeders are deployed from orbit into a planet's airspace by huge speeder transports. The New Republic used these airspeeder-fighters during the Battle of Calamari. [DE]

Vader

See Darth Vader.

Valley of Royalty

🔵 On the planet Duro, the Valley of Royalty is famous for its massive monuments to ancient rulers, including Queen Rana. [MMY]

vaporator

🔵 The inhabitants and moisture farmers of Tatooine employ vaporators to retrieve water vapor from the planet's thin, dry atmosphere. These five-meter-tall multicylinders condense water vapor and store the resulting liquid in large underground tanks. The water is kept for later consumption or sold for profit. [SW]

Varn

🌑 Varn was the chief scout for Tyrann, the Supreme Master of the Serpent Masters. [GW]

Vector

🌑 The popular game called Vector is played in drinking establishments on the planet Bonadan. [HSR]

Veers

See General Veers.

Verdanth

🌑 Verdanth is a jungle planet where Artoo and Threepio became stranded after they were sent to investigate an Imperial messenger drone. [GW]

Verpine

🌑 Verpine are an advanced species of bipedal insectoids. Their thin, sticklike bodies have awkwardly articulated joints and chitinous shells. Two antennae jut from the sides of their heads, which have two large eyes and short snouts. The Verpine live in the Roche Asteroid Field, using great repulsor shells to keep occupied asteroids from crashing into each other and to deflect other bits of space debris. They are innate experts in most fields of technology, and their childlike fascination with all types of machinery has served them well. They hollow out the asteroids for use as colonies, sealing them against space and filling them with all kinds of technological wonders. The Verpine have developed into expert starship builders. The Slayn & Korpil Corporation, named for two neighboring Verpine colonies, has been well known and respected since the days of the Old Republic. It was the Verpine who helped Admiral Ackbar design and build the B-wing starfighter. [SFS, GG4, DFRSB]

vibro-ax

🏵 A vibro-ax is a hand-held melee weapon with a broad blade. Vibrations across the blade give it great cutting power with only the slightest touch. An ultrasonic generator located in the ax handle produces the vibrations that power this deadly weapon. [HSR]

vibroblade

🏵 Another ultrasonic-vibration weapon, a vibroblade is a powered knife or dagger whose reverberating blade edge produces great cutting power with only the slightest touch. [HSE, HSR]

vibro-cutter

⚙️ A vibro-cutter is a heavy-duty industrial version of a vibroblade. [HLL]

vibroscalpel

⚙️ A small, lightweight surgical instrument, a vibroscalpel uses ultrasonic vibrations to excite a small wire blade in order to easily cut through most objects. Controls located in the handle are used to adjust power levels. [HSE, HSR]

vibro-shiv

⚙️ A vibro-shiv is a small, easily concealable vibroblade. [HLL]

Victory-class Star Destroyer

⚙️ The earliest version of the Imperial Star Destroyer, the *Victory*-class Star Destroyer is smaller and less sleek than the newer combat capital ships. While a few still serve in the Imperial fleet, most of the remaining Victory Star Destroyers are employed by local system defense forces and large conglomerates like the Corporate Sector Authority. Measuring a kilometer in length, these space fortresses were once considered to be the ultimate weapons of war. [HSE]

The *Victory*-class Star Destroyer is a 900-meter-long combat starship designed by Republic engineer Walex Blissex near the end of the Clone Wars. Those still in Imperial service carry two squadrons of TIE fighters (twenty-four ships), and have the basic armament: ten quad turbolaser batteries, forty double turbolaser batteries, eighty concussion-missile launchers, and ten tractor-beam projectors. [SWSB]

Vima-Da-Boda

Vima-Da-Boda was a powerful female Jedi who lost her powers after giving free reign to her anger and hatred, then finally succumbing to despair. She did this in response to her daughter's death, and thereby was overlooked during the period of Jedi extermination undertaken by Darth Vader and the Emperor. Princess Leia meets Vima on the streets of Nar Shaddaa, where the old woman is living the life of a beggar. [DE]

Vinda

Vinda is the co-owner of Starshipwrights and Aerospace Engineers Incorporated. Han Solo once owed Vinda credits for the work Vinda's company performed on the *Millennium Falcon*. [HSE]

Virgilio

See Captain Virgilio.

vocabulator

Droids produce sounds through devices called vocabulators (or sometimes vocoders). Usually visible as a grill or orifice, a vocabulator allows a droid to produce speech. The most sophisticated vocabulators on the market can be found within protocol droids. These sensitive devices are capable of producing the sounds necessary to converse in millions of different languages. [SW]

voice manipulation

One of the most frequently used manifestations of the Force by Jedi Knights is voice manipulation. This ability allows a Jedi to verbally implant suggestions into the minds of others and cause the appropriate responses. The Jedi employed voice manipulation to peacefully achieve their objectives. [SW, RJ]

Voice Override: Epsilon Actual

Voice Override: Epsilon Actual is a verbal command that immediately supersedes a droid's primary programing. This override function is activated by a verbal code, usually delivered in the form of a word or phrase. [SWR]

Vonzel

The smuggler Vonzel was an associate of Han Solo from his early days on the fringe. After injuries sustained while making an emergency landing, Vonzel had to be permanently attached to a life-support system to keep him alive. [HSR]

Voren Na'al

Voren Na'al joined the Alliance after a brief stint in the

Galaxy HoloNews Service. He was assigned to Arhul Hextrophon's historian corps, working as an assistant historian. He was one of those charged with preserving the record of the Alliance's war against tyranny. He was especially vigilant in charting the adventures of the Heroes of Yavin: Luke Skywalker, Han Solo, and Princess Leia. Later, he served as the Director of Council Research for the New Republic. [GG1, DFRSB]

vornskr

The vornskr lives on the planet Myrkr. This violent, long-legged quadruped has a vaguely doglike muzzle, sharp teeth, and a whiplike tail. In the day, vornskrs are sedate and inactive. At night, they become nocturnal hunters. The vornskr's tail is covered with a mild poison. It can inflict painful welts, and its poison has the capability to stun its prey. Vornskrs display an unnatural hatred of Jedi, often going out of their way to hunt and attack Force users. Talon Karrde keeps two domestic vornskrs, Sturm and Drang. These guard animals have had their tails clipped to reduce their normally aggressive natures. [HE, HESB]

Vrad Dodonna

Shortly after the destruction of the first Death Star, Vrad, General Dodonna's son, retreated from an encounter with Vader's new battle cruiser, the *Executor*. Vrad made up for his cowardice at a later time when he rammed his ship, which carried a power gem, into the *Executor* and destroyed a section of the defense shields. When Vader shifted his shields forward for greater protection, Han and the *Millennium Falcon* disabled the destroyer from the rear. [GW]

Vuffi Raa

⊛ The astrogation/pilot droid called Vuffi Raa traveled with Lando Calrissian for at least a year shortly after the young gambler had won the *Millennium Falcon* and set off to see the galaxy. The droid was technically Lando's property, as the gambler had won him in a game of sabacc, but after a few adventures Lando came to regard the droid as his friend. Vuffi Raa stood a meter tall, with five multijointed tentacle limbs that it could move at various angles and even prop itself up on to achieve more height. Vuffi was the shape of an attenuated starfish with sinuous manipulators that served as both arms and legs. These were connected to a dinner-plate-sized pentagonal torso with a single, softly glowing deep red vision crystal. Vuffi's entire body was covered in highly polished chromium. [LCM, LCF, LCS]

W

Wadda

Wadda was the humanoid employee of Zlarb the Slaver. Wadda's species remains unknown, for few members of his race have become integrated into galactic society. He was distinguished by his great strength and height, standing nearly 2.2 meters tall. He had a jutting forehead, protruding vestigial horns, and glossy brown skin. [HSR]

walker

See All Terrain Armored Transport and All Terrain Scout Transport.

wampa ice creature

The wampa ice creature is a terrible carnivorous beast that fearlessly hunts the snow-packed tundra of Hoth. Over two meters tall, the bipedal wampa has white fur, yellow eyes, and sharp claws and teeth. Wampas carve lairs out of the ice, forming huge caves in which to nest. When they hunt, they can take their prey by surprise due to the natural camouflage provided by their white fur. Wampas never hunt when they are hungry. Instead, they capture living prey and store it in their ice caves for later consumption. Luke Skywalker was wounded by a wampa ice creature while he was patrolling the frozen wastes of Hoth. [ESB]

wandrella

A wandrella is a huge, wormlike beast that lives in the rainforests of the planet Mimban. This gigantic omnivore has cream-colored flesh streaked with slashes of brown. The creature's blunt end is covered with eye-spots and holds a terrible maw filled with sharp, black teeth. The wandrella moves by using the suction organs located on its underside. [SME]

war droid

War droids, or war robots, are ancient mechanicals designed for combat. Less refined in appearance than modern droids, war droids have heavy armor plating, inefficient power delivery systems, and generally less intelligence and self-awareness than their more-sophisticated descendants. War droids can still be found operating in isolated and remote sections of the galaxy. [HLL]

In the *Dark Empire* comic series, weapon-equipped war droids that have been sold as salvage have been refitted by the Scavs. They employ these droids as extra muscle and protection for their scavenging forays. [DE]

warming unit

See condenser unit.

wave walker

⚙ The new Imperial wave walker is a light attack vehicle designed to operate above the surface of water. During the Battle of Calamari, wave walkers were designed and constructed aboard the World Devastators, then unleashed upon the Mon Calamari and their New Republic allies. [DE]

Wayland

⚙ The planet Wayland, site of one of the Emperor's private storehouses, figured prominently in Grand Admiral Thrawn's plan to destroy the New Republic and reestablish the Empire. On Wayland, Thrawn found what he needed deep inside Mount Tantiss—a working cloaking shield and plenty of Spaarti cloning cylinders. He also found the Dark Jedi Master Joruus C'baoth.

The planet was originally discovered during the Old Republic's second wave of expansion. A colony ship crashed on the planet, and due to an improper entry in the official astrogation charts the colonists were left on their own. Besides the human colonists, Wayland was inhabited by two intelligent species, the Psadan and the Myneyrsh. With only bow-and-arrow technology, the two species were no match for the blasters and repulsors the colonists brought with them. However, power cells do not last forever, and the colonists were forced to take up the technology of the natives. Centuries later, the Empire rediscovered the planet. The Emperor himself ordered the planet's location stricken from all records, then had a special storehouse built there within a hollowed-out mountain. [HE, HESB, LC]

weapon detector

⚙ Weapon detectors use sensors that scan for power cells and clearly identifiable weapon profiles. The sensors feed data directly to a dedicated computer for nearly instantaneous analysis. Detectors are routinely employed in restricted facilities, military bases, detention centers, and spaceports to scan for unauthorized weapons. The Corporate Sector Authority uses them on worlds such as Bonadan to maintain order. [HSR]

webweaver

⚙ A webweaver is a large, deadly arachnid that dwells on one of the lower ecolevels of the planet Kashyyyk. [HLL]

Wedge Antilles

⚙ The Corellian-born Wedge Antilles is a starfighter pilot serving the Rebel Alliance. He is an expert X-wing pilot, often assigned to the Alliance's most important missions. He was in the X-wing squadron that went up against the original Death Star battle station at the Battle of Yavin, fighting alongside Luke Skywalker and Biggs Darklighter. When Luke took over the squadron, Wedge became his friend and one of his top officers. Later, when Luke decided to resign his commission, Wedge took command of the group. He led not only his squadron but an entire battle group on the assault against the second Death Star during the Battle of Endor. [SW, ESB, RJ]

⚙ Wedge accepted the rank of commander after Luke resigned his commission, taking control of the elite starfighter group he and Luke had built over the years. Rogue Squadron was first attached to the Alliance's Headquarters Frigate; over the years, the group became the Rebel fleet's premier squadron. In the five years after the Battle of Endor, Wedge continually turned down promotions in order to stay with Rogue Squadron—he wanted to remain where the action was. He has no desire to step into a political role like the one Admiral Ackbar occupies. [HE, DFR, LC]

Wedge finally accepted the rank of general six years after the Battle of Endor, right before the start of the events depicted in the *Dark Empire* comic book series. [DE]

Weequay

⚙ The Weequay are a humanoid species with coarse, leathery skin and bald heads. By tradition, they wear a single braided topknot on one side of their heads. Jabba the Hutt employed two Weequay as skiff guards. [RJ]

Western Dune Sea

See Dune Sea.

Whaladon

⚙ Whaladons are a species of intelligent, whalelike mammals who inhabit the deep oceans of the planet Mon Calamari. [GDV]

Whaladon hunting ship

🌑 The huge Whaladon hunting ship is a submersible vessel the size of a great capital ship. The hunting ship illegally roams the oceans of Mon Calamari in search of Whaladons. It is equipped with stun weapons and tractor beams to incapacitate the whalelike beings and pull them into recessed storage chambers, where it can store more than a dozen Whaladons at a time. The ship is under the command of Captain Dunwell, and crewed by Aqualish hunters. [GDV]

Whiphid

🌑 The Whiphid, or Toothface, species is a race of hulking, fur-covered bipeds who stand about 2.5 meters tall. With a prominent forehead, long, bowed cheekbones, and two up-turned tusks rising from the jaw, a Whiphid is easy to spot in a crowd. They come from the bitterly cold planet of Toola in the Kaelta system. These ferocious predators have a true love of the hunt, enjoying the whole process of tracking something down and killing it. They also appreciate the luxuries that advanced technology brings, and often take on lucrative bounty-hunting contracts from law-enforcement agencies, criminal organizations, and the Empire. [GG4]

Whistler's Whirlpool

🌑 The Whistler's Whirlpool is a tapcafe on the planet Trogan. Situated on the coast of Trogan's most densely populated continent, the tapcafe is built around a natural formation called the Drinking Cup. This bowl-shaped rock pit is open to the sea at its base, and six times every day the tidal shift causes the water level to rise and fall. At these times, the bowl is filled with a violent white-water maelstrom. The tapcafe's tables are arranged in concentric circles around the bowl, striking a nice balance between luxury and spectacular natural drama. Unfortunately, the noise made by the water striking the natural breakers within the bowl was quite uncomfortable for most of the clientele, and the Whistler's Whirlpool has been largely abandoned. Talon Karrde held a meeting for his fellow smuggling chiefs at the Whirlpool in order to discuss Grand Admiral Thrawn's campaign against the New Republic and its implications for the smugglers and their businesses. [LC]

Wicket W. Warrick

The Ewok named Wicket was the first of his tribe to find and befriend Princess Leia Organa after she crashed a speeder bike and became lost in the moon's great forest. Wicket was influential in convincing the rest of his tribe to aid the Rebel strike team that sought to disable the shield generator located on the forest moon. When Leia and the Rebels attacked the Imperial installation, Wicket fought at their side, helping them gain access to and destroy the guarded facility. [RJ]

Wicket W. Warrick

Wild Karrde

🌑 Talon Karrde's personal space vessel is a dilapidated-looking Corellian bulk freighter he named *Wild Karrde*. This freighter looks like any of a thousand Corellian Action VI Transports plying the space lanes. But Karrde has extensively modified the 125-meter-long vessel, making it faster and more powerful than it appears. The freighter serves as Karrde's base of operations when he is on board. It has combat-rated shields and three turbolasers when offensive punch is called for. Its warship-class sensor package and armor-reinforced hull are definitely not standard issue, and its sensor stealth travel mode rivals the best Imperial spy ship in the fleet. The interior has undergone modifications as well. A large portion of the forward hold has been converted into living quarters and offices, and a permanent kennel has been installed in the main hold for Karrde's pet vornskrs. [HE, HESB, DFRSB]

Wild Space

🌑 Wild Space is the galaxy's true frontier. Once considered part of the Unknown Regions, this area of space was opened to exploration and settlement as one of the Emperor's last acts. Grand Admiral Thrawn was charged with taming this wilderness, and he declared it part of the Empire. However, as the Empire has been too busy to enforce its subjugation, much of Wild Space remains free. [HESB, SWRPG2]

Wiley

🌑 Wiley is an infant Ewok on Endor's forest moon. [RJ]

Willard

See Commander Willard.

Windy

Windy was one of Luke Skywalker's childhood friends. They grew up together on the planet Tatooine. [SW]

Winter

The woman named Winter is tall and regal, with silky white hair and an aura of confidence. She is Princess Leia's aide and companion, and grew up with Leia on Alderaan. As a child, Winter was often mistaken for the true princess as she always looked the part. The two became close friends, and when Leia took her place in the Senate, Winter went along as her royal aide and executive assistant. In addition to her normal organizational skills, Winter has a perfect memory. Everything she sees, hears, smells, or otherwise senses is recorded in her memory. She can forget nothing, even should she want to.

Winter was off-planet when Alderaan was destroyed. Bail Organa had sent her to help Rebel agents, temporarily removing her from Leia's side. This separation lasted throughout the Galactic Civil War as Winter was assigned to Alliance Procurement and Supply, where her perfect memory was used to create maps and gather intelligence information for the Rebels charged with gathering supplies for the Alliance. Her reputation became so well known in intelligence circles that the Imperials began to call her "Targeter." Her perfect memory has its bad points. Where other Alderaan survivors have been able to let the pain of the planet's destruction fade with time, Winter's memories are still clear and bright, as though the terrible event happened only yesterday. She currently serves as Leia's aide in the Provisional Council; she is the princess's companion and friend, and nursemaid to her newborn twins. [HE, DFR, LC, DFRSB]

Wistie

🜨 The Wisties, or firefolk, are tiny, giggly, pixielike beings that glow brightly and can fly. They live on Endor's moon. [EA, ETV]

womp rat

🜨 Womp rats are carnivorous creatures that inhabit the canyons of Tatooine. These vicious, hair-covered rodents grow to lengths of more than three meters. They travel in packs and use their claws and teeth to bring down prey. Luke Skywalker used to hunt womp rats in Beggar's Canyon, targeting them at high speeds from the cockpit of his skyhopper. [SW]

Wookiee

🜨 Wookiees are an anthropoid species native to the planet Kashyyyk. Tall, strong, and covered by soft, thick fur, Wookiees are known as ferocious opponents and loyal friends. The average member of this species grows to over two meters in height and has a much longer life expectancy than a human. On Kashyyyk, Wookiees live in cities situated high within giant trees. Though they appear to be primitive in nature, they are quite comfortable with high technology, combining natural features with modern conveniences. The Wookiee language is made up of a series of grunts and growls. They can understand other languages, but their limited vocal ability makes it impossible for them to speak anything other than their own language. Chewbacca, Han Solo's copilot and partner, is a Wookiee. [SW, ESB, RJ, SWWS]

The galaxy at large knows Wookiees as lethal combatants with ferocious tempers. From the very beginnings of the Empire, the Wookiees, their world, and their colonies were placed under martial law and enslaved to labor for the Imperial effort. Free Wookiees were extremely rare, and few were ever encountered along the galactic spaceways. It wasn't until after the Battle of Endor that the Alliance was able to finally set the Wookiees free. As tree dwellers, Wookiees have wickedly curved claws that pop from hidden fingertip sheaths with the flex of a muscle. With the aid of these claws and their strong limbs, Wookiees can travel through the upper reaches of the great wroshyr trees of their homeworld, clinging to vines and branches with agile ease. While feared as opponents, Wookiees employ no obvious fighting style. They seem to simply charge forward, arms swinging, shattering whatever they hit with their huge, powerful fists. Wookiees never use their claws in combat, however, as this is considered a serious breach of the Wookiee code of honor. [SWSB, HE, HESB]

Wookiee honor family

Wookiees form special bonds of friendship that join one Wookiee with a group of other Wookiees, or even with members of other species. This honor family comprises a Wookiee's true friends and boon companions. Members of honor families pledge to lay down their lives for each other, and they extend this protection to the honor families of each individual member. Chewbacca the Wookiee considers his companions Han Solo, Princess Leia, Luke Skywalker, and the droids R2-D2 and C-3PO to be part of his honor family. [HLL, SWSB, HESB]

Wookiee life debt

The most sacred Wookiee custom is the life debt. Wookiees pledge life debts to those who save their lives, forming a bond that can never be broken. Not slavery, a life debt is a sacred act of honor to repay that which is without measure. When a Wookiee enters into a life debt, he often decides to travel with his savior in order to carry out what he considers to be sacred obligations. Chewbacca has pledged a life debt to Han Solo for acts that Solo performed when the pair first met. [HLL, SWSB, HESE]

World Devastator

The great Imperial war machine known as the World Devastator appears even more terrible than the Death Star. World Devastators inflict massive amounts of destruction, then salvage and use the destroyed material to create new war ships to bolster the Imperial fleet. These machines are also referred to as World Sweepers, World Smashers, and City Eaters. Designed by Imperial engineer Umak Leth, these kilometers-high, kilometers-wide machines are powered by massive ion engines and repulsorlift gravity transformers. The open maws on these machines contain raging molecular furnaces that are powered by microscopic black holes. Whole cities are pulled into these furnaces, where the raging power breaks the material into simple molecules.

World Devastator

These molecules, in turn, are reassembled within the onboard factories as new Imperial war ships.

Each Devastator is different in appearance, as the machines are self-constructing. Within a Devastator's core are the materials processing plants—blast furnaces, testing laboratories, foundries, metal works, stamping mills, and chemical vats. Not everything a Devastator destroys is used by the machine; some raw materials are stored for transport to specialized industrial planets. What is kept is fed into the factory levels, where slave labor and droids construct an unending supply of TIE fighters, ground-assault vehicles, arms and armament, and other items needed to further the war efforts of the Empire. The upper decks of a Devastator house control towers, command stations, living areas, and hangar bays. The outer surface is covered with gun towers and missile launch ports. Shield generators cloak the entire vessel, though selected portions of the shields can be raised and lowered by the command personnel.

World Devastators have complex computer and guidance systems, which are regulated from the planet Byss by means of a hyperspace-transmitted Master Control Signal. [DE]

Wormie

⚛ Camie and Fixer, two of Luke Skywalker's childhood friends, called Luke by the nickname Wormie. [SW, SWR]

wroshyr trees

⚛ The giant trees of the jungle world of Kashyyyk are called wroshyr trees. The branches of wroshyr trees have a unique property: the separate branches meet to form one interlocked branch, which then sprouts new branches of its own. These reach out in all directions to find other branches to join with. This tendency toward unity makes wroshyr trees stronger, and is a natural symbol of the Wookiee concepts of honor and family. The wroshyr trees in the Rwookrrorro city grouping are actually a single giant plant with a unified root system. [HE, HESB]

X

X-222

⊛ The X-222 is a sleek, high-altitude atmospheric fighter craft. [HLL]

XP-38

☻ The XP-38 is a popular landspeeder model. It is one of the newer landspeeder models to hit the galactic market. [SW]

X-wing starfighter

☻ Incom Corporation's T-65 X-wing is a small, single-pilot starfighter that measures 12.5 meters from nose to engine block. Those who fly them sometimes refer to X-wings as snub fighters. With powerful sublight ion engines, a targeting computer, defensive shields, four wing-tipped laser cannons, and a limited supply of proton torpedoes, the X-wing is fast, highly maneuverable, and extremely well armed. These starfighters are also equipped with hyper-

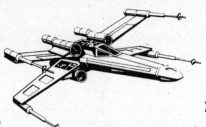

X-wing starfighter

drives for lightspeed travel. A recessed socket, situated on the outer hull behind the cockpit, is designed as an interface for an R2 astromech droid. An R2 unit assists the starfighter's pilot by monitoring onboard systems, performing routine and emergency maintenance, and even flying the craft when circumstances permit. Astromechs also augment the craft's computer capabilities, assist with astrogation, and hold preset hyperspace jump coordinates. The X-wing's double-layered wings split open into an X shape for atmospheric travel and when the starfighter shifts into attack position. The Alliance to Restore the Republic uses these starfighters. [SW, ESB, RJ]

xenoarchaeology

⊙ Xenoarachaeology is the study of vanished off-world or alien cultures through the scientific analysis of the artifacts left behind. [SME]

Xim the Despot

⊙ Before the Old Republic stretched its brand' of justice across the galaxy, the tyrannical Xim the Despot conquered a vast region of space. Some histories claim that the star systems he ruled numbered in the thousands. His conquering armies plundered and subjugated world after world, filling Xim's coffers with wealth beyond imagining. His royal guard consisted of war droids who were programmed to guard him and his stores of treasure. Ruthless and unscrupulous, Xim committed atrocities against those he conquered, including mass spacings. Xim ruled for thirty Standard Time Periods before the conquered star systems were finally able to overthrow him and end his reign of terror. [HLL]

Y

Y-wing starfighter

⊕ The twin-engine, sixteen-meter-long Y-wing starfighter is an old model still used by the Rebel Alliance. It has room for two crew members: one serves as the ship's pilot while the other handles the ship's offensive and defensive systems. This hyperdrive-equipped starfighter is armed with two forward-mounted laser cannons, a rear-mounted twin ion cannon, a limited number of proton torpedoes, and a droid-interface socket. It has combat-rated deflector shields, and its rugged construction allows it to take a considerable amount of damage before its systems fail. [SW, ESB, RJ]

Yaka

⊕ The Yakas are a species of near-human cyborgs. When their home planet was invaded centuries ago by the superintelligent inhabitants of Arkania, a neighboring star system, the Arkanians forced the Yakas to undergo transforming surgery. They implanted cyborg brain enhancers in the Yakas, increasing the species' intelligence to genius level. Now the brutish-looking Yakas are much smarter than they appear. One side effect of the implants is a twisted sense of humor, which all Yakas possess. [DE]

Yak Face

(✪) Yak Face is the informal name given to the bipedal species characterized by a whiskered, broad-snouted face. At least one of these aliens worked for Jabba the Hutt. [RJ]

Yavin

(✪) Yavin is a gas-giant planet in an Outer Rim Territory star system of the same name. Numerous moons orbit the planet, including the fourth moon, which once served as the location of a hidden Rebel base. This lush, tropical moon features the extensive ruins of a now-dead civilization called the Massassi. The Rebels established a base in one of the massive temples, and it was from this location that they launched their desperate assault on the first Death Star battle station. The resulting combat has come to be known as the Battle of Yavin. [SW]

(✪) The Yavin star system has three planets: Fiddanl, Stroiketcy, and Yavin. Fiddanl is a hot, toxic world. Stroiketcy is probably a large comet that was captured by the system, as it follows an extremely ellipsoidal orbit. It supports no life. Yavin itself is a gas giant with dozens of moons. Yavin Four is a lush, jungle moon with wide rivers and diverse forms of life. Yavin Eight is a mountainous moon with stretches of tundra and many varieties of rodentlike life. Yavin Thirteen is a desert moon with two forms of intelligent life: the reptilian Slith and the mammallike Gerbs. Both are still in the primitive stages of technological development.

Yavin Four is also the site of the Lost City of the Jedi, an ancient city built long ago by Jedi Knights deep below the surface of the moon. Droids have cared for the city and its hidden secrets for untold ages. The young Jedi Prince named Ken was found here shortly after the Battle of Endor. [GG2, LCJ, PDS]

yayax

A yayax is a fierce, pantherlike beast that lives in the forests of Endor's moon. [ETV]

Yoda

The Jedi Master Yoda lived to be approximately nine hundred years old before he finally died. For most of those years, Yoda served as mentor and teacher to Jedi Knights. A member of an as-yet-unidentified alien species, Yoda spent

Yoda

his last years in seclusion, hiding from the eyes of the Emperor on the swamp planet Dagobah. Two of his best students were Obi-Wan Kenobi and Luke Skywalker. [ESB, RJ]

ysalamiri

⊕ Ysalamiri, one of the indigenous life-forms of the planet Mrykr, have the unique ability to push back the Force. These salamanderlike creatures grow to a length of fifty centimeters long. Furry snakes with legs, these creatures live in the branches of Mrykr's metal-rich trees. The sessile ysalamiri's claws grow directly into the branches, making it difficult to remove them from their perches without killing them. A single ysalamiri creates a bubble ten meters in radius in which the Force does not exist. Those who have studied the creatures theorize that ysalamiri push the Force away from themselves as a bubble of air pushes away water. Within this bubble, a Force user cannot call on his or her powers or otherwise manipulate the Force.

Grand Admiral Thrawn's plans to destroy the New Republic included the use of the docile ysalamiri. He ordered Imperial engineers to build frames of pipes to support and nourish the creatures so that they could be removed from their branches and transported off-planet. The nutrient frames were designed so that they could be worn by Thrawn and others as a mobile defense against those who can manipulate the Force. The creatures also figured prominently in Thrawn's plans to grow clones rapidly in the Spaarti cloning cylinders he retrieved from the Emperor's storehouse on Wayland. [HE, DFR, LC, HESB]

Yuzzem

⊕ Yuzzem are humanoids from an unrevealed planet.

They are noted for their great strength and volatile, unpredictable temperaments. Characterized by long snouts, long arms, heavy fur, and large black eyes, Yuzzem are often found as slaves in Imperial labor camps, or as hired hands employed for physical activities like mining. A pair of Yuzzem aided Princess Leia and Luke Skywalker during their mission to the Circarpous star system. [SME]

yuzzum

The yuzzum is a creature that inhabits the forest floor of Endor's moon. These strange-looking beasts have round, fur-covered bodies, long, thin legs, and wide mouths full of sharp, protruding teeth. [RJ]

In the Ewok animated television series, Yuzzum are an intelligent though barbaric spear-wielding species who are the natural enemies of the Ewoks. [ETV]

Z

Z-95 Headhunter

The Z-95 Headhunter is a compact, twin-engine atmospheric fighter craft that can be modified for space travel. A single pilot controls the fighter. These outdated ships can still be found in service on backwater worlds—a testament to their durability and construction. The Incom Corporation used the Z-95 as the starting point when it set out to design and build the X-wing starfighter. [HSE]

ZZ-4Z (Zee Zee)

ZZ-4Z, or Zee Zee, is a housekeeping droid who cares for Han Solo's apartment on Nar Shaddaa. The droid was seriously damaged during a recent battle with Boba Fett. [DE]

Zardra

The tall, dark-haired woman named Zardra appears strikingly sensual, with more than a hint of danger about her. She carries a force pike and wears a flowing cloak. Not much is known about Zardra, except that she is a bounty hunter of exceptional skill and daring. She often teams up with Jodo Kast and Puggles Trodd, though only when a bounty catches her interest. She enjoys personal combat and appreciates the fine things that credits can buy, but the hunt is the most important thing in her life. She fears that she will wind up dying senselessly—to her, this means naturally and not in combat—so she often tempts disaster by taking huge risks. [TM, OS]

Zatec-Cha

⚙ Zatec-Cha was the grand vizier of the planet Tammuz-an during the early days of Imperial rule. He hoped to usurp the throne of Mon Julpa, even going so far as to cause the leader's memory loss. [DTV]

Zebulon Dak

⚙ Zebulon Dak was the wealthy and influential founder and owner of the Zebulon Dak Speeder Corporation. [DTV]

Zeebo

⚙ Zeebo, a four-eared Mooka, is the furred and feathered pet of Ken the Jedi Prince. [LCJ, PDS]

zenomach

⚙ A zenomach is a powerful ground-boring machine that looks like and operates in the same way as a giant drill. [MMY]

Zev

Zev was one of the Rebel Alliance pilots assigned to Luke Skywalker's squadron on the ice planet Hoth. It was Zev, flying his snowspeeder over the frozen plains, who found and rescued Luke and Han Solo after the pair was forced to weather a cold Hoth night on the desolate tundra. During the Battle of Hoth, Zev sacrificed his life to give the Rebel forces time to evacuate the secret base. [ESB]

Zev Veers

Zev Veers, son of the Imperial general who commanded the ground assault against the Rebel base on Hoth, disowned his father and went against his wishes when he joined up with the Rebellion. During the Battle of Calamari, Zev was the chief gunner aboard the New Republic Star Destroyer *Emancipator*. [DE]

Zlarb

The slave trader Zlarb is a tall human with fair skin, white-blond hair and beard, and clear gray eyes. He once commandeered the *Millennium Falcon* and its crew when he needed to deliver contraband to the planet Bonadan. [HLL]

Zorba's Express

Zorba's Express is the ancient, bell-shaped starship owned by Zorba the Hutt. [ZHR]

Zorba the Hutt

Zorba the Hutt is the father of Jabba the Hutt. Zorba did not immediately learn of his son's death due to the fact that he was imprisoned on the planet Kip for more than twenty years. Zorba resembles his offspring, though he has long white hair braids and a white beard. All of Jabba's possessions were bequeathed to his father, including his desert palace on Tatooine and the Holiday Towers Hotel and Casino on Cloud City. [ZHR, MMY, QE, PDS]

Z'trop

The planet Z'trop, a scenic and romantic tropical world, is noted for its pleasant volcanic islands, its wide beaches, and its clear waters. Han Solo, Princess Leia, and their companions took time for rest and relaxation on this world. [MMY]

Zuckuss

Zuckuss was one of the bounty hunters commissioned by Darth Vader to locate the *Millennium Falcon* and its crew after the ship escaped from Imperial forces during the Battle of Hoth. [ESB]

Zyggurats

The terrorist group known as the Zyggurats operated on the fringes of the galaxy. Believed to have come to the galaxy from outside known Imperial space shortly after the

Clone Wars, the terrorist group was quickly suppressed by the rising Empire before its activities could cause much damage. [DE]

Zuggs

See Commodore Zuggs.

Zut

🌑 The male Phlog named Zut is the mate of Dobah. [ETV]